Juliette Hyland began crafting heroes and heroines in high school. She lives in Ohio, USA, with her Prince Charming, who has patiently listened to many rants regarding characters failing to follow their outline. When not working on fun and flirty happily-ever-afters, Juliette can be found spending time with her beautiful daughters and giant dogs, or sewing uneven stitches with her sewing machine.

Also by Juliette Hyland

Mills & Boon Medical

The Prince's One-Night Baby
Rules of Their Fake Florida Fling
Redeeming Her Hot-Shot Vet
Tempted by Her Royal Best Friend

Boston Christmas Miracles miniseries

A Puppy on the 34th Ward

Mills & Boon True Love

Royals in the Headlines miniseries

How to Win a Prince

Discover more at millsandboon.co.uk.

DATING HIS
IRRESISTIBLE RIVAL

JULIETTE HYLAND

HER SECRET
BABY CONFESSION

JULIETTE HYLAND

MILLS & BOON

First published in Great Britain 2024
by Mills & Boon, an imprint of HarperCollins*Publishers* Ltd,
1 London Bridge Street, London, SE1 9GF

www.harpercollins.co.uk

HarperCollins*Publishers* Macken House, 39/40 Mayor Street Upper, Dublin 1, D01 C9W8, Ireland

Dating His Irresistible Rival © 2024 Juliette Hyland

Her Secret Baby Confession © 2024 Juliette Hyland

ISBN: 978-0-263-32156-2

04/24

This book contains FSC™ certified paper and other controlled sources to ensure responsible forest management.

For more information visit www.harpercollins.co.uk/green.

Printed and Bound in the UK using 100% Renewable Electricity at CPI Group (UK) Ltd, Croydon, CR0 4YY

DATING HIS IRRESISTIBLE RIVAL

JULIETTE HYLAND

MILLS & BOON

For found families everywhere.

CHAPTER ONE

DR. KNOX PETERS grabbed the soda from the bar and pointed to the back wall. "Game of darts? Loser buys the next round?"

Jackson Peters, his best friend, roommate and for all the purposes Knox cared about, brother, rolled his eyes. "You haven't lost a game since before we met in the boys' home. That hustle might work on the unsuspecting but come on, Knox."

They'd been thrown together in foster care. Bunkmates because of a shared last name. A twist of fate that led to a lifelong friendship.

"Fine. Winner buys the drinks." His buddy was down. Had been down since he returned from Hawaii almost a year ago now. The longest melancholy streak ever. After a vacation. And he wouldn't tell Knox why.

"If you want to play darts, you can just ask me to play darts." Jackson held up the beer he'd been nursing for the past hour in a mock toast.

Knox rolled his eyes before heading to the dartboard. Jackson was right; it wasn't much of a competition. Knox had started playing darts as part of a hustle for one of his less than stellar foster parents. His eye for detail and need for perfection driving him to master the skill, even though his foster father was using it to fleece money from unsuspecting bar patrons.

The fact that the underage Knox was allowed in the bar

and on a first-name basis with the bartender should have been a major red flag. But it never seemed to register with the people his foster father targeted.

Knox passed Jackson the set of red darts. Jackson stepped to the line and tossed the first dart, landing close to the bull's-eye. But not close enough.

That was something Knox loved about Jackson. The man had never beaten him at a game. But he never gave up trying. Never threw a game intentionally to make it go quicker.

The game progressed as it normally did. A few people stepped up to watch them toss the darts.

"Such precision!" A young white woman clapped as she moved toward Jackson. His brother wasn't going to win, but the black man was beyond attractive. Still, Knox knew the beauty's attempt was doomed to failure.

Jackson had never been a playboy, but the man had enjoyed regular dates. Something else that had stopped after the vacation.

"She was cute." Knox grabbed his dart from the bull's-eye.

"You should ask her out." Jackson tilted the beer bottle in his direction again.

Knox shook his head. He'd dated three women since becoming a surgeon. All three had broken up with him when he made it clear that his patients were his first priority. That wasn't fair to them. He understood that.

In a relationship, your partner deserved to know that they were first in your life. Maybe something was broken in him that he seemed incapable of giving that. The universe battered him in his early days. Abandoned by his mother at eight, in and out of foster care until he'd aged out. Hell, he'd graduated high school top of his class to prove to his last foster family that he wasn't a loser.

Not that they'd ever known. They'd dropped him at the boys' home after he failed eighth grade English. Never mind

that he'd spent the year hopeful his mother would finally regain custody only to learn she'd actually given up all parental rights. Not an excuse for failure, however.

They'd promptly forgotten him. Knox would never forget, though. He'd been the best at nearly everything he'd
done since.

"She didn't hit on me. She hit on you. Getting out a bit
more wouldn't be the worst thing to happen." Knox tossed
another dart. Bull's-eye.

"I'm not the only one who could do to spend more time
out of the hospital." Jackson threw his dart, striking into the
heart of the board where only Knox's darts found purchase—
usually. "Bull's-eye."

"Lucky throw." Knox chuckled. Even with the bull's-eye
there was no way for his brother to make up the deficit. "The
last time one of us took a vacation, he came back grumpier
than ever. Maybe it's not the hospital."

Knox was a general surgeon and Jackson a nurse anesthetist. They practically lived at the hospital. Prior to tonight
they'd been on shift for nearly a week straight. It was only
because of hospital policy demanding they take a night off,
that they were here tonight.

"Yet, a vacation still wouldn't hurt you. Your patients
would be fine." Jackson tossed his final dart, just off center.

His patients would be fine. Rationally, Knox knew that
but so many of the surgeons and staff saw Hope Hospital as a
stepping stone. The focus was on next steps, even if it wasn't
in the forefront of their minds. Their hospital was small; it
saw many patients that were struggling to make ends meet.
They deserved stability, too.

But Knox understood. He'd viewed Hope that way, too—
once upon a time. And one day he'd leave, but every time a
good opportunity opened, he found an excuse not to put in.

"Hey! Take it outside!" The bartender's voice rose above

the cacophony of the bar. Knox saw a few heads turn toward the entrance. No doubt cell phones and crowds would follow the action. He needed no part of it.

"Someone's had too much." Jackson grabbed the darts from the board, handing Knox his.

"Someone has always had too much." Knox raised his final dart. It was a sad truth that many of the people he met in the surgical recovery room were there because of a bad decision, overindulgence in alcohol or drugs...or someone else's overindulgences.

His mother had struggled with addiction. Knox understood the disease from a medical perspective. But understanding the dopamine resistance, the tie-in to stress, anxiety, depression and other untreated mental health conditions didn't negate the consequences for those who loved you.

The sound of glass shattering and screams echoed from the front of the building. Jackson was moving beside Knox. Years of medical training kicking into gear before they registered the cries for medical attendants.

"Call 911." Jackson pointed to a young white man holding up his phone. "Now."

The bartender had likely called, too, but it was too crowded for them to make sure. Besides, another call to emergency services wouldn't hurt.

Three bodies lay outside on the sidewalk; blood was already pooling around them.

"Damn." The expletive slipped from his mouth as he took in the scene. The movies made falling through glass look like a quick hit. Maybe a scratched cheek or blood traipsing down the arm before the hero got up and beat the villain.

The actual result was nothing like that.

A white woman was bent over one of the patients, dark curly hair falling over her face as she held pressure on a wound that was seeping blood and fluid. "I'm a doctor. Those two went through the window. She has a stab wound."

Her voice sounded familiar, but it might be the adrenaline. Knox took in the appearance of the two men on the ground. One was conscious. He pointed to him, and Jackson bent to assess while Knox focused on the young white man who was unconscious.

He heard sirens in the distance and hoped they'd sent more than one ambulance. "I've got an unconscious man who is probably midtwenties. Head wound, cuts on the back. Looks like he was first through the window. Pulse rapid but steady. What's her situation?"

Triage in the field was not something surgical staff did often, but they needed to prioritize the first transport.

"I've got a twenty-three-year-old female. Two stab wounds, one to the side and another to the lower abdomen. Pulse thready. She goes first." The female physician's voice was strained. Stab wounds were bad, stab wounds to the abdomen very bad. The young woman would need emergency surgery, and even that might not save her.

"Agreed." Knox looked to Jackson. His patient was sitting up, his face pale, sweat pooling on his forehead, a nasty cut on his left forearm and cuts along his legs. The man's gaze never left the female patient. He was the third transport.

"Will she be all right?" The man had tears running down his cheeks that Knox thought were because of the woman on the ground, not his wounds.

The female doctor didn't look up. Pressure needed to be kept on the woman's wounds. The fact that she didn't answer was not a good sign.

"She'll go to Hope Hospital. It's closest. They'll do the best they can." Knox knew the words weren't comforting, but offering false hope wasn't a great idea, either.

"That's her ex-husband. The bastard was mad she was out with me."

"Take a deep breath for me. I don't want you going into shock." Jackson's voice was soft, but Knox knew his brother's tone. One did not work in healthcare without seeing the effects of domestic violence. DV cases always got to him, but he never let anyone except Knox know that.

Jackson looked at Knox before turning his attention back to the man he was treating. "The police will be informed, but right now our priority is taking care of you all."

There was truth in that. If the man Knox was treating had committed a crime, even a deadly one, it was still their responsibility to treat him.

First, do no harm.

The first ambulance pulled up and the female doctor raised her head. Recognition poured through Knox. Miranda Paulson. No. She was on the East Coast. Working at a fancy research hospital with huge donors. His dream job.

The one he'd have left Hope for—if it had been offered.

"She goes first! Let Hope know to have a surgical suite on standby." Miranda's orders were staccatos in the night. She stood, keeping pressure on the wound like a pro as she walked beside the paramedics and climbed in behind them.

Another ambulance pulled up. Good. Hopefully, one for Jackson's patient would arrive shortly. "My guy next." Knox called over the paramedics. He gave the basics to them and relayed that there might be law enforcement at the hospital.

When the third transport arrived, he waited while Jackson repeated the same measures as he did and passed his patient off to the paramedics.

"Hey, anyone know whose purse this is?" A young black man was holding up a large bag. One that no one would carry into a bar. It was professional, boring and it screamed Dr. Miranda Paulson.

If she had ever cracked a smile during residence, Knox hadn't seen it. And the two were together most of the time. Competing for surgical time, positions and then the follow-on at the research hospital.

Jackson had joked once that they spent more time together than many married couples—and fought like them, too.

"It's Dr. Paulson's."

Knox held out his hand and the man started to give him the purse before pulling back.

"Your hands are covered in blood." The young man shook his head as he held the purse against his chest.

"Right." Good call. Miranda had great taste in clothes. The bag was probably some fancy thing. "Let me clean up, then my colleague and I will head to the hospital. Dr. Paulson will be there. Just give me one minute." Knox looked at his jeans, blood covered the knees, and his shirt was likely ruined, too, but at least he could wash his hands.

"Expensive night out." Jackson ran his hands under the faucet next to him. "Did you say Dr. Paulson?"

"I did." Knox swallowed the other words that bubbled up. He'd recognize Miranda until the day he died. The soft dark curls. Chestnut-brown eyes. Lips that looked like the universe designed them to smile but were in a constant frown. A brain that worked faster than any he'd ever seen.

Jackson cleared his throat but didn't say anything.

"I assume she'll be at the hospital and once the adrenaline wears off, she'll realize she doesn't have her purse. So we'll run it to her." Knox laid out the plan, ignoring the pinch in his belly at the thought of seeing Miranda again. The woman had gotten the thing he wanted most.

Granted, she'd earned it.

He might have grumbled for weeks about losing the opportunity, but he couldn't ignore that she'd been a good choice.

The better choice.

And he'd redoubled his effort to prove himself. To make himself the best general surgeon at Hope Hospital. Completed his surgical critical care certification and several others, too. Outside of the chief surgeon, Knox had more certifications than any other general surgeon at the hospital.

They headed out of the bathroom. The young man with the bag held it out. "You'll make sure it gets to her?"

"We will. We go way back with Dr. Paulson." Knox heard Jackson cough, but he ignored the sound. They did go way back. Maybe not as besties, but there was a history there.

"Can you play nice?" Jackson looked at the bag in Knox's hands then met his brother's gaze.

"Of course. She's probably just passing through town. Maybe visiting family." She'd had a big family. Three sisters and two happy parents. He remembered them standing together after the white coat ceremony.

Posing for pictures. Jackson had stood in the place of his family that day. Jackson's presence was far better than if his mother had decided to show. But as he saw others basking in their families' warm glow it was hard to ignore jealousy's pinch.

"All right. Let's go find Dr. Paulson."

This wasn't the way Dr. Miranda Paulson planned to return to Hope Hospital. Well, she hadn't actually planned to return at all. No, this was a setback.

A necessary one, maybe. But that didn't change the fact that she'd burned bright at Parkins Research Hospital in New York—a private research hospital that claimed to only employ the best. And she'd flamed out in a well of burnout following her divorce.

Well, actually, the burnout started long before the divorce. Stepping back, coming home. Restarting. This was not the plan for the former valedictorian of every graduating class she'd been in.

"Dr. Paulson." Hugh Lawton, the head of surgery at Hope, looked far more tired than she remembered. She and Knox Peters had served under him as residents.

Knox. He'd been at the bar tonight. Jackson, too.

Where one went the other followed. Some things never changed. That was oddly comforting. The men weren't brothers, but they were closer than she and her sisters. Blood might be thicker than water, but love was thicker than anything.

And its absence... Its absence was felt through generations. Though they were trying to break that generational curse now. Thirty-plus years late was better than never.

"I'd say it's nice to see you again, before I officially start tomorrow but..." She held up her hands. They were free of blood now, but there were stains on her jeans, and her white tank top was already in the trash. Luckily, a nurse had offered her a fresh shirt from the Hope Hospital laundry. It didn't fit well, but it was free of blood. That was all that mattered.

"Yeah. Riding in on an ambulance with a stab-wound patient might be one for the record books."

"One I'd happily never repeat. Any word on Jill?" The woman had drifted in and out of consciousness in the ambulance. But each time she was awake, she'd begged Miranda to save her.

Words that never got easier to hear.

"Surgery will take hours. Two abdominal wounds..." Hugh's voice floated away.

She knew the stats. He knew she knew the stats. Pulling through surgery was just the first hurdle. The good news was Jill was young. If given the chance, her body would heal faster.

Her surgeons just had to beat the fates for that chance.

"Starting tomorrow you will be on the floor full-time. It's nice to have you home."

"Happy to be here." They were the words Miranda was supposed to say. That they didn't ring true didn't matter. She'd said some version of them many times since turning in her notice at Parkins Research Hospital.

Excited for a new chapter.

Here's to new adventures.

Stepping back will be nice.

Platitudes people expected. Words that hid the imposter syndrome and failure that crawled through her mind nearly every waking minute. The reminder that she had been good, but not good enough.

Hugh nodded. "Never thought we'd see you back in our regional hospital. But I'm glad you're here."

"Miranda!" Knox's voice echoed behind her.

She turned and her body did what it always did. Locked down.

The man was mouthwateringly handsome. Smart. Humorous. She always told friends that doctors didn't look like they did on television. Not all six-packs and smoky gray eyes that made you want to strip the scrubs from their bodies.

Dr. Knox Peters would fit in perfectly on the set of any television drama. Except he was a brilliant surgeon.

They'd competed for everything from college through med school and residency. Her first. Him second…barely. The man should have done a year or two at Hope and then moved on to a bigger hospital.

Hell, she'd half expected to find him next to her at Parkins someday. Maybe if he had…

She forced her mind to walk away from the what-if. Knox was here, walking up to her. Jackson beside him. Holding her purse.

Her hand went to her hip. She'd changed her shirt and not realized her purse was still at the bar.

Brains on autopilot could do miraculous things while dumping all information it deemed unnecessary during fight-or-flight mode. Like not having her purse.

"Thank you. How are your patients?" She took the purse from Knox's hands, careful to avoid touching him. Her body had lit up once upon a time when he touched her. Light touches, professional. Nothing sexual, but her body hadn't been able to tell the difference.

She was not risking the discovery that the crush was still alive and well. Or rather, she wasn't looking for confirmation.

Her divorce was finalized a year ago. The separation had occurred a year before that.

"One is under arrest, but expected to make a full recovery. The other is getting patched up outside the OR waiting room."

Knox blew out a breath before running a hand through his blond hair. "Rough night." If this was a TV drama, the moment would have been captured on a long camera. The audience sighing at the sight of the hot doc looking troubled over patients. It was so cliche...except Knox wasn't acting.

"It was good the three of us were there. You staying in Phoenix long?" Knox smiled. His top teeth were still just a hair uneven. Her ex-husband would have put caps on them. They didn't take anything away from Knox, though. In fact, she thought they added to his beauty.

"Oh." Miranda looked at Hugh. Had he not told Knox that she was starting tomorrow? Was it because their rivalry had been more than a little too much as residents? That was years ago.

Time might not heal all wounds, but they were hardly student competitors anymore.

"Dr. Peters. Dr. Paulson is our new general surgeon. I told you Dr. Paulson would be shadowing you when she started."

"I didn't think you meant Miranda. She is supposed to be some hotshot on the East Coast."

Was that an inflection on the word supposed?

Miranda bit the inside of her cheek to keep a neutral look on her face.

Don't read into things.

His dark blue eyes caught hers, lightning seeming to flash through them. "Paulson isn't exactly an uncommon name."

Jackson shifted. If frustration was a vibe, it would be Knox's best friend in this moment.

"You got the fellowship. You worked at Parkins Research Hospital. You—"

"Failed and came home." Miranda nodded. "Yep. They should have given it to you." She hefted her purse onto her shoulder. "Hindsight really is twenty/twenty."

"Knox," Jackson's voice was soft but she saw Knox flinch at the tone. A soft-spoken reminder.

Miranda bit her lip. "If you don't want me to shadow you—"

"It's fine." Knox shook his head. "You really gave up the Parkins job? Really?"

"*Gave up* is a relative term." She'd not been fired, but her performance appraisals made it clear they weren't going to renew her contract. So she'd resigned and taken the vacation she'd put off for forever before coming back here.

He cleared his throat. "Sorry."

"Don't be." Miranda crossed her arms. It wasn't much of a defense, but it gave her a small sense of control. "I failed. A first." Her eyes drifted to the floor.

Why did it have to be Knox witnessing the failure? Her parents were gone. Her sisters were happy she was home. They viewed the setback as a gain. A chance to start over.

Only Miranda knew what her failure meant. And it was easy to see when it radiated back from the colleague she'd strangely missed. "Maybe if you'd been there, I could have focused on beating you."

"No one beats me these days."

A startled laugh escaped her chest. "I meant it as a joke." She looked at Hugh and pulled her phone from her back pocket to order a car through the mobile app she'd downloaded when she landed.

"So much for playing nice." Jackson's words were barely audible, but the fact that Knox must have talked about how he would behave before they'd arrived saddened her.

She'd seen them as rivals. As two skilled colleagues trying to best each other. Not enemies.

Of course, I won everything, though.

Maybe that clouded her memories. Either way it didn't matter. "I'll see you tomorrow." Then she pushed past them without looking back. Her soul was too bruised to continue the verbal sparring.

Tomorrow she'd be Dr. Paulson, don the mental armor she'd used all her life. Tough surgeon. No-nonsense physician. Top of her class.

Rather than the broken woman she felt like when she was alone.

CHAPTER TWO

MIRANDA SAT IN her car, mentally prepping herself to walk through the doors of Hope Hospital. Today was the first of a new chapter. That this was a chapter she hadn't wanted was irrelevant.

She needed to do her best.

Best. Her parents' favorite word.

Miranda had grown up answering the question: Did you do your best? She'd heard so many parents say some variation of it. But in the Paulson family, *best* had one meaning. Perfection.

The thing was that until she'd left Arizona, Miranda had always met the metric. Exceeded it. Blew past it. Made it look easy when she was breaking inside.

And it hadn't mattered.

Even perfection wasn't enough to make her parents proud. At least not for Miranda. Her sisters weren't as focused on perfection. Maybe it was eldest-daughter syndrome. She'd read that in one of the self-help books she devoured.

Whatever it was, her life had fallen apart at Parkins Research. She had fallen apart. She couldn't hack it.

She closed her eyes, pinching them tight. That was the past. And she was moving forward. No one needed to know.

Except I told Knox last night...and Hugh was there, too. And Jackson.

Just blurted everything out. Hopefully, the hectic events would drown out the memories.

She held her head high as she walked through the doors of Hope. Dr. Miranda Paulson was not going to fail—not again.

"Good morning, Dr. Paulson." Knox's voice was calm as he stepped beside her, waiting for the elevator to arrive in the garage.

"Morning, Dr. Peters." Miranda kept her tone even, waiting for the inevitable questions from last night. Her ex-husband seized on any sign of weakness. Knox had, too, when they were residents. Though in a different way.

Lance was cruel. Knox just used any advantage he could find to come in first. Even if he'd always only managed second place when Miranda was in the game.

"Hugh wants you shadowing me." His words were crisp as the elevator doors opened.

"That was what he said last night." Miranda raised an eyebrow as she met Knox's gaze. She watched his lips move, just a little. Like he was running his tongue over his teeth. A nervous habit?

Knox shifted on his heels. "Yes." He pushed the button for the surgical floor before leaning against the wall of the elevator.

The picture of handsome. So relaxed, though he made the same motion with his mouth again. Maybe she wasn't the only one acting like nothing bothered her.

"However, after you walked off, I recommended the standard two weeks shadowing be reduced." He crossed his arms before continuing, "After all, you've worked here before."

And it means we have to spend less time together.

Perhaps he wasn't thinking that, but it stung that he'd immediately requested to shorten the time he spent with her.

"True." What else was she supposed to say?

The elevator doors opened, and she sucked in a deep

breath. Time to move. Though that wouldn't stop the next week of spending every work moment with Knox.

She started to turn left, but Knox touched her shoulder. His fingers were gone so fast, but Miranda found herself looking at where they'd been.

"Where are you going?"

Pointing to the left she looked at him. Was he tricking her? "The locker room?"

Knox followed her hand then shook his head. "They remodeled the floor two years ago. Locker room is down here now."

"Ah." A remodel. That was nice. The former facilities had been clean, but the old pink tile a clear reminder that the hospital really only funded projects patients saw. Staff locker rooms, supply hallways, storage rooms, those were always decades out of date.

"Maybe you do need two weeks."

"Maybe I do." Miranda knew Knox hadn't expected her to hear his muttered words, but she'd been gone eight years. Things changed. That was good. Change was good. At least according to all the self-help books on her shelf.

Knox's blue eyes held hers, and she stood there, waiting for him to say something. "Let's get changed, then rounds."

"Fine."

Maybe I do.

Knox laid his head against the locker as he tried to force himself to focus on the plan for today. Show Miranda around. Make sure she understood what she needed then let Hugh know that one day was actually enough.

Sure, most got six, two weeks total, since they did three days on and three days off at Hope, unless you picked up extra shifts. But Miranda had been here before. She knew the routine.

She could pick up anything, effortlessly. It was what had made her top of class. Her brain was a machine. His was fast, but most of that was hard work that he hid from everyone but Jackson. Smoke and mirrors designed to look effortless.

Being around her again brought out feelings he hadn't felt in forever. Miranda had always made him try his hardest. She was his foil. Part of him missed the banter. The drive. The need to beat her.

Last night, though, she'd looked different.

Still beautiful. The woman was the definition of gorgeous. Maybe there were a few extra creases around her eyes, but they added to her glory. She still looked like Miranda but the fire, the spark that made her *her*, seemed diminished.

I failed.

Two little words that made him so uncomfortable. He could not imagine a world where Miranda failed. That place didn't exist.

He pushed off the locker. Whatever thoughts were forcing their way through his brain wouldn't do him any good right now. Get Miranda through the day and make sure she was good enough not to need him. That was his only goal.

"I heard your guy from last night was arrested as soon as he regained consciousness." She was leaning against the wall in the hallway, the blue scrubs that seemed to drape over everyone else hugging her so perfectly.

How did she manage that?

"Not surprised." It was unfortunate but not the first time he had a patient with law enforcement escorts. One bad choice could alter everything.

Not enough people thought that through. Or considered who else might be impacted by their issues. His mother never had...or if she did, it didn't make her change her actions.

"My patient came through her surgery." Miranda looked to her feet before looking back at him.

He heard her unstated *but*. Abdominal wounds were tricky. Something every general surgeon knew. With luck, she was done lying on their operating table.

"And her date?"

Miranda smiled. "You can tell Jackson that I saw him on his way to find a cup of coffee. He had sixty stitches spread out on all his appendages but otherwise he is fine. He's stayed with Jill all night. Not the greatest first date."

"First date!" Knox knew his mouth was hanging open. "Man, I've had more than a few rough starts but that really takes the cake."

"Rough starts?" Miranda let out a small chuckle. "How can *you* have a rough start?" Her cheeks darkened as she met his gaze but she didn't withdraw the question.

"It happens to us all. Though maybe not to you." Miranda's strive for perfection probably touched every aspect of her life, dating life included.

"First dates… I can count on one hand the number I've had."

"Only one hand? I've got at least two handfuls of bad first date stories." Yep, perfection, thy name was Miranda.

"Oh." She grabbed a tablet chart from the nurses' station and shrugged. "No, I've only gone on four first dates. Always too busy, then I met Lance."

"Lance. I remember him. Neuro, right?"

"Right." Miranda didn't look up the from the chart. She wasn't wearing a ring, but then surgeons typically didn't. Still, there was something in her body language.

The set of her lips. The tightness in her shoulders. He'd seen many divorces in his life. Though he didn't remember his mother and father's, more than one foster family had imploded while he was there. And several residents had married and divorced before they'd managed to land at the same hospital.

It happened. Only psychiatry had a higher divorce rate than surgeons.

"So, back at Hope. Must feel like a step down from Parkins Research?" He was proud of the work Hope Hospital did. It was a regional hospital, not internationally known, but the hospital did good work.

"Do you think it's a step down?" Miranda tilted her head, a loose curl falling over her left eye.

He didn't. This place felt nice—that wasn't quite the right word for the feeling that made him turn down every new opportunity offered.

"We've got two crash victims coming in!" Lisa, the charge nurse on the floor called over the radio. "Teens, drag racing. Both have arrested once en route."

All thoughts disappeared as he and Miranda headed for the surgical suites, listening to the stats come over the radio.

"Jackson here today?" Miranda asked over the hum of the water as they scrubbed up.

"Yeah. He'll be in with us. Hugh and Mitchell have Beth as their nurse anesthetist." They gloved up and moved into the OR. The minutes ticked by.

Jackson nodded as he sat monitoring anesthesia equipment that wasn't needed yet.

"I hate this part." Miranda's voice was soft, barely carrying over the light music in the room.

"Me, too." Jackson nodded as he triple-checked the equipment he would use to keep the patient sedated.

Knox wasn't fond of the wait, either. General surgeons saw more trauma than other specialties. That didn't mean the wait was easy.

Commotion echoed in the hallway and the professionals in the surgical suite seemed to take a deep breath together.

"Sixteen. Had to use Jaws of Life to get him out." The

ER team rushed the kid in. Reciting stats that weren't great. "Collapsed lungs, internal bleeding…"

The list went on.

Typically, a general surgeon operated with a resident. But since it was Miranda's first day, she was standing opposite him. It was a weird feeling. They'd never worked like this. They'd each stood in the spot where she was, but it was Hugh or one of the other surgeons standing where Knox was.

Her dark eyes met his as he took the scalpel, and a sense of calm settled within Knox. He looked to Jackson and waited for him to give the thumbs-up that the patient was fully under.

"All right, Dr. Paulson, let's get to work."

The teen, Fritz, was in recovery. Touch and go was the name of the game and would be for the next forty-eight hours. She and Knox had closed three lacerations in his abdominal cavity and removed his spleen. His friend had lost his foot above the ankle.

A terrible day for all involved. But the boys were alive.

"Ready to talk to the parents?" Miranda pulled the cap off her curly hair. Her feet were sore, and her lower back ached. It was weird how surgeons just got used to it.

"Nope. But that is what we have to do." Knox pulled his own surgical cap off.

She understood his statement. There was no easy way to tell parents that they still weren't sure if their child would make it. Still, there was something in Knox's eyes, a look that made her heart clench.

"I can do the notification, if you want?"

Knox's eyebrows pulled together as he shook his head. "I was the lead surgeon. It's my responsibility."

His shoulders straightened a hair on the word *responsibility*.

"All right." She walked beside him. A weird sense of home

settling around her. She'd notified hundreds of loved ones in the course of her career. Told people the best and worst news. Today's notification was somewhere in between. But delivering it with Knox—it felt different.

"If you're son hadn't dared my son, he wouldn't have lost his foot!"

"I don't even know what has happened with my son! And your boy has always been a troublemaker. Fritz is a good kid. Straight-A student."

"Oh, please. That's because you can afford to pay off teachers."

"I do not!"

The argument poured through the doors to the waiting room. Adult voices blending together in a cacophony of blame.

"Blame game already started." Miranda sighed. Both boys were alive. That was no small miracle considering they'd crashed at high speeds. But it was human nature to want to blame someone.

"Never a good sign." Knox rolled his head from side to side, then stepped through.

Two white women were standing, noses nearly touching, both with tearstained cheeks. They turned almost in unison and Miranda knew her eyes were wide as the identical twins stared at her and Knox.

"Fritz?" The woman on the right teetered and her sister wrapped a hand around her waist. The argument forgotten, at least for the moment.

"He came through surgery but the next twenty-four hours will be touch and go." Knox took a deep breath, his body shifting a hair closer to Miranda. "We had to remove his spleen."

"His spleen." The woman who was clearly Fritz's mother slipped to the floor. "Can you live without that?"

"Yes," Knox stated and Miranda looked at him, waiting for him to expand on that a little more.

When he didn't, she took a step forward. "A normal life, though he might be more prone to infection. My sister had hers out due to a car accident a few years ago. She has a scar but otherwise no issues."

"So he will be all right?" Her watery eyes met Miranda's and she realized her misstep.

Kelly's accident wasn't as extensive as Fritz's and her recovery took months. Fritz wasn't stable enough for her to make promises. It was a misstep she'd have never made a year ago. Her ability to distance herself from the trauma, from the reactions, a necessary trait in surgeons, was broken.

"We will be better able to give a prognosis tomorrow afternoon. Right now, he is stable." Knox's words were controlled, commanding, but Fritz's mother refused to let her gaze leave Miranda's.

"Promise me he is going to be okay."

There was no way for Miranda to offer that promise. "We are doing everything we can." Words that she doubted were much comfort in this moment, but were the truth.

"You can see him, if you'd like." Knox gestured to the door they'd come through. "He's in the intensive care unit, but if you follow the hallway behind me, it will take you to the desk. A nurse will take you to him."

She gripped her sister's hand and stood. Then she walked past them, her head held high, her sister right beside her.

"Sorry." Miranda crossed her arms. Talking to family in this situation was a delicate game. If you couldn't make promises, you didn't talk of the future.

"It happens." Knox looked at her, his eyes saying what so many had said in the past two years.

But not normally to you.

Once, she had been the picture of perfection. Yes, behind

closed doors she sometimes cried for hours. There were days where she felt more robot than person. But that robot was a better surgeon than the emotional physician who made mistakes. Who failed…

"At least the argument stopped." Knox was trying to make her feel better.

"No, it didn't. They tabled it." Knox gave her a look that made her chuckle. "I grew up with three sisters. Trust me. That argument will kick-start again as soon the crisis settles. And be renegotiated through the years."

She loved her sisters. Miranda never felt the call to motherhood, but Kelly and Olive had three each. The cousins were all around the same ages; it made family gatherings loud. If their oldest were in a car accident, the sisters would support each other and argue about fault.

"Renegotiated?"

"Yeah. If you ask Olive and Kelly about the winter of ninety-nine they will each claim it was the other's idea to go 'sledding' on the sandhill. The concussion Olive got is why her memory is fuzzy, according to Kelly. The six stitches Kelly needed to close the wound in her head, Olive's excuse." It was the way of the world amongst sisters.

"Siblings." Knox shrugged. "But are you okay?"

"You and Jackson are brothers." Miranda preferred this topic to his question. It sucked to not give patients' families too much hope. But it was necessary when the odds were still tumbling. Her slip was one others might look past, ignore as first-day jitters, but Knox knew her.

Or he had once.

"Surely the two of you have fights that get started and have to be put aside for a while?"

"No." Knox shook his head, his blue eyes staring at her in a way that made Miranda want to shift away. She wasn't the woman she'd been. And there wasn't even a good reason.

That was the thing she'd told her therapist. She'd just burned out. No catastrophic cause. No major life change. Her marriage was a disaster. Lance was cruel behind closed doors. Manipulative. A masterful gaslighter.

But she'd handled it. In fact, it was he who'd left. Saying he'd taken a new job three states over without telling her, then handing her divorce papers.

That was one thing she'd change if she got a do-over. She and Lance should not have married. A truth she'd suspected on her wedding day.

People divorced all the time. Particularly surgeons. None of the divorce stress caused her burnout.

It was like one day the switch that kept her perfect just switched off. And nothing she'd done could flip it back on.

"Miranda—"

"I'm fine." The words were spoken too fast. The defensive stance creeping through her. "Really. Just first day back. Fine. Really. Fine."

"Three fines?" The concern flipping through his blue eyes made her want to lean toward him. To confide the truth. She felt lost.

She had everything she'd wanted. A good career. Enough money in the bank to be comfortable. Happy family time with her sisters and her new role as the fun auntie. Complaining felt wrong.

"Yep. Three fines. Just to reinforce it." She tapped her nose, offered a smile she hoped looked real, before turning and heading to the locker room. Miranda kept an ear open in case Knox said anything else.

As she entered the women's locker room, she tried to convince herself that it was all right that he didn't.

CHAPTER THREE

KNOX LOOKED OVER the interns. The fresh batch of baby doctors trying to figure out their next paths. He and Miranda had stood in a similar gaggle. That gaggle had been doctors across a wide range of specialties and across the nation for more than a decade. It was weird to feel so old and see yourself in the next group, too.

He picked out the Miranda of this group. The perfectionist already writing notes with her stylus on a tablet. A young woman stood next to her, mimicking the motions. Though she didn't look quite as determined. Had people looked at him and Miranda that way?

Picked out the two over-overachievers in a group of overachievers?

"Ready?" Miranda yawned as she stepped next to him.

"I am. Are you?" She'd disappeared after the blunder with the family yesterday. A minor misstep. Sometimes emotions got in the way when talking to family. But Miranda had always been too hard on herself.

"Yeah. I just need another cup of coffee." She held up the reusable mug and tilted her head toward the future doctors. "Ready to convince some of these kids that they want to do surgery?"

"How could they not want to!" Knox chuckled as they started toward the group. He'd joined surgical because it was the most prestigious. At least that was what the doctors who had stood where he and Miranda stood now had said. He'd stayed general rather than specializing because he liked knowing some of everything. He had his critical care certifications, and surgical oncology, and pediatrics and just about everything else, too. He worked on all sorts of cases.

"Spoken like a true surgeon." Miranda took a sip of her drink.

Her eyes were far away. Like she was looking at the interns and thinking of their time, too. But coming to a different conclusion than he did. Like maybe this wasn't the life she'd choose in a do-over.

"Good morning." Miranda raised a hand as all the interns' faces turned toward them.

Now all the tablets and styluses emerged from oversize pockets or satchels. Dutiful note takers even if they already knew this wasn't the specialty for them.

"Morning." The group's harmonized greeting made him smile.

"So who already knows surgery is for them?" Knox clapped and gave a thumbs-up to two interns on the right. The woman who'd started taking notes before they'd even walked over started to raise her hand, hesitated, then raised it fully.

Knox saw Miranda tilt her head at the hesitater. The first two hands had shot up. The third…

"Is there anyone who knows this isn't the specialty you're choosing? It's okay. Dr. Peters and I will not take it personally."

"Speak for yourself." Knox nodded before gesturing for anyone to raise their hands. "Let us know."

Three hands from the back shot up.

"Which specialty are you three looking at?"

"Pediatrics."

"Ophthalmology."

"Radiology."

"All right." Miranda smiled. "You can still ask questions. With the exception of radiology, there are surgical specialties for both."

"Some of us like to live in the dark!" The hopeful radiologist's joke let out a chorus of chuckles.

"The lights are pretty bright in surgery." Knox crossed his arms. "But what questions do you have for us?"

He and Miranda fielded the standard questions for the first twenty minutes. How to handle placements? Was it better to think of two specialties you might like in surgery? What was the best lesson to take away? Questions each class asked and surgeons and other doctors answered multiple times a year.

"How much trauma does a general surgeon see?" The question came from the hesitater.

"Quite a bit." Miranda's tone was controlled but forceful. "We are the frontline. Car accidents, ruptured appendix, fights. General surgeons see a little of everything. I am technically a general with a certification in trauma surgery and pediatric trauma care."

"And I have those and surgical oncology, and vascular surgery. And I am considering hand surgery, but most of those go to the ortho guys. All the little bones." Knox chuckled, trying to relieve the tension this question always created.

"But," Miranda added, "all specialties have great days and lows deeper than you can possibly imagine."

"Surgery seems so competitive." The woman pursed her lips as she made another note.

Knox saw the flush of the resident's cheeks and wondered if she'd meant to say it.

"Surgery is competitive no matter the specialty. General surgery is least competitive than the others and matching into it is still difficult." Miranda's answer was the textbook one. He'd read some variation on the theme on the blogs he'd searched when trying to determine his own match choices.

"Competition makes you better, though." Competition drove you to be better. It let you reach goals that you might not reach without fighting someone else for them. It was how he'd reached the point he was at.

Mostly because of the woman beside him now.

"Competition *can* be healthy."

Miranda's inflection on *can* nearly made Knox's head bounce back. They'd competed for everything; she'd won everything. It had gotten her everything.

There was no way she could regret that...right?

"Would you choose a different specialty if you could go back in time?"

That question wasn't for him. Knox found himself as interested in Miranda's answer as the young intern.

"I think the choice of specialty is an important one. If you are choosing because someone else thinks its best, or because an online post says this is the best one, or the top moneymaker, or for any reason other than it is where I feel I can spend the next thirty to forty years of my life, you open yourself up to regrets. You should make that choice for yourself, not because someone else wants it."

She hadn't answered the question. In fact, she'd fairly well avoided it. With a good speech. The interns did need to focus on things that made them happy. They'd been in school with kids who choose a career because that was what mom or dad wanted for them. That was a rough road.

Luckily for Knox—no one had wanted a say in what he did.

"Was that a yes?" The hesitater raised an eyebrow as she held the stylus. Knox would give her credit. She wanted an answer. A full answer.

"No. I would not choose a different specialty. General surgery is rewarding. The adrenaline rush of saving someone experiencing trauma is real. That isn't just a television drama moment." She took a deep breath, and the faraway look he'd seen earlier reappeared.

"But…" She looked at him then at the group of students. "I cannot look out at you and tell you there aren't changes I would make. I took a fellowship after graduating, a coveted one, that I shouldn't have. Sometimes it's easy as you compete with each other to focus on what the world says you should want, instead of what you want for yourself."

His ears buzzed and his jaw ached as he forced himself to unclench his teeth. How could she say that she'd change it? How could she acknowledge she hadn't wanted the fellowship? It was the one job he'd have taken to leave here. The one he absolutely would have said yes to.

What would his life be like if she'd realized that years ago?

"Time to start rounds." Knox cleared his throat. He needed to move, needed to push away the discomfort coating his skin. Anything to focus on something other than the what-if.

"You're very fortunate." Miranda stood next to Jill's bed. The young woman still had two tubes draining the fluid buildup in her stomach, but over all her prognosis was positive.

"He got upset sometimes, but I never thought Doug would…" Jill looked out the window. The view was a dirty roof, nothing one would actually enjoy, but she'd worked with domestic violence victims before. It wasn't the view Jill wanted; it was the avoidance. But she hadn't done anything wrong.

"It's not your fault." Miranda said words she knew Jill had heard. Shame came with the territory. It wasn't fair, only the perpetrator was responsible for intimate partner violence, but the victim always felt like they'd done something.

At least for a little while.

"When do I get to leave this floor?" Jill bit her lip before looking at Miranda. "I'd like to get out of PCU."

Progressive Care Unit or the PCU was in between the intensive care unit and a standard floor unit. The stepdown schedule for the unit varied on the severity of disease and injury. "I know you want to get off the PCU, but the fact that you aren't in ICU two days after the attack is a small miracle."

Jill brushed a tear from her cheek. "I want to go home."

"I understand. The comfort of your own bed—"

"No." Jill interrupted. "Not my own bed. Home. I moved to Phoenix for a job. For Doug's job. And then we got divorced and I stayed because..." She threw her hands in the air. "I don't know why I stayed."

"I stayed because it was easy. Until it wasn't." Miranda took a deep breath and moved to the chair by the window. If Jill wanted to look out at it, that was fine, but she wanted her to know that she was sitting opposite her.

"Are you about to tell me it's not my fault again?" Jill pinched her eyes shut. Those words were good for some people, triggers for others.

"There is no roadmap for this." Miranda barely resisted the urge to pull her legs up. "I wish there was. I wish I could give you a magic pill or something to know how to build your life around the trauma you've experienced. From before the attack and through it. Only you can figure out what that path looks like for you. But if you want to leave the city, there are programs that help you with funding if you need it. Counseling services."

"I want a fast-forward button. A way to just fast-forward six months and things be different."

"In six months, your body will be healed. Life will be different, but that doesn't mean everything will be all right. Give yourself time, Jill. You are worth it." She stood. "If you need more pain medication make sure the nurses know." Miranda planned to request a visit from the hospital counselor. Jill could always send them away. But talking to someone...

It had helped her. Once she'd finally reached out.

Lance had never raised his hands, though Miranda suspected he was capable of it. He had used emotional manipulations. Made her feel so unworthy that she pushed herself and pushed herself. Their careers were the things they focused on. Two over-overachievers. But she'd wanted an actual marriage, to come in at least second to his career goals. Unfortunately, she hadn't even been in his top ten. All slots were reserved for his career. And she thought if she just worked harder it might change.

And when she broke, when the burnout became too much for her to focus on anything, when she'd gone to administration to ask for a sabbatical, he'd called her crazy.

Denigrated his wife's mental health, using what many referred to as an ableist slur.

The worst part was that in those days she'd believed him. After achieving her entire life. Competing and winning to feel nothing when she entered the hospital. Numb to the job, her mind wandering when it needed focus. What other answer was there?

Lying in bed, depressed and feeling like she was worthless and her husband had agreed with the dark demons of depression. He'd fueled the lies her mind had told her in those days.

And she'd stayed. That rankled her far more than she wanted to admit. Then he'd left her.

Most days she still felt like an imposter. A failure hiding under a mantle of a fancy résumé and quick talking. She wanted the feeling to stop. Wanted to find a way to prove she was fine.

Knox was putting in notes at the computer workstation. He tilted his head a little as she walked up but didn't say anything. If he clenched his jaw any tighter, she worried he might pop out a few teeth.

The man had been professional today, but the relative ease they'd had yesterday seemed to evaporate this morning.

Her mind immediately jumped through their interactions, looking to see where she might have made a mistake. Then she shut the thought train down. She was not responsible for Knox's bad mood. Or if she was, that wasn't fair and not her concern. He could work through it…or not.

She'd taken on all the responsibility in her relationship with Lance. Done her best to please him. To make him happy while making herself smaller and smaller. Not happening again.

"Jill is getting restless. And she has at least another two days in PCU. Does Hope have any programs for restless patients?"

"What kind of programs?" Knox continued typing.

Miranda bit back the question, *Are you mad at me?* She was not asking that.

"Well, things like volunteers that play cards, craft materials. I had a patient that loved doing diamond paintings. Maybe a video game console to borrow, paper to write a story or letters." Each room had a television but there were only so many hours of television some could stand. Smartphones helped pass the time but they got old, too.

"Hope is not a very big hospital, Miranda."

"You don't have to tell me!" She laughed, hoping to change the direction of conversation. "Climbing the stairs here isn't as much of a workout but finding a parking spot in the garage is super easy."

"The point is," Knox said, turning toward her, "if you wanted fancy things, you should have stayed at the fancy hospital."

"Out with it." She crossed her arms. Whatever he needed to say, life would be easier for them if he let it go now.

"Excuse me?"

"No. You are not playing the fool now, Dr. Peters. You are being short with me. You've been short all day. I am asking if there is anything I can do for a patient, and you are being snarky. So, what is it you actually want to say to me?"

Knox's eyes widened and color flooded his cheeks. Embarrassment or anger, maybe a hint of both.

"You had everything. Everything. The fellowship. The fancy job. How could you not want it? How, after working so hard to beat me, could you tell an intern this morning you'd change it?" He pinched the bridge of his nose. "You got the thing I wanted most, and you didn't even want it in the end."

Miranda blinked. She doubted Knox had meant to let all of that spill out. But now that it was here, there was no going back for either of them.

"Are you the same person you were when we were residents?" Life had changed her. Whether she wanted those changes or not was irrelevant.

"Yes." He crossed his arms. "I am still the hardworking, competitive man I was when you were last here."

Miranda looked at Knox. The muscles in his shoulders were tight and his forearms flexed. The man was tightly wound, whether he realized it or not. "Well, I had to change. I'll see you tomorrow." Then she turned and left.

What else was there to say?

CHAPTER FOUR

HE'D NOT NEEDED Jackson to tell him he'd been an ass. At least on this, Knox was self-aware. Though his brother had agreed with the analysis when he outlined what he'd said. Then helped him gather some of the things for his apology.

Knox looked at the small cabinet in the break room that had been stocked with a mishmash of things that really belonged in the trash can. He'd run Miranda's idea past Hugh via text. The head of surgery had agreed that Knox could have this cabinet.

He put a label on the cabinet and leaned back, admiring his work.

"If you lean back any farther and fall over, I will laugh before I help you up."

Miranda's light tone stunned him. He was prepared for an understandably angry morning shift.

"I'm sorry for yesterday." Knox turned, and her dark eyes met his. There were circles under them. He'd caused her to lose sleep. All because she'd changed life paths.

A pivot could be healthy. He had never pivoted, never changed paths, because this one worked.

Other people changed directions all the time. And she was back here. That was nice. Standing across from her in surgery, he'd not realized how much he'd missed her presence until she was there. And he'd screwed it all up with an overreaction!

She'd been the best candidate for the job. If it was offered today, he was sure he could come in first. But then… Then, she'd been the right choice.

"I appreciate the apology. Why are you admiring the cabinet?" Miranda's raised eyebrow made him smile.

"I stole your idea." Knox pointed to the small cabinet. It had seemed bigger when he was cleaning it out. And even with the few things he'd picked up from the store with Jackson, it was very empty.

Still, every plan had to start somewhere.

"I haven't had any ideas." Miranda crossed her arms and rolled back on her feet.

The twitch of her lips, the frown hidden not quite quick enough, stabbed through him. He'd hurt her more than he'd realized yesterday.

"Not true." Knox opened the cabinet, adding a flourish to his hand motions.

Miranda chuckled, the rich sound bringing out his own laugh.

"You look like a bad game show model. In this corner you've won an ugly living room set, but you could have chosen a nearly empty cabinet!" Miranda mimicked his motions, her smile infectious.

"It's not an empty cabinet." Knox stuck his tongue out.

"I said nearly empty," Miranda countered.

He looked at the pack of cards, diamond paintings and adult coloring books that took up almost no space and had to give her that assessment. "All right, fine, nearly empty, but I figure we can work on that."

"We?"

"Yes. You were right. We should have some options for patients that are stuck here. There is a library near the cafeteria, too. I should have remembered that yesterday. But I was too focused on…" Knox took a deep breath.

"Too focused on being angry at the past. Which is dumb. You can't be angry at the past. It's done." He laughed, but the chuckles stopped as he saw Miranda wasn't laughing.

"You are allowed to have feelings about it. You aren't allowed to take those feelings out on me." Miranda's hip buzzed.

"That sounds like something a therapist said." Knox had seen a range of counselors and therapists when he was in foster care. None of them had had much to say for a young boy who knew his family didn't want him.

They'd offered platitudes. Told him it wasn't his fault. Given him pamphlets and books. Things he was certain their textbooks said would help him.

None of it did.

What finally had was graduating close to top of his class. Getting his own place and knowing that no one would ever find him lacking again.

"I might have had a therapist say it." Miranda shrugged as she looked at the pager. "Doesn't make it not true."

She looked up, "We have a consult down in the ER. Where is your pager?"

Knox pulled his off his hip. The battery light blinking. "Right here…and not holding a charge." It was a problem they'd had with them lately. The pagers were old but administration felt they could make do.

"I'll grab another as we head past the nurses' station." He tossed the dead weight. "I bet your other place didn't have issues with pagers."

"Parkins had issues and so did the two other hospitals I've worked at." Miranda held open the door. "Those hospitals were fancy, no way around that. But administration is the same everywhere. Cut corners to maximize profits."

Knox shook his head. "Always administration."

"The bane of all US hospitals." Miranda sighed, the frustration of a doctor who only wanted to treat patients but also had to make administration and insurance companies content. Two goals that were too often in opposition.

They walked down the flight of stairs into the ER. The buzz of the floor always reminded Knox of a well-choreographed play that dangled a little too close to full chaos. "The page said bay four."

"Dr. Peters." The young ER physician, Dr. Hinks, stepped between him and Miranda. Miranda raised a brow but stepped to the side to give them a little bit more space.

Dr. Hinks and Knox had had a few run-ins. The man believed his position as a doctor made him better than others. And he had a chip on his shoulder because he'd not matched into his chosen specialty. He'd matched into emergency medicine through the supplemental offer and acceptance program, commonly called SOAP.

That chip, and the idea that because he'd spent years in school meant his word was all that mattered, made him an incredibly difficult colleague.

His old-school belief that he shouldn't be questioned by patients, that he always knew best, was a principle most physicians were doing their best to root out. The fact that Dr. Hinks was so sure of himself despite only working in the field for a year unnerved Knox.

That level of confidence, mixed with a bitterness at the universe for not getting what you thought you were owed, could be dangerous.

"Child in bay four. Was pushed off the roof." The physician crossed his arms and shook his head. "Single mother and she wasn't home when the incident occurred. Clearly not fit to parent."

"That's quite a statement. What are you basing it on?" Miranda's question was the right one.

Which was good since Knox's head was buzzing as he saw disdain pass the physician's features.

"A feeling." Dr. Hinks rolled his eyes. "Sometimes that is all you need."

Healthcare workers saw unfortunate cases all the time. Social services was an important network to provide support to families. It was also underfunded and strained. Adding to it because of a *feeling* based on a bias was a horrid practice.

One that could have lifelong consequences.

"A feeling?" Miranda made a note on the tablet chart. "And the reason for the surgical consult?"

Dr. Hinks looked from Miranda to Knox. "She doing all the talking?"

"Excuse me?" Miranda's eyes flashed with a warning Knox doubted Dr. Hinks would take.

"I said…"

"We heard you." Knox interrupted before the physician could say anything else. "Are you planning on answering Dr. Paulson's question?"

Dr. Hinks let out a heavy sigh. As much as Knox hated getting administration involved in things, someone needed to talk to them about this man.

"He was pushed off a roof. He has a broken arm and big bruise on his side. Internal bleeding is your job."

"What's his blood pressure?" Knox checked his watch. If the kid was conscious that meant he likely wasn't hemorrhaging. The body could repair a minor internal bleed.

"Normal." Dr. Hinks shrugged.

"Normal?" Miranda's frustrated taps on the tablet mirrored Knox's thoughts. One of the main indicators of internal bleeding was low blood pressure. A large bruise might just happen with a fall. In fact, it likely *would* happen.

"When was the MRI ordered?" Knox suspected the answer but the furrow of Dr. Hinks's brows made it clear.

"Order it now." Before the man could say anything else, Knox opened the curtain and walked to bay four with Miranda, pulling it closed without waiting for Dr. Hinks.

A little boy lay on the ER bed, his mother in tears beside him, and a boy a few years older than him that had to be his big brother stood as they walked in.

"Good morning, I am Dr. Paulson." Miranda raised a hand.

"Dr. Peters." Knox nodded. "What happened?"

"I didn't mean to push him. Our cat climbed the tree and was up on the roof and..." The brother wiped a tear from his cheek.

"He told me not to follow him." The boy on the bed clenched his eyes shut and took a deep breath.

"Neither of you should have been on the roof." Their mother's stern look was softened by the tears in her eyes. This wasn't a parent who didn't care.

Knox had grown up with several of those. It was something he knew how to identify and quickly. One tiny benefit to a childhood steeped in trauma was his brain recognized it in others.

That was also one of the worst things.

"Let's start with basics." Miranda's voice was calm. "I'm Dr. Paulson, what is your name?" Miranda looked at the boy on the bed with the air cast on his right arm.

"Leo." He frowned. "It's my cat. Sprinkles is my responsibility. If I hadn't left my window open."

"Blame games don't help anyone right now. You can spend years pointing fingers at each other." Miranda waved a finger.

Was that what happened with her sisters? He and Jackson weren't bound by early-childhood memories. Just teenage years trying to break the cycle they'd been thrown into. Two young men bent on proving everyone wrong.

"When you fell, you tried to catch yourself?" Miranda gestured to the air cast.

He needed a real cast. But the priority was the MRI, even though, based on the steady blood pressure reading on the monitor in the corner, the child's coloring and the fact that he seemed completely lucid, Knox figured it would come back clear.

"I did."

"And the bruise." Miranda moved as Leo used his left hand to lift his shirt.

Knox shook his head. "That is a shoe print."

"Yep." Leo glared at his brother. "Sprinkles, my cat."

Knox could have guessed that by the name.

"She scratched Ben and he kicked me. Next thing I knew I was on the ground, my right arm screaming in pain."

"If you'd stayed inside…" Ben crossed his arms, but the tears in his eyes made it clear this was an accident.

"Well," Miranda said, looking at Knox, "I think Dr. Hinks was being overly cautious."

Knox nodded. Miranda's diplomacy was far better than the thoughts running through his head.

"So he doesn't need the MRI?" Leo's mom looked at her son, her bottom lip trembling as she ran her hand over his dark hair.

"I think we should still run it," Knox stated. "Dr. Hinks already put the order in. That bruise is nasty-looking. Based on Leo's vitals, I don't think we will find a bleed, but if it is slow, you could be back here in a few hours or days. And that adds complications."

"Right." His mother leaned over, kissing Leo's head. "That makes sense."

She hadn't wanted to challenge them, but Knox could see the relief in her face. She wanted to make sure Leo was fine, other than the broken arm.

Miranda tapped out a few things on her tablet. "If it comes back clear, Dr. Peters and I won't see you again, Leo."

Leo wiped a tear from his cheek. "At least I get a fancy cast." He pointed to the wall where there was a display of cast colors.

"I broke my ankle when I was about your age. What I wouldn't have given for a blue sparkle cast. Choose well, because you will have it for weeks." Miranda smiled, then turned to Knox. "Anything else, Dr. Peters?"

"I never broke any bones, but I would caution against the yellow—it gets dirty-looking fast." He gave Leo a thumbs-up. "Unless the grungy look is what you are going for."

"Ma'am—" Knox looked at Leo's mother "—can we talk to you for a minute in the hall?"

Leo's mother looked at her boys, her features falling.

"Just the hall, promise." Knox could see the worry. "If Leo or Ben need anything, you'll hear them."

She kissed Leo again, offered a watery smile to Ben and then led the way out of the room.

Miranda closed the curtain, and Knox turned his attention to Leo's mother. The woman's shoulders were straight. Tears coated her eyes but her lips were set. A woman ready for battle.

That confirmed that Dr. Hinks had said something unsavory.

"I am a fit mother." Her voice wavered. "I am also a single mother. We are in the twenty-first century. I will not be treated like some pariah because my ex-husband wants nothing to do with the family he helped create."

He saw Miranda's head turn out of the corner of his eye, but Knox didn't break eye contact with the boys' mother.

"I am not doubting that." Knox held up his hands. "Let's start at the beginning. I am Knox, this is Miranda." Titles were fine, but they could put some people on edge, particularly if they'd been weaponized.

"Stacy."

"It's nice to meet you, Stacy. The main reason I wanted to talk was about Ben."

"He didn't mean to kick his brother. He was trying to get the cat...who would have jumped off the roof and been fine." Stacy sucked in a sob. "I swear, they are good boys."

"Of course they are." Knox shook his head. "But I think Ben might do well to talk to one of our counselors while you wait for the MRI and its results. He's upset, which is understandable. But having him talk to someone who can reinforce that this was an accident may help."

Kids internalized a lot more than adults often realized. Ben was worried. He'd wanted to do the right thing for his pet and now his brother was waiting to find out if he had internal bleeding. None of that was the plan, but the rethinking, the rehashing, the wondering how you might have changed the outcome. It could stay with a kid for years.

Particularly if his and Miranda's initial assumption about Leo not needing surgery was wrong.

"We can put in the request for the counselor."

"Okay." Stacy looked to the closed curtain. "That might be good. But you said main reason. What else?"

Knox looked behind him, no sign of the other reason he wanted to discuss. He leaned against the wall, his hand falling in line with a poster most people ignored.

"I wanted to make sure you knew what all Leo's rights are as a patient." His hand tapped the line he was drawing Stacy's attention to. Miranda's smile was so big, he thought her teeth might radiate down the hall. This was important, but if admin asked, he could also say he hadn't technically recommended it.

Her mouth opened, then shut. "I can get Leo a new doctor. But I like you and Dr. Paulson."

"We aren't Leo's physicians of record. Dr. Hinks is." Miranda's tone was controlled, but he saw the twitch in the corner of her eye. Miranda wasn't impressed by the man, either.

"So if I wanted another doctor for Leo, I can ask?"

"Yes." Knox tapped the printout on the wall one more time before standing. The patients' rights poster was required to be prominently displayed. It clearly outlined her entitlement to choose a new physician, if there was an issue.

It wasn't talked about much, but it was state law.

Administration could be difficult, but with Miranda and Knox backing her, they'd make the change. Better that than a lawsuit. "Mention it to one of the nurses and let them know they can talk to me or Dr. Paulson, if they have questions."

"Thank you." Stacy closed her eyes, a little of the worry decreasing from her cheeks.

Stacy moved past him, and Knox clenched his fists. The emotional drain of dealing with abuse situations was terrible, but threatening a mother when it was clear an accident had occurred was also wrong. A power play from a man who wanted to prove he had more power than others.

"Knox?"

Miranda's dark eyes were trained on him, kindness, and he feared pity, clear in them. He couldn't explain the blend of emotions rocketing through him. He'd been the one without power for his entire childhood. Watched bullies, kids and adults pick on him because he had less power than them. That a health professional would do the same...

He'd not solved problems with his fists since grade school. But the urge was there. "I need to get some air. I'll catch up with you."

Knox walked past Miranda without looking back. He needed a breather. In a few minutes he could put back the feelings of unworthiness, the memories of having to deal with an unfair system, the hurts he kept buried—unless he was using them to push himself forward.

* * *

Miranda grabbed an adult coloring book and the crayons. The owls and flowers would take a while to color. It would give Jill something to do.

The gesture from Knox was sweet. An acknowledgment that he'd messed up. An apology with thought behind it. Her parents never apologized, and the few her ex-husband delivered had been tinged with insinuations that it was Miranda who should apologize.

"Dr. Paulson." Leah, the charge nurse on Med-Surg, passed her the tablet chart. "The MRI results are back and Dr. Hinks is at the nurses' station. He's looking for Dr. Peters."

"Dr. Peters is removing an appendix." Miranda had seen the twenty-something male come in. Dragged by his roommate, who told him that his pride would kill him. It would have, too. The appendix had ruptured. If left untreated the man had only a day or so left in the mortal plane.

Knox had been out of sorts since the ER consult. An appendectomy, even one that had ruptured, was basically routine for a general surgeon. Knox had jumped at the opportunity for the surgery. Looking for a reason to let his mind focus on anything other than the issues Dr. Hinks had raised before.

She knew that need. Knew the desire to focus on healing someone else. But was he letting himself heal?

Easier said than done—she knew that, too.

"I know. I was hoping you might be able to defuse him." Leah looked over her shoulder. "Dr. Peters doesn't deserve to be yelled at by Dr. Hinks."

"And I do?" Miranda winked, making sure the nurse understood that Miranda was kidding. "Let me run this to Jill—"

"I can do that." Leah held out her hands. The unspoken *Dr. Hinks needs to be gone now.*

Miranda handed the nurse the coloring supplies. "Ask Jill what else she might like. I'm going to talk to administration about getting a few more things. I'd like to get things people want."

Leah nodded as she headed out.

Miranda pulled up Leo's results. Knox was right. The bruise was deep but there were no signs of internal bleeding. He'd enjoy hearing that when he was out of surgery.

Closing her eyes she took a deep breath, then opened her eyes and straightened her shoulders. Walking out the door, she mentally planned her speech.

Most physicians were inherently good people. They went into the profession because they wanted to heal the sick and injured. A small handful were in it for the money—not the reason she'd choose, but she understood it. A tiny fraction were here for power.

Because knowledge of the healing arts made them feel superior. Those doctors were dangerous, and even with only a few minutes of interaction, she knew Dr. Hinks fell into this category.

"Dr. Hinks, I just checked the results of the MRI. Good news. No internal bleeding." Miranda offered a smile she knew he didn't want. But in her experience playing extra nice with these types often made them uncomfortable.

They thrived on terror. And she refused to play into that desire.

"I am *here* to talk to Dr. Peters." He crossed his arms and looked behind her. "Where is he?"

"In surgery." Miranda kept her smile in place. At least her marriage had trained her not to respond in these situations. "The MRI showed no sign of bleeding. There is nothing you need to discuss with Dr. Peters you can't discuss with me."

"I want to discuss why he told the patient's mother to request a new doctor."

The root of the issue. Dr. Hinks didn't care about Leo. Or his mother's situation. Or his brother's guilt. It was about his image.

"I was there. Knox did not tell her to request a new doctor."

"Then tell me why she did." Color flooded Dr. Hinks's face.

Miranda's stomach tumbled but she didn't flinch. He was trying to intimidate her. It wasn't going to work.

"She has the right to request a new doctor if something isn't working. It is her right as a minor patient's mother." Miranda kept her tone level; Lance had used any inflection of emotion against her.

Calling her reactions crazy. A term used to demonize those with mental health issues since its invention. The only good to come from that relationship was her ability to deal with bullies and abusers. Dr. Hinks certainly fell into the first category, and it was possible he fell into the second, too.

"She is just mad because I said she was unfit."

Gee. How would that make her angry?

"Accidents happen, Dr. Hinks. That is the way with children. And for what it's worth, parents who've hurt their children, or who don't care about them, do not bring them to the emergency room until it's almost too late." It was something her mentor had told her as a first-year medical student.

"Social services can clear her, if there is nothing there." Dr. Hinks crossed his arms. "And I made sure the social worker knew she'd requested transfer after I suggested there was a problem."

"Clear her!" Knox's voice was tight as he stepped to Miranda's side.

He still wore his surgical cap. "Clear her? Do you know how overworked caseworkers are? Do you know what filling the system with biased reports because you have an agenda does? Do you know the trauma of foster care? Even when it is in the best interest of the children, it is trauma."

"Knox." Miranda didn't realize a body could be that rigid. His neck muscles were tight, his jaw was clenched and his fingers were digging into his arms as he stared down Dr. Hinks.

He ignored her soft words. "If you look at your patients this way, maybe you shouldn't be seeing them."

"Is that a threat?" Dr. Hinks looked like he hoped it was. A bead of fear pressed at her neck. This man was dangerous to more than just patients.

Miranda stepped between the two men. "I think it's time we take a breather. Tensions are high and our jobs stressful. Leo is all right. That is what's most important. Right?"

Knox nodded. Dr. Hinks didn't respond.

"This isn't over." Dr. Hinks pointed a finger at Knox. "Tell another patient of mine to request transfer and I *will* speak to the board about you."

He turned on his heel and stormed out of the Med-Surg bay.

"Knox?"

He stood there, his eyes focused on the closed door where Dr. Hinks had disappeared. "I'm fine."

"I might believe that, if your jugular vein wasn't visibly pulsating on your neck."

Knox didn't look at her. He just took a deep breath. "I need to talk to Julio's roommate. Infection was spreading from the rupture. He'll be here a few days. And his roommate is listed as his emergency contact."

"Good thing he came in, then."

"Yep." Knox blew out a heavy breath then walked through the same doors that Dr. Hinks had gone through a few minutes ago.

CHAPTER FIVE

"Good morning, Knox." Miranda waved as they walked from the garage to the elevator.

"Morning." His tone was soft and there were circles under his eyes. So today did not herald the return of the fun Knox.

That was fine. She understood. Though she wasn't sure why the argument with Dr. Hinks last week was still weighing on him.

"Are you getting any rest?" It was a question she wished people had asked her when she was in the final stages of work before burnout stole her ability to function. People often only saw the productivity, not the pain or worry behind it.

"Enough."

Miranda tilted her head as the elevator doors opened. "Enough rest or—" she lowered her voice, trying to sound silly, while expressing concern "—enough…stop talking to me?"

Knox's blue eyes widened and he smiled. The first she'd seen since the argument with Dr. Hinks.

Was it weird that she was tracking his smiles? That was a question she might want to investigate another time.

"Is that supposed to be a cartoon villain sound, Miranda?"

"No. Although maybe it fits. I didn't watch cartoons growing up. Did I do it right?" This wasn't the conversation she'd planned to have with him. Or anyone ever. But he was finally giving more than one-word answers, and she'd take whatever topic made that happen.

"You didn't watch cartoons growing up? What did you do?"

"Study." She shrugged. The only television in her house was in her parents' room. They did not permit their children to "waste" time in such a way. And once the girls had gotten laptops, they'd installed spyware on the computers under the guise of keeping them safe.

Control was what her therapist called it. Miranda had to agree, though she still wondered if they hadn't pressured her to be her best if she'd be standing where she was now.

"Seriously, Miranda. What did you do for fun?"

"Math games." She saw the same look she'd seen so often from friends when she mentioned how she was raised. It was weird what you could find normal, if you didn't know anything else.

"But we aren't discussing my childhood." She winked as the elevator doors opened. "We are talking about if you got enough rest."

Knox looked away as they started toward the locker room.

"Knox, what is it about Dr. Hinks that has thrown you so far off?" The man was an ass. A certified bully who clearly liked his position of power over his patients. That was terrible; sadly, he wasn't the only doctor she'd met who felt that way.

Hell, she'd been married to one.

"Did you know he is the CEO's nephew?"

"No. But that doesn't surprise me." Nepotism was a part of nearly every professional organization, unfortunately. "His comment on speaking to the board was pretty telling."

"What do you mean?" Knox leaned against the wall, his face finally free of some of the stress she'd seen there over the past week.

Man, even tired and stressed the man was hot as hell.

"Would you ever threaten to talk to the board?" Miranda knew the answer. Knox might talk to admin, or Dr. Lawton if there were problems, but only a very specific kind of person threatened to go to a hospital board.

"Of course not."

"That's because of who you are." Miranda tapped his shoulder and felt her eyes widen at the contact. The touch had been instinctual but the fire of need it brought made her clear her throat. Knox was hurting; she was offering comfort. That was all.

Or at least that should be all.

"And his reaction is all about him." Knox looked at the spot where her fingers had lain just a minute ago. "Easier to drop if he wasn't so bent on hurting patients he thought were less than him."

"Agreed." Miranda shook her head. Unfortunately, she wasn't sure there was anything they could do about that, other than ensure if anyone asked about Stacy, Leo and Ben that they were honest. The boys were fine. All indications were that it was an accident.

"Hey, you two! Hanging in the hallway. It's a fun pastime." Jackson's grin was huge as he slapped Knox on the shoulder. "Good to see you not just grumpy facing everywhere. Thanks for that, Miranda."

"Not sure I had anything to do with it." Though if she did, she wouldn't mind. Making Knox smile was oddly rewarding.

"It's tots night at Mulligan's, we going?" Jackson was nearly bouncing. "I'll even let you play darts."

"You realize that you can get tots at the store and just use the air fryer, right?" Knox laughed, "But I will take you up on the offer of darts. Want to join us?"

Knox's blue eyes held hers. A look in them Miranda

wanted to believe was something other than surprise that he'd asked her.

"What is tots night?"

"Now you've done it." Knox shook his head. "You should come, but I am going to change into scrubs to avoid listening to Jackson wax poetically about his favorite bar night."

"It's amazing." Jackson waved at the departing Knox, clearly unconcerned about his statement regarding whatever tots night was.

"We're talking about tater puffs. The little fried pieces of potato that you serve school children?" Somehow it felt like this should be some kind of euphemism, but for what, she couldn't even hazard a guess.

"Yes!" Jackson clapped. "Mulligan's hosts it once a month. It's all you can eat tots for five dollars. Tots and beer. It's the best."

"Is it?"

"Yes." Jackson shook his head. "And that doubt I hear just confirms what I already know. You need to come. Once you experience tots night, there is no going back."

"All right. Sure." It was silly and something she'd never usually do, but Jackson seemed so invested. And it wasn't like there was much in her schedule to keep her away.

Jackson clapped. He legitimately clapped.

"Wow. You are passionate about tots."

"Yep. And Knox is passionate about darts. You should play a round with him. But be advised, he always wins."

"Does he?" Miranda looked to the closed door where Knox had disappeared a few minutes ago. "Well, maybe I will give him a run for his money."

"Tell me you are secretly great at darts." Jackson's eyes widened, the hope in them shocking.

"I might be." Miranda winked. She hadn't lied to Knox. She did study and do math rather than play or watch television like most kids. However, her parents had allowed the girls to play pool to demonstrate geometry and physics components and darts for adding and subtracting, and hand-eye coordination.

Skills the girls could use, rather than just fun pastimes.

"Tonight. Mulligan's Tot Night. You will be there."

"Sure, Jackson. I'll be there."

"You know she probably isn't going to show up." Knox took a small swig of the beer before him as he looked at the door. The door where Miranda had yet to walk through.

"Funny. I'm not the one watching that door like a hawk." Jackson slapped him on the back before grabbing another tot.

His brother only ate the potato variants at Mulligan's. The one time Knox purchased an actual bag of them and fried them at the house, Jackson hadn't even tried one.

He wasn't wrong about the door watching, though. Knox had watched the front door from the moment he'd walked in here. Jackson swore Miranda planned to come, but he couldn't quite believe she might show up.

Miranda belonged someplace much finer than Mulligan's.

Which is why when the door opened and she walked in wearing a yellow sundress and low heels, he nearly went to his knees with desire. She stood out in most places but, dressed as a literal breath of fresh air in a dive bar, damn.

"Your mouth is hanging open, Knox." Miranda gave him a playful nudge on the shoulder as she moved between him and Jackson. "These the famous tots? Can I steal one or do I have to buy my own, Jackson?"

She'd leaned against the bar, her tan legs brushing his. She'd called him out, and she'd not been wrong. Miranda looked lovely any day. But with her curly hair down, in the sundress that hugged her in all the right places, she was mouthwatering. And he was far from the only one in this joint to realize it.

"You can steal one. But only one." Jackson chuckled, "Then you have to buy your own. At five dollars for all you can eat, they are a steal."

Miranda looked at Knox and shook her head. "I thought he was kidding about the tots. He really meant just plain tater puffs."

Knox leaned a little closer, the scent of lemon and sugar wrapping through him. Of course she smelled as good as she looked. "He never kids about the tots."

Miranda took one and popped it into her mouth. Her eyes showed what Knox expected. It was just a fried potato. His brother loved them, but most people were here because it was a cheap beer and bar food night. Not because there was something heavenly about the tots.

"It's good." Miranda looked at Jackson, and Knox saw his brother shake his head before walking off to talk to one of the paramedics from the hospital.

"Did I upset him?" Miranda leaned past Knox to get a better view of the beers on tap.

"He loves the tots here. I find them over oily but don't tell him I told you that. I can't deal with the drama it might cause." Knox put a hand over his heart, enjoying the smile lighting up Miranda's eyes.

"Can I get the cider please?" Miranda started to hand her card to the bartender but he waved it away.

"Wha—?"

"Jackson paid for your first drink about ten minutes ago." The heat rushed to Knox's face as he tried and failed to clear his throat.

"Jackson?"

Was that a twinge of sadness he heard? Or was he imagining the slight downward tilt of her lips?

"Yeah. He said I was watching the door too much. I told him you probably weren't coming and he bet me you would by buying your drink."

What he did not add was that Jackson told Bill, the bartender, the first drink for the woman that made Knox swoon was on him.

The blush in Miranda's cheeks as she took a sip of her cider made his insides rush. She truly was the definition of gorgeous!

"I thought you promised me a game of darts." Miranda's hand brushed his shoulder as she slid off the stool. "I bet I can give you a run for your money."

He doubted that, but he wanted her to try. "I will never turn down a round of darts."

"All right." Miranda handed him his darts; her fingers touched his hands for a millisecond but it burned. The small crush he'd had on her when they were interns was roaring back and he didn't quite know how to put it back in the mental cage he'd forgotten about until she'd returned.

Or nearly forgotten about. One did not forget Miranda Paulson.

"You want to go first or me?" Miranda held up a dart, looking at the board like a pro.

"Go for it." Knox stood and watched as her dart landed dead center in the bull's-eye.

Her eyes were bright as she grinned. "Your turn."

Was that a lucky break? No. He didn't think so. The hustler in him, the kid who had grown up taking so many adults for their cash at this game, knew when he met another. If he was still playing for coin, Knox would toss this game and walk.

But they weren't competing for anything more than bragging rights—and for the first time in forever someone might actually beat him.

Knox tossed the dart. Bull's-eye.

Miranda stepped up to the line. Bull's-eye.

They repeated the pattern for all three throws. And the next three and the next three.

"Someone is finally keeping up with Knox!" He wasn't sure who'd called it out but he saw Miranda smile as she stood beside him.

He'd beaten every one of the regulars, and the gathered crowd was enjoying this almost as much as he was.

"It's your turn, Knox." Miranda's voice was soft and her hip brushed his.

"Trying to distract me?" Knox raised a brow as he raised the dart. He threw it without looking—bull's-eye.

"If I was, it doesn't seem to be working." She winked, holding his gaze as she raised her dart and threw it the same way he had. Bull's-eye.

"All right. Now they are just showing off."

The comment buzzed around him, but Knox didn't take his eyes off her.

"Are we just showing off?" Her dark gaze was a rush he'd not experienced in so long. "Your turn."

He dared not take his gaze from hers, fear that this moment, whatever it was, would vanish if he blinked. Raising his final dart, he tossed it. He knew it was close to the bull's-eye but not a direct hit.

She raised her hand and let her final dart fly. He knew from the crowd's cheer that it hit dead center. Miranda Paulson won.

He'd come in second to her, just like he always had. And Knox couldn't care less.

Her lips. Her full, kissable, perfect lips were so close. The urge to dip his head, to chase whatever heady connection was pulling through them, was almost overwhelming.

Before Knox could give in to the moment, Jackson's hands slapped his back. "That was the best thing ever!"

"Even better than the tots?" Miranda high-fived Jackson but her gaze didn't leave Knox.

"Even better than the tots."

"Best two of three?" Knox raised a brow.

She stepped a little closer. "Think you can beat me?" The last shot had been luck. Her hands had shaken so badly as she stared at Knox's mouth. She'd let it loose just to end the game. When the crowd cheered, she'd known she'd won, but her eyes had refused to abandon the man before her.

"Scared the first time was a fluke?" His eyes glittered with the challenge.

Miranda stepped a little closer, lifting just a little on her toes. "You might regret challenging me." She whispered the words, enjoying the flush of color on his neck.

She was flirting with Knox Peters. It wasn't the plan for tonight. Or maybe it was. Miranda had picked the sundress and heels, knowing she'd be out of place but wanting to see the look on Knox's face.

And she'd not been disappointed. The man's mouth had literally hung to the floor. She'd meant to make a joke. She thought she had, but the funny jaunt she'd designed to make them laugh had escaped her.

No. When she'd seen his face, Miranda had almost swooned herself.

"I will never regret challenging you."

Wow. She didn't know what to say to that. "I'm going to get a drink." Miranda stepped back. She needed a moment. And something cold to chill the heat pouring through her.

Sliding up to the bar, she waved for the bartender. Knox joined her almost immediately.

"Drinks are on me."

"Only—"

Knox held up a hand. "It's a standing rule that the loser pays."

Loser pays. Of course. She'd almost joked that he could only buy it if this was a date. The words hadn't tumbled out before he cleared the actual reason. Of course it was just a dart rule.

Miranda might have the hots for the doc but Knox was just keeping up with rules.

"Another cider or do you want a fancy drink since it's on me?"

Miranda leaned her head against her hand, careful to make sure they didn't touch against the crowded bar while they waited for the bartender. "Does this place have fancy drinks?"

Knox's chuckle lit up her soul. "I mean, they can make some cocktails that they will charge you an arm and a leg for."

"Technically, they'd be charging you an arm and a leg. Since I won and all." Miranda winked. She'd never bragged about winning. The win wasn't the main goal, after all. Her entire life, she'd tried to come in first to earn her parents' love. And no amount of winning had ever achieved that.

Not that they would have cared about winning a dart game in a dive bar. Still, the challenge felt nice as she nearly leaned toward Knox.

Knox laid a hand over his heart, leaning back just a hint, in playful hurt. "You were victorious, but next time it shall be me."

She opened her mouth to respond, but before she could a drunk white man pushed into her. The distance she'd kept between her and Knox evaporated and his arm went protectively around her waist. Heat molded through her, and she bit the inside of her lip to keep her sigh contained.

"Watch it!" Knox held up his free hand, not pushing the drunk but making sure he didn't come closer to Miranda.

Protection wasn't something she needed, but Miranda couldn't deny how nice it felt.

"It's getting a little rowdy." Miranda looked around. As much as she wanted to stay with Knox, she had no desire to see a repeat of the night they reunited.

Knox looked down the bar, disappointment clear on his face. "It isn't usually like this, but you're right." He raised his free hand to wave to Jackson.

It was only then that Miranda registered his other arm was still wrapped around her waist. She should pull back, but the drunk was still right next to her, waving at the overloaded barkeep. It was a good excuse to stay exactly where she was.

"This is a little much." Jackson's voice was risen, and if he thought anything of her in Knox's arms he didn't say it. "Even for tots night."

"I'm going to walk Miranda to her car. See if you can close out our tabs." Knox shifted her away from the bar.

She waved at Jackson. "Thanks for the invite."

Jackson's dark eyes focused on Knox's arm around her waist before meeting her gaze. "Anytime, Miranda. Watching you beat him at darts might be this year's highlight."

"I hope not. There is still a lot of year left." Miranda waved, then let Knox guide her through the crowd.

"Where did you park?" Knox's hand dropped from her waist as soon as they cleared the front door.

It was the right choice. They were out of the crowd, but she wished he'd kept it there. Wished there were a reason to keep it there.

"Parking lot two streets over." She looked at him then started toward her car. Silence dragging between them.

As they got close to the second street, the flashing lights of emergency vehicles came into view. A bouncer was talking to several uniformed police officers.

"Guess that explains why Mulligan's was overcrowded." Knox stuffed his hands in his pockets. "This is a college bar. Doesn't matter the night, it's always packed."

"Oh." Miranda didn't know what else to say. She hadn't spent any time at bars in college. In fact, even with her trip to Mulligan's this evening she wouldn't need all her fingers to count the number of bars she'd been in.

"You didn't visit college bars, did you?"

"That obvious?" Miranda laughed as she shook her head. "I swear there must be a sign around my neck that screams I'm not fun."

Knox reached for her hand. "I did not say that!"

"No. I did." Miranda shrugged. How many times had Lance told her she wasn't fun? That she didn't know how to have fun? Of course his idea of fun was schmoozing with colleagues who might help his climb up the career ladder.

"Miranda—"

"It's not a big deal, Knox. Did you spend a lot of time in college bars?" She could see him dancing with college girls. Enjoying himself but also making sure everyone got home on time and safely.

"Yes, but I was behind the bar." He said the words with such coolness.

She'd known several people who worked their way through school that way. "I had a job at lab."

"That does not surprise me. Were you doing tests and running scans?"

"No." Miranda pointed to her car. "I followed the cleaning staff, construction workers and anyone else who wasn't an employee." She saw the surprise on his face and understood. It was a weird job, one she'd found out about from a friend of a friend's dad.

"I guess they did work for the Department of Defense or one of the national labs or something. I had to have a security clearance but I have no idea what the actual place did. The job let me study while getting paid."

"Nice."

"This is me." She leaned against her car, not quite ready to say goodbye. "Thanks for walking me to the car."

"No problem." Knox started to lean toward her.

For the briefest second she thought he might kiss her. Then he shifted and looked over his shoulder. "I should get back to Jackson. I'll see you at the hospital on Thursday. Enjoy your day off."

"Thanks." Her cheeks were hot. Thank goodness the dark parking lot hid the color seeping through her cheeks. Of course Knox wasn't planning to kiss her.

She'd beaten him at darts and had a fun night with colleagues. That should be enough.

CHAPTER SIX

THE SUN WAS barely over the horizon as Knox pounded the pavement. He'd gone three miles already and still hadn't driven thoughts of Miranda from his mind. Her lips, the pink full lips that had haunted his dreams, flashed in his memory. He'd nearly leaned in to kiss her last night.

It had felt so natural. Like what he was supposed to do. But they weren't on a date. He was simply walking her to her car. A friend looking after a friend.

He looked at his phone, pushing the button to change the song. He needed something faster. Something strong to drown out his thoughts. Knox briefly considered raising the volume but he was already getting a warning from his smart watch that he was over his recommended volume usage for the week.

Knox sucked in a deep breath, letting the burn in his lungs and limbs be his focus. It nearly worked, until he caught sight of the runner coming down the path.

Miranda.

She was in black Spandex and bright yellow sports bra with pink headphones on her ears. Delectable did not even begin to cover the descriptor. Brilliant and beautiful.

"Knox." Miranda blew out a breath and pulled her left leg behind her, stretching while stopped on the path by him. "Out for a run, too?"

He pulled the earbud from his ear, his mind doing its best

to focus all his attention on her face. She was stunning, and her smile was intoxicating. She did not deserve to be ogled when out for exercise.

"Yeah. I just finished three miles. You still going?"

"I still have a chapter left before I call it quits." Miranda tapped the headphones around her neck.

"Chapter?" The question slipped out even though it shouldn't shock him that Miranda listened to books while working out. Did she ever just have fun?

She pulled her other leg up, her eyes looking away from him. "Just a book I downloaded from the library."

"Any good?" He never listened to books or podcasts while working out. He needed music, something with a heavy beat, otherwise he had no interest in moving. But he enjoyed audiobooks for when he was cleaning or just hanging about his condo.

"Yeah. It's fine." Miranda cleared her throat.

"What's the title? I'm looking for something new to add to my library." He enjoyed science fiction, fantasy and the occasional romance novel. Anything that let him leave the world of trauma he often worked in.

"From Lazy to Nearly Perfect."

"Lazy. Who do you know that's lazy?" Knox chuckled then caught it. "Miranda."

"That was my buzzer. I need to keep my pace up." She put the headphones back on and darted off.

He waited until she was around the corner before closing his eyes and mentally kicking himself. Damn it. How did he manage to say the wrong thing around her so often?

Knox looked at his watch. He'd done more than he'd planned this morning. It was time for a shower and then a coffee at the shop on the corner of his and Jackson's condos. They'd lived together from the time they were teens. Rented out Jackson's condo for years. Then when the adjoining unit went up for sale, Knox had bought it. Jackson owned his now, too.

He ran to his door, not surprised to see no sign of life in Jackson's windows. The man said he'd earned the right to sleep in. He wasn't wrong, but Knox had never managed to stay in bed past six.

Knox did a few stretches then jumped in the shower. His mind going back to Miranda—listening to a self-help book while running. Who did that?

Miranda Paulson. That was who.

But lazy. That was not a descriptor that could be placed on her. Ever!

I failed...

Her words from that first night pummeled against his chest. What had happened on the East Coast? There were no answers today, but Knox was going to find a way to figure it out.

He dressed, walked out the front door, enjoying the fresh morning air. Now to add caffeine to his already pulsing blood. Maybe some people-watching would let him get Miranda out of his mind.

Pulling open the coffee shop door, Knox took a deep breath. Roasted beans were one of his favorite scents.

"You're blocking the door, Dr. Peters. Always risky at a coffee shop."

"Miranda." Knox grinned. Clearly, the universe planned for them to spend time together today. Who was he to question that on the second unexpected encounter?

"Fancy seeing you here." She had a large bag with a giant book sticking out. This one titled *Working on Yourself: Find the "You" You Were Meant to Be.* She certainly had a reading niche going.

Knox stepped to the side to let her pass. "Funny isn't it. Let me get your coffee."

"Knox, you don't need."

"Do I or do I not owe you a drink for losing at darts last night?"

Miranda shook her head. "I wasn't planning on calling that debt in." She leaned toward him then seemed to catch herself. "Besides, I think my coffee might be more expensive than a beer."

"Miranda Paulson drinks fancy coffee!" Knox crossed his arms to keep himself from playfully nudging her shoulder. "I had you pegged as a black coffee drinker."

She made a face, sticking her tongue out and shuddering. "Absolutely not!"

"I happen to enjoy a black coffee." Knox stuck his own tongue out, mimicking her.

"And I am happy for you. I want cream and sugar and sometimes even whipped cream on top. If you plan to *judge* me on that, then, oh, well."

Her emphasis on the word bothered him. "You get what you want, but I am buying. Who knows when I can convince you to come to Mulligan's again." Last night was not the bar's best showing. Add that to the disaster before…

At least it looked like they visited the same coffee house. Seeing Miranda outside the hospital was a gift Knox didn't feel like giving up.

She ordered a fancy Frappuccino, with whipped topping, her eyes daring him to say something. All he did was order his regular and pay. Her shoulders relaxed a little and he wondered who would say something about a coffee order that might make her so defensive.

"I'm going to get a table. Want to join me?"

His plans to head home, curl up on his couch and watch old game shows disappeared in an instant. "As long as I won't be interrupting your reading?"

Miranda's hand moved to the book as she shook her head.

"Nope. I've already read it. Just looking over some of the notes I made in the margins."

Knox opened his mouth but no words materialized. Notes in the margins... He read medical journals and made notes. The field moved too quickly to throw away learning when you finally earned the title of doctor. But his own free time never included note taking.

And that's why she beat you at everything.

She waited a moment longer then wandered to a table in the corner. Knox turned, waiting for their coffees. Her frilly one with whipped topping and caramel drizzle was a work of art. Was this the one extravagance she let herself have?

Surely not.

"One caramel mocha frap!" Knox handed her the drink as he sipped his own.

Miranda's fingers brushed his as she took the plastic cup; a delicate rose flowing into her cheeks. Maybe she was as interested in him as he was her.

"All right, why the self-help books, Miranda? You are one of the most accomplished people I know. What else could you possibly hope to achieve?" He made sure the grin on his face was genuine. If she didn't answer, he'd drop it. Talk about other things or just sit quietly with her in the corner.

"It's nice that you think that." Miranda bit her lip, then took a deep sip of her drink. "It's not true, though."

"It's not?" He didn't believe that for a second, but it was clear in the downturn of her lips, the far-off look in her eyes and the small slump in her shoulders that she believed it.

The world had beaten her down. He'd been that person once. The kid no one believed in. The fact that people had done the same to Miranda... Knox took a deep breath, letting the smell of roasted beans calm him. Going on a campaign of rage at the injustices of the world wouldn't solve anything.

And it wouldn't help Miranda.

"I burned out. I know I said that, but I mean I really burned out. I had days I couldn't even get out of bed." Miranda's fingers fidgeted on the table, drawing little patterns as she refused to look at him.

"That doesn't sound like burnout."

"Sounds like failure, right? That's what Lance said." The monotone words were knives. Only someone who'd been told that repeatedly—and believed it—could say it so blithely.

Now his fury had a target. Her husband, the man who'd sworn vows for better or worse, had said such a horrible thing.

"It sounds like clinical depression, Miranda." He fought the urge to point out that she was a doctor, a surgeon; she knew the signs. And so had her ex-husband.

Around thirty percent of individuals developed depression post-surgery. Surgeons and counselors were trained to remind patients that the isolation and edema caused during recovery were temporary. The good news was most patients' depression resolved within months of surgery.

"My life was good, though. What did I have to be depressed about?"

"Did Lance say that?" Knox took a drink of his coffee to keep from balling up his fists.

Miranda shrugged. "He might have mentioned it. I know that he was an ass. My counselor helped with that after the divorce. I know I was depressed. I know it's a serotonin issue. I understand that, but it was more than that."

She blew out a breath. There was more on the tip of her tongue, but she seemed to have run out of words.

The mood around the table was far too tight. Leaning across, he made a silly face. "I read one self-help book. It was all about keeping lists and staying organized. I mostly remember the raised lettering on the cover. It felt nice." Knox shook his head, horror at the memory of trying to read it returning. It had been recommended by one of his teachers, a way to focus his tasks.

She'd meant well. One of the few adults in his young life who saw through the mad-at-the-world kid to the well of potential beneath it. *If* he turned in his assignments.

If it was surgery or medical knowledge, he kept everything locked in. If it was something else, there was a good chance that he'd forget. Thank goodness for auto bill pay and a monthly subscription for Post-it notes.

"I take it from the sour look on your face you were not a fan." Miranda tapped his knee.

Knox looked down. Her fingers had already disappeared but part of him still felt her touch. "I prefer fantasy. Wizards, dragons, magic."

"Wizards and dragons?"

Her smile made his heart leap. "Yep. The more fire magic the wizard uses, the better!" He made a few motions with his hands and she giggled.

He finished his coffee, hating the sign that their outing was nearing an end. "I can't listen while running, though. For that, I have to have a beat. I tried listening to podcasts that I enjoy since there never seems to be enough time for all the ones I love, but I couldn't make myself actually run at a good clip."

"Why do you have to run at a good clip?" Miranda raised her eyebrow as she used her straw to pull the last of the whipped topping from the bottom of the cup.

"I—" Knox sat there, trying to figure out the answer. "I—"

"You already said that." Miranda laid her hand on his knee and this time she didn't pull it away. "Just something to think about."

"Want to get dinner Sunday?" The question popped out, and he placed his hand over hers on his knee. He had no idea what this was, but he wanted to spend it with Miranda.

She looked at his hand then back at him. Her dark eyes holding his. "Like a date?"

"Yeah. Exactly like a date." He watched the wheels turn in her eyes. Saw the heat dance across her cheeks.

Say yes.

"All right."

The urge to pump his fist was nearly overwhelming but he kept it in check. "I'm looking forward to it."

CHAPTER SEVEN

"MIRANDA!"

Lacey, one of the floor nurses, walked up with a look she knew spelled dread.

"Jill has an infection in the wound on her left side."

Miranda took the tablet from Lacey and glared at the admitting notes under Jill's name. The woman had been discharged to a rehab facility only two days ago. Miranda was hoping not to see Jill again.

That was the weird part of being a trauma surgeon no one talked about. You saw people at their lowest. Saw them crushed and got to witness miraculous recoveries. And you hoped, fervently, that when they walked, or were wheeled from your care, that you didn't see them again.

"How is she mentally doing?" Infection in abdominal wounds was not uncommon but any setback was unwelcome, particularly because she knew how much Jill wanted to get home.

Lacey looked to the closed door of Jill's room. "Not well. I mean, no one likes coming back, but she seems down on herself."

"All right." Miranda made a few more notes in the chart and then moved to the door, knocking before opening it slowly.

"Jill?"

"Dr. Paulson." She blew out a breath.

Miranda couldn't see her face in the dark room. "Would you like me to turn on a light?" There'd been no mention in Jill's file about a headache or sensitivity to light, but it happened. It was also a key indicator for depression.

"If you like." The unenthusiastic response barely made it to Miranda's ears, even in the small room.

All right. Address the infection, then address mental health—at least as much as she was able.

"Tell me about your pain."

"Didn't the rehab send along the notes?"

Bitterness after a major life-altering event was not uncommon but she'd hoped Jill might avoid it. "They did. But you are the one living in your body."

"And I am the one responsible for what it can and cannot do."

The tone made Miranda see red. "Who told you that?" Jill had had major abdominal surgery. She needed at least a week in the rehab facility to help her regain strength in her abdominal area. People didn't realize how much the core muscles did until you had to slice through them!

"No one." Jill pushed a tear off her cheek. "It's just something I know. I mean, as you said, I am the one living in the body. If I cannot make myself do it, then who else's fault could it be? If I fail…" She pushed herself up on the bed, glaring at her stomach.

"It's like it won't do what I say!" Jill gritted her teeth then burst into tears.

Miranda sat on the edge of the bed, waiting for Jill to collect herself. This was a difficult time but beating herself up wasn't going to make the healing go faster.

"Sorry." Jill swiped at her nose as Miranda offered her a tissue.

"You don't need to apologize. You've had a setback."

"Setback. Such a diplomatic word, Dr. Paulson." Jill bit her lip. "Man, I really am being a bitch, and I don't even mean to. I am just so frustrated."

"Understandable. You aren't even close to my most difficult patient, but we do need to get the infection under control. Based on the notes I saw in your chart it looks like you might have overdone it at rehab."

"That place stinks. I don't mean like I don't want to be there, I mean it has a barely covered antiseptic odor that is not working at covering the scent of decay." She squeezed her eyes shut, balling up her fists. "I just want to go home."

Miranda understood. And she even understood the comment on the smell. Just like hospitals, rehabs had a unique aroma that made some patients uncomfortable.

Taking a deep breath, Miranda tried to keep her words kind but forceful. "You have an infection. It's easier for your body to get infections if you are tired, or pushing yourself harder than you should. I know you want to go home, I do, but your body is not failing you. You are not failing. You are healing."

"Okay." Jill's lip wobbled a little more. "I don't suppose there are any paints in the cupboard you pulled the colored pencils and coloring books from?"

"There aren't but I will see if I can dig some up." Miranda was looking for things to add to the cabinet Knox had started. She'd seen a few people adding to it. Before long, they'd need another cabinet, or a closet.

"Thanks." Jill sounded more upbeat.

However, that could be so that Miranda wouldn't ask any more questions. She put in a psychology consult. If depression was at play that would slow Jill's recovery, too.

"If you need anything, let the nurses know."

"Just for my body to do what it needs." Jill smiled, but it didn't touch her eyes.

"Give it time." Miranda nodded before heading for the door.

Stepping out, she rammed into Knox.

His arms wrapped around her waist to keep her from falling over. "Careful." He raised his brows in a playful manner. "We have to stop meeting so abruptly."

"Do we?" Miranda chuckled as she stepped back. As much as she enjoyed his hands around her waist, they were at work. Tomorrow, though. Tomorrow they'd be on a date.

A date with Knox Peters. If someone had told her when they were interns they'd be going on a date she'd have laughed at them. And privately celebrated.

She wasn't the same woman she'd been, but the crush on Knox, that was unchanged.

"At least in the hospital." Knox lowered his voice. "Outside of it..."

He shrugged and she was sure there was a joke that wasn't work appropriate in his unstated words.

"How is Jill?"

"Blaming herself." Miranda let out the frustrations she hadn't wanted her patient to see. "She is blaming her body for failing, or more accurately blaming herself for her body failing."

"Let me know if you want me to do a secondary consult for psychology. Those guys are the definition of overbooked. Sometimes a secondary consult request speeds things along."

Miranda looked at the door. "Do you need to wait a few hours for that?" At her last hospital, the general rule was to wait two hours before doing the secondary consult for psychology. It wasn't the doctor's fault; the specialty was overburdened and not enough med students were finding their way in.

"Played this game before?"

"Who hasn't?" Miranda leaned against the wall and rubbed her back. "Even with the warnings that you will do so much more than just cut and heal patients, you never realize how much literal red tape there is just to get your patients the support they need."

"Back sore?"

She appreciated the change of subject. Complaining about administrative headaches wasn't going to fix anything—unfortunately. "Always. Isn't yours? We aren't exactly young guns anymore."

Age wasn't something that bothered her. Work in trauma surgery and you figured out really fast that getting old and creaky was a blessing so many didn't have.

"It's like my bones are screaming some days. Don't tell ortho!"

She let out a giggle that died as soon as both their pagers went off.

"Damn it." Knox looked at his pager. "Three GSW inbound."

She took off as soon as he did. Gunshot wounds...three of them.

It was going to be a long night.

Knox hit the elevator at the same time as Miranda. Three hours after their shift was supposed to end. They'd lost all three gunshot victims. A fight over less than fifty dollars had cost three young men their lives. It was the roughest way to end a shift.

The door opened and Miranda and he stepped in without saying anything. What was there to say when three lives were cut so short? Still, he scooted a little closer to her, and she did the same to him. They weren't quite touching but it was nice not be alone in the horror.

The doors opened on the parking garage and Miranda pushed off the back wall. "I hate days like these."

Knox wrapped an arm around her shoulder, then shifted and pulled her into a hug.

"I'm sorry." She hiccupped as the sobs started.

"Why on earth are you apologizing?" Knox stroked her back, tears coating his own eyes. Today was rough. So very damn rough.

"For crying." Miranda let out another sob and then a hiccup. "For getting emotional at all. I used to be able to control it. Now... Now it's like a monster let loose that refuses to go back in its cage."

"Miranda." Knox pulled back a little, making sure she saw the emotion in his own eyes. "There is nothing wrong with getting emotional over losing patients. Our surgeries were perfect. The fates just weren't in our favor tonight."

"The fates." She let out another sob. "Really?"

"Sure." Knox wiped a tear from her cheek then pulled her back into his arms. "We can do everything right, and sometimes it simply won't be enough. And the amount that sucks is immeasurable. Particularly when it was so avoidable. If any of them had walked away, or pointed differently or gone to the movies tonight or something..."

Playing the what-if game was never a great idea but it was difficult in times like this to ignore the possibilities. A millimeter to the right in his patient might have made a difference. He wasn't sure the difference for Miranda's patient but it probably wasn't much. The third had never made it out of the ER bay.

"Want to come to my place for a bit? I plan to pop some popcorn, eat candy and watch pointless television for a while." The offer flew from his mouth but he didn't want to yank it back. Going home to an empty place after a day like today could be a lot.

"Popcorn...not beer?" Miranda pulled back, shifting the bag on her shoulder.

"I have beer in the fridge if you want one." As a rule he didn't drink after a rough day. Knox trusted himself, mostly.

But he acknowledged the addictive traits his mother displayed were in him, too.

He just made sure they were trained on things like besting others at darts and academic achievement.

"Come on, Miranda. Today sucked. It's well past dinnertime, but I doubt either of us is really hungry. So come eat popcorn and some chocolate at my place."

He waited for her to say no. Waited for her to make an excuse. Instead, she nodded then waited while he punched his address into her phone's GPS.

The drive home felt like it took no time and all the time in the world as he kept checking his rearview mirror to see Miranda behind him. Part of him expected her to change her mind. Instead, she pulled into the parking space behind him on the street in front of his condo.

"Is Jackson going to mind us watching television?"

"As long as it's not so loud that it echoes into his condo, no." Knox opened the door to his place, a sense of home settling through him as he dropped his keys on the tiny table he kept for that purpose right by his door. This was his sanctuary. His place. After a life lived out of trash bags operating as suitcases, owning his own place would never get old.

"Somehow I thought you two would always be roomies. A bit silly considering it's been more than a decade." Miranda followed his lead, taking off her shoes. The bright pink socks with kittens on her feet were a bit of a shock.

"Well, we are close. He's next door in the one we used to rent together. I bought this place when it went up for sale. He bought the one we lived in when the owner finally gave in to his pestering. So now it's just neighbors."

Knox headed toward the kitchen as he heard Miranda chuckle.

"I love my sisters, but I am not sure us living next to each other would ever be a good idea." She leaned against the counter as he pulled the popcorn off the top of the fridge and stuck it in the microwave. "Though I enjoy when Kelly and Olive stop by. And we have brunch on the first Sunday of every month. And given the six littles I play aunt to, it seems like there is almost always at least one birthday party each month. Family time is one perk of failure."

"You aren't a failure." Knox squeezed her shoulder, the motion not overly satisfying. "I'm glad you came back, too. But right now you're in front of where I keep the candy." Knox grinned as he slid an arm behind her. Her scent made him pause; he'd expected her to shift, to move over. Something. Instead, her dark eyes met his and his body nearly melted into her.

The one scrap of willpower he had from the day kept him from asking to kiss her. It had been a day. A terrible day. She was here for company, not for kisses.

He pulled the bag of mini chocolates from the cabinet, his fingers skimming her hips as he shifted. "Do you mind if I dump the candy in the bowl with the popcorn or do you want it in a separate bowl?"

Miranda's eyes held his, a look he hoped wasn't disappointment floating across them. "I am crashing your downtime. Whatever you like best."

"Not crashing—a guest." He pulled the popcorn from the microwave and felt his body start to relax. This was something he'd done since med school. Though now instead of reading tomes of information trying to keep up with the woman beside him, he watched game shows or reruns to television shows he'd seen so often he could quote them.

"This way!" He held up the bowl, marching toward the couch, before realizing that his small couch was only really designed for him to sit on. As a rule, Jackson was the host. The one who wanted people to visit his place.

Knox gave it all at the hospital, then kept to himself here.

"I…um…" He pulled at the back of his head as he looked at his couch.

"Don't host much?" Miranda grabbed the bowl from his hands and sat on the sofa. "Guess we are just going to be comfy, then."

I guess we are.

Knox slid beside her, enjoying the feel of her next to him. "This does make it easier to share the popcorn."

He grabbed the remote, trying to ignore the rush he felt as her body leaned close to his.

Focus on the television.

"So what does Miranda Paulson like to watch? Documentaries?"

She made a face. Her nose scrunching so tightly her eyes closed.

"Okay, no documentaries. How about game shows?"

Miranda shrugged. "I had to watch a lot of game shows growing up. They are fun, provided you're not going to have me try to beat the buzzer."

So nothing in her family was done just for fun.

"All right, so I will show you my favorite game show, provided you tell no one. Not even Jackson."

"Not even Jackson." Miranda's eyes widened and her mouth fell open. "I promise. I swear." She put her fingers over her heart. "I swear."

"You already did that."

"I know." She grabbed a piece of popcorn, her grin wider than he'd ever seen. "But a secret that Knox Peters hasn't shared with his brother and best friend. I swear I will take it to the grave."

Knox shook his head and pulled up the show. Three women stood on one side of the stage while a man stood on the other. Nine suitcases stood between them, each bigger than the last.

"What kind of show is this?" Miranda grabbed more popcorn, her fingers touching his.

The contact brought a sigh to his lips that Knox barely managed to catch. She was here, at his place, eating popcorn and about to watch Baggage...the worst train wreck of a game show he'd ever secretly loved.

"Dating game show...sort of. The idea is that each piece of luggage has some piece of personal baggage in it. The person choosing the dates throws out the one they don't think they can deal with and the person with that baggage leaves. There are two sessions—one with a female picker and one with a male. Winners get a date paid for by the studio."

Miranda looked at the television as the first suitcases opened, revealing some very personal details. "These are the little pieces of baggage?"

"So they say." Knox chuckled and threw his arm around her shoulder. The motion had been so simple, felt so right, but that didn't stop his heartbeat from pulsing in his ears.

Miranda's gaze held his before she slid just a little closer. "This is ridiculous."

He wasn't sure if she was talking about the show or the feelings racing between them. "It is. But everyone has a guilty pleasure."

"I never liked that term." Miranda leaned her head against his shoulder, started to lift it, then let it stay. "If you like something, it can just be something you like. And I guess it is nice if your partner tells you up front they cheated on their ex-fiancé with the fiancé's twin brother. How is that the small baggage?"

Knox laughed and leaned his head against hers. "The things people admit to on this show will absolutely make you feel better about your life choices."

They sat on the couch letting three twenty-minute shows play out before the popcorn and chocolate were exhausted.

"Do you want me to get more?" He wasn't hungry, but Knox wasn't ready to say goodbye to whatever this evening had turned into.

"No." Miranda's voice was soft. She lifted her head off his shoulder.

Her gaze was like water to his parched soul. His eyes fell to her lips, the pink mounds calling to him. "Miranda." Her name fell unbidden from his mouth.

"Knox."

Time hung between them.

"I want to kiss you." His hand rose, his fingers caressing her cheek.

"Kiss me."

Miranda's body sang as Knox's lips connected with hers. The fantasies she'd let herself indulge in during their residencies were nothing compared to the feel of him holding her. He felt safe, and luscious and like the world was calling for them to never part. Fantastical feelings, but indulging for a few moments couldn't hurt.

Her plans for tonight had not included sitting on Knox's couch watching the weirdest "game show" she'd ever seen. But it was far better than sitting alone in her place reading.

His hands slipped down her back, and she let out a soft moan. "Knox." She wanted to lose herself in him. Wanted to throw away all the reservations her brain had no trouble spewing constantly and beg him to take her upstairs.

"I should get going." Those were not the words she wanted to say, even if they were the "proper" ones.

Today was a lot. Finding comfort in the arms of another was a stereotype for a reason. She liked Knox. If she went to bed with him, she wanted it to be because they both wanted it, not because they were reminding themselves that they were alive.

"All right." Knox dropped another kiss on her cheek.

"All right." She smiled and leaned her head against his. "Thank you for tonight. It was perfection. And now I know you like trash game shows where people spill far too personal secrets."

Knox's chuckle carried through her soul. "Well, I know that under your very professional-looking orthopedic shoes you wear pink kitty-cat socks. So we both know something about the other. Though your socks are hardly blackmail material."

Miranda looked at her feet; the cute cats always made her smile. "I love cats. Their little noses and snuggles."

"What was your cat named?"

She shook her head, kissed his cheek then forced herself to stand. If she stayed beside him any longer, she'd kiss him again and they would end up in bed. Miranda's dating record wasn't long, but she knew what her body was craving.

"I've never had a cat." She wiggled her toes as she headed to the foyer where she'd taken off her shoes. "Lance wasn't a fan of animals and my parents—" She waved a hand. She'd begged her parents for a cat. Promised to take care of it and they'd told her that if she got a perfect score in math her freshman year that they'd consider it.

A perfect score.

She'd nearly done it, too. But she'd missed one question on the final. One question. Ninety-nine percent was not perfect. So no cat. They'd never again made such a promise—though she'd gotten a perfect math score every year after.

"You could get yourself one now." Knox's hand was on her back as he opened the door.

It was warm and the urge to lean into him pulled at her.

She ached to close the door and rip the man's shirt over his head and worship his taut body.

"Hospital hours." She bit her lip. She'd looked several times, fallen in love over internet pictures, celebrated each time they were adopted and told herself they were better off with someone else.

"Cats are pretty self-sufficient. Heck, you could even get a dog. After all, doggy day care is a thing. Dr. Protes takes his lab every shift. The dog loves it, and he shows us the live videos of the dogs playing in the yard. Frequently! Don't ask him about Potato unless you want to hear *all* about him."

"Potato? How did he come up with that name?"

"Ask that question at your own risk, Miranda. A dog named Potato kinda make sense, but cats are typically more dignified." Knox kissed her cheek then leaned against the doorjamb.

The sexy pose made her mouth water. It was time to go but her feet refused to move off the front step.

"You like cats?" Somehow that didn't surprise her as much as she thought it would. Knox would look adorable with a big dog, but a cat curled in his lap? That brought tingles to her soul.

"Yeah. I had a senior cat adopt me right after med school. Lenny was an orange bundle of love that cried for food at all hours and thought sleeping on my face was the best place to be. I lost him about two years ago and the universal cat distribution system hasn't sent me another yet."

Miranda laughed. Her sister swore that was how she got her two cats. Sometimes the universe decided you needed a cat, and one would show up and make your place its home. Miranda didn't think that was how it worked, but who was she to judge?

"I need to go." She looked toward her car, then pressed her lips to his one more time. "Thanks again."

"Anytime, Miranda. See you Sunday. Wear comfy clothes!" He watched her walk to her car and was still standing in the doorway when she drove off.

CHAPTER EIGHT

"YOU HEAR THE NEWS?" Jackson took a sip of the giant water bottle that seemed to be connected to him when he wasn't in the OR.

"News or rumor?" Knox didn't bother to look up from the computer screen where he was entering surgical notes. He'd yet to meet a surgeon who enjoyed doing any of the paperwork that came with the job, but unlike others, he never put it off. No use letting this pile up!

"Is there a difference in the hospital?" His brother shook his head and held up a hand. "Hey, Miranda!"

Now Knox looked up. Miranda was rolling her shoulders, then pulling one arm across her body to stretch. Hours on your feet felt like a lot more once you were in your forties. "You okay?"

"Just tired. Looking forward to my day off tomorrow." She winked at him then turned her attention to Jackson. "Hi, Jackson."

"So I am not invisible." His brother laughed and gave Miranda a high five.

"No." Miranda shook her head. "What are you two discussing?"

"Hospital rumors." Knox hit the final button and closed out the notes of the surgery he'd done this morning. For the moment, his paperwork was finished.

"Rumors?" Miranda raised a brow.

"Or news." Jackson took another sip of water. "I heard it as news."

"Is there a difference in the hospital?"

Miranda's words were perfect. Knox raised his hand and she high-fived it, though he could see her confusion. It wasn't the connection he wanted, but they were at work. Kissing a colleague was frowned upon, though if they were alone, he'd at least brush his lips across her cheek.

"How are you two one mind?" Jackson rolled his eyes.

"It's obvious we haven't heard, Jackson." Miranda moved to the terminal and pulled up the notes section for the surgery she'd done in the OR next to him this morning.

"And equally obvious you are desperate to spill the beans. So what is the news?" Knox typed out a few more notes.

"We are getting a new head of surgery." Jackson held up the water bottle in a *ta-da!* moment then frowned as neither Miranda nor Knox responded.

Miranda's dark eyes met his and Knox shrugged.

"That is quite the rumor." Miranda looked at Jackson.

"Seriously, neither of you heard it?" His brother frowned and looked at his watch. "I would have thought you'd both be in the running to take the position."

Knox's stomach clenched. He and Miranda were competitors. It was what their residency was based off. Always pushing the other to be better.

And she'd won, each time.

"I am sure if Dr. Lawton was leaving, he'd have told Knox." Miranda tapped out a few more things on the computer then turned.

Knox looked at her; there was no hint of competition in her eyes.

Her beeper went off at the same time his did. "ER consult. With ortho…"

Knox looked at the ceiling. "I swear the bone guys are all the same."

"Not always," Jackson murmured.

Knox looked at him, but he didn't say more. "Let's go."

"The ER is crowded," Miranda whispered, but he could hear the concern in it.

The crowd was doctors, nurses and staff members. That meant whatever was here was unique. Unique was interesting in medical journals. Not when you were the operating surgeon.

"Yo!" Dr. Patrick O'Sullivan raised his hand as he stepped beside Miranda. "You two know why we're consulting together?"

"No." Miranda looked at the orthopedic surgeon then shifted her head to the people in the room. "But given the crowd…"

"Something fun."

"Patrick." Knox liked the doctor. He was fun and incredibly knowledgeable. He was also one hundred percent the definition of an ortho bro.

Orthopedic surgery was the only rotation he'd done where they told him he didn't need a stethoscope and meant it.

"I mean fun in the best way."

"I need the surgeons in room five." Alex, a nurse who'd been in the ER longer than anyone else, shooed people away. "If you stay, I will put you to work in the ER. We can use some help."

The exodus happened immediately.

"Never fails." Alex handed Miranda the tablet chart. "Twenty-one-year-old male, impaled rebar through his left thigh."

Impalement. Unusual, but not unheard of. Particularly around construction sites. That didn't explain the crowd.

"Oof." Miranda looked at the chart, her eyes widening before she looked up at Knox.

Alex handed Knox a chart. "Twenty-two-year-old male, impaled through his right thigh." She read the words out.

"Are they connected?" Patrick's words were soft, but his stance had shifted. This was the professional who had moved to Hope last year to get a bit of a break. Dr. O'Sullivan was one of the top surgeons in his field in Dallas, Texas.

"Yes." Alex let out a breath, her shoulders slumping a little.

"Wow." Knox hadn't meant to say the word but this was a first.

"They were daring each other to jump off the second floor of the construction site on Lincoln Street. Not sure the exact events but…the paramedics didn't want to separate them until you guys saw the X-rays and decided what to do."

"And why am I here?" Patrick raised a brow. He was right; if it was through the meat of the thigh it wasn't good but it didn't require ortho.

Alex pulled up an X-ray on the other tablet. "The femur of the twenty-one-year-old."

Knox covered his mouth. The man's femur was shattered. The femur was the hardest bone in the human body to break. Shattering it usually involved high-impact car accidents and the recovery took months.

"All right." Miranda looked to Knox. "You want to cut with Patrick or want me to?"

"I'll take the solo. Is anesthesiology already here?"

"Yep! Anesthesiology first, then you guys. I know Dr. Mitchel paged Jackson to get ready in the other surgical suite." Alex reached behind the nurses' station and handed the saw to Dr. O'Sullivan. "They should be out enough for you to separate them."

"Ready?" Patrick looked to Miranda and then Knox.

Ready or not, it was time to cut.

* * *

Miranda rubbed the back of her leg with her other foot as she started to close the wound on Carter Telers's thigh. The young man had been out when they'd cut him and his best friend apart, but the dirt stains on his cheeks had tear tracks.

Patrick had put pins through the bone and the boy would be in traction for at least three weeks. Then rehab. With luck, he'd be back to himself by the end of the year, but it was likely he'd have a limp for the rest of his life.

"You applying for Lawton's job?"

Patrick's question caught Miranda off guard. She saw Jackson raise his head in her periphery. Clearly, the rumor was well and truly loose. If Hugh wasn't retiring, he needed to nip the rumors in the bud fast!

"I wasn't aware that a position was coming open." And she had no plans to apply. Once upon a time she'd wanted to be the head of surgery. Wanted it more than she'd wanted nearly anything else. In fact, she'd considered applying at her old hospital even when burnout was chasing at her heels, convinced that that would make everything better.

Maybe it would have.

She mentally pushed that thought away. It wouldn't have made it better. She wasn't cut out for that. She'd learned that the hard way. No need to repeat the mistakes of the past.

"Oh, it's the hospital's worst-kept secret." Patrick's face was bright and she could tell he was smiling behind his mask.

"I see." Miranda wasn't sure that was true. After all, Knox wasn't in the know, either, and the man seemed to live here.

"So, you my top competition?" Patrick tilted his head as he closed the wound on the other side of Carter's thigh.

"No." Miranda had been back at Hope for less than a month. She had no intention of putting in for a promotion anytime soon. Or anytime at all, really. One failure was enough.

"Really. That opens the field quite a bit, then."

"I suspect Knox will put in."

"He isn't competition, though." Patrick put the tools on the side tray. "Done."

"Of course he's competition." Knox didn't need her to defend him. He was a great surgeon. Knowledgeable on so many different trauma types. Cool under pressure. Dedicated to his patients. He'd be a good boss.

Patrick shrugged. "He's never left Hope."

That was true. She didn't risk looking at Jackson. No doubt he had his own thoughts. It wasn't technically a requirement that surgeons moved around. But typically, they transferred at least a few times. Dr. O'Sullivan had run a successful practice in Dallas and before that he'd been at a regional hospital in Ohio. He was also experienced as a level-one trauma center. Hope was good. It just didn't see as many patients.

Knox had nearly every additional certification a general surgeon could achieve. And he'd been loyal to Hope his entire career. But loyalty wasn't rewarded as much as it should be.

"I thought you were at Hope to take a step back?" That was what she'd heard, but people had all sorts of reasons for taking new positions.

Patrick's eyes met hers. "I am, but I'm not passing up an opportunity. Head of surgery here would be a nice stepping stone to something bigger."

That was true. Though her body curled at the words *stepping stone*. Hugh Lawton had been head of surgery for over twenty years. It wasn't likely they'd get that again.

"Closed." She set her own tools to the side.

"If you change your mind, you'll let me know?" Patrick tipped his head as he looked at the stats on the monitor.

"There isn't even a position to consider at the moment." How could no one pay attention to that piece of the scoop? "And Knox will give you good competition, should he choose to put in."

Maybe he wouldn't be the top candidate, but she didn't like that Patrick was just tossing him out because his breadth of experience outside Hope wasn't as large. Knox would make an excellent head of surgery.

Patrick's dark gaze held hers for a moment. "I didn't realize you two were so close."

There was nothing Miranda needed to say to that. "Carter needs to head to ICU. I'm going to check on his friend." She'd actually expected Knox to find them first. After all, their surgery had been the one with the shattered femur.

Nothing about the impaling was good, but on scales of disaster, Carter's case had looked worse.

Knox was sitting in the staff lounge; his head slung over the back of the couch. Eyes tightly shut.

She didn't say anything. There was no need. Whatever had happened, what he needed in this moment was not to be alone. Miranda sat close, letting her hand rest on his knee.

It was several minutes before Knox finally opened his eyes. "It took six units of blood to stabilize him."

Six was a lot. Anything over four was considered major blood loss, but she'd seen worse. "Six isn't—"

"The first time." Knox let out a breath. "It took six the first time to stabilize him."

"Did he make it?"

"I beat fate today." Knox looked at the clock and shook his head. "I think."

Touch and go was the nature of their game far more often than they wanted to admit. A consult that looked like the easier case could turn into a nightmare. And it had for Knox.

"He is alive. Thanks to you, Dr. Peters."

"For now." Knox shifted, putting his arm around her shoulder. "And your case?"

"In traction." She leaned her head against his shoulder. "It was standard pins and closing."

"Standard." Knox let out a laugh that held no trace of humor. "They were jumping off a second-floor construction site. Nothing about this was standard. It was stupid and reckless and just plain stupid."

He'd said stupid twice but she wasn't going to point it out. "Eighteen is considered an adult. But as science now indicates, the human brain isn't finished developing until the mid-to late-twenties."

"And the prefrontal cortex is the last to finish. Why on earth does the part of the brain responsible for making good choices develop last? What kind of a design is that?"

Miranda didn't disagree. It was something that scientists and doctors knew well, but the average person was just beginning to understand. And it differed depending on life experiences.

"At their age you were putting yourself through college, but surely you did some dumb things." Miranda hadn't done much besides study but her youngest sister, the rebel of the family unit, had made some very questionable choices. Her youthful criminal record had been expunged but that didn't wipe the memory away. Luckily, Olive's indiscretions hadn't hurt her or anyone else.

"I didn't have the luxury of doing dumb things."

Such a heartbreaking statement. She understood, but not in the same way. Olive had basically been cast out by her parents. They'd given up on her, and demonstrated to Miranda and Kelly they had the capacity to do what they threatened.

However, she'd had a roof over her head. Her parents had largely quit talking to her, but she'd not been shipped off.

"You did your best." Miranda squeezed his hand.

"What if your best isn't good enough?" Knox rolled his head from side to side then slapped his knees. "All right, I want some coffee to push the gloom away. Any chance I can convince you to get something sugary?"

Miranda saw the compartmentalization. Every medical professional had to develop it. It was the right choice, but she still worried for him. "I'm getting extra whipped cream."

She'd found out what it meant to learn your best wasn't good enough. It had crushed her, and rebuilding her life was still in phase one. What would happen if Knox couldn't compartmentalize anymore?

CHAPTER NINE

A DATE WITH Miranda Paulson. He was headed on a date with Miranda Paulson!

Knox practically danced up the stoop to her condo. The woman lived less than three blocks from him and Jackson. Frequenting the same coffee shop was going to happen on the regular. And he was looking forward to it.

The door opened before he even raised his hand.

"Can you give me one second?" Miranda pointed to the phone in her hand. "Knox, so good to see you. Come on in. Yes, Olive. I was talking to you about giving me a second. And yes, Knox is here. I told you I had a date. Yes, a date with Knox. Yes, that Knox."

Rosiness coated her cheeks as she motioned for him to step in and mouthed an apology.

That Knox.

So she'd talked about him. The warmth in his belly bloomed, and Knox couldn't keep the smile off his face.

Her condo living room looked like a library. There were six bookshelves overcrowded with books. He stepped to the first shelf and saw the standard medical journals and text-books. He preferred to read these on a tablet. That let him make notes in margins and pull up the images to huge sizes. Jackson thought it was hilarious and enjoyed commenting on "old" eyes needing larger fonts.

Getting older was something many of their friends in the

youth home hadn't gotten to do, so Knox wasn't overly concerned by the need to make a picture bigger or the few extra lines around his eyes.

The other bookshelves. All five of them were stacked with self-help books and journals. Titles like *Be Your Best, Organize Everything to Ease your Life, How to go from Zero to Hero.*

The only thing missing was one called *How to Exhaust Yourself!*

He had a room dedicated to an old television show he'd watched growing up. Jackson got him a memento or a toy associated with it for every holiday and birthday. A treat for something he loved but couldn't have as a kid.

These shelves… It was more than just listening to podcasts and audiobooks while running. More than not watching television. At least part of Miranda believed she needed these.

Believed she wasn't already the best version of herself.

"Sorry, Olive's youngest has a fever and rash. It's fifth disease, but she's worried." Miranda shook her head as she grabbed her bag from her purse. "The pediatrician is booked with flu patients, and Olive was worried so it's doctor sister to the rescue."

"I'm sure she appreciated that." Knox dropped a kiss to her cheek, enjoying the soft scent of lemon and sugar that seemed to cling to her. If he had any siblings, he wasn't aware of them. He never got to play the role of family doctor.

"It's weird to see Olive with kids. She is so overprotective. The rebel sister turned nurturing mother who will go feral if anyone tries anything on her kids."

She let out a sigh that Knox knew well. The sigh that said *If I'd had that…*

It was weird, heartbreaking and sometimes cathartic to realize you'd be a different person—a happier person—if you'd been raised in a happy home.

Wrapping an arm around her shoulder, he kissed the top of her head. "Ready for our date?"

"Yes." Miranda kissed his cheek.

For a first date they were already so comfortable. Thank goodness because after their first kiss, he needed her. Not in a sensual way—though that was there, too. Just in the way she fit with him. It was a weird feeling, one he'd never experienced before.

"So, now can you tell me where we are headed?"

"Nope. Still a surprise." He held her car door open with a flourish. He'd planned this from the moment she'd said yes. Well, not actually. The first plan he'd had was a fancy and expensive dinner date. Something he still wanted to take her on. But today, today was about the Miranda he learned about the night she came to his place.

The drive to the location took about ten minutes. If she liked this, perhaps she'd finally let one of her dreams come true.

"A cat café?" Her dark gaze glimmered as she shifted her head from him to the café over and over.

Knox had found the place as soon as she left his house the other night. He'd heard a few of the nurses mention it but hadn't put much thought into coming. Another cat wouldn't be his Lenny but he could love on a rescue for a bit.

"The cats aren't actually in the café part." Something he'd learned from the nurses when he'd questioned how they maintained their food licensing with animals roaming around. He could still recall Petra's look of absolute shock that he couldn't figure that out on his own.

"I assume they are in their own room."

"Yep, with a window so we can watch them play and probably sleep." He squeezed her hand, not surprised that she hadn't needed the explanation. "You have to have an appointment to meet the cats."

"Oh." Miranda nodded. "Of course. You can't just let everyone wander in."

"Our appointment is—" Knox looked at his watch "—in five minutes...then we can get coffee after."

"Knox!" Miranda laughed and nearly bounced out of the car. "You brought me to meet cats for our first date."

He exited the car, enjoying her brilliant smile. "It's different."

"It's perfect!" She pulled the door open and Knox wondered if she might dance her way inside.

He checked them in, and they filled out paperwork before following a young white woman with purple hair through the side door. She gave them instructions, which basically came down to let the cats choose what to do, and told them they had thirty minutes.

They stepped into the room and Miranda let out a soft sigh. "They are all so pretty."

She was definitely a cat mom. Because there were several of the rescues that were not what the average person would call pretty. More than one had at least one ear with a piece taken out, and two had chopped tails. Indicators that while this was a cat café, it was also a rescue.

Miranda sat cross-legged in the room and an orange tabby that looked so much like Lenny climbed into her lap.

His heart pounded in his chest as he watched her rub the cat's head. The rumbling in the cat's chest while the beauty he was with cradled the feline made Knox want to freeze this moment forever.

"His name is Inferno." Miranda made a face as Knox slid beside her.

"Not a fan of the name." Knox raised a brow. It wasn't what he'd name such a sweetheart, but rescue names were often temporary things that they hoped caught enough attention to get the cats adopted.

"This is a Cinnamon if I ever saw one." Miranda rubbed her head against the cat's. "Though he doesn't smell like cinnamon."

Knox laughed. "She just called you stinky, Inferno!"

Miranda opened her mouth, then playfully glared at him. "Don't listen, Inferno. You are very handsome."

The cat meowed, yawned then sashayed away.

"You hurt his feelings." Miranda tsked.

"I believe you called him stinky." Knox pet the head of a tiny gray cat nudging his leg.

"Careful, Miranda, thinking of names for a cat, even a stinky one, is a good way to adopt a cat." Knox personally thought Miranda should think of adopting. The woman had wanted a cat since she was a child. At forty years old she should grant herself that dream.

The gray cat climbed into his lap and started purring. It was an addicting sound.

"These little guys deserve better than my place." Miranda dropped a kiss on Inferno's head.

"Miranda—" How could she not think that a cat would love roaming her place?

"I just mean that I am gone a lot." She laughed as a black-and-white cat named Fred dropped a play mouse in her lap, clearly waiting for her to throw it. She did, and shook her head as the cat brought it back and dropped it in the same place. "I thought dogs were the ones that played fetch."

The point of this date wasn't to get her to adopt a cat. Though he'd stop at the pet store on the way home if she decided to fill out an application. But he wished she understood that what an animal needed was love. Miranda had that in abundance.

"What is that little one's name?" She looked over at the gray one. "Smokey?"

Knox knew from their website that the café only had adult

cats; that meant the little one in his lap was probably the runt of her litter. But she was sweet.

Looking at the name tag, Knox let out a laugh. "Nope. This is Bitsy."

The gray cat let out a yawn.

"I think she likes it." Knox rubbed her chin, grinning as the cat lifted her head, directing him exactly where she wanted to be petted.

When the woman came to let them know their time was up, it felt like only seconds had passed.

"It was so nice to meet you guys." Miranda threw the mouse one more time for Fred and then waved to the room. "I hope you all find the best homes ever."

Her eyes were bright and she was beaming as they walked out of the room. "That was so fun! Maybe we should come back next week."

He'd bring her back anytime.

Knox wrapped his arm around her waist as they walked to the coffee counter. "You want the biggest frap with whip?"

She lifted onto her toes, capturing his lips. When she pulled back, she grinned. "You know me so well, it seems. Yes. I want the whipped topping."

Compared to most, Miranda didn't have a lot of experience with first dates. Her and Lance's first date had felt more like a job application—red flag number one of thousands. And the few others she'd had, if there'd been a spark, it was buried so deep no one was going to bother even looking for it. But tonight, tonight felt like it was the kind of date movies said everyone would experience.

The cat café, the dinner after, walking around the park and talking until the streetlights came on. Knox had thought of everything.

"Thank you for tonight." Miranda slid the key into the

lock of her door. They'd been together for almost six hours, and she still wasn't ready to say goodbye.

"Thank you." Knox leaned against her doorjamb. His trim body so relaxed and delicious-looking.

"Do you want to come in? I can make some decaf coffee."

Or we can just go right up to my bedroom?

Her face was hot even though she hadn't let that last thought out.

"I'd love some coffee." His eyes sparkled with what she hoped was desire.

Opening the door, she slipped her shoes off, aware that he glanced at her feet. "Yes, I have a whole drawer of cat socks." These were blue with gray cats that looked very similar to the tiny cat that had sat on Knox's lap for most of their time in the café room.

"Nothing wrong with that. It makes me happy to think I chose right for the date."

She wrapped her arms around his neck, pulling him so close. "You chose right." She brushed her lips against his. The soft, playful kiss she'd meant to give him morphing into something more immediately.

Knox's hands pulled her closer, her hips brushing against his. She wanted him, now.

Pulling back just a little, she looked to her kitchen. "Do you really want coffee?"

"If you do." Knox's fingers danced along her back, tiny sparks of need lighting with each touch.

If this was how her body reacted to his touch over her clothes, how would it react to him touching bare skin? Only one way to find out.

"I want you."

The smile spreading across his face was the sexiest thing she'd ever seen. "The feeling is very mutual." She pulled away, grabbed his hand and led him to her bedroom. Her condo was nice, spacious, but in this moment she wished there were fewer steps from her foyer to the bedroom.

She opened her bedroom door and immediately pulled her shirt off. "I want to feel you touch me." The words were fire but the blink of fear spread through her. Lance had not enjoyed her taking any form of control in the bedroom.

Knox tilted his head and let out a breath. He raised a hand, letting his finger trace along her belly. "You are gorgeous."

"Says the handsome surgeon who looks like he belongs on a movie set instead of a surgical suite." Miranda lifted his shirt over his head, her eyes catching on the tattoos covering his chest and arms. There was a caduceus, a stethoscope and a bird breaking out of a cage.

"Damn, Knox. I didn't think it was possible for you to be hotter."

"You're going to make me blush." Knox bent his head, his lips trailing along her neck.

His hands found her bra strap, pulling it off. "Seriously, Miranda. You are breathtaking."

Knox's thumb circled her nipple, his eyes watching her as she melted in his caress.

The urge to strip him naked, join their bodies and ride the wave of fire pulsating through her warred with the need to draw this out as long as possible.

Knox's tongue flicked the raised bud of her nipple. Her hands ran along his back, where more tattoos were blazed across his body. She wanted to explore him but her mind couldn't focus with the masterful strokes of his tongue.

His fingers undid the button of her pants, slid them over her hips, then he slipped to his knees. He pulled her panties off and licked her.

Miranda let out a soft cry. His tongue found exactly where she wanted him. His hands gripped her butt, holding her in place for him to worship her.

Letting her hands run through his hair, Miranda lost herself in the sensations Knox was driving through her. Heat, desire, need, everything poured through her as he drove her closer and closer to the edge.

"Knox." His name on her lips as she crested felt like a cry to the heavens.

His arms were around her as he lifted her, carrying her to the bed. "Miranda." His lips brushed hers as he unbuttoned his jeans. "Sweetie, tell me you have a condom. I need you. Badly."

She grabbed the condom from the top drawer of her nightstand. She ripped the wrapper open and slid the rubber down his magnificent length. When she got to the end of his shaft, Knox let out a guttural noise.

Knox sat on the bed, pulling her onto his lap. She wrapped her legs around him as her mouth worshipped his. They moved as one, as though they'd done this thousands of times. Their bodies seemingly knowing exactly what the other needed, what the other wanted.

His fingers dug into her hips as she rode him to completion, her name echoing around them as Knox found his own orgasm.

CHAPTER TEN

KNOX KISSED MIRANDA'S BACK, letting his hands trace her body. Waking next to her felt too close to a dream. The date he'd planned yesterday had gone on for hours longer than he'd planned. Yet, it hadn't been long enough. Even now, as he was lying in her bed, he wanted more time.

"I could get used to waking up in your arms." Miranda rolled over, her breasts pressing against his chest.

They'd spent all night worshipping each other. He shouldn't be able to get hard again, but his body had no desire to listen to the biology notes his brain had learned through med school.

"I would never guess you had so many tattoos." Miranda's hand traced over the caduceus on his left biceps. He'd gotten that one the day after he'd graduated from med school.

"Body art is personal, or at least mine is. Still, people make judgments about it. I spent my entire childhood judged as lesser. The stereotypes of the bad guy having the tats have shifted with the younger generations, but they don't sit on hospital boards. Yet."

Her fingers ran along his hip. Her lips caressing his chin. "I understand the medical stuff, it's you. Why the bird in the broken cage?"

How did discussing personal topics feel so right even when they were lying naked in bed after their first date?

"As a kid in the system I felt like everything was a cage.

Making mistakes was one step closer to delinquency, and everyone seemed to expect that we'd end up in the prison system. I did slightly better as a white kid. Jackson heard from more than one foster parent that he was just a choice away from parole."

"That's awful."

He could tell from the look in her eyes that she wasn't surprised, either. It was an unfortunate truth that humans were biased creatures. Othering made people feel safer, and the consequences were lifelong.

"It is. I got this the day I turned eighteen. And then I had it redone after college when I had the money to pay a proper artist."

"It's beautiful." Miranda's lips traced the edges of it.

"You're beautiful."

She made a noncommittal sound as she started to trail her lips down his body. Her fingers seemed to have memorized every little spot that made him ache even more for her. And she found them with deliberate speed.

When her mouth covered him, Knox couldn't help arching. His body seemed to react on its own around her. She took advantage and gripped his backside just like he had done to her last night. "Miranda."

His hands wrapped through her dark curly hair. His mind was lost to all thoughts but pleasure.

"Sweetheart, don't make me beg."

"What if I want you to beg?" Miranda's dark gaze held his, her hand stroking his balls as she ran kisses up his shaft.

She was going to be the death of him—but what a way to go.

"Please, Miranda. I need you baby. Now."

Her eyes glittered as she sheathed him and climbed on him. He let his hands roam her taut body as she kissed him.

Her movements were slow, they'd spent so much time joined, but the need, the need wasn't diminished at all.

"You didn't come home last night." Jackson raised a brow as Knox stepped onto his stoop.

"I wasn't aware you were tracking my comings and goings." Knox winked as he opened the door. "Everything all right?"

"I got this for Miranda's closet." Jackson held up two bags of goodies.

"Whoa." Knox grabbed the bags. "That was nice of you."

"Wasn't me. I told Patty about it and the next thing I know…" Jackson shrugged as he looked at the bags at his feet.

Patty was an ancient white woman at the free clinic Jackson volunteered at. The woman looked the same today as she did when Knox and Jackson had visited the free clinic as patients. The woman was a walking contradiction to medical science. She'd smoked at least a pack of cigarettes a day since she was sixteen and drank whiskey every night. She said if it hadn't killed her by eighty-eight, she wasn't giving it up now. She ran the "arts" program on her own shoestring budget for the local kids in her neighborhood.

Mostly it was crochet and cross-stitch because that was what she could do, but the kids in the neighborhood had all learned. Jackson still crocheted occasionally, and Knox swore that the cross-stitch lessons had prepped him for surgical sutures.

Knox looked in the bag. Crochet needles and yarn filled one and the other had cross-stitching materials. "That was kind of her."

"She knows." Jackson winked and Knox laughed.

Patty did not suffer from a lack of self-confidence.

"So, did Miranda get a cat?" Jackson sat on the tiny couch.

"No." Knox tilted his head, looking at his brother. "Out with it."

"What?" Jackson raised his brows, but he rolled his shoulders, clearly getting ready to deliver bad news.

"Word in the surgical unit is that Miranda came back for Dr. Lawton's job. That she knew he'd be retiring in a few months, and this is her next stepping stone."

"Miranda came home..." Knox cleared his throat. Her reasons weren't his to share. And weren't a cover for a next career ladder climb. "That isn't why she came home."

"Besides, has Hugh actually said he's retiring?" Why did everyone forget that? Hugh would tell Knox. He would.

"No. But you know how the rumor mill is."

"Wrong. At least fifty percent of the time." Knox understood office gossip. It was even more pronounced in the hospital. Long shifts in high-stress situations resulted in people talking to pass the time or to ignore the pressure to scream, or cry, after a tragedy.

"But when they are right..." Jackson let out a breath. "There's more."

"Of course there is." Knox shook his head. "There is always more. But it's gossip."

"People say they don't think you'll be competitive for the job." His brother's words were rushed. Jackson held up his hands. "I didn't say it. But it's being said. I want you to know in case you hear it."

"If I want it, I can make it mine." Knox didn't doubt that. He'd been at Hope longer than anyone else. He knew the inner workings better than the entire board and most of the administrative staff. Hell, he was the one people asked to shadow most often. The fact that people would think he wasn't qualified, that they'd rule him out before the competition even started, stole a little of the past twenty-four hours of joy, but he wouldn't give it any more.

That wasn't fair, but he wasn't going to engage in rumors. "I appreciate the heads-up, Jackson."

"Not sure I believe that." Jackson sighed as he stood. "See you at the hospital."

"Good morning, sweetheart." Knox handed her a coffee. "No whipped topping since it's the start of the day but if I guessed wrong..."

"You didn't." Miranda dropped a kiss on his cheek as they stepped into the elevator. "Careful, Knox. I might get used to this."

Her mouth was hanging open. She knew her mouth was hanging open. She'd had a great time on their date and in the hours past it. But it was one date. Her ex-husband hadn't bothered to do anything that didn't progress one of their careers...usually his. But she'd clung to scraps of kind words and tiny gestures.

The small amount of affection she'd craved after a lifetime of trying to earn it in her family had made her accept less than she was owed. At least according to her therapist. Miranda had agreed with the assessment and sworn she wouldn't fall into the trap again.

And she could. It would be so easy to get used to this. To him. To silly game shows and cat café visits and maybe even a cat. Jumping from one date and hot sex to getting a cat together. Talk about leaps.

She'd spent her life trying to be better. To get good enough. Nothing was ever enough. It was easier to stay on her own than want more and never reach it.

"Miranda, what thoughts are rattling around your brain?"

"Nothing. Well, nothing important. Just chastising myself for saying out loud that I could get used to this. I wasn't trying to put pressure on you."

That was the line her ex had used so many times. The second he felt like she was asking him for something he made her feel like she was weak for asking.

"Would that be so bad? If you got used to it?" Knox raised a brow, then pressed his lips to hers for just a moment. It was a soft kiss, a reassuring one.

Hesitation stole through her. She wanted to say no. Wanted to say it wouldn't be a big deal if she got used to it. But no one took care of Miranda. She handled herself. She'd needed to handle herself.

She was rebuilding her life. It wasn't rubble anymore, but she didn't quite feel steady yet.

"Miranda, I had the best time the other night. I want more of that. If you don't…"

"I do. I do want more. That terrifies me." Had he snuck truth syrup into her coffee this morning? Those were not words she planned to say in the quiet of her own head, let alone out loud to the man who'd explored every inch of her body this weekend.

"Ah." Knox let out a breath, reaching for her hand. "It doesn't terrify me. Not sure if that helps."

"It does." She squeezed his hand, happy for the connection before taking a sip of the mocha he'd gotten her. A little of the worry leaking away.

She'd never had passion. Part of her had worried that deep love could combust. So she'd dated men, even married one, who didn't make her want to lose herself. Logic kept you safe, if mildly unfulfilled.

"It's just a coffee, Miranda. It's not like I'm trying to plan our future children's names. Just getting your coffee." Knox hit her hip.

I'm not having children.

Four little words that she felt very strongly but the elevator opened before she could say them.

Which was good since the hospital elevator was not the

place for this conversation, but before their next date she needed to at least let Knox know. At forty, she was entering the final years of her fertility metrics but Knox could technically have children for many more years. If he wanted children, then she wasn't the right person for him.

"Miranda, you're needed in surgical consult now!" Jenny the duty nurse's eyes were frantic.

Miranda took a giant gulp of the coffee Knox had gotten for her as she turned to pass it to him. "Thanks."

He held it up and smiled. "Good luck."

"All right, Jenny, what is so urgent?"

"We have a patient refusing treatment." Jenny blew out a breath.

Miranda understood the frustration, but it was a patient's right to refuse any treatment. "That is her right, Jenny."

"I know. But Dr. Reedy is older and a male and he's trying to convince her, and I think she is right to refuse. But…"

Jenny stopped right outside the consult room door. "She's asked for a surgical consult several times and Dr. Reedy keeps delaying it. She deserves to control her own body and choices."

Miranda nodded, then knocked on the door. "Come in."

The older male voice was craggy and the tufts of white hair on his head were well past the "thinning stage."

"Good morning, I'm Dr. Paulson, general surgery."

"We do not need general surgery." Dr. Reedy crossed his arms, his eyes darting to the nurse in the corner then behind Miranda, where she was sure Jenny was standing. So this was a medical standoff. Three women, a female patient and an elderly OB/GYN.

"What is general surgery?" A young white woman sat on the exam table, her thin legs hanging out of the blue hospital gown, her face pale.

"It means that I do all sorts of surgeries rather than specialized surgeries. What is your name?"

"Amber. And I want a hysterectomy not another round of hormone shots or birth control pills that make me feel suicidal." She glared at Dr. Reedy before wiping a tear from her eyes.

"A hysterectomy is major abdominal surgery." Miranda kept her tone level. This was not a request many people made, and those who did often felt quite strongly about it.

"And you are not even thirty. What if your husband wants a baby?"

Dr. Reedy's words were not overly surprising. It was shocking the number of professionals who asked what a woman's male partner wanted. Something that was only a deciding factor, if the patient wanted it to be.

"I do not have a husband."

"Future husband, then." Dr. Reedy looked at Miranda, clearly hoping to convince her to chime in.

"Amber, why do you want a hysterectomy?"

Amber pushed a strand of dark hair behind her ear. She really did look too pale. "This is my third trip to the ER *this year* for blood loss during my period. I know that if I took birth control that it would lessen the flow."

"If it is giving you suicidal ideations, hormonal birth control isn't an option."

"Was it really that bad?" Dr. Reedy asked rather condescendingly.

"Yes." Amber's cry broke Miranda's heart.

Medical professionals had a lot of training, but they were not living in their patients' bodies. Only the patient could tell you what they were going through.

"There is the copper IUD." Dr. Reedy looked like he wanted to roll his eyes.

"Those can increase menstrual bleeding. What about an

ablation? That procedure destroys the lining of the uterus and drastically reduces menstrual bleeding or even stops it completely."

"Then she still couldn't have children." Dr. Reedy looked at Miranda like she was out of her mind.

That was not technically true, though women who had the procedure were warned to avoid pregnancy due to complications should an egg attempt to implant on the thinned wall of their uterus.

"Do you want children?" Miranda looked at Amber. She'd never wanted them, and she'd known that from the time she was a teen. Amber was in her late twenties. Old enough to know what she wanted and for that choice to be respected.

"No."

"You might change your mind."

"Dr. Reedy." Miranda pinched the bridge of her nose as she took a deep breath. "It is not your concern if Amber doesn't want children. She is so pale, that I suspect she is anemic."

"Her hemoglobin is at eight. The last time she was here, it was eight point one, the time before that seven point six," the nurse in the corner stated, nodding to Amber.

They were united in their fight for their patient.

"So not just anemic but severely anemic. Have you ordered blood for her?"

"It's being typed now." Dr. Reedy pursed his lips then looked at Amber. "I think it best if I am no longer your physician."

"Wha—? Are you firing me as a patient?" Tears streamed down her face. "Because I don't want children?"

"I will notify the practice that you are discharged." Dr. Reedy shuffled past Miranda.

"Sorry." Amber let out a sob. "I'm just so tired. So tired."

"Some of that is anemia." Miranda made a few notes in

the tablet chart Jenny passed her. She requested another OB/ GYN consult, but she planned to talk to Knox.

"Can you do the ablation?"

Miranda wished there were a way to say yes. Wished she could offer Amber a fix now. She steeled herself to deliver the bad news.

"No. You will want an OB/GYN to do the procedure."

"Except every OB I go to says the same damn thing." Amber pitched her voice, "You're too young. What if you change your mind? What will your future husband think?"

She took a deep breath. "Dr. Reedy is not the first to tell me he won't help me."

Miranda grabbed the chair and slid next to Amber. "Amber." She kept her voice low, soft, controlled. "I know you haven't felt supported, but look around you. Two nurses made sure I was here. I'm going to find you someone who will look at your whole history and wants. It may take another few months and I know that hearing that is not helpful. But we will get this worked out."

A knock at the door made them each turn; the phlebotomist stuck her head in. "The blood typing is done. I'm here with the transfusion."

"I have a transfusion every time this happens. Not sure why we have to type my blood each time. I am A positive."

"Safety." Miranda and Jenny said at the same time.

"Get a little rest, and we'll check back in on you shortly." Miranda nodded to Jenny, who followed her out into the hall.

"Who do you know who will do the ablation? I'm not sure I know anyone who'd be willing at her age." Jenny made a disgusted noise.

Miranda wasn't sure. She'd been back in Phoenix less than a month. The contacts she had were mostly located on the East Coast. But Knox had been in the area his whole career. With luck, he could give her a starting point.

* * *

"Knox!" Miranda's voice carried down the hallway, but she didn't seem like she was in a race to the surgical suite. Hopefully, that meant the surgical consult had gone well.

"No cutting?"

"Not today. Or at least, not right now." She took a deep breath, squaring her shoulders.

"What are you preparing for?" Knox tilted his head as she adjusted her stance again.

"Do you know any OB/GYNs that will perform an ablation on a patient under thirty with no children and no spouse?" Miranda looked at the tablet chart in her hand. "Patient has had abnormal menstrual cycles since she was twelve. Routinely seen in our ER for blood transfusions."

"Dr. Elaine Matre." Elaine was whom he always recommended. "And if she isn't seeing patients, all the staff at her clinic are top-notch."

"The patient doesn't want children."

"You already said that. And that is good, since getting pregnant after an ablation is counter indicated." Knox reached for Miranda's hand, squeezing it gently before letting it go. "Why the surgical consult?"

Miranda let out a breath and then launched into a story that Knox wished he were surprised to hear. Dr. Reedy, and many others, had a tendency to play the what-if card when a woman asked for a procedure for sterilization. What if you change your mind? What if your future partner wants kids? What if…

"No one ever asked me what my wife would think when I got my vasectomy. And I wasn't even twenty-five." Knox shook his head as he pulled up some notes on his tablet.

"You had a vasectomy?" Miranda coughed as she looked around the hall, her cheeks darkening.

"You don't need to worry. It's something I am pretty open

about." It was a choice he'd made and never regretted. He'd spent his life in the system. Knox loved the life he had now, but it did not include a calling for children. His life was his patients. That was enough for him.

Some men were squeamish about the procedure. Worried that it might "affect" their abilities. So he answered any and all questions. It was simply a medical procedure he'd elected to have performed.

"You joked in the elevator about naming our children." Miranda's eyes were wide.

He had said that. She was panicking over him getting her coffee. He'd gone to the furthest extreme he could think of—children. "It was a joke. If you want kids—"

"I do *not*." Miranda laughed then covered her mouth. "Maybe I shouldn't laugh at that."

"Don't see why not. Kids aren't for everyone. If people realized that—" Knox cleared his throat. His mother should never have had a child. She hadn't wanted him, and even when she was in her short bouts of sobriety, she'd made that quite clear.

"But it makes sense why you would feel so strongly for Dr. Reedy's patient."

"He just dismissed her." Miranda leaned against the wall, rubbing her back. "I hate that. But luckily you know everyone in the area."

"Been here long enough." Knox chuckled.

"Some might say too long." Dr. O'Sullivan hit Knox's shoulder as he chuckled. "Just kidding, Dr. Peters."

"Right." Knox shook his head. "What is it with ortho and their jokes?"

"The bone guys seem to be the only ones that really get them, too." Miranda's head turned, following the orthopedic surgeon until he was through the doors of the employee lounge.

"Ever think of moving?" Miranda's tone was low.

"Not since a very cute doctor beat me out of a coveted position after residency." Knox made sure that his voice was solid. "I've had offers, but nothing that really struck my fancy." It was weird how you could blink, and years could go by.

"Why?" He nudged her hip with his. "Trying to get rid of me?"

"Not at all." Miranda leaned forward and kissed his cheek. Then her hand returned to her lower back.

"Why don't you let me massage your back this evening?" Knox ached to touch her. To run his hands on her. A massage, a quiet night in. It sounded like bliss.

"I think I might just let you do that!"

CHAPTER ELEVEN

"YOUR FINGERS FEEL DELICIOUS!" If she could purr, Miranda knew Knox's massage would have drawn the sound out of her. His thumb dug into the exact right spot on her back, and tingles radiated down her legs.

"How are you so tight?" Knox put a little more of the massage oil on her back and continued his slow, circular movements.

"On my feet all day, stress of surgery, hitting forty. Take your pick." She said the words and let out a groan as he found another knot in her back.

"You are just a ball of stress, sweetie."

Knox moved his hands onto her butt and Miranda let out a sigh. The massage had been nice, and longer than any other a male partner had given her. Now the hanky-panky was starting.

"Why are you moving?" Knox lifted his hands. "Did that hurt?"

She looked over her shoulder, raising a brow. "You touched my butt."

"Yep. Your low back muscles connect to the piriformis muscle. We may not be bone bros but we know the muscular system. Lie still."

Miranda laid her head back on the table and sucked in a breath as Knox's fingers dug in. "Oh, my God."

"Not said in the way I like most." Knox kissed her cheek.

"Take a deep breath. Let's get the knot out and your back will feel so much better."

His fingers pushed and pulled across her butt, finding knots she'd had no idea existed. But as his fingers released them, her low back seemed to align more, too.

"All right. Now the shoulders." Knox ran his hands up her back using his palms to apply pressure and she sank into the realm of pure pleasure again.

"Miranda." Knox kissed her nose. "Miranda, sweetie."

"I like being called sweetie. No one ever calls me a nickname." The words were heavy on her lips; her whole body felt like it was floating.

"Well, sweetie, I think it's time for bed." Knox lifted her off the table he'd borrowed from Jackson—who'd put himself through nursing school as a massage therapist. The brothers were full of surprises.

Miranda yawned; her eyes seemed incapable of staying open. "Knox—"

"Yes, sweetie."

She smiled against his shoulder.

"You shouldn't have still been here, but I'm glad you were." Miranda didn't think she'd said the words. Her thoughts were mush after his fingers tantalized her so much.

All she knew was she was glad he was here.

Miranda rolled over in Knox's bed. Her body was sore, but not in a bad way. Her muscles felt like they were relearning what it meant to be comfortable. Had she ever been comfortable?

Probably not. After all, if you were comfortable that meant you weren't working. Not working meant you were slacking.

When she'd finally slept in during her marriage, from fatigue and depression, her ex had told her that her new-found "laziness" was the reason she was struggling.

But mornings like this seemed designed to lie in bed at least for an hour or so before starting the day's activities. Particularly when there was a sexy man who made your body sing next to you. She was glad that he'd been here when she walked back through the door. He was like a grounding force. She rolled onto her side and stared at the man in the bed next to her. She was so glad Knox was here.

Dr. O'Sullivan was right, though. If Knox cared about advancing his career, staying at Hope was the wrong move.

Air seemed to rush through her ears as she lightly ran her thumb along the sleeping god's jawline. She was falling for him. Maybe the crush she'd had on him so long ago was more than she'd realized.

They'd always seemed to act almost as one. Even as competitors. In a world where there wasn't a valedictorian and salutatorian, a number one and a runner-up, a winner and a loser, they were nearly perfectly matched.

She let her hand run down his thigh, enjoying the swell of his manhood. Miranda kissed his cheek, stroking his chest.

His hand moved to her hip, cupping her buttocks. "I don't think there is a better way to wake up." Knox turned, pulling her leg over his hip.

His fingers stroked her, finding her core, and Miranda let out a moan.

"I was trying to turn you on." Her lips trailed along his chin.

Knox grabbed her hand, placing it on his manhood. "Mission accomplished."

She cupped him, enjoying the intake in his breath.

His finger skimmed her nipple, and she arched against him. His erection pressed against her and she guided him toward her.

"I have condoms."

"You've had a vasectomy. I've had an ablation. I'm comfortable if you are." Miranda wanted him.

Knox didn't hesitate. He slid into her, cradling her as he gently rocked them. This wasn't a rush to completion. A drive for orgasm.

It felt deeper. More primal.

"Miranda." Knox's mouth captured hers, his tongue dancing in rhythm with his fingers as they skimmed across her electrified skin.

She'd never felt anything like the sensations he was driving through her body. His shallow strokes drove her closer to the edge but weren't quite enough.

"Knox." His name came out as a plea. A desperate one.

"Sweetie." He lifted her leg a little farther up his hip. It still wasn't enough.

Miranda arched her back and hooked her leg around him, pulling him on top of her. Her body sang as he entered her fully.

"So demanding." Knox brushed his lips against hers but still didn't change his pace as he slowly drove into her. The slow strokes were pleasure and the most blissful torture imaginable.

She wrapped her legs around him. "Faster, Knox." Bliss was so close, so close but she couldn't quite reach it.

"I like you demanding, sweetie." Knox dipped his head, sucking one nipple, then the other. "But I want to enjoy this for as long as possible."

His tongue flicked the base of her neck, and electricity shot through her whole body. She arched with him as he cradled her through the orgasm. When it was over, he started building another.

"Knox!"

"Nope. No better way to start the day."

* * *

"Want to go for a run?" Miranda kissed his cheek as she grabbed a banana off his counter. "It won't take me long to run home and grab my stuff."

"A run?" Knox let his hand run along Miranda's excellent ass. She was wearing cotton panties and one of his T-shirts. There was no sexier outfit in the world. "I'm a little surprised you can think of that. My body feels like it's made of rubber. Maybe I need to spend more time pleasuring you."

Her dark eyes widened as she laid a hand on his chest. "My body also feels spent. And my muscles are so relaxed from the massage yesterday. I feel like I'm walking on air."

"So what do you say we spend the day snuggling on the couch?" Knox kissed the back of her neck as he mentally calculated ordering in food and spending the entire day with Miranda.

"But we relaxed the other night." Miranda turned in his arms, her eyes bright with a smile.

The sincerity in her voice sent a chill down his back. "The other night?" Was she talking about when they watched movies…almost a week ago? She couldn't be.

"Yeah. The 'game show.'" She used air quotes around the words *game show*. It would be adorable, if it wasn't so sad.

"That was almost a week ago and we lost multiple patients that night. You can just relax."

She blinked and opened her mouth, then closed it.

"You know that, right?" Knox reached for her hands. "You can just spend time reading a book *for fun*." A designator he wouldn't have to make for most people. But even her reading habits were kind of work.

"When was the last time you just did nothing for the day but have fun with no purpose?" Knox squeezed her.

Her eyes shifted to the side; her teeth dug into her bottom lip. "I don't understand the question."

He was humbled by her honest answer. Even as it broke his heart. Miranda didn't know how to relax. The woman's body had been a ball of knots last night. As much as Knox enjoyed loosening her up, he hated that she was so tight.

"I know you don't, sweetie." He kissed the top of her head. "But today we are not going for a run. We are going to have fun. Lots of fun."

"Doing what?" Miranda's brows narrowed.

"Well, that depends." Knox playfully tapped her nose. "Do you know what you like doing?"

"I liked beating you at darts." Miranda raised her chin, the dare in her eyes clear as anything.

"Because you like playing darts?" Knox enjoyed darts. It was therapeutic, even though he'd started playing for all the wrong reasons. Though those reasons weren't his.

Miranda twisted her lips. So the answer to that question was no.

"All right." Knox playfully turned her, tapping her butt. "Today is operation figure out what Miranda likes doing just for herself. Step one. I get dressed, then we run to your place, get you dressed for the day. Then…we try a pottery place."

"Pottery?" Miranda looked over her shoulder.

"Sure." It was fun and you got to create. That might make her feel like she was accomplishing something. It was a start at least.

"When you said pottery, I thought you meant making the pottery." Miranda looked at the paint your own pottery studio and laughed. "I was already planning how to get pottery clay out from under my fingernails."

Knox squeezed her hand as he opened the door. "If you want to try making a pot we can. But to get studio time you need more than an hour to schedule it."

"I'm surprised you even know of these places." Miranda's smile was big; hopefully, this was a good idea.

Knox shrugged. "I wanted to have a birthday party here when I was a kid. Well, not here. But in a place like this." He'd known enough not to beg his foster parents for it. The answer wouldn't have just been no. It would have been hell no.

"So as an adult you came here to treat yourself?" Miranda hit his hip with hers.

"Honestly—" Knox looked at the walls of ceramics waiting for their glazes to turn them into something beautiful "—I've never actually come in."

He'd driven past the location so many times. Never pulling in.

"Well…" Miranda wrapped her hand around his waist. "Then what are you picking?"

He wasn't surprised when she chose a cat figurine, but he just kept staring at the options. The plates, the banks, the figurines. It was all so much.

"We can always come back and do it again." Miranda kissed his cheek as she handed the cat figure to the woman.

She was right. Knox was an adult, with adult money. If he wanted to spend his free time at the art studio he could do that. He reached for the turtle piggy bank, then pulled his hand away. What would he do with such a thing?

"Get it." Miranda grabbed the turtle piggy bank, placing it in his hands. "It's clear you want it."

Knox moved it around his palms. "One of the kids in one of the foster homes I was in had something like this. We weren't allowed in his room—he was the biological son. That mattered a lot in some homes."

Knox ran his fingers over the turtle's face. "It's silly to even remember it. But he had a turtle bank. I wanted it and I must have been seven or eight. I got caught looking at it.

He claimed I was trying to steal his money. That was when I learned it was a bank."

He pulled his head back. That wasn't a story he ever shared, and it just slipped out with Miranda.

Miranda's eyes flashed but there was no pity in them. Instead, she raised her chin. "If you do not get that and paint it, I will put my cat back, go home and listen to an audiobook on organizing."

"Quite the threat." Knox kissed her cheek as he led her toward one of the tables, the turtle bank hot in his hands. This might seem silly but there was no way he was letting her walk out without the cat and having some fun.

CHAPTER TWELVE

KNOX RANG THE BELL TO Miranda's condo and entered as soon as she said to come in. The past two weeks had flown by in a series of date nights in and stolen conversations at the hospital. And tonight he had a surprise for her.

"I have something for you," Knox called as he slid his shoes off by the door. His eyes immediately going to the romance novel on the side table next to her couch. The fantasy and sci-fi books he'd recommended were a bust, but one of the nurses had recommended a romance. Miranda had devoured it. And the three others in the series.

It had gotten out that she liked romances, and a stack of recommendations was appearing from so much of the hospital staff. Apparently losing yourself in happily-ever-afters was a pastime many enjoyed.

And there were options for everything. Though he'd barely kept a straight face when she waxed lyrically about an alien romance that she'd devoured in a day. Whatever made Miranda happy was great!

Miranda came around the corner and leaned against the doorway between the living room and her kitchen. "Dinner is on the table. Street tacos from Julio's."

"That sounds right domestic." Knox laughed as he moved in to kiss her.

She deepened the kiss. When she pulled back, Miranda

playfully pushed at his shoulder. "No one will ever call me domestic and mean it."

There was a tone to her words, one that made him reach for her hands. "Does that bother you?"

"No." Miranda shook her head as she moved to pour some wine. "I should have made margaritas but I don't have tequila."

"It doesn't bother you?" Knox took the wineglass. He didn't care what she offered him. They were together; that was all that mattered.

"It bothers me that it is supposed to bother me. I've achieved a lot. I'm rebuilding after burnout and divorce. But at forty I'm not married, don't have or want kids. Breaking all the unspoken rules of society." She rolled her eyes. "What did you bring me?"

She held out her hands, her eyes sparkling as she looked at him.

Knox pulled the gray kitten she'd made on their date day out of the bag. The squeal coming from the beauty across from him was childlike, melodic and rattled the windows all at once.

Miranda took the kitten figurine and laughed. "I don't know why this makes me so happy."

"Just think what a real cat might do." Knox pulled the turtle bank out of the bag.

"Your bank." Miranda set the cat on the counter and reached for the turtle. "Did seeing it make you as happy as the cat made me?"

No. It had made him happier. He hadn't squealed. Hadn't danced in the little studio, but a piece of his heart seemed to stitch into place when he held it. A little piece of childhood that he could gift himself. Those were a lot of words and emotions and he wasn't sure how or if he ever wanted to voice them.

"It's something special."

Miranda's eyes caught his. For a moment he nearly shifted under her gaze. Nearly spilled how the turtle made him feel deep inside. But it was a turtle bank. Something so insignificant. It felt ridiculous to give it that much power.

"Maybe I should put the cat on the cat tree I bought?"

"Cat tree?" Knox knew he hadn't hidden the surprise on his face, but who bought a cat tree and then didn't get a cat?

"Bought it on a whim." Miranda's cheeks were pink and he suspected that she hadn't meant to share any of that.

It was past time she had a cat. So now he knew his next mission; get Miranda a cat.

"Taco time!" Her phone dinged and she made a face that wasn't hidden quickly enough.

"Do you need to take that?"

"No." Miranda stuck her tongue out. "Just another hospital rumor text. I guess Dr. Lawton is retiring."

"That rumor is just a rumor. I talked to Hugh." Knox followed Miranda into the kitchen, his mouth already starting to water in anticipation of street tacos.

Knox wanted to roll his eyes. This rumor really was getting out of hand. Hugh had blown it off. Said not to worry too much over rumors. "I swear, hospitals are hotbeds of gossip but this is getting out of hand."

"Knox." Miranda's voice was level as she held up her phone.

Know three people on the selection panel. I will give you a run for your money, Miranda.

Dr. O'Sullivan's text had two emojis at the end. Somehow Knox hadn't pegged the bone bro as an emoji guy.

"Selection committee. Hugh hasn't even announced his

retirement." Knox pinched the bridge of his nose. "There must be some misunderstanding."

"I don't think so." Miranda pursed her lips as she passed him the plate of street tacos. "I think Hugh is retiring."

"He told me he wasn't." Knox had been at the hospital longer than anyone else. He'd stayed when everyone else left. Hugh would tell him. He would.

"Did he say he wasn't? Or did he say not to worry?"

Miranda's questions made his stomach sink. "Not to worry." Knox had taken that to mean Hugh wasn't retiring, but that wasn't technically what he'd said.

"I've been at Hope longer than anyone else. When others have used it as a career peg to other things, I've built a career there. He should have told me." The tacos on his plate looked great but his urge to devour them had evaporated.

Miranda's fingers wrapped around his wrist. "You're right. But it's possible his contract means he can't tell us until the selection committee is set."

Her words rang true. Hugh was a stickler for protocols. He followed every rule, while Knox followed the letter, but not always the spirit. Like when he'd let patients know they could switch physicians. Technically, something that was allowed and guaranteed under the patients' rights, but not really something the hospital advocated for.

It was one of the things the board loved Hugh for and reminded Knox of when he teetered close to the line. If they'd told Hugh not to tell anyone that would include Knox. No matter how much that hurt.

He took a bite of the taco, trying to force away the emotions pooling in his stomach. "And Dr. O'Sullivan plans to give us a run for our money, huh?"

"I have no plans to put in." Miranda took a sip of her wine. "Do you?"

"Of course." Knox didn't know what stunned him more.

That she wasn't planning to throw her name in the ring or that she had to ask if he was?

Miranda would excel at the position. Losing to her wouldn't sting nearly as bad this time. Though he still thought he had the edge.

Knox had been at Hope longer than anyone. The surgical suite was practically his second home. Hell, there were days it felt like it was his primary residence.

"Does Dr. O'Sullivan mention who is on the selection board?" Knox wasn't surprised the orthopedic surgeon was interested. But he wouldn't stay at Hope. Not for more than a few years. Hope was one stop on his career ladder, not the pinnacle rung. Something Patrick had not kept quiet.

Which was fine. People got to move on. But the patients and staff deserved someone like Hugh. Someone devoted to the hospital. Someone staying.

They deserved Knox.

"No." Miranda kept her eyes trained on her plate.

He waited for a moment, hoping to push away the uncomfortable feeling that she was avoiding meeting his gaze.

"I'll have to ask Hugh." Knox waited but she only nodded without looking at him. His belly twisted. Maybe tacos hadn't been a good idea.

Her phone dinged again. She looked at it and grinned.

Knox didn't want to act like a jealous boyfriend. Particularly because they hadn't officially discussed any labels. That was the actual plan for tonight in his head—before Patrick O'Sullivan's texts arrived on Miranda's phone. Still, he wanted to know what had caused such a grin on her face.

"More information from Patrick?"

"No." Miranda held up a photo. A tiny gray kitten was curled on the front stoop of a house.

He hated the sigh of relief that echoed out of his mouth.

Miranda's eyes met his, but she didn't ask any questions about his sudden exhale.

"Cute cat. Whose is it?"

"That is a good question." Miranda ran a finger over the image on her phone before setting it aside. "Kelly has posters up around the neighborhood, but we suspect that it is a feral cat's kitten. It can't be much more than three months old. Kelly will take it to the shelter if she can't find an owner. Her dog is *not* a fan."

So it could be Miranda's kitten. If she wanted it.

"You could adopt it."

Miranda didn't acknowledge that statement; instead, she put her elbows on the table and leaned her head on them. "Why did you sigh with relief when I showed you a cat? Were you jealous that Patrick was texting me?"

"I want to say no. That I don't care if he's texting you." Knox shrugged; may as well address this head-on.

"But you do?" Miranda bit her lip and the worries about Hugh's potential retirement disappeared.

Her eyes were bright. There was a tint of pink in her cheeks, a hopeful sparkle in her eyes. "Do you want me to be jealous?" Knox reached for her hand, enjoying her fingers wrapping through his.

"No but also yes." Miranda let out a giggle. "Such a ridiculous response for a woman many years past her teenage self. Since we're on the subject, though, I'm not seeing anyone else." She took a deep breath. "And I don't plan to while we are dating."

"I feel the exact same." Knox leaned across the table, his lips brushing hers. "So do we label it? Boyfriend and girlfriend?"

More pink spilled into her cheeks. "It's funny. Some days I feel too old for such a label, but I want it."

"Then you have it." Knox stood, walked around the table

and pulled Miranda to her feet. "We can clean up the dishes later. Right now I want to take my girlfriend to bed."

"Miranda, can we talk?"

She knew what Hugh wanted to talk about. The surgical floor was buzzing with the news. Confirmation of what everyone already knew.

"Have you talked to Knox yet?" Miranda wanted him to hear this as close to first from Hugh as possible. He'd been on the floor longer than anyone other than the surgeon in front of her.

Knox hadn't moved around like most of the staff. He'd done his residency here. Then gotten a position and earned certificates that made him competitive as hell at other places. Yet, he'd stayed. So he deserved to hear it early.

"No." Hugh looked down at the floor. "We had a patient come in with gangrene on the foot. Diabetic. He's doing the wound debridement, hoping to save the foot."

It was not an uncommon injury in diabetics. Nerve damage related to the diabetes could cause the loss of feeling in the extremities. If an injury occurred it could easily get infected, but the patient might not feel the pain.

"Think it will work?" Miranda was delaying Hugh's announcement. She knew it. He knew it. But she watched the older surgeon step into the role of head of surgery. His shoulders a bit straighter as his eyes held a truth he wasn't ready to admit yet.

"Not sure."

Which meant no. Knox was trying and it might work. But the odds were stacked hard against him. Today was going to be a hard day for her boyfriend.

"I'm retiring, Miranda."

"So I heard." She tipped her head then raised a hand

and patted him on the shoulder. "We'll miss you. Do you have plans?"

She hoped so. Miranda had seen far too many people retire, not know what to do with themselves and return. Her father had signed retirement papers three times. And all three times he'd returned to another company doing similar work because staying home and relaxing wasn't an option. The only thing that stopped his work was the grave.

At least she knew where she'd inherited the inability to relax.

"My wife and I have three cruises scheduled. She loves them and I haven't been able to go with her much. It's time for me to party on the high seas." Hugh looked down the corridor, then leaned back on his feet.

"But it's not my plans I want to talk about."

Nope. She wasn't having the conversation she saw dancing in Hugh's eyes. "Hugh…"

He held up a hand and the resident in her that had hung on every word the man said shut her mouth. "You would be an excellent head surgeon. Hope would do well under your supervision."

It was a kind thing to say. Two years ago it was exactly what she'd wanted to be told. She'd spent her life achieving. Head of surgery was as high as she could go and still spend time cutting. Any further up and it would turn to admin work.

The absolute bane of a surgeon's existence.

Today, though, this version of Miranda wasn't ready. She overthought getting a cat; she gave patients and their families hope when it wasn't warranted yet. She didn't function at the level she used to.

Was her work solid? Yes. Was she still good? Yes. Better than most, even? Probably. But the certainty she'd had in herself, the belief that she could fix anything, had poofed out of existence in her soul.

The running joke in med school was that surgeons had God complexes. She'd once heard a surgeon say, *"Only because we are godlike."*

She'd never believed she was godlike, but the complex was real for a reason. You had to be certain in your duel with the fates that you would win more than you lost. That you were the conqueror.

Besides, she was happy with the life she was building. Maybe career was coming second, but she had Knox and her sisters, and her nieces and nephews. The dreams looked different now, but that didn't make them bad.

"You'd be great at this, Miranda."

The tiny ball of flame in her soul that brightened every time she could achieve flickered. If she tried, really tried, Miranda probably could make this a reality. Her chest tightened and her palms itched. The urge to achieve burned next to the withering cold reminder that she'd burned out so brilliantly not that long ago.

That should be enough to force the urge away.

"Hugh!" Jackson's voice was bright behind her.

Thank goodness she wasn't alone anymore.

"I just heard the good news." Jackson offered his hand to Hugh, gripping it tightly as he slapped the surgeon on the back.

"I feel like this was the worst kept secret in Hope Hospital's history."

Jackson nodded. "It leaked weeks ago. It is the way with big news." He sighed. "Retirement, man. You better enjoy it."

"I plan to." Hugh beamed. "I'm trying to convince Miranda to put in for the job. They selected the recruitment team. Which, for reasons I don't understand because I refused to do any unnecessary admin stuff, was the reason I had to play it cool despite everyone asking."

"Don't worry about it." Jackson parroted the line they'd all heard Hugh say over the past few weeks.

"You'll help convince Miranda to look at the job opening? She has refused to say anything. Which is shocking! The resident I knew would have jumped up and down at this opportunity to compete."

"That resident would never have returned to Hope." Jackson winked at Miranda.

She smiled at Jackson, appreciating the look he gave her. Not giving advice or asking if she wanted to put in. A simple acknowledgment of the woman standing here now. Unfortunately, it was clear from the look Hugh was giving her that he was waiting on a response.

A simple *I'll think about it*. That was noncommittal and easy. Or she could be honest and admit that she didn't feel ready for it. That she didn't really want it.

That was the right answer. But her tongue refused to utter the words that she knew would have disappointed so many in her past.

"Dr. Paulson." The nurse walked up, a smile on his face. "There is a patient demanding to see you."

Typically, Miranda didn't give in to demands. She'd run into more than a few patients who felt that because she was a female surgeon they could bully her. But she'd do anything to get out of this conversation.

"Of course." She turned, following DeMarcus. "What are the demands?" She mentally calculated her patient list. No one currently on it was someone she'd have pegged as difficult. But surgery had a tendency to bring out the worst in people. Pain did that—whether it was physical or mental.

"Just to see you." DeMarcus grinned. The black man's face was brilliant. Not exactly the face one expected when they were being harried by a disgruntled patient.

"DeMarcus?"

"Dr. Paulson!" Jill's voice was strong as she waved from the nurses' station.

"A difficult patient?" Miranda raised an eyebrow.

"I said a patient was demanding to see you. Never said they were difficult." The man winked as he slid behind the nurses' desk.

"Jill." The woman looked good. They'd discharged her after her return from rehab almost two weeks ago. She looked better than Miranda would have guessed for this stage in her recovery. Though it had been more than a month since her attack. Her body was healing, and the smile on her face made Miranda's day.

She held up a platter of Dorothy's Cookies. The iced shapes made her mouth water. The cookies were a staple in the area. They were made by one woman—ironically named Betty—in her small bakery. She swore the buttery treats were named after her mother, who loved sweets more than anyone.

Miranda had no idea if that was a marketing strategy or the truth. What she knew was these were the best cookies in the city.

"I wanted to thank the staff for saving my life." She set the cookies down, then picked one up and placed the cookie in Miranda's hand. The cellophane-wrapped stethoscope was beautiful, and it would taste even better. "And I wanted to make sure *you* got one."

There were tears in Jill's eyes. "I wouldn't be here without you."

"I was just in the right place at the right time." Knox and Jackson were at the bar. They'd have saved her life.

"Not just the night at the bar. The talks and the information to help me get home. My bags are packed." Jill bit her lip then straightened her shoulders. "The counselor you recommended gave me a list of places. My mom is letting me move back into my old room. It's temporary and I was so afraid it was failure but it's not. Just a new dream, a step in a new direction."

A step in a new direction.

It was a good phrase. One she should start using with her patients…and herself.

"I am glad to hear that, Jill." She opened the cookie and broke it in half, popping one piece into her mouth. Miranda closed her eyes automatically, the sweetness of the cookie blending along all her senses.

Opening her eyes, Miranda smiled. "And thank you for the cookies. They weren't expected but I know everyone will appreciate them."

"Thank you again, Dr. Paulson." Jill looked to DeMarcus. "Tell the staff sorry I was a grump sometimes."

"You were fine." DeMarcus grabbed a cookie from the tray and put it in the pocket of his scrubs.

"I think getting stabbed is a good excuse for being grumpy." Miranda raised her hand and smiled as Jill returned the handshake. "Good luck. Have a great life. You've earned it."

CHAPTER THIRTEEN

"So, I did something." Knox bit his lip and pulled an adoption form out of his backpack as they walked to the elevator bank. An approved adoption form.

Miranda eyed the paper in his hand but didn't reach for it. "Meaning?"

She wanted a cat. Needed a cat. The little gray figurine still sat on top of the cat tree. It was such a sad little reminder that her home was ready for a furry companion. She'd be the perfect cat mom, if she'd just let herself.

"You are approved to adopt from Old Farm Cat Sanctuary." Knox shook the paper, hoping she'd take it.

Instead, she crossed her arms.

"You got me a cat?"

"Nope." Knox had not taken that route. She needed to pick a cat or rather a cat needed to pick her. But more importantly, animals weren't presents. "Though I will pay the adoption fee if you go and find a buddy."

"Find a buddy." Miranda's dark eyes held the paper in his hands. "I like the sound of that."

"But?" Knox raised a brow. He could hear the word hovering on the end of her sentence.

"But the hospital, but my life, but..." Miranda let out a heavy sigh that he was sure contained so many unnecessary worries.

Knox put the application back into his backpack and pulled

her into his arms. "The world is always going to have buts, sweetie. It is the way of life." He ran his hand along her cheek before pressing his lips to her forehead.

There were a million reasons not to do things. Hell, he'd found excuse after excuse to not leave Hope Hospital. But that didn't mean you shouldn't jump at opportunities, either—like the head surgeon job for him and a cat for her!

"This is just an approved application. And I was honest about everything. Your hours, how long the cat might be alone, the job you have, everything. The rescue reached out in less than two days—which is a minor miracle for an all-volunteer organization. They think you would be a good cat mom." He kissed her forehead again, wishing they weren't at the hospital so he could truly kiss her. "Only you are stopping it."

Miranda squeezed him tightly. "Lance hated animals."

The words were soft. Ones he wasn't sure she'd meant to speak. "Lance isn't here."

If he was, I'd give him a piece of my mind.

"I wanted a cat when my depression was bad. I thought it might help with burnout. Or at least give me a cuddle buddy on the days when getting out of bed felt too hard."

It probably would have. And even if it didn't, she clearly loved cats. A loving spouse would want their partner happy.

"Lance told me that expecting another living creature to help me was selfish."

Knox had never worked so hard biting his tongue. "I think we should go see the cats. If nothing happens, nothing happens. You don't have to take a kitty home."

"But I can." Miranda's smile was brilliant as she held her hand out for the application. "I can take one."

"You have everything you need, and even some things you don't!" Knox squeezed her.

"I don't have food." Miranda stepped back.

The wheels were turning. She'd rebuilt so many areas of her life. The woman was amazing; she just needed someone to help with this last step. And now she was off and running with ideas of what the till-now fictional cat might need.

"The rescue will give you enough food for at least a week. You don't know what cat you are getting. Kittens, adults and seniors have different dietary needs."

"Right." Miranda nodded. "When are we going?"

Knox looked at his watch. Maybe he should have waited until closer to their scheduled appointment. But on the random chance that Miranda wasn't sure about this, he'd wanted to be able to give the rescue a heads-up that they were canceling the appointment. "We don't have to leave for another two hours. We can head to your place, get the litter box ready and fill the water bowl."

"And after that, we can make out a bit, so I don't watch the clock the whole time until it's time to leave." Miranda clapped, the crinkles in the corners of her eyes deepening as she danced up to him and kissed him.

"That sounds like an excellent way to fill the next few hours!"

Miranda held on to the edge of Knox's car seat to keep herself from bouncing up and down as they pulled into the small rescue location. She was a forty-year-old woman but in this moment, she felt five.

When Knox told her he wanted to talk as they were leaving, she'd expected him to ask about putting in for Hugh's job. It felt like over the past two days everyone in the hospital had asked if she was throwing her name into the ring. Everyone but Knox.

They'd not broached the subject once. In the old days, they'd have started competing for the job right away. They'd have quietly and not so quietly started mapping out plans.

Miranda would have pushed herself to the bone to make sure she came out on top. Whether she wanted the job or not.

And she didn't want this job.

She was back at Hope, finding herself again. Stepping back. That was what she was doing, what she planned. It was a good choice—it didn't mean that she was letting failure get the best of her. Just that she was choosing her path.

And her path was at Hope. But not as the head surgeon. She rebuilt her life and for the first time ever, she was the only designer. Not her parents, not her ex-husband. Miranda was deciding.

She tapped her foot, grateful when Knox pulled the car to a stop. She wanted to see the cats. Hopefully, she'd even take one home. Knox had dusted off the soft carrier she'd picked up years ago. It had moved back to Arizona with her, even though she hadn't even visited a cat rescue.

"Ready?"

Knox's smile filled his face. He was so excited. What happened if this was a bust? Would he be disappointed?

"I'm not sure. I mean, I want to see the cats. Obviously." She blew out a breath trying to keep inside the torrent of words racing through her mind. "I just don't want to upset you if I don't find my cat."

Knox leaned toward her, his heavenly scent wrapping her senses. "You can't upset me, Miranda."

Miranda looked at the little cottage with cats painted along the door. Old Farm Cat Rescue was written on a hanger and there were two cats sitting in the window. Knox put in the application. He got her approved.

The air in the car was thick and for just a moment Miranda wondered if he was going to say *I love you.* Her soul craved the words but when he squeezed her hand, she knew the moment had passed.

Which of course it had. They'd been together, officially,

less than a month. One did not just shout out *I love you* after so little time. And what would she have even said if he'd said the words?

Miranda knew the answer with more certainty than she'd felt in forever. Her heart recognized his. Knox was the person she wanted to talk to first in the morning and last before her eyes slipped into slumber. He was the one she wanted beside her.

She'd fallen for him. Maybe years ago when they were competing. Or maybe in the weeks since she'd returned. Either way, she loved him.

"Let's go meet some kitty cats." Miranda opened the door, hesitated for a moment then pulled her hand away from his and grabbed the soft carrier. She didn't have to come home with a cat. But taking it with her was a good omen and she was using that.

The entry of the rescue smelled like cat—but in a good way. There were kittens in several kennels on the wall and a door with a bubble letter sign reading *Cat Room—Fluff Guaranteed!*

An older white woman stood, her eyes trained on Knox. "I'm Kitty Resen. Yes. My parents named me Kitty. No, I don't think that is the only reason that I started a cat rescue. Yes, I do see the irony. Yes, I get these questions a lot."

"I bet." Knox held out a hand, offering Kitty his winning smile.

The older woman put her free hand over her chest as she shook his hand. "My, my, you are a gorgeous young man. Quite the keeper." She winked at Miranda.

"Hear that, Miranda? I'm a keeper."

"You are, and he'll be bragging on that all afternoon Ms. Resen." Miranda gave a playful exasperated noise.

"First time in my life I've ever been called a keeper. You

better believe I'm going to brag on it." Knox was grinning but she could see the hint of pride, too.

It probably was the first time. He rarely talked about his time in foster care. But his reaction to Leo, Ben and their mother was seared in her memory. His need to walk away after, his withdrawal.

"You are very much a keeper, Knox." She reached for his hand and squeezed it.

Kitty sighed. "Well, you seem thoroughly taken, young man. But if she cuts you free..." She wagged a finger and laughed.

"You'll be my first stop, ma'am."

"All right, let's get to the real reason you're here." Kitty clapped her hands, turning her full attention to Miranda. "A cat for you, my dear."

If she spoke, Miranda worried she might say she was just looking. Or something that would make Kitty realize she wasn't the best choice for a cat. So she nodded and held her breath.

Kitty picked up a piece of paper and read over it. "Surgeon—fancy. Not home at regular hours but able to keep water and food out all the time. Do you plan to declaw?"

"Oh, no." Miranda didn't keep up with much veterinary medicine but as a cat lover she'd seen the studies on declawing. It was detrimental to a cat's mental health and their longevity. They had to relearn how to walk and she doubted the rescue would allow an adopter to adopt who said yes.

"Right answer." Kitty tapped her nose. "Do you mind an adult cat?"

"No." As cute as kittens were, she didn't think she had the right home for one. "I think my home is better suited for an adult cat."

Kitty wrote a few things on the adoption paperwork. "How do you feel about one that is a little more aloof?" Kitty looked at Miranda and she could tell there was a specific feline that she was thinking of.

"As long as the cat likes me, aloof works. After all, the cat will be alone, sometimes for almost twelve hours."

"Right." Kitty sat the paper down. "I think you are perfect for one of the cats. Assuming she likes you."

Miranda's stomach turned as Kitty led them into a meet-and-greet room. There were cat toys on the floor and pillows for her and Knox to sit on. "What if the cat doesn't like me? She said she had one. One cat that fit me. Maybe this wasn't the best idea."

"Sweetie, take a deep breath." Knox inhaled and waited for Miranda to follow. "If the cat doesn't like you there are others. Their website literally has twenty. And if you don't find one today, well, it's nearly always kitten season. More will come. You can't fail this."

You can't fail this. Miranda latched on to the words. He was right. There was no way to crash and burn on meeting a rescue cat.

"I think another massage may be in order tonight." Knox kissed her cheek.

"Maybe. Your fingers are super delicious."

The door opened on the last phrase and heat flooded Miranda's cheeks. "Oh, uh—"

"No need to apologize for young love. Despite my flirtations I still remember what it was like when my Harold and I were together before he departed this level of existence."

"Young love." Knox hit Miranda's side. "Did you hear that?"

Miranda held her breath. She had heard it. *Love.*

"Young." Knox grinned.

"Right." Miranda's throat was tight. Of course he was talking about the word *young*. Getting older was weird. At forty she didn't feel old.

There were more lines around her eyes, and her back ached in the morning. Society noticed, too. The few times she'd logged in to a dating app most of her potential matches were men in their sixties.

Before she could think too much on the young love comment, Kitty opened the carrier and a bright white cat with brilliant green eyes hopped out, turned and promptly glared at Kitty then walked past Miranda and Knox, twitching its tail.

"Meet Icy."

Icy twitched her tail but didn't turn when Kitty said her name.

"I take it the name is due to personality." Miranda held out her hand, surprised when Icy sniffed it then let her run her hand on the top of her head.

"I would love to tell you that it's because of her color, and if I was prone to lying I might." Kitty let out a chuckle. "But honestly, I am a little surprised she's letting you touch her like that. Typically, she runs into the corner."

Icy's bright eyes focused on Miranda. She tilted her head, and Miranda could see the cat weighing her options.

Miranda ran her finger under the cat's chin and the creature let out a soft purr. The rumble was gone in an instant. "Can't change that it came out Icy." Miranda winked at the cat, knowing the girl didn't understand. The animal may not speak her language, but she could hear Miranda's happy tone.

Icy let out a meow then climbed into Miranda's lap. The cat turned three times then settled down, laying her head on Miranda's knee.

"I think you have a cat." Knox chuckled as he held his hand up. Icy sniffed it, then let him rub her ears.

"I think y'all have a cat." Kitty sighed.

Miranda's ears were buzzing on Kitty's words that she almost missed her next statement. "I love filling out adoption paperwork." The older woman clapped, ignoring Icy's glare. "You'll take her with you today?"

"I will." Miranda kept her gaze focused on Kitty. If she looked at Knox, she'd look for all the ways he might be reacting to Kitty's comment on *them* getting a cat.

So many thoughts, questions and hopes hung on that statement. He hadn't corrected Kitty. Knox also hadn't confirmed it. After all, pointing out that it wasn't their cat would be uncomfortable for Kitty—and maybe them, too.

"You are going to be so spoiled, Icy." Knox kissed Miranda's cheek and stood. His posture was relaxed, his face beaming. The man was aware of what he'd accomplished, and she doubted he'd stop crowing about it for at least the next week.

"You'd think we were torturing her!" Knox opened Miranda's door as Icy screamed bloody murder in the cat carrier.

"I think she thinks we are torturing her." Miranda rushed toward the laundry room. "I want to release her by the litter box so she knows where it is."

"I'll order dinner." Knox moved to the kitchen and found Miranda's stack of takeout menus. It was in nearly the same location as his. And he already knew what she preferred at most of the locations.

They'd slipped into this so fast. Yet, it felt—perfect. When Kitty had called them *young love*, he'd wondered if his feelings for Miranda were so easy to see. He loved her. Though sitting across the floor from her at a cat rescue was hardly the place to make such an announcement.

So he'd joked about the word *young*. And her face had fallen just a touch. Or he thought it had; maybe he was just imagining things. Everything was tumbled together in a puzzle that made no sense but was perfection.

Whether it happened in the past few weeks or years ago when they were competing with each other, he wasn't sure.

And it didn't matter.

"She's inspecting her new kingdom." Miranda stepped behind him, wrapping her arms around his waist and laying her head against his shoulder. "Thank you. She is perfect."

"She likes you. That's what matters." Knox kissed the top of her head as he pulled out three menus for her to choose from.

Miranda squeezed him. "She likes you, too. Maybe not as much as me, but you are well passed tolerating."

"Maybe before I pushed her butt into the carrier." Icy had screeched and Miranda had been using her soft voice, trying to calm her. The cat may not have obliged but it was clear Icy blamed him not Miranda.

"She'll forgive you." Miranda kissed his cheek, more hope showing in her eyes than Knox thought right.

"Hmm." Knox doubted Icy was the forgiving kind. Hopefully, once she was fully settled in, she'd remember she tolerated him at the rescue once upon a time.

Miranda tapped the menu for the Italian place. "I feel like lasagna. And their portions are big enough I'll have leftovers for tomorrow."

"What if we order the family size and we can eat it for a few days?" The question was out of his mouth before Knox could think through the implications. He'd just invited himself to stay...for a few days.

His mind wandered to the ways he could pull the words back but his heart refused to say them. He wanted to be here. When he wasn't at Hope, with Miranda was where he wanted to be.

"That sounds like a good plan." She moved to the fridge, grabbing a bottle of white wine.

It was such a small moment. One they'd hopefully do thousands more times. But it felt monumental.

Knox quickly ordered on a delivery app, then accepted the wineglass.

Icy wandered from the laundry room, her gaze taking in her new surroundings. Her tail twitched as she walked past them. And he swore she'd glared at him.

"I guess she approves of her new domain?" Miranda tipped her wineglass toward the cat. "Right?"

"Based on her reaction to the cat carrier, I think we'd know if she didn't." We. Two little letters. One little pronoun. All containing a world of possibilities.

"When you said you did something, this was not what I thought you meant. Not in any universe, but I'm glad you filled out the application for me, Knox. Thank you." Miranda's gaze was focused on Icy, who was sniffing around the couch in the other room like she owned it.

"What did you think I meant?" Knox took a sip of the wine. It was drier than he typically preferred but had a good body.

"I figured you wanted to talk about Hugh's job. I swear everyone is trying to get me to put in for it. Hugh was as pushy as I've ever seen him. Dr. O'Sullivan made a comment about me being his main competition—he is so sure of himself." She tsked her tongue. "What is it with bone bros?"

The rest of what she was saying was lost on him. He could see her lips moving, knew there was more, but his brain had locked down. No one had talked to him about putting in. Jackson had made a random statement about it, but no one else. Not even Hugh. He'd assumed that people weren't seriously talking replacements yet.

But they were.

They just weren't talking to him.

No. He had to have misunderstood. There had to be a mistake. "Hugh spoke to you?" He'd stayed at Hope. He'd been there the longest. He had the certs. Knox was good at his job.

No, Knox was damn great at his job.

"Yes."

His fingers tingled as Miranda squeezed his hand. This wasn't right.

"Has he not talked to you?" Her dark gaze held what he knew was the truth. She wasn't surprised he hadn't talked to Knox.

That was a bigger blow than Hugh not speaking with him.

"Don't pretend, Miranda." Knox set his wineglass down. He needed to do something. Something…but he wasn't sure what.

Setting her glass beside his, Miranda pressed herself against him, hugging him tightly. "Knox, take a breath."

He didn't want to follow her command, but he did. The air filling his lungs was tinged with the sweet scent he'd come to think of as hers. Instead of calming him, it drew frustration.

Why had she not talked about this with him? Why was she not plotting the competition? It would be friendlier now. But this was what they thrived on.

Because she doesn't think I'm competition.

The truth slammed his chest. What had happened? He was better than he'd been before. So much better. And he was still coming in second…or rather last.

"I should be a top candidate." Knox tapped his fingers against the counter. His whole body was vibrating.

Miranda's hands pressed on either side of his cheeks. "Look at me."

His gaze focused on her before he leaned his forehead against hers. "Why has no one talked to me?"

"Because you aren't a top candidate for the board." The soft words were hammers to his soul.

"That isn't fair." He pulled back, his body wanting to flee, his heart wanting comfort, his mind wanting answers. "And it can't be true. I'm accomplished. I have all the certs. I've been at Hope longer than anyone besides Hugh."

"It's that last one that's the issue. The board wants a 'well-rounded' candidate. One with a few hospitals on their résumé. Loyalty deducts points, not adds them." Miranda crossed her arms and shrugged. "You were right the first time. It's not fair. But life isn't fair."

Life isn't fair.

How he hated that phrase. Hated how everyone accepted and how there was nothing he could do to change that.

"I know that, Miranda." Knox pushed a hand through his hair, not caring that the motion was too rough and a few hairs came loose from his head—not pain-free.

He closed his eyes, trying to gain some bearing. "I grew up in the system. I didn't have a loving home. Parents who encouraged me. Sisters who had my back. I didn't have the advantage you and others had."

"I didn't grow up in the system but I didn't have a loving home, Knox."

"Not a competition, Miranda." He choked back a sob. "Sorry. I know you had it rough in a different way. I know that." This wasn't her fault. Nothing she was saying was wrong. It simply wasn't what he wanted to hear.

At least not right now.

"I need to leave." He grabbed his keys off the table and moved to kiss her cheek, hating how rigid she was. "It's not about you. It's me. I need a night. I'm sorry."

"Stay."

The word hit his back and he paused. "I feel like I am coming out of my skin, Miranda. I just need a night." He kept moving toward the door, waiting for her to call out again. But the word never came.

CHAPTER FOURTEEN

"THINK THE FAMILY-SIZE platter was a universal joke?" Miranda asked Icy as she cut a square for her breakfast and placed another in her lunch box. Getting a chance to eat on shift was hardly guaranteed, but she could always eat it cold.

Icy flipped her tail and then walked out of the kitchen.

Miranda reached for her cell phone for at least the hundredth time since Knox walked out last night. She'd typed so many messages and deleted all of them. He'd wanted time to process.

She understood that. She agreed with him. It was a crappy thing to not at least talk to him. She knew in Hugh's mind Knox should be a top candidate. But Hugh wasn't on the board. And the board liked to brag about doctors from "high profile" hospitals choosing Hope.

Longevity should be rewarded. And when it wasn't going to happen, Hugh should discuss it. Talk to Knox about his options so they could chart his next move.

Being hurt was a natural emotion. But they weren't competitors anymore. She wasn't even applying. This was what partners helped each other with.

Lance never discussed his plans with her. Just delivered the news of his latest new job with divorce papers. Her parents showed little emotion in their union. United in making their daughters, and themselves, as great as possible, no matter the consequences.

Miranda had little experience in this, but she knew what she wanted. A partnership that shared. There were several hospitals in the local area if Knox wanted to move on. Or he could accept his role at Hope. Maybe it didn't come with a fancy title and a few more dollars an hour pay, but it did come with more free time. Assuming he took it.

"What should I tell him?" Miranda held the phone up to Icy, who did not bother to look at it on her way to the laundry room. "Not helpful."

The cat twitched her tail but didn't offer anything.

Miranda looked at her watch; time to get going. "I'll see you when I'm home," she called after the white floof whose tail had just rounded the corner cabinet. "One day with a cat and I am already talking to her."

Miranda looked at her phone one more time then slid it into her backpack. She'd see Knox at the hospital. Hopefully by then she'd know the perfect thing to say.

"Miranda!" Knox's voice was bright and airy as it called across the parking garage.

That was not what she'd expected.

"Knox." Miranda smiled as he placed a quick kiss on her cheek. "So you're better?"

"Much. And I am so sorry, sweetie. I shouldn't have left like that and I absolutely should not have compared our childhoods. That was a terrible thing. I am sorry."

She wrapped an arm around his waist, some of the tension leaking from her. "You said you were sorry twice."

"Is that not enough? Do you want a third sorry?" Knox pressed his lips to her head as they waited for the elevator.

She playfully pushed her elbow into his ribs. "You know that isn't necessary. Are you doing better?"

"Yep." Knox used his free hand to tap his head. "Cause I have a plan."

His eyes were bright but his body tensed on the words. She'd seen this Knox. Worked beside him for years. The competitive man was here now. Except this wasn't a prize he could win.

"Knox."

"I'm applying, Miranda. I will make the board tell me I'm not the best candidate. From this moment on, I will be one of Patrick O'Sullivan's top competitors."

"All right." Miranda suspected he'd make it to the final round, if just for looks. But if this was what he needed, then she'd support it.

"It also means I'm going to put in extra shifts."

Ah, the unwritten "rules of the game." Extra shifts might not be explicitly stated as a necessity, but anyone currently on staff who wanted to throw their name in the ring would be expected to live at the hospital as much as possible.

"Not sure that is actually possible, Knox." The man was already pushing all the hours he was legally allowed to work most weeks.

The real reward for good work was more work. Not promotions. Not recognition. Just asking you to deliver more than you already were.

No matter how hard she'd pushed herself at her old hospitals, it hadn't resulted in anything more than an increased workload. And when she'd broken under the system, they'd pushed her work off on another high performer. Restarting the cycle.

Knox tapped his foot. There were words dancing around his brain. She could practically see them forming in his mind. But none escaped.

"You already work the maximum hours."

"I've stepped back over the last two weeks." He pushed the button for the elevator, like forcing the number the second time would make the thing magically appear.

Miranda leaned her head against his shoulder, weighing the different paths she could take here. If Knox wanted to put in, he should. Would the hospital board interview him? Almost certainly. Would they select him? Almost certainly not.

"Two weeks of one less shift is not slowing down, Knox. Not really." She doubted anyone even really noticed.

"I also plan to talk to Hugh about why he didn't talk to me."

That was a good plan. Hugh had chickened out on this one. Calling him out on it wasn't a terrible thing. Knox had deserved more, and standing up for that was good.

"So. When do we start the competition?" The elevator doors opened, and Knox stepped on.

"We don't." Miranda wasn't interested in the competition. Not anymore. And she really wasn't interested in it with her boyfriend. She'd support him with the application. Listen to any strategy he wanted to put out there. But she had no intention of putting in.

Knox hit her hip with his. "I know you had a bad time before, but you should put in. If I have to lose to anyone, I'd rather lose to you. At least I know how to do that."

"Knox." Miranda pulled at the back of her neck. She knew he meant it as a joke. Their past was them competing. Challenging each other. It had made them better surgeons. She believed that deep in her core. But over the past month they'd become partners.

That was a blissful state she had no desire to upset with competition.

"Miranda." He put his hands on his hips. "I'm serious. You are perfect for it."

Perfect. Knox's words radiated in her. He thought she should put in. Perhaps she should at least consider it.

"I appreciate that. I really do. But I like my life here. I've rebuilt my relationship with my sisters. I like Hope. I have what I want here. I'm happy. It's enough for me. And now, because of my very sweet boyfriend, I have a cat."

"So, tell me how Icy is."

She appreciated the shift in conversation. Icy was something she doubted she'd ever tire of talking about. "We made it through the night just fine."

The elevator doors opened, and Hugh was standing just outside them. "Good morning, Miranda. Knox, do you have a minute?"

"I do." Knox crossed his arms then uncrossed them as he stepped off the elevator.

"Good luck." Miranda whispered the words under her breath, not sure who needed it more.

"I am surprised you didn't want to talk to me sooner." Knox heard the frustration in his voice. Maybe that wasn't a fair way to start off the conversation but it was all he could muster in the moment.

Hugh looked at his feet, his gaze hovering on the floor.

Knox waited a second then let out a breath. Hugh was his mentor. A man who'd believed in him. Counseling him when he needed it, comforting him on days that felt like the end of the world. He didn't deserve Knox's frustration. "I didn't mean that."

"I think you did." Hugh crossed his arms, then finally met Knox's gaze. "I knew you'd ask about putting in."

"Oh, I'm putting in." Knox was qualified. Maybe the board wouldn't choose him, but that didn't mean he couldn't make them consider him. And if they considered him—well, Knox was nearly certain he could win the position.

The tips of Hugh's lips turned down and a pit opened in Knox's belly.

"Take a walk with me." Hugh started moving down the hallway without waiting for Knox to reply.

He caught up quickly. "You don't think I've got a shot?"

"I don't."

The words may as well have been hammers. Or knives. Tiny bullets shattering the self-confidence Knox prided himself on.

"I am a damn fine surgeon."

"I know." Hugh shook his head as he opened the door to the hospital courtyard. Or what the hospital claimed was its courtyard. There were a few flowerpots, currently missing any flowers, and some uncomfortable benches. But at least the sun was shining and no one else would hear whatever his mentor had to say. "You are a great surgeon, Knox. But the board doesn't really care about that."

"How could they not?" He was great in the surgical suite. Great at bedside. Great with the irritable parents, spouses, kids of parents. He was great at his job. How could that just not matter, according to Hugh?

"You've only ever worked at Hope."

"That should make me the top guy. I'm the expert." Knox couldn't seem to stop interrupting. He felt like he had all those years ago in state care. How many times had he been told his best wasn't good enough? He'd done everything he was supposed to. This wasn't the way his story was supposed to go.

Knox grabbed his phone and pulled up the emails he'd gotten this morning. "I reactivated my online job portal less than twelve hours ago. I have two hospitals and a headhunter reaching out. In *twelve* hours." Others wanted him. Why not Hope?

Hugh stopped in the small circle in the center of the "garden." The word *breathe* was carved into the stone. A reminder that once upon a time someone planned for this area to be used more. A plan that had not come to fruition.

"My position is more than cutting." Hugh held up his hand,

but Knox had run out of words to interrupt. "It's admin. It's fundraising. It's training interns. It's mentoring." Hugh held up his hand, ticking off the list of things he did.

Knox could do all those things. Knox had done all those things.

Hugh laid a hand on Knox's shoulder. "You could do all those things. Have done them."

It was like he was reading Knox's thoughts. If only Knox could do the same, he might understand why his mentor seemed to be saying he was the perfect fit and yet not even a candidate.

"But…" Knox held up his hands. This would be easier if Hugh would just drop the hammer.

Instead, his mentor bit his lip and looked over his shoulder.

Knox knew this moment. He'd seen it in caseworkers who were trying to find a way to lessen the blow they were about to deliver. The truth was that hard news was always hard, no matter how you said it.

"Just say it." Knox pulled his hand along his face.

"You haven't left and that is the problem. Leaving broadens your networking ability. It means there are candidates who will have colleagues around the nation."

"I have that, too." Maybe not to the same level, but in the local area, he knew everyone. Literally.

"So I'm going to be punished for loyalty? Where exactly is it written that I have to have worked in multiple hospitals to get this promotion?" He pushed his hands into his pockets, then pulled them out. He needed to be professional but his brain also wanted to revert to the scared kid he'd been once upon a time. The one who'd yelled that life wasn't fair. That had believed if he just worked hard enough there was no ladder too high to climb.

"Unwritten rules are often more important than others. You know this."

He did. His childhood was a list of unwritten rules. Constantly changing ones, too. This family didn't like it if you ate a snack without asking; that family got mad if you asked too many times for snacks when you could just grab them from the pantry. Silly little things that didn't matter in the real world. That didn't change who he was as a person.

Working in other hospitals didn't make Miranda or anyone else a better doctor. Having worked at Hope his whole career didn't make him less qualified. But on paper one was better than the other. For reasons.

Reasons that meant nothing. Even if Hugh could explain them right now they would mean nothing. They were reasons to score someone. And once more he was being found lacking.

"I'm still putting in." Let them tell him no. Let the committee look at his résumé; his work, and tell him no.

"If you decide you want a reference for another hospital, I'd be happy to give you one. I think you would make an excellent head of surgery. And I think it's unfair that your long tenure here will be held against you by the board."

A reference to leave. Not a reference for the position.

Miranda walked past the courtyard. Even through the glass, he could see the concern in her body language. Was she looking for him? Or concerned for a patient? Both?

"You told Miranda to apply." He hadn't meant to say that. But may as well lay all the cards on the table.

"I did." Hugh took a deep breath, then looked at his watch. They needed to wrap this up. There were patients to tend to and surgeries to handle. "I think she would make an excellent head surgeon."

"And I would, too, just not here." Knox blew out a breath, then looked at his own watch. He wasn't going to accomplish anything else with this. And he appreciated Hugh's candor.

Still, there had to be a way. He just hadn't figured it out yet. "Thanks, Hugh."

The older man nodded and tapped his shoulder a few times. Knox hoped the gesture was born of kindness but part of him feared it was pity.

He looked at the emails. One hospital in Nevada, another in Maine, and the headhunter told him he had openings in four states. He looked at his watch one more time, then sent three emails. It didn't hurt to at least talk to them.

What did he have to lose?

CHAPTER FIFTEEN

"You really aren't interested in putting in for the position?" Olive's youngest daughter was on Miranda's hip as her mother pulled the cookies Miranda had asked for from her bag. Her sister's home bakery had grown by leaps and bounds over the past year. Living close enough to get fresh deliveries was definitely a perk.

"Nope." Miranda jiggled Rose, enjoying the one-year-old's laugh.

"I am worried about Knox, though." The statement was out, and she regretted it. He looked broken when she'd seen him in the garden with Hugh. But he wouldn't talk to her about what was said on their short breaks.

Just waved away her concern. Tonight she wanted him to talk to her.

"What's wrong with Knox?" Olive raised a brow as she pulled the lid off the cookies.

Miranda leaned over the box as her face heated. He'd had an understandably bad reaction to a bad situation. He was stressed and this was their problem, one she wanted to discuss with him, not someone else, even her sister.

"Those look so pretty." The chocolate cookies had ribbons of white through them. "Did you put white chocolate in these?"

Knox loved chocolate cookies. These were her *I know you had a bad day and I want to hash out next steps* cookies. It was a new category, one she hoped not to use very often. Though any excuse for Olive's cookies was a good one.

"It's marshmallow. These are my hot cocoa cookies. I'm planning to make batches for Christmas. This is test number four. I do need your and Knox's honest opinion please. Now, answer my question, Miranda. What's up with Knox?"

Her sister put her hands on her hips. The same motion she'd seen so often growing up as her little sister took on their parents. Olive was the one who'd never cared what their parents said. She'd wanted to be a baker.

Miranda was a doctor; Kelly, her middle sister, a lawyer. Olive was meant to be the CEO. And in many ways she was. Her bakery was doing well, but it wasn't the penthouse suite her parents had wanted for her.

"He isn't a candidate for the head surgeon position. Not really." Miranda handed Rose back as the toddler reached for Olive.

"That sucks." Olive put her hand on Rose's mouth as the little one started to repeat the word. "That is just for Mommy, Rosie."

Rose didn't really understand words other than mama and daddy and no, yet. But she was becoming a real parrot. Miranda needed to watch herself around the little ones now, too.

"It does. And he won't talk about it." Miranda took a deep breath and recounted how he left the other night. "Walked out, like Lance."

"Did he?" Her sister dropped a kiss on her daughter's nose then looked back at Miranda. Her eyes held a statement that she didn't say. Sisters.

"I want a partnership. I can help him. If he'll let me." She'd run him through interview questions. Make sure meals were packed for his long shifts. Hold him when it got overwhelming and when the job went to someone else.

"If he won't let me..." Her voice caught. Not sure she wanted to travel down that path.

"One bad night and you are already worrying? Wow, Miranda. Take a deep breath."

"Take a deep breath? That all you got? Not super helpful advice, sis." Miranda stuck out her tongue—something Olive had done repeatedly as a kid. Her sister was right, though.

Which, based on her sister's expression, she was well aware of.

"I'm the little sister. The oldest is the one who is supposed to have all the answers."

The door to her town house opened and Knox stepped in. His eyes went to Olive and Rose before he went over and kissed Miranda. "I'm Knox." He held his hand out to Olive.

"You weren't kidding. He is hot." Olive winked at Miranda, clearly enjoying the horror she knew was on her face.

"Olive is my youngest sister. She takes great pride in being the baby of the family." Miranda didn't stick her tongue out again, but she wanted to.

"Enjoy the cookies." Olive waved. "It was nice to meet you, Knox."

"You, too."

Olive squeezed Rose. "Time for us to head home, Rosie. Think about what I said, Miranda." Then she headed out.

"Cookies?" Knox kissed the top of her head.

Good. Better for him to focus on that than Olive's parting shot.

"I thought you might like some cookies after shift." Miranda pulled away and headed for the kitchen to grab the cookies. "Olive wants our thoughts on these hot cocoa cookies."

Miranda handed him one, but Knox didn't look as thrilled

at the cookies as she'd expected. "Do you not like chocolate cookies anymore?"

"I love chocolate cookies, and I'm stunned you remembered that."

He and Jackson had joked about Knox's obsession with chocolate during his residency. Jackson had even playfully kept chocolate bars in his locker and thrown one at Knox anytime he was off. Telling him to eat it and become himself again.

The running joke hadn't happened since she'd returned. But back then they were exhausted residents operating on caffeine and adrenaline. Work balance had shifted in the past few years. Med students got breaks, not enough, but more than they'd had. The grueling hours to become a surgeon still meant people were hungry more than they often realized on shift.

"I remember a lot about our residency." Miranda grabbed her own cookie. "We were constantly together. I don't think this—" she waved a hand between them "—would have worked then. But maybe." There was no way to know for sure.

They'd been competitors but not enemies. Maybe even then the spark had been there.

"I…" Knox hesitated. He looked from the cookie to her. "I almost want to say no. Because if it would have worked then—" he reached for her hand "—then we lost years."

Years… Miranda's heart nearly exploded. Years. A single word with so much meaning. If they'd lost years, it meant he felt they had years together. "We have now."

"We do." He leaned over, his lips meeting hers. He tasted of chocolate and fun. His body molded to hers. "And right now, I am taking you to bed."

There were things to discuss. His day. The conversation with Hugh. The unspoken *I love you* she felt hovering in her heart. But it was impossible to focus when his lips were on hers and his thumb was tracing her nipple through her cotton shirt.

Maybe putting it off wasn't the best idea, but they had time. Lots of time.

She put the rest of her cookie on the counter. "Knox." His name on her lips felt so right.

He lifted her, carrying her to the bedroom.

Knox ran his hand over Icy's head as he grabbed two more cookies and glasses of milk. Miranda was pulling up a television show. A night in after his rough talk with Hugh was exactly what the doctor ordered. Miranda was a mind reader.

"These cookies are amazing." Knox set the plate on the table by Miranda's couch.

"I figured they were the perfect way to end a tough day." She stretched, the T-shirt she was wearing lifting to show her stomach...where his lips had trailed just an hour or so before.

But it was her words that caught his attention. Tough day.

Their patients today had all had standard outcomes. Everyone would recover. It was the kind of day everyone wished for. There was no reason for him to have a tough day...except for his conversation with Hugh.

He hadn't told her what Hugh had said. Yes, he'd been frustrated that Hugh had spoken to Miranda, and everyone else he thought was a candidate. But today's conversation could have been Hugh telling Knox that he was the top candidate. That he'd told everyone to put in because it looked good.

Part of him had hoped Hugh might say he hadn't thought it necessary to talk to him. Because of course Knox would put in and be competitive.

"You knew Hugh would tell me he didn't think I was competitive for the position." His blood cooled.

"I told you that the other night." Miranda's dark eyes held

his as she tilted her head. "You've been at Hope too long. You need to move on if you want that role."

I put in for two jobs this afternoon.

Those words ping-ponged in his mind but he didn't say them. The job in Maine was for a lead general surgeon with pediatric oncology credits and HR had sent a follow-up email almost immediately. It was nice to be wanted.

But he kept those words buried. No sense rushing any more than he already had. Rage applying for a new position was one thing; actually considering a whole other.

"So you got me pity cookies?" He closed his eyes, took a deep breath. He wasn't mad at Miranda. There was no reason to take his frustration out on her. "I'm sorry."

"These aren't pity cookies. These are delicious chocolate cookies."

He raised a brow and she shrugged.

"Fine. Maybe they are a little bit pity cookies. But they are commiserating pity cookies. Because I agree you should be competitive for the job." Miranda laid her hand on his chest as he sat down. "It should only matter how well you cut, how you deal with patients and how you manage. All things you're great at."

"They are good pity cookies." Knox kissed the top of her head, trying to push away the feelings in his belly. None of this was Miranda's fault. "But I am not ready to admit defeat just yet."

"Help me plot the best strategy to make the board rue the day they didn't consider me a top candidate?" Maybe he didn't have a shot. But Knox Peters had been down a lot in his life and always came out on top...or damn close to it. No reason for this to be different.

CHAPTER SIXTEEN

"So, I THINK Dr. O'Sullivan will crash and burn in his interview. He is so sure he's the best for the position that there is no way he is prepping the way he should. That's good news. The bad news is I was able to confirm that Leah Kilio from Southland is applying." Knox didn't even look up from the tablet that seemed attached to his hands the past week as he walked up to her by the elevator bank.

If he was not seeing a patient or consulting this seemed to be all he thought of. If he was like this during their residency, she'd not seen it. The man was working constantly and tracking whatever he could regarding the job opening otherwise. And she doubted it was going to make a difference.

And was he even enjoying this? Did he want it that badly or was it only because he'd been told he wasn't a top candidate?

Miranda had done so many things she didn't want to. Done them because she thought that was what was expected of her. And it led to soul-crushing burnout. And Knox was headed down that path.

"Why do you want this job?" The question was out before she'd really contemplated it. But she wanted an answer.

"Miranda?" Knox laid his hand over hers as his tablet dinged.

"What was that?"

"Nothing. Just an email." Knox turned his tablet over and leaned a little closer.

A twinge raced down her spine but she took a deep breath. It was an email and she wanted to focus on the job.

"Do you really want this job? Or do you just think you should want it?" Miranda watched his features, saw the tightening in his lips, the appearance of tiny lines around his eyes. Nothing about what he was doing appeared to be for fun.

Grabbing his tablet Knox tapped a few things out then flipped it around. "My résumé is fantastic."

That wasn't an answer.

"I think we should take a night off from all the prep." Before he could argue, she held up a hand. "Just a night. Some rest and relaxation." Miranda winked, but knew he didn't see it. All his attention was focused on the tablet she was beginning to truly hate.

Pulling the tablet to her, she pulled up the calendar app. "Schedule some downtime."

"Downtime? What do you mean? This is prime prep time. Dr. O'Sullivan is already working all the shifts he legally can."

And he's grouchy as can be about it.

Miranda kept that observation to herself. She was not derailing this conversation by talking about Patrick. He'd made his choice. She hoped he was happy no matter the outcome. If she had to work for him it would be fine.

Not as good as Hugh. But then those were shoes whoever got the position would need to grow into.

"I want downtime from this." She tapped the tablet and rolled her eyes and he pulled it away, correcting whatever she'd just messed up.

"We don't know when the interviews will start."

Miranda grabbed his wrist. "But we do know they will be after the position is posted. Which to date, it is not. You cannot apply for a position that is not open. So I ask again. Can we schedule some time for us? Just the two of us?"

"How will Icy feel about that?" Knox leaned over; his mouth was so close that if they weren't at the hospital she'd close the distance.

"Icy will insert herself as she sees fit." Miranda chuckled. The cat was very comfortable in her new role as empress of the condo.

Knox looked at the tablet. She could see him wanting to argue. He was so focused, so intent. But it felt like a war to prove he belonged, rather than a battle for something he truly wanted.

Or maybe I'm putting my feelings on this.

"Knox? Downtime?"

"Of course." He nodded his head, but there was a look in his eyes.

Her hip buzzed. A distraction!

The joy was immediately tempered by reality. A consult for the ER meant someone was having a terrible day.

"I'm needed downstairs." Miranda squeezed his hand. "Schedule it." Then she turned and headed for the elevator bank.

Part of her couldn't shake the idea that he didn't really want it. If he did, he'd have left Hope. It was admirable that he'd stayed, providing continuity for patients and staff alike. But Knox knew what it took to advance past certain levels. Corporate medicine wasn't ideal, but it was the life that physicians lived too often.

That was something they should talk about. But how?

And her brain refused to provide any answers on the short elevator ride down to the ER.

"Dr. Paulson." Dr. Hinks raised a hand; the smile on his face made her uneasy.

"You paged me?"

"Yes, I have a consult in bay four. The man is in his eighties, got into a motorcycle accident." Dr. Hinks rolled his eyes then caught himself and cleared his throat.

So the tendency to judge his patients hadn't miraculously fixed itself over the past six weeks. Shame.

"I ordered the CT and MRI scans. They are loaded. Looks to be a bleeder in the stomach. Maybe a burst ulcer. He's pretty beat up."

"A motorcycle accident will do that." Miranda grabbed a tablet from the charging station and pulled up the results. Clifford Douglass, eighty-one. Motorcycle accident. Broken right wrist. Bruised ribs. Contusion on cheek. No concussion, thank you, helmets. What looked to be a bleeding ulcer in the stomach.

She pulled up the scans and saw the notes that he'd been seen by gastro for symptoms eight weeks ago. The bleeding looked about the same. But no worse.

"Let me go take a look." Miranda started for the door, but Dr. Hinks stepped in front of her. "Yes?"

"I was wondering if you knew who might be putting in for Dr. Lawton's position—I was thinking of cross training and just wanted to wish people luck."

Wanted to find out who to suck up to was more like it. If Dr. Hinks wanted to figure out who to schmooze, he'd have to do it himself.

"I have a patient with internal bleeding. That takes priority." She moved around him and knocked on the patient's door before entering the room. "Mr. Douglass. I'm Dr. Paulson. Nice to meet you."

"Call me Clifford, please. You'll excuse me if I don't say the same." The older white man chuckled then grabbed his side. "Boy, you never realize how much you don't want to feel your ribs until you have to feel your ribs."

"That might be the truest statement about those bones as

I've ever heard." Miranda smiled and offered the man her hand. "So you were on a motorcycle?"

Clifford shook his head and sighed. "Let me guess, you can't believe someone my age would even bother."

"I never said that. Motorcycles are…" She patched too many people together after an accident to have a ready platitude.

"For young people."

"No. I would say they are for no one." Miranda gestured to Clifford. "You have the bruises and injuries to show why I think that. Age has nothing to do with it. But I am not here to talk broken bones and achy ribs."

She tapped a few things on the tablet and watched the television screen light up with Clifford's MRI. It hadn't been looking for the ulcer but all the indicators were there.

"I think you have an ulcer. And it's bleeding."

"Its name is Bertha."

Miranda blinked, opened her mouth but didn't quite manage to make any sounds.

Clifford hit his belly in the upper right quadrant where the ulcer was located. "She and I have been friends for at least three years according to my gastro doc. Nice man. Very interested in my fiber intake. Did an endoscopy to confirm a few weeks ago."

Miranda smiled and nodded. All physician specialties had certain traits and it was funny when patients picked up on them, too.

"That annoying lady is why I was on the motorcycle." Clifford glared at the screen.

Now she was truly lost.

"I'm sorry. What?"

Clifford chuckled and his face showed the instant regret. "I spent my whole life in the office. Always going for the next big promotion. Hell, I'm not even sure why. To prove I could. To make more money—had enough."

He cleared his throat and closed his eyes. The room was silent for a moment before he reopened them and smiled. A grin Miranda was sure he didn't feel.

"Bertha has probably been with me for a decade or so. Though she got super angry about a year ago. That was when I actually got help for the constant feelings of exhaustion. So I could work more."

The elderly man closed his eyes and a tear slipped down them. "So I could work more. What a statement to make. My kids don't talk to me and my ex-wife. Well, she hasn't picked up the phone in nearly thirty years. I demonstrated that work was more important than everything else and they took that lesson to heart."

Miranda nodded. It wasn't as uncommon of a story as one wanted to believe. Elderly people were often without family. Some of that was because family was too busy to deal with the effects of age. But some of it was because the person hadn't given attention or love to others when they'd needed it.

"Anyways. I understand why I am alone. I accept the choices I made. I can't change them. But I can change myself. So yeah. That is Bertha. My ulcer. The thing that finally got me out of the office. It seems small, but I didn't want my only accomplishment to be the thing my family left me for. A thing I'm not sure I ever enjoyed." Clifford pulled at his neck.

"My father hated motorcycles. Said only bad boys and gang member rode them. Such nonsense. Took me eighty-one years to realize I am more than my folks' expectations. But I guess better late than never. So I will be getting back on the bike."

"Not for a few weeks at least." Miranda pointed to the broken wrist. "And the ulcer?"

"Doc's got me on meds. It's bleeding less. I might have to do surgery but to be honest I don't want to."

"It's laparoscopic now. Three little holes."

"Yeah. Yeah." Clifford waved her notes away. Clearly, that was something his gastroenterologist had explained, too. "Took me eighty years to live. Don't want to miss a moment."

"That sounds like a good plan." Miranda took a big breath. "A very good plan."

She and Knox were talking tonight. She wanted to know exactly why he wanted this. If it was just to prove he was good enough, well, she wasn't sure how to make him realize he was already pretty perfect. But that was an issue to cross later.

Rumor is that someone named Ryann Oliver is putting in.

Ryann Oliver. Knox frowned as he read the name again. His friend in human resources wasn't in charge of hiring but he'd let Knox know when he heard rumors.

Ryann Oliver? That wasn't a surgeon he knew. Wasn't a surgeon he'd even heard of. What was their specialty? What did their CV look like?

His eyes floated to Miranda's front door. She'd asked for tonight to just be about them. He wanted to honor that, even though the competition was making his blood pump. He hadn't realized she needed a break.

The old Miranda wouldn't have.

Knox pinched the bridge of his nose, forcing the thought from his mind. It wasn't even accurate. The Miranda he'd competed against as a resident would have needed the break; she just wouldn't have asked for it.

And this wasn't even her competition.

One quick Google search and Ryann's name popped right up. Great. He'd get the basics about Dr. Oliver and then start his actual search tomorrow. Anything to get a leg up.

Ortho. What was it with the bone docs putting in for the position?

Knox read over Ryann's CV and his stomach sank a bit with each line. The woman was impressive. In fact, he'd argue that she was easily the top candidate.

His phone dinged again, an email notification coming across the screen. HR at Beacon Mountain in Maine was asking when he could come out to interview.

Would having a counteroffer make a difference at Hope? Maybe...

A knock echoed on the window. Knox jumped and his cheeks heated as he met Miranda's gaze.

He watched her dark eyes scan his phone and saw the slight shake of her head.

Opening the door, he slid out, ready to make his case. "Listen, I wasn't looking at other women. Or I was but just one in particular."

Nope, that sounded worse than anything he could possibly have come up with.

Miranda put her hand over his mouth and shook her head. "I am not worried that you are looking at other women." Her eyes rolled and she pulled her hand back. "I am disconcerted that you are reading a CV in front of my place on the night I specifically asked for no job talk."

Miranda pulled the phone from his hand, biting her lip. "Let me guess. Ryann Oliver is your latest competition?"

They'd talk about this for ten minutes then he was all hers tonight. No more job talk. That would be a nice compromise. He leaned against the hood. "According to the rumor mill."

"The rumor mill?" Miranda raised an eyebrow. "Please. I know you mean Pedro Garcia in accounting."

"Yes." But Pedro wasn't who he wanted to discuss. "This is where all my focus should go."

"Why do you want this job?"

She'd asked that question this afternoon, too. And he'd answered. Why were they back to this?

"You know why I want this job."

"No." Miranda shook her head. "I know that you were hurt not be considered and have thrown yourself headfirst into this." She gestured to his phone then to the tablet that was poking out of his backpack. "Why do you want this job?"

Knox paused, sucking oxygen in. He must have needed a breath for longer than he realized. His brain blanked. "What do you mean?"

"It's not a hard question, Knox. Or it shouldn't be. You haven't left Hope."

I might. Others wanted him. Wanted him bad, but he wasn't yet willing to voice that.

He wasn't even sure why he was so tense about bringing it up. He was the unusual one. People moved all the time.

Knox pointed to her door. "Why don't we go in, order some pizza and chat?"

Miranda looked like she wanted to argue but she started for the door.

"Fine. Pizza and we talk while we wait for it." Miranda walked into her condo, grabbed her phone and ordered. "There, that's done. Now spill. Why do you want this job?"

"Why do you keep asking me that?" Knox crossed his arms, mirroring her defensive stance.

"Why don't you give me an answer?"

"Because it's obvious. Of course I want the job. It's the head surgeon job." It was what surgeons aspired to. How many times had he heard that over the course of his career? That was the pinnacle location. One only a few got to.

"Why don't you want it?" Two could play the question game. Pulling his hand across his face, he looked at her. "You should want this."

"No." Miranda's eyes floated to the bookshelf where her

self-help books resided. "No. I am allowed to be happy where I am."

Fine. That was true. She had a good point.

"What happens if you don't get this job that you want so bad you can list all these reasons?"

Frustration flared. Why did she keep pushing this? "If that happens then maybe I take the job in Maine." That would show the Hope board.

"Maine. Job. What?" Miranda's head tilted then shook as she placed a hand over her heart.

He hadn't meant for that to pop out but in for a penny, in for a pound. "The day I had a conversation with Hugh a headhunter reached out. It happens."

"It does." Miranda pursed her lips then motioned for him to continue.

"I was frustrated and pissed. I'll admit it. So I reached back. One thing led to another and I have an interview at Beacon Mountain." It was weird to say the words out loud. He hadn't even decided if he was taking the interview. He'd rage applied. But if he didn't want the job, he would have turned down the interview like he'd done so many times before.

The color drained from her face. "Maine. Like the state, Maine." It was clear she needed some time to process.

"Yes." Knox nodded, and keeping his voice upbeat, he added, "Instead of heat like here, it's lots of snow. At least that's what HR told me."

"HR told you about the snow. Wow. So you've had more than casual chats with them. A rage apply is one thing but..." She pushed her hand through her hair. "When were you planning on telling me?"

"Now."

"Really? This was really the plan."

All the words were stuck in his throat. He wasn't sure.

The Beacon Mountain job was moving much faster than the Hope one. He'd never really considered a job anywhere else.

Not for long anyway. It just happened, and for once he hadn't stopped it.

He reached for her and she stepped back. "Miranda."

"Applying for a job without telling me. In a state thousands of miles away." She bit her lip, then closed her eyes for a second. "Okay. I hope you get what you want, Knox. I do. But my life is here. And I want a partnership."

"We have a partnership, sweetie."

She flinched and his heart broke. "Miranda." He wanted to stop time. Pretend for a few minutes that she wasn't ending things. "It's a job. People apply all the time. You came here."

"I did. My sisters are here. My life, the one I want, is here."

"If I want to be a head surgeon, I can't stay here." The words were out and with it the truth he hadn't let himself acknowledge. "I can look at a place closer."

"Closer than Maine," Miranda laughed but there was no humor in the sound. "A world of possibilities and the first one you applied to is forever away. And you didn't tell me. I've lived that life. The one where I find out the major decisions at the end. Where I am not consulted. I'm not doing that again."

"I deserve the job, Miranda. I compete. I better myself. I reach for more. If I stop trying, then am I still me?"

"You do deserve it. And I can't answer that last question, only you can." She laid a hand on his cheek then pulled back. "I want you to get everything you want, Knox. Everything you deserve. If you go to Maine, you'll have to send me pictures of the snow. I miss it sometimes."

The camera notification on her doorbell went off. The pizza was here. Pizza for the night they were supposed to have.

"You should take the veggie with you." She didn't catch the sob on the end of the statement.

"Right." A flood of words rushed through his brain. Pleas, cries, promises he wanted to believe he could keep. Instead, he opened the door, tipped the pizza delivery person and passed her the meat pizza.

Knox looked at the veggie pizza pie in his hands, then turned and walked out, his heart cracking into a million pieces as he stepped into the early night air.

CHAPTER SEVENTEEN

"YOU STILL NOT TALKING?" Jackson slapped Knox's back as he stepped into the condo with a cup of coffee for him.

Jackson passed Knox the coffee then shook his head at Knox's small couch. "I'd say you need a bigger one but this one fits the two of us just fine."

And that was all he needed.

His brother was nice enough not to point that out. But the truth still stung. It had fit him and Miranda, too. Though they'd spent most of their time at her place. With Icy.

Two days ago. Two days since he'd seen her. Forty-eight hours and an eternity.

"Want to play darts?"

Jackson's pity question made Knox sigh. And it meant he must look nearly as bad as he felt. "You don't want to play darts."

"Never do. But you do, so I thought I'd offer." Jackson took a sip of his coffee. "You like competition."

"Not exactly a secret, brother." Knox was glad he didn't have to worry his surly mood was going to impact Jackson. They'd been through hell together. "An intricate part of my personality that not everyone can accept apparently."

"Mmm-hmm." Jackson took another drink, his dark eyes holding Knox's.

"Something you want to say?"

Jackson shrugged. "Is there something you want to say? You're the one that's sat over here in silence for the last two days."

"I haven't been silent." Close. But not completely silent. The difference wasn't really important, but still.

"Mmm-hmm."

He hated that noise. It was one Jackson made when he had a lot of thoughts but planned to say none of them. "Ever thought of moving to Maine?"

"Umm, no." Jackson cleared his throat. "Not the direction I thought this conversation was going, I'll be honest. Why Maine?"

"Beacon Mountain Hospital is there. They offered me an interview and sent me virtual tickets for next week to fly in and see the facility." Knox gripped the coffee cup so hard he wondered if the lid might pop off. This was further than he'd gotten in any interview process. By his choice.

If Hope didn't want him, others did. So why did the idea of even stepping on the plane send chills down his back? Why had he nearly said no thanks a hundred times? The tickets were refundable; he could back out anytime he wanted.

Jackson still didn't say anything.

"Nothing to add? Nothing?"

Jackson tilted his head, his dark eyes showing so much wisdom that Knox suddenly wished there was a way to retract his statement. "Wow. I can't believe you'd leave."

"I mean I'd miss Hope. And living next to you. And the summer heat. And this place—first place I've owned. And Sally's Donuts and the Mulligans and tot nights and you. And—"

"And Miranda," Jackson added.

"And Miranda." He'd miss her for the rest of his life. "I need this. I think."

"You think?"

"Miranda kept asking me why I wanted the position yesterday."

"It's a good question." Jackson sipped his coffee but didn't add anything further.

"I'd be good at it." Knox stated the obvious, not sure why nothing else would come to his brain.

"Miranda would be great at the position, too, but she doesn't want it." Knox took another sip of his coffee, trying to piece together any of the rapidly firing thoughts through his brain. "I've never left. This is my home."

Home.

He looked around the condo, at his brother, the little turtle bank he'd painted with Miranda, the pictures of him with staff and friends from Hope. This was his home. Not the condo but Hope Hospital and Phoenix.

And Miranda.

His ears buzzed and his heart wanted to bust out of his chest. Why the hell hadn't this realization come forty-eight hours before?

"I love working at Hope."

"But you can't be the head surgeon working at Hope." Jackson tapped his fingers on the edge of the couch. "Not without experience elsewhere. You could take a job for a few years, then compete when whoever they hire moves on."

"I don't want—" He caught the words before they exited his mouth. He didn't want to move on. He loved his life. After a childhood proving himself, he'd earned the right to just be happy with himself. It was his ego that was bruised by Hugh's assessment that he wasn't a good candidate.

His ego that had driven him to apply for positions he didn't truly want.

Applying to hospitals without even talking to the woman he loved.

His heart bled as his brain pummeled him with memories of Miranda wishing him the best. Telling him she hoped he got everything he wanted. When everything he wanted was standing in front of him.

"I think a battering ram just pushed through my soul." Knox pulled up his phone, deleted the apps he'd downloaded to help with job prep. Then he went to the kitchen and grabbed his tablet. The battery was close to dead. He plugged it in and started deleting the CVs and info he'd gathered.

His neck flamed as he saw how much was there. She'd been right to ask for a free night. Right to voice her concerns. Then he sent his apologies to Beacon Mountain. He was staying at Hope.

"Patrick O'Sullivan will do a fine job." Jackson grabbed his keys from the table by Knox's front door, already surmising that Knox needed to leave—now.

Knox chuckled. "He might if Ryann Oliver wasn't putting in. She's Patrick's true competition."

"Ryann?" Jackson turned, his brother's eyes brighter than he'd seen in forever. "Ryann with two ns?"

"Yeah. Dr. Ryann Oliver. She's from the Pacific Northwest. Orthopedics. Do you know her?"

"Probably not."

There was more to that story, but Knox didn't have time to peel the layers back on the looks passing over his brother's face.

"I need to see Miranda, but we're going to talk about whatever—" he pointed to Jackson's face "—is making that smile reappear."

"I don't know a Dr. Ryann Oliver." His brother pushed the phone into his back pocket.

"Maybe not. But you do know a Ryann. And I am guessing she is the reason you haven't dated since you got back from Hawaii—over a year ago!"

Jackson looked at his wrist, hitting an imaginary timepiece. "I thought you had someplace to be."

His brother was right, but sometime soon he was going to find out who Ryann was.

Her phone dinged. Another note from a colleague reaching out to make sure she knew the position had opened this morning. Hugh, Patrick, three nurses and the ER tech so far had sent her messages.

She wasn't making a mistake but the fact that she knew they weren't blowing up Knox's phone infuriated her. Miranda had been back at Hope less than six months.

Yes, she had worked at three other hospitals. Yes, following residency she'd taken a prestigious fellowship. Yes, she was good at her job.

But Knox was great at his job. He knew everyone in the area. Had good working relationships with nearly every doctor. He cared about the patients and staff. By rights he should be a top choice, the one glaring at his phone as another ding went off.

And instead of throwing his hands up and storming off, something Lance would have done in an instant, he'd buckled down. Trying to find a way to prove them wrong.

And he'd applied for the job in Maine.

But was he really serious about taking it?

Miranda looked at the wall of self-help books she had. The wall where she reached when her life wasn't turning out the way she thought it should. When she doubted herself. There was no book for this, though.

Knox hadn't told her about the interview. About the rage applying. He'd shared so much with her. Things she knew he hadn't told others. If the interview in Maine was *that* important, he'd have told her.

She suddenly knew that with crystal certainty.

He wanted recognition. Deserved it. And he was hurt—which was normal.

And rather than address the hurt, rather than comfort him, she'd asked if he really wanted Hugh's job and then panicked when he'd told her about Maine.

Instead of thinking through why Knox wouldn't tell her, she'd leaned back on her old life. On the hurt Lance caused. And she'd reacted to protect herself. Instead of comforting the man she loved.

Rebuilding her life was fine but not if she built its foundation on the past.

And if Knox needed to leave? If what he needed was someplace new?

She looked at Icy and then around her condo. Then they'd try somewhere new and she'd come back here as often as possible.

Miranda took a deep breath and walked into the kitchen to grab her keys. She wanted to talk to Knox. Now.

The front door dinged and she called, "Come in," over her shoulder. One of her sisters was probably dropping something off. They'd checked in three times in the two days since she and Knox had parted ways. Each coming up with a different random excuse for why they "just happened to be in the neighborhood."

That was something she loved about being back here. Something she'd miss if they left. But hey, there were viral videos of family reunions for a reason. That could be fun, too.

Her phone dinged and she threw her hand up in the air, unintentionally releasing the book in it. "Why won't people stop texting me about that stupid job? They should be texting Knox. Begging him to apply."

"That is nice to hear." Knox's voice was smooth as his arms wrapped around her waist. He laid his head on her shoulder and just held her. His arms tightened as she turned in them.

He was here.

"But you're right. I don't want it, either." His lips pressed against her forehead.

"Come on." She must be imagining things. Knox was here, gazing at her as though she was the sun in all its glory. "It's okay to want it, Knox. Okay to rage apply and be ticked that your phone isn't ringing off the hook."

"Yes. But I'm happy where I am. This is my home. I'm content, and I like that. I like the feeling of being sure in my place in this world. Of not needing anything else. I just didn't like the idea of people saying I wasn't qualified.

"I am so sorry that I didn't tell you about Maine, sweetie. I didn't expect it to move so fast. I rage applied then just kept going. It was nice to be wanted."

"Of course it was." He was saying all the right words. Everything her heart needed to hear.

"And the righteous anger on my behalf, that feels better than anything else. I love you. This is home. And I'm happy, with you. And without that job we can watch more trash game shows together."

"I love you." Miranda kissed his cheek. "But I should have talked rather than wishing you well when I found out about Maine. It made no sense, and rather than dig into it, I just sent you on your way. I let the hurt from my past tarnish my future." Miranda squeezed him tight. "Forgive me?"

"Absolutely." Knox let out a sigh. "So, I guess now we get to watch Patrick work a ton of extra shifts for the next few months while the board looks across the nation for the hire."

"And we can work our regular already long shifts, then eat pizza and veg on the couch with a judgy cat monitoring us."

"Sounds pretty perfect to me." Knox dropped his head, his mouth capturing hers.

"Me, too."

* * * * *

HER SECRET
BABY CONFESSION

JULIETTE HYLAND

MILLS & BOON

For my furry co-author, Abby,
on our last book together.

Run fast, sweet girl. Catch all the balls.
See you on the other side.

PROLOGUE

TWELVE HOURS. That was all the time Jackson Peters had left to spend with Ryann with two *n*s and no last name.

They'd agreed when they'd met on the plane to Hawaii, both catching a layover in LA, that this week was fun and nothing more. No strings, no attachments, just bliss.

And bliss it had been.

They'd shared nothing too personal. He knew she was a surgeon and lived on the West Coast. She knew he was a nurse living in the southwest. That was as deep as they'd gotten conversation wise.

He did know that she smelled like summer rain, tasted like morning dew and made his body hum with the lightest touch of her fingers.

She knew every inch of his body and nothing about his past. It was ecstasy.

Jackson's story wasn't a happy one. It wasn't one he wanted to dwell on, particularly on vacation. This was supposed to be his time away. The "honeymoon" he hadn't gotten because Marie had decided she'd prefer to marry someone without so much childhood baggage. A week to forget the pains of the past and loneliness dwelling in his condo.

Part of him—the part that still hoped someone might not look at him as though he was somehow broken—wanted to share with her, wanted to believe that maybe Ryann wouldn't care about his past, wouldn't treat him differently because of it. But once someone knew, it was like they couldn't help but pity him.

And the last thing he wanted was to watch the pity dart into Ryann's eyes when she broached questions he didn't want to answer.

"Hmmm." Ryann ran a hand over Jackson's thigh as she sat up in the bed they'd shared for the last week.

The sheet dropped from her perfect breasts, and his hand automatically went to her brown, already perky nipple. *Beautiful* did not come close to describing the breathtaking creature before him. "Do we bother going to get dinner or just spend the night doing this?"

Her hand cupped him, and his body sprang to life. This was heaven. A temporary heaven that his soul was soaking up.

Jackson continued to twirl a finger around her nipple as her hand stroked him. Both of them so familiar with what made the other purr that they were drawing pleasure close but not making it impossible to think of nothing else.

"We could always do room service." Jackson lifted his head, running his tongue over the places where his finger had just traced, enjoying the tiny hitch in Ryann's breath. "Unless you want to spend the final night walking on the beach."

As much as he wanted to spend tonight crystalizing the memories of every single part of Ryann's body, this was the first vacation she'd had in a decade. One of the lone pieces of personal information the beauty had parted with. If she wanted to spend tonight walking the sandy beaches and running through the tide, he'd make that memory, too.

Her fingers curled around his manhood as she pressed her lips to his. "We could always enjoy each other, then walk on the beach, grab some fish tacos and come back for a final round."

Had her breath hitched on the words *final round*?

Did it matter if it did?

Not really.

No strings attached. Pleasure. Vacation memories. Stolen time away from the real world. That was all this was.

"Sound like the perfect way to say goodbye." Then he captured her mouth, devouring her before she could say anything else. He wasn't wasting a single minute.

CHAPTER ONE

DR. RYANN OLIVER covered a yawn as she walked toward the elevator bay at Hope Hospital. It was her first day on rotation at the hospital since accepting a private-practice gig earlier this month.

The Arizona desert was as far removed from the green of Washington State as possible. Moss had grown on her home there, the sun not daring to peek its head out of the clouds most days. The greenery was like walking in a forest paved with roads—at least according to Ryann's mother, Lydia.

The woman prided herself on never settling for the "normal" way of life. She'd seen a different side of everything.

Sometimes it was nice…but when *different* meant running off to find herself or chase some new soul calling…it was Ryann who suffered.

Chaos never benefited anyone.

At thirty-nine Ryann might not have known exactly what normal was, but she knew it was more than just doing whatever you wanted when you wanted to, with whomever you wanted. That lifestyle might've been fine if you didn't have a child to care for.

When Ryann had been a child, Lydia—the only name her mother would answer to—had disappeared for weeks at a time. Ryann had been left in the care of the multitude of stepparents who had entered her life for months to a year or so at a time. If her mother had been between partners, Ryann had stayed with "friends" or acquaintances.

Lydia had always seemed to return just before social services had gotten really involved. The overworked system had let Ryann slip through the cracks again and again.

There'd been some good moments—night trips for ice cream, road trips where they'd stopped at the "biggest spoon this side of the Mississippi" or alligator farms or haunted farms. Ryann still got giddy whenever a roadside attraction popped up.

But stability, the knowledge that she was safe, that the lights or water wouldn't be cut off because Lydia had forgotten to pay the bills… Ryann had not known that until she'd created it for herself.

She yawned again. Her reason for taking the private-practice gig and moving to Arizona had kept her awake most of the night with what had turned out to be a gassy belly.

Around three this morning she'd let out a toot so loud it should have come from a grown man rather than Ryann's not-so-tiny-anymore six-month-old daughter. Ayla had let out a sigh, then yawned and fallen asleep. Ryann had slept in the rocker in Ayla's room, ready to react to the smallest sound, but her daughter had slept until the alarm sounded at six thirty.

Then she'd fallen asleep as Ryann had been driving to the babysitter's, comfortable in the knowledge that she was safe and loved. Ayla might have been unexpected, but she would never doubt that she was cared for.

Ryann's job was to protect her daughter. To control the world's chaos as much as possible. Ayla would never fear the way she had. Never know rotating caregivers or worry her mother might forget to pick her up from school.

Private practice paid well, and the hours were considerably better than staff hospital work. She was in the office two days a week, in surgery for two days and on rotation at the hospital for a day. After spending so much time at her old hospital, a regular schedule with two days guaranteed off was close to heaven.

The world of orthopedic surgery was competitive. There were more women in the field now, but they still made up less than ten percent of all practicing surgeons.

When Hope Hospital had hired Dr. Patrick O'Sullivan as the new head of surgery over her, it turned out to be a blessing. After all, he was at the hospital at all hours, and she kept close to a nine-to-five.

Her phone buzzed twice—the sign of a personal email.

Ryann's stomach dropped. It had been five months since she'd first contacted her daughter's father through a DNA-matching website. Five months of radio silence. Yet on the first of every month, she sent the same email through the online portal she was supposed to reach out on and stupidly hoped that this might be the one he'd respond to.

She and Jackson, if that had been his name, had shared a blissful week in Hawaii. The first vacation Ryann had taken since completing her residency. It had been a fling, the most unstructured thing Ryann had done since leaving her mother's side.

Pure chaos with the hottest man I've ever seen.

It had felt good. So very good. There were nights when she still woke from dreams of his dark lips trailing along her body. She'd never regret that week; it had given her Ayla.

And as she saw the latest email—from her mother, with an image of her on a sandy beach with a new partner—she was reminded why she didn't plan to repeat the wild-and-free days she'd spent with Jackson.

Not that she'd get the option. Ryann took a deep breath

as tears coated her eyes. She was not going to cry over this. Months of silence from the man who'd fathered Ayla was nothing new. She was just tired and already craving foods she'd decided to give up to help with Ayla's gassy belly. That was why the frustration was bubbling too close to the surface.

It wasn't like she even needed him to co-parent. She'd been very clear in her notes that he didn't need to be involved if he didn't want to be. But she wanted a family health history for Ayla—and for him to know that he had a daughter.

Had part of her hoped that he might want more? Maybe. But she'd buried that feeling months ago. Not that it mattered.

Because five months and six days after the first note had been emailed there was still nothing from Jackson.

"Good morning." A white woman with curly brown hair smiled as she offered her hand. "I'm Miranda Paulson, one of the general surgeons at Hope."

"Ryann Oliver, orthopedic surgeon with the Lowery Group." Ryann pushed the elevator button again, wondering how long it took the parking-garage elevator to arrive.

"The button is funny." Miranda moved a little closer, pressed it twice, then held it until it lit up. "The hospital keeps telling us they will have maintenance look at it." Miranda shrugged as she stepped beside Ryann. "But since only staff park in this lot…"

She let the words run out, but Ryann knew what had been unstated. Since only staff used this entrance, it was not a priority. Technically it functioned. Profit over everything else.

"Thanks. I guess I look pretty dense standing here waiting for something that won't arrive." Ryann was tired enough that she'd have stood here for several more minutes before finally searching out a stairwell.

"No." Miranda shook her head, offering a bright smile. "You look new. I was the newbie not that long ago."

"The elevator hasn't worked for months?"

"This only started two weeks ago. My issue was with the pagers. They did finally fix that—though since you are private practice you won't get paged as often."

The elevator arrived, and they stepped in. Miranda lifted her mug, and the sweet scent of coffee nearly made Ryann weep. She hadn't had a drop of caffeine since learning she was pregnant. And since she was breastfeeding and Ayla was prone to tummy issues, she was still avoiding it.

She could hold off until her daughter was weaned, make it to at least a year of breastfeeding...more if Ayla was willing.

Just a few more months. *Few*...six or seven...ten...who was counting?

"You okay?" Miranda raised a brow, and Ryann knew the image she saw.

An exhausted mom...one craving the liquid that was in her cup.

One that had come darn close to beating the new head of surgery...if the rumors floating around the practice were right. Ryann needed to be on her game today. And she could do that without coffee—after all, she'd done without for so long now.

She plastered on the smile she wore whenever exhaustion was on her doorstep—so most days. "My daughter was awake well past her bedtime with a gassy tummy. She's fine, but I'm operating on less sleep than usual and your coffee smells delicious."

"It is. My boyfriend likes to joke that I prefer a little coffee with my sugar and syrup."

Ryann laughed. She did not enjoy sugar in her coffee— at least she didn't think so. Her first cup had been from the creaky machine in the library at her local college. A machine that should have retired to appliance heaven a decade before her arrival at the college but was probably still there.

It had functioned, but the coffee had been less than stellar. At least according to the others who'd partaken with her. It had tasted fine—ish—and woken her up. That was all Ryann had wanted. The coffee she'd drunk was the cheapest, with the highest caffeine count possible.

The elevator doors opened, and Miranda stepped out. "The locker room is this way," she said.

Ryann heard the words. They registered, vaguely, as she forced her feet to move in step with Miranda's. Her feet obeyed the commands of her brain, but her eyes stayed rooted to the black man standing behind the nurses' station, his head bent over a tablet.

The distance between the staff elevator and nurses' station was probably over five hundred feet, but even from this distance she recognized the shoulders, the stance, the black-rimmed glasses that he had to push up his nose.

It couldn't be. It wasn't possible.

Blood pounded in her ears. Heat coated her cheeks, and her mind was torn. Part of her was already plotting to run back to Ayla. Scoop her up and find another new start. Jackson hadn't returned her emails, and yes, she'd craved that just a few minutes ago, but seeing him now?

Her fight-or-flight instinct had definitely picked flight!

Ryann's mother had taken that route with her second step-father. Lydia hadn't been prepared for that move. Even her fly-by-the-seat-of-her-pants mother, who figured everything would work out fine, had felt the hardship of starting over with basically nothing.

Ryann wasn't prepared for a move. It would be disruptive for Ayla. This was just panic, her nervous system overreacting.

She had a good job and a mountain of med-school debts. Protecting Ayla meant staying here. At least for now.

That was the main thought running through her mind. The other, the thought that made her chest burn and embarrassment wrap around her spine, was the impulse to run to Jackson and hope his silence was just some misunderstanding.

Her mother would do that. Pretend the silence was the universe's way of giving her a big moment. Gush that karma had led her back to her soulmate and rush to him. Which was why Ryann wouldn't give in to that notion, either.

Control. That was what was needed here.

"That's Jackson Peters," Miranda said. "He's a nurse anesthetist, so you'll be working with him regularly. He's a good guy." Her voice was silky smooth, clearly misreading the reasons for Ryann's interest.

Ryann bit back all the words that threatened to tumble forward. She'd met Miranda less than ten minutes ago. It was better for the other woman to think she was ogling the hot nurse than to spill the truth.

She'd spent a week memorizing his body and come home with a baby surprise, followed by months of silence since their daughter's birth. Not exactly knowledge you laid at a new colleague's feet.

"Is he the hospital's only nurse anesthetist?" A certified registered nurse anesthetist, or CRNA, provided anesthesia during operations just like an anesthesiologist. Instead of holding a doctor of medicine, they held a doctorate in nursing and passed different exam boards.

Many rural hospitals employed only CRNAs, but Hope wasn't rural. Not huge, but far from rural.

"Yes. He got the degree about two years ago. Jackson worked his way from certified nursing assistant to APRN. I joke with him that he's running out of degree advancements."

That was impressive. Ryann had met many nursing assistants, or CNAs, that went on to become registered nurses. But an advanced practice registered nurse, or APRN, took years of schooling and exams on top of the requirements be a registered nurse.

The time, *and cost*, meant many qualified and passionate professionals stopped at the RN stage.

"So you know him well?" She hadn't meant to ask the question, but there was no good way to shift the conversation as they stepped into the women's locker room. It didn't matter if Miranda knew Jackson, didn't matter if he was great at his job.

He hadn't responded to her contact on the DNA-matching site. The entire reason for being in that database was to find family. To reach people. To make connections.

Their daughter deserved a response.

"He's my boyfriend's best friend. Knox is one of the other general surgeons here. Jackson and Knox grew up together—basically brothers. They used to joke the universe gave them the same last name to make sure they found each other. Always together." Miranda chuckled as she closed her locker.

Information to file away. Jackson had a friend close enough to consider him family. And he was close friends with at least two of the surgeons here. How was he going to react to seeing Ryann in person?

She was the outsider. The one who would need to move on, if necessary.

"Ready to meet the rest of the crew?" Miranda's smile was bright—hopefully she'd dismiss any hint of uncertainty on Ryann's part as first day jitters.

"I met a few people when I did the hospital orientation last week. Not a lot, and I didn't have to do the full thing."

"The joys of private practice," Miranda said as she clapped.

"You ever consider it?" Ryann hadn't until the offer had come through from Lowery. She'd worked for hospitals her entire career; the switch was nice. She had her own office, a better schedule and a paycheck that was quite nice. Overall, the pros far outweighed any cons.

"Not really." Miranda opened the door of the locker room and gestured for Ryann to leave first. "I like the fast pace of the trauma-surgery suite. I know how that sounds, but it gets me going."

Spoken like a true trauma surgeon. That was the one specialty Ryann had never sought out. The wins in that field were brilliant—the losses...earth shattering.

That specialty dealt with everything. You had no control over the type of cases landing on your surgical table.

Ryann took a deep breath. She was about to see Jackson, about to make contact with the man who'd made it clear by ignoring the outreach she'd made that he wanted nothing to do with her.

And because the universe was the way it was, she was at work. Which meant she had to have no reaction, tamp down on all the emotions raging through her.

"Knox!" Miranda waved to a man walking down the hall. "Meet the new orthopedic surgeon."

The white man smiled at Ryann and offered a hand. "Dr. Knox Peters. Nice to meet you."

"Dr. Ryann Oliver." Ryann hoped she looked professional, that the interest she was giving to the periphery of her vision wasn't clear. And that no one was noticing her heart attempting to jump out of her chest.

"I'm off shift. I'll have dinner ready when you're home, sweetheart." Knox leaned forward, placing a quick platonic kiss on Miranda's cheek.

So, this was Jackson's friend. What would he think when

he learned that Ryann wasn't just the new ortho surgeon but the mother of his best friend's vacation baby?

A worry for another time.

Knox moved through the locker room door, and Miranda watched him until he was completely out of sight.

"Right, then, let's go find Dr. O'Sullivan. Patrick should be the one to introduce you to staff you didn't meet during orientation."

Ryann nodded, not sure she could trust her voice. They rounded the corner, but Jackson wasn't by the nurses' station. That was good.

So why was disappointment coating her soul?

"Meet the new ortho?" Knox, Jackson's best friend in the whole world and the closest thing he had to family, asked, already wearing his street clothes.

"Not yet. But shouldn't you be heading to your new home? You know, the fancy one." Jackson threw a hand over his heart. He wasn't really upset that Knox had moved in with Miranda last month.

Though the new neighbors, a young couple that probably shouldn't have been living together, had upset the quiet ambiance he'd cultivated living next to Knox. Their fights were epic. Last night it had been over the lack of broom use. At least that was what he thought they'd been screaming about.

The walls weren't that thin, but he'd listened to make sure there were no sounds to indicate the argument had turned physical. Jackson hadn't wanted to involve the authorities for a noise complaint. But for intimate partner abuse? That was something he wouldn't ignore.

After an hour, whatever cleaning decision they'd been angry about had been overcome, or set aside for another time, and make-up noises had rumbled on the other side of the wall.

"It is weird not being right next door. But Icy was already comfortable at Miranda's place." Knox hit Jackson on the shoulder. "Want to come over for dinner tonight? I promised Miranda I'd make something."

Jackson made a face. Bad enough that Knox was using his girlfriend's cat as an excuse, though he understood not wanting to upset the feline princess. But he was not eating anything his brother cooked.

Not now. Not ever.

"I'm warming up one of the premade dinners that Miranda orders in bulk." Those services were what Knox had lived off of after he'd moved out of Jackson's place. It was a little funny that the woman he'd fallen for also refused to use the kitchen for more than reheating leftovers. They were perfect for each other.

"Oh, then yeah, I'll stop by," Jackson said.

He looked over Knox's shoulder and blinked twice. A woman with curly black hair and olive skin was walking next to Dr. O'Sullivan. They passed down the hallway, out of sight before Jackson could register more about the new doctor.

The new doctor.

Dr. Ryann Oliver.

The woman he'd refused to look up online after learning about their new hire, not wanting the disappointment of knowing it wasn't *his* Ryann when he found her picture.

She'd only been his for a week. A blissful, beautiful week almost two years ago didn't matter. *Ryann* wasn't a common female name, but it wasn't uncommon.

Now, from a distance, it felt like she was here.

It couldn't be. What were the odds? Such things happened to other people.

Others got miracles. Others got stories that sounded like the plots for television stories. Others got happily-ever-afters.

Not Jackson Peters. All life ever delivered Jackson was disappointment wrapped in hurt and coated with trauma. Hoping for anything had only ever left him wanting.

It wasn't his Ryann. Wherever she was, it wasn't Hope Hospital, but he sent a thought into the universe wishing her happiness.

"We'll see you after the shift, then," Knox said. He raised a hand and headed down the hall.

Jackson looked to where Dr. O'Sullivan and Dr. Oliver had gone. Better to get the introductions out of the way, let the dim light of hope playing in his brain snuff out.

Besides, he'd be working with the new surgeon at least a few times a week. The Lowery Group contracted with the hospital to use their anesthesiology staff so the practice didn't have to pay for a few of their own.

He turned the corner, hoping to get a glimpse of the doctor before he arrived at the nurses' station, but Miranda and Patrick were blocking his view. Of course.

Stepping up to the group, he tapped Patrick on the shoulder, and the doctor moved aside to let him in.

People always talked of the world standing still in these kinds of moments. But as he met Ryann's eyes for the first time in more than a year and a half, the axis holding the world in place seemed to rush forward.

"Good morning. I'm Dr. Ryann Oliver, the new orthopedic surgeon with the Lowery Group." Ryann held out her hand, the words as sterile as an operating room.

Was she really going to pretend they hadn't spent the week together? That he hadn't held her every night, kissed every inch of her skin? For that week they'd breathed the same breaths, their hearts thumping with a single beat.

The memory meant the world to him. The fact that he hadn't asked to break the pact they'd made and give each other their contact information was the biggest regret in his life.

And the handshake and greeting seemed like her way of saying *We're not talking about this.*

His chest moved as his lungs preformed their function, but it felt like the weight of the entire hospital was sitting on him. And he had to act normal. Unbothered.

Damn.

"Jackson Peters, CRNA."

He saw Miranda move her head, but if he looked at his best friend's girlfriend, his friend, his tongue might unleash all the thoughts running through his brain.

"I need to see to a pain patient." Jackson nodded to Miranda and Patrick, then turned his focus to Ryann. "It's really good to see you."

Meet you. I should have said "meet you."

He cleared his throat, "Welcome to Hope."

Then he made himself walk away. He didn't turn to look at the woman behind him, at the person who'd made him feel whole.

He was forty years old. Disappointment had been the only constant in his life. At least he knew the routine. Push down the emotions. Ignore the pain. Move on.

"Is your patient room 242?" Ryann's words hit his back, and she was walking beside him less than a second later, her cheeks tinted with just a bit of color.

From catching up with him or shock that they were in the same place? No way to ask in the hospital, and he wasn't sure he wanted the answer.

"Yes. She had hand surgery—"

"Left hand, Dupuytren's disease affecting the fourth finger. Finger curling toward the middle of the hand. Dr. Jenks performed a fasciectomy—not fully successful."

"Yes." Jackson shouldn't have been stunned by Ryann's systematic recitation of the facts. He'd heard dozens of doctors give the same type of statement—a factual outline with limited thought to the patient attached to the symptoms and outcomes. He hadn't thought Ryann was that way.

However, he'd only known her on vacation—for a week— more than a year ago. The disappointment he felt was his own fault. People were different on vacation, particularly with people they never expected to interact with again.

The part of him that had hoped for more was his own fault. By now he should've known better.

"Tina," he said.

Jackson always used his patients' names. Growing up in the system, he'd too often been referred to by his case number. Even to his face. Everyone was a person, and that meant they deserved to be called by the name they wanted.

"Tina is aware that the surgery didn't have the outcome Dr. Jenks wanted," he explained. "She's hoping that there might be another option for her." The fasciectomy had released a decent amount to the tension in her ring finger, but she still couldn't straighten the digit all the way.

And twenty-four hours after the procedure, she should see more movement—at least from what Jackson had heard the doctors saying yesterday.

And then there was the pain. Jackson had tried to reassure Tina that pain post-surgery was common, that the swelling in her finger was normal, and given a few days it would subside some.

Some. He'd been very clear on that word. *Some*, not *all*. Dr. Jenks believed she'd likely have pain in her hand for the rest of her life.

How debilitating? That was still to be determined. And pain was felt by the patient. What one could live with, another couldn't.

"She isn't going to like that Dr. Jenks isn't here," he said. "I know you're on rotation today." Maybe their first interaction was sterile, but Ryann deserved to know what she was walking into. "Tina isn't happy."

"And she feels like Dr. Jenks is avoiding her. He warned me…via text." Ryann let out a sigh. "She isn't wrong. I told him she deserved more follow-up from him, even if it isn't pleasant. He disagrees."

The words were said in the same formal tone she'd used for everything else. But there was a hint under it. A not-so-subtle disappointment.

That made him happier than it should've. Dr. Jenks was a competent doctor, and when his procedures went well—which they most often did—he was excellent at bedside manner.

That was the easy part of the job. The part Jackson would argue didn't matter as much. Everyone enjoyed good news. Everyone liked a success.

It was the bad outcomes, the less than successful, the ones that came with—sometimes a lifetime of—disappointment that mattered most. The doctors who stood there and took the anger, the tears, the frustration—those were the ones Jackson respected the most.

"How is her pain level?" Ryann paused just before Tina's room. Another good choice—asking the question before and not in front of the patient.

"She says it's a five on the scale of one to ten."

"But she was in pain for years. As a black woman, her pain was dismissed regularly until her finger was so bent there

were no other choices. So, a five for her is likely a seven or
eight for others."

Probably more. But it certainly wasn't a "typical" five.

Jackson was relieved Ryann understood his concern regarding Tina's 'level five'. Women's pain was often dismissed; women of color experienced it even more often.

"Pain is difficult," he said. "Only the person living in the
body really knows, but yes, I suspect she has pain not con-
sistent with twenty-four hours post-op."

Ryann nodded and made a few notes on her tablet. "Right.
Let's go."

Jackson led the way. Ryann was here for rounds; he was
here for pain management. People often thought anesthesiologists and CRNAs only put people to sleep for surgeries.
That was a major part of the job, but the positions were really focused on pain management.

No pain or feeling during surgery, as little pain as possible during recovery.

"Good morning, Tina." Jackson put on a big smile. The
notes in her chart indicated that last night had been rough.
The night nurse had written that she was rotating between
barking orders and tears. The doctor on shift had told her she
couldn't have more pain pills and had indicated in the chart
that he thought she was drug seeking.

That note had infuriated Jackson. Drug-seeking notes
could follow a patient for years. What she needed was com-
passion, not judgment, from her care team.

Tina's eyes welled with tears. She looked exhausted, and
her face was pale. This was not level five pain. Period. "I
hurt. My hand—it feels like it's on fire."

Jackson looked at Ryann. "I can give her something for
the pain, but…"

"No." Ryann shook her head and stepped to the bed.

Tina glared at her, but if Ryann noticed or cared, she didn't respond. "Ms. Priat, I'm Dr. Oliver, an orthopedic surgeon."

"Right, because Dr. Jenks is avoiding me. The man swore my hand would be better. If this is better..." Tina choked and put her head back against the pillow. "I don't know if I can do this."

Her word's flashed a bright red warning signal in his brain. First address the pain, then the mental health concern.

"Jackson, I need her entire palm numb—as fast as you can do it."

"What?" Tina's voice broke; her eyes met his, scared and confused.

Jackson grabbed the phone on the wall that went directly to the nurses' station. "I need a nurse in room 242 with lidocaine and a scalpel tray."

"Ms. Priat, I know your hand hurts. It hurts a lot. I need to relieve the pressure with a fasciectomy."

"That's the procedure I just had." Tina looked to Jackson. "Please don't leave. You're the only one who's listened to me."

"I'm right here." Jackson had no plans to leave. He knew Tina from the local community that had provided him a safe place to study and learn when he'd been at the group home. They'd all learned to take care of each other because no one else would.

"You have every right to be upset with your care. That is your right as a patient," Ryann said, her words soft. "But the pressure from the wound dressing is what is causing the pain. I need to open the wound to release the pressure."

Ryann looked to Jackson, and his breath caught. The look in her eyes was the one he'd seen so often during the week they'd spent together—like they were of two minds. "Can Jackson please numb your hand, Ms. Priat, so I can help you?"

Giving the patient a choice. That was good, though there really wasn't a choice here.

"What if I say no? What happens to my finger if I try to wait it out?"

Ryann sat on the edge of the bed, put her hands in her lap and looked Tina directly in the eye. "The pain will get worse. You're describing it as a five, but I suspect if a man were laying in this bed, they'd be screaming and saying it was an eleven out of ten."

Jackson agreed. As a pain-management specialist, women had higher levels of tolerance than men, on average. By a lot.

"Then the pressure will cut off blood supply. We're within hours, if not an hour, of that happening. Then your finger tissue will die, and it will require amputation to keep the rest of your body from going septic."

Tina blew out a breath. "Thank you for explaining that to me."

"Of course." Ryann's voice was soft but firm. The perfect bedside manner for this moment. "Can Jackson numb your hand for me?"

"He can."

Ryann looked over her shoulder at him.

"I'm going to get washed up and gloved," she said. "I can do the procedure here. It will be fast, once I start, and you'll feel immediate pain relief."

Tina nodded and watched Ryann walk out of the room. "I like her."

Me, too, Jackson thought.

CHAPTER TWO

RYANN KISSED AYLA'S HEAD, smiling as her daughter's hand tapped her cheek. At six months old, Ayla was moving past the newborn stage and starting to show off her personality. Ryann had always loved children.

When she'd been eight her mother had joined a group living in a commune for almost a year. They'd followed some man there. Ryann had had five "stepfathers" and two "stepmothers" during her childhood. Each one swore her mother's choices were hers, that it didn't mean they didn't love her. But they'd eventually floated out of Ryann's life, forgetting all about her.

Ryann had spent her time in the commune helping with the younger children. Playing with the young ones, even though she'd hardly been an "older" child, had given her some peace and structure during that unusual time.

"You and me, sweetie. You and me…" The chorus she sang her daughter every morning caught in the back of her throat. "You and me. You and—"

Tears coated her eyes as she looked at her daughter's smiling face. She had Ryann's curly brown hair, her dark eyes. But the heart-shaped lips, the tilt of her nose—all of that was Jackson.

He was here. Yesterday he'd been so attentive with Tina. The only one who'd recognized the woman wasn't drug seeking, wasn't acting. It was a sad state of affairs that women's pain was often overlooked.

She'd seen a woman in her office with a degenerative bone disease that had sent waves of needles through her feet when she'd walked. Several doctors had told her she'd needed anxiety medication, that it was all in her head.

Old-fashioned ideas that were far too prevalent in modern medicine.

Jackson, though, he listened. He'd comforted Tina while he'd been numbing her hand. In the patient's room he'd seemed every bit like the man Ryann had spent a nearly perfect week with.

Reconciling that with the man who hadn't responded to her outreach on the website, who'd seemingly ignored her requests for information that might help their daughter…it didn't make sense.

She looked at Ayla, pulling her daughter's smile deep into the pool of her soul. Jackson deserved to meet his daughter. Or at least have the option of meeting her.

He got one more shot. One more.

The next time she was at the hospital and saw him— which in theory could be weeks, if they weren't scheduled together—she'd ask him for dinner, make it very clear that it wasn't a date. And then introduce him to Ayla.

Mentally it all sounded so easy. Realistically there were a whole lot of things that might go wrong.

If he wasn't interested in them…in Ayla…then she'd start looking for a new position somewhere else. Her daughter would be protected.

Nothing else mattered.

"All right, sweet girl." Ryann snuggled her close for one more moment. "Time for work."

* * *

Ryann looked at her watch. She'd called the Lowery Group to let them know she was stopping in to look after Tina. It wasn't her day on rotation, but the woman hadn't had the best outcomes to date and Ryann wanted to alleviate as much of the unease as possible.

Jackson had been on yesterday and wasn't scheduled for the day. Twelve hours and she was already keeping tracking of him. She hadn't needed to ask after his schedule yesterday, but she had.

So she knew there was no reason to look for him, no reason for her head to swivel as she walked toward the elevator bank. At least today she knew the trick to getting the elevator to drop.

She pressed the "code" on the elevator's call button, taking a little too much pleasure when it dinged and opened on the first try. Sometimes life really was about the little things.

Stepping onto the floor, she waved a greeting to Nicola, a nurse she'd met yesterday. She wasn't technically here, but she grabbed a tablet chart from the charging station and quickly pulled up Tina's chart. The patient had slept through the night and had not requested additional pain medication. There wasn't a better outcome.

Ryann walked to Tina's door and knocked before walking in. She took two steps in and opened her mouth to say good morning, only to stall out completely when she saw Jackson sitting in the visitor's chair next to the empty bed.

"She's getting an X-ray." He yawned and looked at his watch. "Should be back any second."

The man looked like he'd been here for hours. "Did you sleep here?" she asked.

Jackson rubbed his eyes and rolled his shoulders. "*Sleep* is a relative word in the hospital."

"Jackson." Ryann took a step toward him, then stopped herself. Why was she so drawn to this man?

"Tina never married. She has no children, and her only sister passed away about two years ago."

Information not available in her charts. Knowledge he could only have learned from Tina. How much time had he spent with her?

Ryann had met many patients who were alone in the world. It was far more common than people wanted to discuss. Many liked to imagine they'd grow old together on a front stoop with the one they loved next to them and a bevy of grand-children around them. Reality looked different for many.

"So, she's alone?"

"I'm here." Jackson winked. "And no, she's not alone. She's part of Patty's Community."

"What is that?"

"A community started by a woman I know named Patty for those that need a place. It started in her home, then moved to the community center. It's about a hundred people strong now," he said, rolling his shoulders again. "I started...volunteering there when I was a teen."

She heard the pause. The heaviness in the milliseconds between *started* and *volunteering*. Why? Many teens wouldn't bother with volunteering, and they certainly wouldn't have continued once they were well into adulthood.

Jackson rubbed the back of his neck, the color of his cheeks shifting a little. "I stopped by after dinner last night. I was worried about the notes put in her file about drug seeking."

So he had slept here. "That was kind of you," she said.

"It sure was. But now he has a crick in his neck and needs to go home." Tina was all smiles as she waved at Ryann. She looked like a completely different woman.

Amazing what not being in pain could do for you.

"I see you're feeling better." Patient smiles were a great way to start her workday.

Tina held up her hand. The bandage covered the entire palm, but it was clear from her attitude that the second bed-side emergency surgery had been a success. "You should do all the hand surgeries."

"Funny you should say that," she said. "My specialty is hand surgery. Though I do more than just that." Most ortho-pedic surgeons had a specialty. Some were fortunate enough to only do that sort of surgery, and maybe one day Ryann would be, too.

"It shows." Tina winked.

Ryann felt the heat flood her cheeks. Praise, even from a stranger, always gave her a tingly feeling. "I'm glad you're doing better." She didn't want to look at her watch, but she knew she needed to get moving before her first appointment at the Lowery Group.

Still, she'd made a promise to herself this morning. If she put it off once it would be easier to put off again and again. Excuses were easy. Lydia put everything off...and it had never solved one of her problems.

Now or never. Ryann took a deep breath. "Jackson, can I speak with you? Tina, if you need anything please have one of the nurses call me and if you would prefer to see me for your follow ups just let the office know."

Ryann put her card on the bedside table. "That has my di-rect office line—use it if you need anything."

"Don't suppose I'll need anything. You did a great job." Tina tapped the card. "But thank you."

Jackson stood, and she could see hints of something in his eyes. Hope, exhaustion, worry—she didn't know. And it didn't matter.

There was one person who mattered, and that was Ayla.

"Walk me out? I assume you aren't on today?" She knew that, but she didn't want him to know that she knew that. Besides, he'd have never slept in Tina's room if he were, no matter his concern for the patient. The staff break room had uncomfortable cots, but they were better than the chairs the hospital swore pulled out into a bed.

No, they did not.

"I'm not back on until Tuesday." Jackson followed her to the elevator bank. "So, you want to talk?"

"No." Ryann cleared her throat. He had a right to meet his daughter. One chance. She needed to focus on that.

"What I mean is no, I don't want to, but we should. Damn, that sounded worse. I… I would like for you to come to my place for dinner."

"Your place." Jackson raised a brow. "We could do dinner out if you wanted. Your place seems a little intimate."

Ryann let out a chuckle. "I think we're past that." She started to lean toward him and pulled herself back quickly. "It needs to be my place. I'll explain. Tonight. Six thirty. Um…" She pulled a pad from her purse and quickly wrote out her address. "Park in the driveway. The woman who lives across the street goes ballistic if there's a car in the street. She claims it's in the HOA, but…"

She was rambling. Ryann never rambled. She was cool. She was collected. She was in control even when the world was spinning out of control. That was how she worked. Period.

"Ryann—"

His voice was soft. It called to the places that hadn't been able to resist him all those months ago. Her skin vibrated, and her heart yearned for things it didn't need.

"This isn't a date." The words came out harsher than she'd meant. Maybe she should have put this off. "I mean…" Her brain froze. Ryann's pager buzzed and relief flowed through her—saved by the buzzer. "And now I have to go."

"The elevator isn't here." Jackson pointed to the door that still hadn't opened despite them putting in the right "code."

"Well, I have appointments I need to get to. Six thirty." She pointed to the paper, then turned and walked down the end of the hall. She wasn't exactly sure where the stairwell was, but it couldn't be that far. Besides, that was knowledge she needed anyway.

Stairwell locations were a safety issue. What if they had to evacuate patients? Granted as private practice she would almost certainly never be in that position.

The excuse didn't even sound good in her head. She was running away, pure and simple. But there was no dodging him tonight.

Jackson stood outside the address Ryann had texted him after the most awkward exchange of phone numbers he'd ever been a part of. Honestly, he was not quite sure what he was doing here. He wondered for the umpteenth time if he should walk back and put the flowers in the car. She'd stated…before racing away from him…that this was not a date. But she'd asked him to meet at her place.

Demanded it.

What other reason might there be?

Only one way to find out. Jackson looked at the pink lilies in his hand. They weren't exactly like the plumeria Ryann had worn in her hair the night they'd danced under the moon, just before leaving the island. But it was as close as the local florist could get.

Jackson squeezed his eyes shut, taking a deep breath. When he opened them, he walked deliberately toward her door. The flowers were nice, even if this wasn't a date.

He raised his hand and knocked, his chest tightening with the passing moments waiting for Ryann. Except she didn't answer. Now what?

Most of his younger life had been spent waiting for those who'd never showed up. He'd promised himself that he'd never leave someone waiting for him, that when he was an adult people could count on him. It was a principle he maintained—and the only thing keeping him from walking away when she didn't open the door.

He'd promised to be here at six thirty. So he was here. He'd wait as long as necessary.

Raising his hand, he knocked again. A few seconds later his phone dinged.

Busy. Door open. Be in the living room in a second. No. Seriously. How...?

The last few words read like she was dictating the note and the phone had caught the last of the conversation.

Jackson read it again, then reached for the handle. The door swung open, and the sweet scent of Ryann flooded his system...mixed with a hint of baby powder? That was unexpected though not unpleasant.

Everything was orderly. The entranceway had a place for a coat and shoes. Jackson slid his off, setting them next to Ryann's. The sight gave him too much pleasure. They hadn't seen each other in more than a year. Yes, they'd had a great week, but the ache in his chest...

He'd wanted a family more than anything growing up. There were even a few times he'd thought he'd gotten it. A foster family who'd sworn they'd adopt him, only to choose a baby when given the opportunity and dump him back into care. The fiancée who'd sworn she'd loved him and wanted to create the life he hadn't had, only to leave him three months before their wedding for a businessman who could offer her a better life. A life free of baggage—according to her.

Even his biological family didn't want him. His father and mother, both of whom he'd located through a DNA database…and had sent similar expletive-filled rants telling him not to get back in touch.

A family might've been what he craved, but it was always out of reach. Women always seemed to run when they found out about his unstable youth. One had even asked how he could be stable after all the trauma. And that was with only sharing a tiny bit of what his childhood had looked like.

What other choice do I have?

Even Marie, his ex-fiancée, had changed after begging him to tell her everything—something he couldn't do. She'd wanted someone who shared their past. But what was he to share? All the hurt? No one needed that.

No, his partners were better off not knowing the demons floating through his past.

"Ayla!" Ryann's frustrated call made him look up the stairs.

Jackson left the flowers on the entry table and started toward the sound. He wasn't sure who Ayla was, but it was clear Ryann was upset. Rounding the corner he heard the cries—Ryann's and an infant's.

"What…?" He stepped into the room that was clearly a nursery and stopped as giant watery brown eyes met his—eyes he saw staring back at him every morning in the mirror.

"She's blown out three diapers in the last hour and has a horrid rash that burns. I must have eaten something that upsets her, but I can't figure out what." Ryann pressed her head to Ayla's, tears mixing on their cheeks.

The child let out gas designed to clear the room, then immediately started screeching.

"Oh, Ayla." Ryann looked at her own shirt, then at him. "I've already changed her three time today. She's just so miserable."

Jackson reached for the little girl he knew was his daughter. "Let me. Go change, or take a shower or just fifteen minutes of rest."

Ryann looked at Ayla, then at Jackson. "She needs another diaper change."

"I grew up in foster care, Ryann. In many houses I was basically help for the little ones. I can change her diaper." He ached to hold the little girl. This was the reason he was here.

Her insistence that this was not a date clicked into place. His daughter.

His.

They'd used protection all week, but that was hardly one hundred percent effective, as he'd explained to more than one person when he'd been an ER nurse.

Ryann looked at her daughter, then handed her to him. She hovered by the door.

"Promise, Ryann. I got this." Jackson looked at Ayla, his heart swelling. "Hi, cutie."

She didn't smell baby fresh, but his daughter was gorgeous, even red in the face with tear streaks.

He lifted the onesie off her and dropped it into the laundry hamper right by the changing table. Organized. He took the diaper off and knew why she was so uncomfortable.

He cleaned her as quickly as possible, but she screamed when the wipe touched her raw skin. The best thing for her would be a baking-soda bath. Not so easy with a little one who still couldn't sit up on her own without support.

"Want to play in the kitchen sink?" Jackson booped her nose, knowing she didn't understand the words yet.

He took off his own shirt. Unlike Ryann, he did not have an endless stock here. If the baby got sick between here and the kitchen sink, he could just take off his white undershirt.

Then he lifted his daughter and took her down the stairs, talking nonsense in a fun voice. He might've been her father, but to Ayla he was a stranger.

Filling the sink with barely warm water, Jackson started opening cabinets. He found the baking soda and dumped a healthy amount into the water. In just a few minutes the little bath was ready.

"Here we go!" Jackson made silly sounds as he helped Ayla sit in the sink.

She let out a surprised sound, then sighed.

"Feels good, huh!" Jackson dipped his hand into the water and dribbled a little over her face.

Ayla giggled.

"That was a nice sound." Ryann's voice was tired as she crossed her arms and looked at her daughter.

"Baking soda. Works wonders," Jackson said. He winked before putting a little more water on Ayla's head.

"Was that a trick you learned taking care of foster kids?"

"Yep." And he didn't want to discuss his past, particularly when his future looked so bright. "You have a toy she can play with in here? Ideally she should soak for ten minutes. That will help neutralize the acids."

Ryann nodded and wandered to another room before coming back with a little rubber ducky.

Setting the toy in front of Ayla in the bath, she leaned against the counter. "Not exactly the way I planned to introduce you to your daughter."

Jackson looked at the little girl and couldn't stop his grin.

Your daughter.

There were so many things to figure out. A world of changes this news brought, but those two little words were as close to perfection as he'd ever gotten.

"Nice to meet you, Ayla," Jackson said. Then he looked at Ryann. She was clearly exhausted. Parenting was difficult—parenting alone, even more so. But she had help now.

"She's beautiful. Just like her mother." Turning his attention back to Ayla, he cooed as the little one pushed the duck around the sink. "Sorry I missed so much, Ayla, but we'll get caught up."

"If you'd have responded to *any* of my messages, you wouldn't have!" Ryann's sharp tone echoed in the kitchen.

Messages? What messages?

"Ryann—" His brain refused to supply any additional words. It was overloaded with happiness and trying to process the anger he saw steaming from her face.

She wiped a tear from her cheek and bit her lip so hard he feared she was tasting blood.

"Ryann…" he started again, but no words materialized this time, either.

"I need to get a towel to dry her off. Then I'll feed her and put her to bed. After that…" She blew out a breath. "After that we can talk." Each word was choked with sobs she refused to fully let out.

Jackson was holding up their daughter in the sink, but he ached to pull Ryann in, to hold her tight as she let out whatever she needed to.

But he also wanted to know why she thought he would have ignored any messages from her. He'd have moved heaven and earth to find her if he'd had more than a first name. Hell, he hadn't even had a city until her CV had arrived at the hospital. Seattle…and he only knew that from hospital gossip.

Learning about Ayla would have meant uprooting himself from Phoenix. Leaving his condo—the one place that was his, only his. The place no one could take from him.

And he'd have done it as soon as physically possible to support her.

Ryann came back in holding a baby-blue towel that looked softer than anything that had ever touched his skin. He lifted their daughter and let her mother wrap her in the towel. She kissed Ayla's head and went back up the stairs. Jackson didn't follow.

She dressed her daughter in just a diaper and took a few deep breaths while Ayla cooed on the changing table. The baking-soda bath had been a great idea—one Jackson had thought of within five minutes of learning he was a father.

There was no handbook for introducing your child to their vacation-hookup father.

And no handbook for the butterflies that danced through Ryann's stomach when she'd walked in on Jackson in his white undershirt taking care of their daughter. She'd done this alone every second. She'd been prepared to see Jackson walk away.

Hell, her father, and every stepparent, had walked away because dealing with her mother had been too hard. She knew how to act for that, the armor to don to protect her daughter.

But if Jackson was here, was ready to step up…

I've seen him handle one situation!

How many of her stepparents had handled a few situations, even a few years of situations before walking out on her mother?

And me.

They'd all walked away from Ryann, too. Even the ones who'd sworn that it wasn't her fault and they'd keep in touch. A birthday card, a couple of phone calls, maybe a holiday gift and then silence.

It had happened so often that she'd recognized the pattern each time it had started. Knowing that hadn't stopped her from hoping, at least a little, each time. Never mattered, though. If they didn't love her mother, they couldn't stay in her life.

Picking up Ayla, she kissed her cheek. The way she protected Ayla was making sure Jackson only saw his daughter. There'd be no relationship with Ryann for him to walk away from. No disagreements with his daughter's mother.

They'd shared a wonderful week and gotten the most precious gift from it. That was enough. It had to be.

"Ready, sweet girl?"

Ayla moved her mouth and reached for Ryann's chest. "Yep. Snack time, then sleep."

After breastfeeding, Ayla would be down for a few hours. Up for another feeding, then down again…if her stomach issues calmed down. No guarantees.

When Ryann reached the living room, Jackson was sitting on the couch, his right leg crossed over his left, his arms resting on the back of the couch. He'd put his shirt back on, but if someone snapped a photo they'd could title it *Smoking-Hot Man at Relaxation*.

"She needs to eat," Ryann said as she walked to the rocking chair Ayla liked, lifted her shirt and put Ayla to her breast. Her daughter latched, and the room settled into silence.

Jackson looked at her, a look crossing his face that she didn't know how to read.

"Does my breastfeeding bother you?" It was a normal human requirement. Still, she'd been told by more than one person to cover up. Feeding her baby was not a sexual act, and she refused to feel any shame over it—particularly in her own home.

"No." Jackson smiled as he looked at them. "You and Ayla. You're so beautiful, and this moment…" He closed his eyes and took the deepest breath, his muscular arms moving up and down in a way that was damn near hypnotic in its own way. "I never knew happiness felt so good."

"Jackson…" She looked at Ayla, whose eyes were heavy. Ryann would pump the other breast and put it in storage. "Why didn't you answer my messages?"

She'd done this alone, and she could have continued. Women had done so for centuries, but the fact that he could sit there looking like he'd won the lottery was so at odds with the silence.

"What messages?" Jackson asked, shaking his head. "I never got anything. I swear to you if I had, I'd have been on the plane to you."

He seemed so sincere. But she'd sent one a month. Five total. All unread.

"I sent them through the DNA site," she said. "I was looking for her health history. I told you that I needed to know. I reached out the month after she was born and on the first of every month ever since."

"Oh." Jackson pulled a hand over his face.

"Oh." Ryann was glad Ayla was asleep. It meant there was no way she was going to raise her voice. After months of silence, all she got was *Oh*. "That is really all you have to say—oh. Our daughter is six months old, and you can't tell me you didn't get the results. I get notifications from them weekly. It seems everyone and their mother is taking the tests and registering. Hell, they're even solving murders with these databases."

Ryann sucked in a deep breath. She was usually so good at controlling herself.

Not with him.

In Hawaii, she'd been free, had felt deeply for the first time in her memory.

She wasn't on vacation now. And there were real consequences to her week of no rules.

"Everyone is on those systems these days." Jackson pulled at his face again. "I…uh… I…sent all the notifications to a hidden folder about a decade ago."

A decade. "What?" she asked. "You expect me to believe you've been in the system that long? That would make you one of the first."

"Yes. I've been a member since I was eighteen, but even then, there were several," he said. "DNA tests and databases have been around since the late nineties. I was one of the first to apply to them all."

"All of them? That's…"

"Not as many companies now actually. Most have been acquired. They don't give you back your money when they combine databases." He chuckled.

"Not sure I see the humor."

"There isn't any." He shifted, darkness crossing his features. "I joined to find my parents. They abandoned me in foster care when I was seven. Or at least that's when they stopped trying to earn their parental rights. I was in care most of my life."

His body seemed to shrink, and it made her heart shudder. For a moment, he was far away from them, in another life.

"You didn't find them." That would hurt.

"I did." Jackson shook himself, the self-assured man returning. "Not directly and not for several years, but through a hodgepodge of cousins, half siblings I've never met and a nephew I didn't know existed."

Jackson looked at his hands, lost to her and the world as a whole.

"And they didn't want to be found?" She whispered the words more to herself than anything else.

"They did not appreciate my attempts at reconnection, no." He cleared his throat and blinked quickly. "So that's why I set up any emails to come from there into a hidden folder. I didn't want to see the results anymore but couldn't make myself unsubscribe. It...well... I didn't see you reach out. I apologize."

Ryann looked away for a moment, not sure what to say. She'd been so angry. Furious. The silence had felt personal. And it was, but not toward her. She believed him. The man who'd taken his angry baby and gotten her a sink bath would not have ignored her.

"No apology needed. A misunderstanding, and one that is cleared up now."

"I am sorry I missed the first few months. And your pregnancy, but I want to be involved now." He smiled at the curly haired little girl in her arms.

"I want you involved with Ayla."

"And us?" Jackson tilted his head.

She looked at the flowers down the hall. He'd brought them and dropped them onto the table by the door. Ryann had seen them when she'd come downstairs. From her position here, she could make out the bright pink collection, though not the individual flowers.

Plumeria? The flower she'd worn all week with him in Hawaii.

"There is no us." Her throat burned as she said the words.

If they'd met some other way, if she was sure he'd stick by her forever…

But you could never be sure of that. They'd had lust and passion, but that didn't mean they'd have made it more than that week if it had been an option.

Declaring you were in love had seemed to be the kiss of death for her mother's relationships.

"I want to be in Ayla's life," Jackson said.

"And I want you in Ayla's life." Ryann meant that. She wanted her daughter to have the parental figures she'd lacked, wanted it more than anything.

Which was why it was better if Ryann and Jackson were co-parents. That limited the drama. He'd never hate seeing his daughter because he was upset with her mother.

"Ryann, we had something special."

His words called to her soul. Part of her—a larger part than she wanted to admit—wanted to throw caution to the wind. They could put Ayla to bed together, and she could kiss Jackson, maybe even invite him to stay the night. Not for intimacy, but because she hadn't slept so well since the day she'd left his arms.

Life was short—her mother had said that so often when she'd been giving in to a whim. It was Ryann who'd paid the price each time. Ayla would never feel that. "We had passion," she said. "And we got something special from it."

She looked at Ayla. That was true. Their daughter was a blend of the two of them. Hopefully the best blend. The safe blend. The blend that would never worry about if she was loved.

The protected one.

"If that's what you want."

Ryann nodded. It wasn't. But it was what was best for Ayla. She yawned and looked at the clock.

"Will she be awake soon?"

"No." The change in topic was welcome. "Or at least she hasn't been until lately. I think something I'm eating is upsetting her. I started an elimination diet, but she's still up at all hours. I have a surgery tomorrow, so hopefully tonight isn't one of those."

Jackson nodded, then gestured to Ayla. "Why don't you let me take the night shift tonight? I don't have work tomorrow."

That sounded absolutely delightful. "I couldn't ask that."

"You didn't ask. I offered to take care of my daughter tonight so her mother can get some rest," he said. "She must take a bottle while you're at the hospital. Point me to the supply, then go get some rest."

Ryann opened her mouth to decline. This wasn't what she'd asked him over for. And him spending the night here while she slept felt oddly more intimate than anything they'd done before.

"Ryann—let me take care of *my* daughter."

It was the emphasis on the word *my* that made her smile.

"All right." She stood. "Let's put her down, and I'll show you around."

CHAPTER THREE

JACKSON YAWNED AS he unlocked the door to his condo. Ayla had been up almost every hour. Between the diaper rash and the gas, she'd had trouble getting comfortable. Finally, he'd gotten her off to sleep on his chest in the recliner in the living room.

His back ached. His head throbbed. He felt like he could drop into bed and sleep for hours.

And Jackson had never been happier.

Ryann had gotten a full night's sleep. She'd looked refreshed, and there'd been a gleam in her eye when she'd gently tapped his shoulder before lifting Ayla off him.

She'd gotten Ayla ready for the babysitter, and Jackson had fixed Ryann some oatmeal using the coconut milk in the fridge. Day four of Ryann's elimination diet.

Before sleeping, he'd spend a little time researching what foods she could eat. He hadn't been there for her during pregnancy and Ayla's newborn stage, but he could be there now.

A supportive co-parent. That was the role Ryann wanted him to play, so that was what he'd be. Maybe he wanted more—craved more—but you dealt with what life gave you.

Back at his own condo, he started the coffee and booted up his laptop. The ancient device took forever. Knox kept telling him to upgrade, and he should, but it still worked…mostly.

Maybe he should chuck it, but Jackson had made a conscious decision not to throw out useful things for better options.

If people had treated him the same way growing up, maybe his life would look different. Though he'd done pretty well for himself.

Grabbing a cup of coffee, he slid into his kitchen chair and stared at the screen. First the hard task. Taking a deep sip, he pulled up his email, clicking into the hidden folder he hadn't checked in so long.

Jackson could have unsubscribed from the DNA-matching websites, but part of him hoped maybe his mother or father would reach out. The rational part of him knew that was never going to happen, so he hadn't checked the folder since setting it up.

There were now over a thousand unread emails. He sorted them quickly. The majority, around nine hundred, were notifications that people had been added, of price changes and policy adjustments for the automatic renewal he just couldn't make himself cut off.

About a hundred were direct notifications about people related to him. Second and third cousins. A half brother who'd sent one message asking if Jackson knew where their father was.

That one was from two years ago. Jackson knew where their father had been five years ago and knew that the man wanted nothing to do with any children he'd fathered.

If I'd wanted anything to do with ya, I'd have kept up with ya.

Words engraved on Jackson's heart. The wound might not bleed now, but it would never fully heal. If his half brother had found their father in the last two years, he'd know the man wanted nothing to do with them. If he hadn't…well,

Jackson didn't think anyone deserved to know how much their parents resented them.

But that wasn't his choice to make for another. He sent a short note with an apology for the extremely tardy response. The rest of the message was as gentle as he could make it—a warning that their father wasn't pleasant and had no use for the children, so to reach out with caution if he chose to. His half brother would need to decide for himself what do with the information.

A note that Jackson's daughter was in the system was flagged as important from the company. They were right. If he'd seen it, he'd have contacted Ryann immediately. He'd have known about Ayla from month one.

Been there from almost the start. Not half a year in.

The last four messages were from Ryann. All said the same thing and were dated on the first of the month.

Jackson,

We have a daughter. Her name is Ayla, and she is the most precious gift in the world. You do not have to be involved, but I need to know any medical conditions that might run in the family.

For her sake, I hope you reach out.

Followed by her contact information.

He'd missed the first months of Ayla's life because he hadn't wanted to read the emails in this file, unintentionally letting down the mother of his daughter and his own flesh and blood.

If Ryann hadn't happened to land a job here, he might never have known about Ayla. His past wasn't rosy, but running from it had kept him from his daughter.

And her mother.

He clicked a few buttons and confirmed he wanted the messages to come to his inbox from now on.

The front door opened, and Knox walked in holding a pickleball racket. He'd gotten into the sport a few weeks ago. His partner, Miranda, had no interest in the game, but Jackson had had fun with it a few times.

At least it was something other than darts, though Jackson figured his brother would go back to that game in short order. Outside of the surgical suite and Miranda, darts were Knox's passion.

Jackson had agreed to play a few rounds on the court at the condo complex today, a fact he was remembering only because Knox was here and ready for competition.

"You aren't even dressed." He crossed his arms, the short paddle sticking up out of his elbow.

"I forgot—sorry. Long night."

"Did you and Ryann have fun?" Knox slid into the chair across from him, a smile gleaming on his cheeks, the insinuation palpitating across the table.

"I was up most of the night with my daughter," Jackson said. "She's got some stomach issues. Ryann is trying an elimination diet, but it's only been a few days since she eliminated dairy. It can take up to four to have any lasting effect."

At least that was what Ryann had told him. Jackson had never worked in peds. Kids were great, and he'd always wanted them. But working in peds meant dealing with domestic violence and child abuse. Not often, but not never, either.

And he'd seen enough abuse to last a lifetime.

"I'm currently looking up some recipes that might work for her. Particularly since she's pulling out eggs and soy, too," he said.

"I know you didn't just give me data on breastfeeding and elimination diets while telling me you have a daughter." Knox leaned back in his chair. "A daughter. You hear what you're saying? A kid." He let out a laugh and then a muttered "Wow."

Knox had never felt called to fatherhood. He'd stated more than once that taking care of himself was more than enough. Jackson understood, but he'd always felt different.

Though now that the moment was here, a tiny voice whispered he'd let everyone in his life down. So much so that they'd walked away from him.

But that was not happening with Ayla. He'd never let his daughter down.

"Yes. Daughter. Six months old. A Hawaiian souvenir."

"You're very calm about this."

"I've had a few hours. Want to see a picture?" He'd snapped a photo of her around three this morning.

"Of course." Knox looked at the image on his phone and smiled. "She's cute."

"No." Jackson ran a finger over the picture he'd immediately made his phone's background. Ayla sleeping on his chest, her body relaxed, her mother's curly hair, Jackson's broad nose and lips that had cooed the sweetest sounds—when she wasn't screaming. "She's gorgeous."

He ran a hand over the tiny bundle on the screen. *How is she today?* he wondered. *Any better?*

Probably not. Elimination diets took time, and Ryann still needed to build up her stockpile of elimination breastmilk.

Something that had clicked in his head early this morning when Ayla had been so upset.

"Gorgeous. Just like her mother?"

Yes.

"Ryann and I are co-parenting. The details are still to be worked out. But that is all." The final words were rough as they exited his mouth. His brain was forcing them, but his tongue didn't want to repeat them.

Knox's head shifted, the recognition clear in his eyes. "I'm sorry, man."

"She doesn't want a relationship. A baby doesn't make happily-ever-after." Jackson didn't understand Ryann's intense statements on them only co-parenting. They'd had something special in Hawaii.

At least he'd thought so. But it was only special if two people thought so. If they didn't, well, unrequited feelings were unfortunate, but they wouldn't keep him from caring for their daughter.

"Maybe she'll come around." Knox shrugged.

"She doesn't need to come around." Jackson looked at his phone one more time, his daughter's soft face on the screen. "She gets to decide her life."

He'd spent a lifetime with disappointment. He could handle this, too. If Ryann didn't want anything more than co-parenting, then he'd honor it. Wants and decisions were something he wasn't granted as a child, and as an adult he wouldn't try to take those from another. He'd just adjust himself.

"Want to take out some frustrations on the pickleball court?" Knox held up the racket.

"I don't have any frustrations, Knox."

What was the point of them? They'd never solved anything. He was a pro at letting the emotions go, not rocking any boats or causing others to worry over him.

Jackson yawned and pushed back from them table. "Let me change. Give me ten minutes."

"You can just take a nap," Knox said.

It was a kind option. A good one. But even with exhaustion coursing through him, Jackson didn't think he'd manage to sleep. Maybe after a few games it would be easier for his mind to let go of the last twenty-four hours of material and let him rest.

Ryann looked over the chart in the office of the Lowery Group. Her mind refused to focus on the words on the paper chart. Dr. Lowery, a man who hadn't held a scalpel in more than a decade, didn't like the look of computer charts in front of patients. He thought it made the patients feel like the computer was their doctor, something Ryann couldn't always dispute. But her entire career had been on computer, and the younger patients had a tendency to think the paper was old-fashioned.

Which it was.

It was also not the main system for the office. Each note was copied into the computer system by an assistant whose sole job was to collect the file as soon as the appointment was over.

If Dr. Lowery ever fully stepped away from the practice that would likely be the first thing to change.

And contemplating paper versus electronic was not going to help her focus any better. Jackson would be here in five minutes and their patient in ten.

The sixty-year-old carpenter had done every trick in the book for his basal arthritis. All conservative treatments had failed. So his daughter was bringing him in for a surgical consult.

Forcing him in, if the note from the receptionist was accurate.

It was why Jackson was attending this meeting—trying to give him some reassurance that he wouldn't be in pain during the surgery.

Jackson...

The man had looked downright delicious sleeping with their daughter the other morning. She'd come down to find him sitting up in the chair, his and Ayla's snores synced.

She'd snapped a quick picture and let her heart yearn for what it couldn't have for a few minutes—a dream that would never be hers. Not if she wanted Ayla to continue to have the relationship Jackson was developing with their daughter. That was too precious, too easily lost if her parents couldn't stand to be in the same room if something went wrong between them.

"You ready for this?" Jackson was smiling as he entered her office. He let out a whistle. "This is fancy, Ryann!"

It was. Her "office" at her hospital in Washington had been a shared space with a framed stock image the hospital had probably purchased two presidential administrations ago. She'd used it for charting and not much else.

"It is nice. How have you never been in one of the office suites here?" she asked. "They all look pretty much the same."

"Never invited." Jackson shrugged. "Just the CRNA, remember." He tapped his nose.

The underlying statement cut at her heart. CRNAs did everything that anesthesiologists did. They held doctorates, too. But there was still a preference in some circles.

And given the little he'd told her about his background, she suspected he'd had many judge him.

"That's not fair, Jackson. I can speak to the partners," she said. She wasn't sure it would do any good but maybe.

"Eh, doesn't matter." Jackson pointed to a picture of Ayla on Ryann's desk. "Besides, this is the only office with a picture of the prettiest baby in the world in it."

"That was snapped by the hospital photographer that offers sky-high picture packages. I think I was taken for a ride, but she was so cute." It was the only professional photo she had. Ryann ran a hand over Ayla's cheek in the image.

"Beautiful, just like her mother," Jackson said, then cleared his throat.

Now was a good time to get to the topic at hand.

No mental pun intended.

"Mr. Nigili will be here shortly," she said. "Basal arthritis in the thumb. Going on nearly three years of failed conservative treatment. He cannot grip anything anymore."

"And it's painful—at least according to the daughter," Jackson added while looking at a tablet.

The small tech in his hands sent jealousy rippling through her. "Where did you get that?"

"Snuck it from Dr. Kelson," he said. "The man has a suite of them on chargers in the storage room next to his office. He and Lowery have been having a go of it over tech revolutions versus necessity versus the role of physicians. Once you're well-established in the practice, I suspect they'll ask you to choose sides."

That would be a simple choice. "I might just steal one."

"Wait at least a year. You're technically still a probationary partner. In a year, Lowery can't vote against your full partnership and you can side with modernity all you want." Jackson winked. "But you can borrow this one while we're in here."

Ryann took the machine, her fingers brushing his for less than a nanosecond. Yet heat and need floated through her.

It was like that moment when he'd first sat down on the plane beside her. Her whole body had hummed. She'd never experienced full-body lust before. Then he'd said hello, his deep, rich voice singing straight to her soul. Ryann had been lost.

It would be so easy to let herself fall into that again. But lust burned bright…for a while. How many partners had her mother claimed were her soulmate, only to hate them six months later?

"Pain is his concern." Ryann's tongue was thick, and her brain had fogged for just a minute. But it was Mr. Nigili they needed to focus on.

She ran her thumb across the tablet chart and watched the images of Mr. Nigili's thumb pop up. She'd seen these several times, but Ryann always looked back over notes before seeing a patient.

"There's no cartilage left in the base of the thumb," she said. "The fact that he's dealt with bone rubbing on bone for at least a year, more likely all three years he was trying conservative treatment, means his pain tolerance is extreme." Ryann shook her head.

"And at its breaking point," Jackson added.

The thumb was used for every movement of the hand. It was the reason humans could do so much compared to other mammals.

A knock echoed on the door, and an older man, his daughter and the office nurse stepped into the room.

Sour-faced was the description Ryann's mother would have used for Mr. Nigili. He was already glaring at her and Jackson.

"Come on, Dad." The woman offered a smile to Ryann and Jackson, but there was more than a hint of resignation in her shoulders.

"It's nice to meet you, Mr. Nigili." Ryann held out her hand, but he didn't take it.

"I don't shake hands," he said. His shoulders were stiff, and he didn't meet her eyes.

It would be easy to find the offense. Hell, as a woman in surgery, a female orthopedic surgeon, she'd faced more acts of misogyny than she could count. Add in that she was a mixed-race woman...

But she didn't think that was the issue here.

"Because you don't like to shake hands, or because it hurts to grip someone's hand?"

Ryann saw Jackson nod out of the corner of her eye. He was picking up on the same energy she was. This was an embarrassment issue.

Mr. Nigili looked at his daughter and shrugged. "A man's grip is important. I ain't got none now."

"Which is why we're here, Dad," his daughter said, patting his shoulder.

"I don't want anyone cutting me." The man looked at his daughter and then at Ryann. "Nothing personal, but I'm only here because Ella will not let it go."

Ella rolled her eyes. "Because you're in pain."

"And surgery is painful." Mr. Nigili shrugged his shoulders.

Jackson shifted, taking a commanding presence beside Ryann. "That's the reason that Dr. Oliver asked me to sit in on this conversation. I'm Jackson Peters, the certified nurse anesthesiologist. Think of me as the pain-management specialist."

"The one who knocks me out."

Jackson nodded, saying, "Yes, but it's more than that. It's about pain management before and after surgery."

"The surgery cannot be worse that the pain you are in constantly now," Ella said. "I hear the moans when you don't think I do. The curses. I see the looks you give your old wood-working tools, the ones with so much dust on them now. I know you miss it." She looked like she was about to cry. This was clearly an argument they'd had more than once.

"Surgery killed your mother." He crossed his arms, not quite covering his flinch as his thumb wrapped around his arm.

That was a problem not listed in his file. They'd not prepped to make an argument about survival rates. Ryann couldn't guarantee anything, but this was about as safe a surgery as possible.

"Mr. Nigili, I monitor your vital signals during the surgery," Jackson said. He moved to the desk, leaning against it—the picture of a man in control of himself, laser-focused on their patient. "This is about as simple a procedure as possible, with limited time under anesthesia. But I understand your concern."

It was like Jackson was reading her mind. Why did he have to be so perfect? It would be easy to keep her distance if he had glaring flaws.

"Tell me what happened with your wife." Jackson's words were soft but commanding. It wasn't a question or request.

Which was good—if they were going to have any hope of helping him, they needed to know the real reason he didn't want to be on Ryann's surgical table. And it looked like this was the first time he was being fully honest with anyone about these hesitations.

Mr. Nigili looked at his daughter, then at Ryann, before focusing on Jackson. "Doctor said she needed surgery for a herniated disk. A routine surgery. Except she coded on the table. Not sure why, but they never got her back." He sniffed and looked at his shoes before looking back up.

His eyes were cloudy, but the tears didn't fall.

"I am so sorry for your loss," Jackson said as he tilted his head. "As Dr. Oliver will tell you, there are never guarantees with surgery, but it is rare for a complication—"

"Rare, until it happens to you. My wife left me a single father at the age of forty-two. My children are grown, but I'm the only parent they have left. My thumb hurts, but leaving them…" He choked back a sob, then cleared his throat. "It is not an option."

"My daughter is almost six months old." Ryann turned the picture on her desk around. "I understand being scared. I can't tell you that there is no chance of complications—there are always risks. What I can tell you is that it is very minimal and significantly less than spinal surgery."

Ryann moved around the desk beside Jackson. "It is admirable that you want to be around for your children."

"And grandchild." Mr. Nigili huffed. "Six months old, just like yours."

"All the more reason to get the surgery," Jackson interjected. "The thumb will get worse—the pain must be excruciating now."

"I make do." Mr. Nigili barely covered the flinch as he made a fist with his hand and immediately released it.

Ryann could almost hear the bones rubbing together. The man was in excruciating pain. And it would only get worse.

"*Making do* and *living* are not the same," Jackson said. "Think of all the things you'll miss with your grandchild— picking them up, swinging them in your arms, throwing a ball with them." He ticked off the items on his fingers as he listed them.

"Teaching them carpentry." Ella rubbed her father's knee. "Some of my fondest memories are of us in your woodworking shop. The smell of sawdust. You showing me how to make something, guiding me." She let out a choked noise. "I want that for Gretchen and any cousins she may have in the future. I want her to tell her grandchildren one day when we're all long gone that the table she's showing them how to build is just like the one her grandfather showed her how to make."

The older man looked at his daughter, and Ryann could

see him remembering Ella as a little girl. You always needed a parent, even if that parent wasn't there for you. Ella'd had that—she was lucky. Ryann also saw the moment he tilted his head and the look she hoped was acceptance crossed his eyes.

Maybe, maybe he was going to agree.

"You can do the surgery?" Mr. Nigili raised his chin as he looked at her, more defiance in the posture than anything. "*If* I decide to let you cut me."

Progress. Not much, but she'd take anything she could get.

"If you decide, yes, I can do the surgery," she said. "It takes about an hour and half in total, but I'm only operating on your hand for about twenty minutes. The rest is Jackson making sure you're out and then bringing you into recovery."

Overall, the surgery would be quick, but she understood the fear. He'd heard "routine" with his wife. That was a word Ryann personally didn't like associated with anything related to the spine. There were too many what-ifs, too many factors that could go wrong, even if you'd performed the surgery hundreds of times before.

But this surgery was about as close to no-risk as possible. And it would provide him relief.

"I'll think about it." He stood, the conversation clearly at an end.

"You can call the office anytime, and they'll get you on my surgical schedule."

Ryann kept the smile on her face until they were gone. "Think he'll make an appointment?" she asked.

Somehow this meeting felt like a failure. He'd agreed to consider it. But thinking on it, away from the office, meant there was a decent chance he'd change his mind. She'd seen it happen again and again with patients.

If they didn't make an appointment when they left her office, the odds of them making one ever went down exponentially.

The words *I'll think about it* were some of the worst for a surgeon to hear.

"I don't know," Jackson said. "He has strong reasons to say no."

"The surgeries are completely different." Ryann crossed her arms. She knew it wasn't personal. The man wasn't doubting her, but that made it worse. He was in pain, and she could fix that. If he'd just let her.

Jackson put his arm around her shoulder and squeezed it. She let herself lean into him for just a second before pulling away.

"I know he lost his wife…" Ryann didn't understand that pain, but she could see that even after decades he still missed her. What was that kind of love like?

"It's not about that," Jackson said. He stood, pushing his hands into his pockets. "It's about the kids. Grown or not, he's the only parent they have. And he can't imagine them losing him. Pain—" His eyes moved to Ayla's picture. "Pain is a price he's willing to pay to make sure he's still in their life. I kinda get that."

Jackson rocked back on his heels. "I hope his kids realize how lucky they are." He waited a moment, then reached for the tablet. "I have a few patients at the hospital today. I'll see you later."

"Come by for dinner tonight?"

Say yes, she begged him in her mind. *For our daughter.*

Jackson smiled. "Of course."

"Not sure you want to smile too much," she said. "I'm making a rice pilaf without flavoring other than pepper and salt. Maybe this weekend I'll have time to research some recipes." It was rough eating from such a limited range of food, but Ayla had been better the last two days.

So it was worth it.

"I don't mind if you want to bring your own food."

"I happen to love rice pilaf." He raised a hand as he walked out of the office.

CHAPTER FOUR

JACKSON GRABBED THE warming bags from the back seat of his car. He had sweet potatoes and wild salmon to go with the rice pilaf Ryann was making. She might not have had time to do the research, but he'd found several recipes online that were quick and easy.

Pulling the bags out of the car, he tried to shake the mental unease that had settled there since the meeting with Mr. Nigili this morning.

"Mental unease. Pfft! It's jealousy plain and simple." He was not in the habit of talking to himself, but Jackson hoped by naming the emotion he'd find a way to release it. That was what his therapist would suggest.

He was jealous of children and a grandchild he'd never met. It wasn't their fault they had a parent who cared for them. And it wasn't Jackson's fault that his parents hadn't cared for him—at least that was what his therapist had told him…repeatedly.

Rationally he knew that was true. But part of him would always wonder why he hadn't gotten what other kids had, why the universe had picked him for the hardships, for the loneliness.

Life wasn't fair. It was a phrase people said all the time. But why the hell wasn't it? He hadn't chosen his parents, hadn't chosen the difficulties.

But those were feelings to handle in his own place, feelings to write in his journal or let explode on his therapist's couch.

They were not emotions to burden Ryann and Ayla with. The front door opened before he could knock. Ayla was on Ryann's hip, her hands wrapped in her mother's hair, and they were both grinning. He mentally snapped a photo.

Maybe his early life had been hard, but this was exactly where he wanted to be. And his past was not going to taint his present. He would not allow it.

He ached to lean over and kiss both of them. But Ryann had been specific about their relationship, and he wanted to honor that boundary.

"That smells divine!" Ryann took a deep sniff of the food bags. "Probably a good thing you brought your own dinner—the rice pilaf looks a little sad. I'm definitely finding time to research recipes this week."

"This is for us, to go with the rice pilaf." Jackson smiled and leaned forward to kiss Ayla's cheek. His daughter squealed. There was no better sound in the world.

"What?" Ryann said as she backed up, letting him through the door.

"Salmon and sweet potatoes." Jackson looked over his shoulder as he headed toward the kitchen. He knew she liked salmon—she'd told him in Hawaii that she'd never met a fish she didn't enjoy eating. "I used a garlic-herb blend for seasoning instead of lemon. No citrus in the elimination diet, but this should be good."

"And sweet potatoes." Ryann's sigh was a good sign.

That one he'd guessed on. White potatoes were not part of the diet, but people seemed to have very distinct opinions about sweet potatoes. Love or hate—there was little in between.

"I had some time, so I looked up a few recipes. I'm no culinary master, but I can manage an easy dinner."

"Thank you, Jackson." Ryann pursed her lips, burying her head in their daughter's curly hair for a moment. "This was a really sweet gesture."

"Any time." He meant the words more than she understood. She'd given him the best gift. He'd take care of her, too. After all, Ryann was the mother of his child.

They were a family. Platonic co-parents still equaled family. And he'd do anything for his girls.

"Want to hold her while I get the plates ready?"

He didn't answer, just held his hands out for Ayla to come. The little one looked at her mom, then came to him. She wasn't scared of him, but Jackson was still a stranger. Not for long, though. *Hopefully.*

"So, now that we're several hours from it, any new thoughts on Mr. Nigili?" Ryann asked. "I keep running through reasons I might give him to get him on the table. I have his daughter's contact number, and I can reach out from the office tomorrow. Assuming I have something new." She clicked her tongue as she grabbed the rice pilaf from the stove and put it on the plates. "Right now, I feel like everything I've come up with are simple twists on what I said today."

Work talk. That was safe, at least usually. It wasn't Ryann's fault that Mr. Nigili was the last patient Jackson wanted to discuss. He was overreacting—he knew that.

Yet his brain refused to cut off the jealous feelings. It shouldn't matter, particularly when he was holding his daughter. Life was pretty amazing for Jackson Peters these days.

"Jackson?"

"Sorry." More time must have passed than he'd realized. "No ideas." Mr. Nigili would schedule the surgery, or he wouldn't. The only ones who might be able to change his mind were his kids.

Kids who had a father who loved them so much he was

willing to live in pain—constant pain—rather than risk them losing him. Hopefully they knew what a gift that was, that people would change places with them in an instant…if given the chance.

"Why the frown?"

He looked at her, raising a brow.

"Don't play me like that," she said. "Your frown was so deep I was a little worried your handsome features might stay frozen that way."

"Handsome." Jackson made a fun face for Ayla. "Did you hear that, baby girl? Mommy thinks I'm handsome."

"Don't change the topic." Ryann wagged a finger at him as she plated the salmon, rice and sweet potatoes. "And clearly I find you handsome—that's why she's here." She laughed, then her features took a serious look. "Why the frown?"

"It's dumb." Jackson kissed the top of Ayla's head and moved toward the table where Ryann had set up a high chair a few days ago.

Almost six months old and starting solids before too long. But tonight, the plan was just to let her play with some toys while they ate, let her get used to sitting in the high chair and with them at the table. The next season of Ayla's life was already here. So much happened in the first year. He'd missed her newborn stage; he wasn't missing any more.

Whether the toys entertained her at all, let alone long enough for them to finish dinner, they'd soon find out.

"So it's dumb. So what? Why the frown?" Ryann said. "Did you see something in Mr. Nigili's records I should know about?" She set his plate in the space next to hers before sliding into her chair.

Sitting between Ayla and Ryann…it made the jealousy seem so pointless. He was happy in this moment. Getting upset about what he hadn't gotten wouldn't do him any good.

"There was nothing in the records," he said. "If there was, I'd say something. Some physicians might not trust their nurses, but I always speak up for the patient." He'd run into more than a handful of physicians who'd thought their degrees made them masters of the universe.

Never mind that he had a doctorate, too. He was never quite enough.

"Anyone who doesn't trust their nurses shouldn't be in the field. You speaking up for the patients is the least surprising thing I've ever heard." She smiled, then motioned with her hand. "So why the frown? I'm not letting this go."

"Your mother is very stubborn," Jackson said to Ayla. He took a bite of his salmon. Then he took a sip of water and finally a deep breath. "I'm jealous of his kids."

"The ones who forced him to come in?" Ryann chuckled. "I suspect he's quite cranky with them."

"Probably." Jackson took another drink of water. Cranky, but not furious. Not 'drop them off and forget about them' furious. Not 'refuse to acknowledge any connection, even when they were adults and didn't need anything from you' furious.

"My mother was never cranky with me," Ryann said. "She was flighty and forgetful. Neglectful. But I can't remember her ever getting mad."

That was fortunate. Though neglect manifested trauma, too.

"What about your parents?" she asked.

This was not a topic he discussed. He'd already told her the reasons he hadn't seen her emails. That was more than enough of a burden for Ryann to know about.

He cleared his throat. The past was the past. He'd beaten the system. He'd put himself through college working as a nursing assistant and massage therapist. He'd gotten his nursing license and eventually a doctorate in nursing.

It didn't matter that his fiancée had left or that the mother of his child didn't want a relationship with him. There was a wall between his past and now. And he wasn't letting any breach occur.

"They were absent." He looked at Ayla. "Do you like the blue ball or rattle better?"

"We know the answer to that." Ryann chuckled as Ayla shook the rattle right in Jackson's face.

"I can't imagine a parent loving their child so much they would take the pain rather than a simple surgery with almost no risk," he said.

"You can't?" Ryann leaned forward and looked from him to Ayla and back again. "Wouldn't you risk anything for her?"

Jackson smiled at their daughter. Ayla blew bubbles with her lips, soaking up the attention. "I know the answer I am supposed to say is that I wouldn't risk anything for her. But that isn't the case."

Ryann's eyes widened. "Wha…?"

"I would risk everything for her." Jackson ruffled Ayla's curls. She'd get to have everything he had learned early not to even ask for.

Gymnastics lessons—sure. Learn to play guitar—give it a go. Drama class—he'd be in the front row of every performance and bring roses at the end of the play no matter the size of her part.

Ayla would get a world of experiences.

"I would have the surgery without even thinking about it too hard. For me it would the easiest choice," he said. "I would want to throw balls and pick her up and swing her. Those things I ticked off, they were my wants. And I would want the pain-free experience I know you can give him, so I can show her the whole world."

Ryann tilted her head, a host of questions floating through

her eyes, but she didn't ask them. "You accept risks." Her voice was soft, a lilt to it he couldn't quite place.

He didn't see it as risks, more as experiences. After a childhood devoid of fun experiences, how could he want anything else? He wasn't risky by nature, but if something fun was available or an exciting opportunity dropped in his lap, hell yeah, he took it.

"I want a world of experiences. Remember hang gliding over the ocean?" He reached for her hand but pulled back before they connected. She'd asked for this to be platonic. If it changed it would be on Ryann's terms.

Which was why it was good that he caught the comment about the bright pink two-piece she'd worn that day being one of his favorite memories before it dropped off his tongue. Most of his favorite memories revolved around Ryann and Ayla.

Ryann looked at Ayla and shuddered. "I cannot imagine her hang gliding. The guy who hooked us up to that contraption was clearly just some random guy doing it as a side job. We got basically no instruction. The fact that we didn't crash into the ocean or the side of a volcano is a minor miracle."

It wasn't that bad, though she was right, they should have gotten more instruction! "It was fun." Jackson pointed his fork at her. "Fun—and I dare you to say otherwise."

"It was fun. But also dangerous." She held up her fork, pointing it at him just like he was doing to her. "Admit it was dangerous."

Ayla giggled at the display in front of her.

"Are Mommy and Daddy silly?" Ryann asked, then she held the fork up a little higher, shaking it at him. There was a gleam in her eye that made everything a little better.

Jackson laughed enjoying the sound of his chuckles mixing

with the wonderful sounds of Ayla and then her mother joining in. Goose bumps rose on his arms as he drank in the happiness.

Pressing the call button for the elevator, Ryann frowned when the pattern Miranda had shown her didn't deliver the elevator. She looked at her watch. There were stairs…at the other end of the garage. But it was hot and she didn't want to be all sweaty for rounds.

"The metal box giving you trouble?" Jackson's deep voice made her insides jump. Not from surprise, either.

The other night she'd nearly leaned over and kissed him when he'd brought her dinner—something he'd repeated every night for the last week. It was such a simple declaration of care, but no one had looked after Ryann in so long.

It would be easy to start craving it, start expecting it…

But they were maintaining a platonic parenting partnership. That was best for Ayla.

At least their daughter was sleeping better now. Ayla was only up once a night since her belly no longer gurgled all evening. Yet Ryann's nighttime routine still wasn't restful.

Instead of infant cries of pain, the tossing and turning in her bed was caused by dreams—all focused on the hunk standing next to her. The urge to lean against him, invite him to come over tonight for dinner, then ask him to stay was clinging to her chest.

Taking a deep breath didn't help. His scent wrapped through her—hints of maple, wood and male that was just Jackson made her mouth water. Memories rushed at her.

Running her hands down his hard body had been the highlight of her vacation. No, kissing him—that was the highlight. The sweet touches that had escalated to heady need…

"Ryann?" Jackson leaned closer, the scent of coffee and him pulling her from the indecent thoughts.

"Sorry."

"It's still early." Jackson winked and held up a travel mug of coffee. "Brain not quite functioning."

Her brain was functioning fine. It just wasn't focused on work appropriate topics. "Mmm…coffee," she said.

"Actually," Jackson said, lowering his backpack from his shoulders, "it's tea."

"Not unless my sniffer is off!" Ryann tapped her nose. Just because she hadn't drunk the stuff in months didn't mean she couldn't identify it.

He pulled out a second travel mug and handed it to her before putting his backpack back on. "It's herbal coffee— caffeine-free," he said. "Miranda mentioned you looking longingly at hers. I thought you might like this. Chocolate-mint flavored."

"You really are too good to be true." She took a sip just as the elevator arrived. "Finally."

They stepped on together as they waved goodbye to two night-shift nurses who looked like they wanted to dart to their cars.

"This is good," Ryann said. She took another sip as Jackson pushed the button for the surgical floor. It wasn't quite coffee, but it satisfied most of the craving.

"Right?" He held up his own mug. "I admit that I wasn't sure when I bought it. I was worried it might taste like roots or dirt or worse, but figured it was worth a try."

"What's worse than dirt?" Ryann giggled, then took another sip.

"Not sure. But I bet it's one of those things that you know it when you taste it. And then you think, *I bet eating dirt would be better.*" Jackson winked and leaned a little closer to her.

Her skin buzzed. Surely he wasn't trying this just for her? "When did you get this?"

The skin of his cheeks darkened.

"Jackson?"

Before he could answer the elevator shuddered, then dropped a floor. "Jackson!"

He was by her side, his arm wrapping around her waist just as the lights went off.

The elevator shuddered again, then stopped moving. What the hell?

"Ryann?" His arm tightened on her waist. "You all right?"

"Yes." The word was chirpy, but it was true. Physically she was fine. Mentally, her brain was already spinning. Both Ayla's parents were trapped in this tin can. What if the worst happened?

Jackson's refusal to discuss his parents the other night had made it clear they were not an option if something happened to him and Ryann. And her own mother wasn't much better. She was somewhere on the East Coast with a new partner, wholly uninterested in her granddaughter.

At least she had been two weeks ago. By now she could be in Europe, India or headed to Arizona for an unannounced visit. She was not a good option in case anything happened to them.

"Take a deep breath," Jackson said. He held her tightly as they slid down the wall.

"I'm fine."

"Your teeth are chattering." Jackson pressed his lips to her temple. "You're not alone. We're going to be fine."

"You don't know that." Now was not the time to argue. She didn't want to, but it was easier than letting the worry consume her.

"Stay here," he said.

Where exactly am I going to go?

She bit back the retort as Jackson slid across the floor,

used the flashlight attached to his phone and pressed the emergency button.

"Compton Elevator Security line, what is your emergency?"

"Never realized that the red button called an elevator security line." Ryann leaned her head against the wall, tapping it gently in a rhythm. The motion wasn't likely to wake her from a dream, but just in case...

Jackson didn't respond to her comment—the right move. He gave the information to the operator and then slid back over to her.

"Hopefully it won't be too long for them to send someone out," Jackson said as he sat beside her. His body heat called to her, and she leaned her head against his shoulder.

He turned off the flashlight on his phone, the elevator blinking back into darkness. "It will drain the battery."

"Right." The flashlight app wasn't meant to actually replace flashlights, which was a nicer thing to worry over than if the elevator was supposed to have emergency lights. And what it meant if they didn't kick on.

"Think this will make the hospital fix the elevator?" Ryann laughed, though she could hear the hint of hysteria in the sound. If you couldn't be hysterical in pitch black after falling a floor in an elevator, when could you be?

Jackson chuckled. His laugh did not sound like he was fighting back panic. "I think so, but honestly, who knows. The corporation that took over last year seems hell bent on cutting costs."

"Capitalism in medicine. Fun!" Ryann rolled her eyes, even though she knew he couldn't see her.

Jackson wrapped his arm around her shoulder and leaned his head against hers. If they weren't in this tiny box, it would be very sweet.

Of course if they weren't in this tiny box she wouldn't let him hold her. She liked it too much.

"You never answered my question," Ryann said, placing her hand on his leg. She needed him to talk, needed something to distract her from imagining the elevator plummeting to the basement.

"I fear I have forgotten the question." Jackson squeezed her arm, then started to pull away. "A lot has happened in three minutes, after all."

"Hold me." The two words slipped out, but he didn't say anything, just put his arm back in place.

"All right." He took a deep breath and moved his feet, probably trying to find a comfortable position, but he didn't let go of her. "What was the question, Ryann?"

She held up the travel mug, knowing he couldn't see it in the pitch darkness. Somehow she'd held onto it during the drop—reflexes were weird. "When did you start drinking this?"

And was it for me?

"Yesterday." He whispered the words.

"So you'd have an option for coffee if you took this on with me too?" He was eating the same food as she was. At least around her.

It was sweet, given the limited options she'd have until she figured out exactly what was causing Ayla's issues. Many partners didn't take that on, and Jackson wasn't her partner.

Because I told him I didn't want that, she thought.

Jackson's leg moved like he was tapping his leg in the dark. The silence hung between them. "I wanted to give you an option," he said. "You've done everything by yourself for over a year. Cooking, finding a coffee alternative, staying up with Ayla when she isn't feeling well…it's not too much to do for you."

"You are perfect, aren't you?"

She covered her mouth. *Like that could force the words back in!*

"I fall pretty far short of that. But I try." His head leaned against hers. "Is that why you want to keep everything platonic between us? Because I'm so close to perfection?"

His tone had a jokey vibe to it. Would he have asked it if they weren't sitting in the dark, trapped in a metal box waiting for rescue?

"Yes." Ryann took a sip of the herbal coffee.

Jackson moved, and she could tell he was looking at her face.

"Yes," she said again, "the reason I want us to remain coparents is because you are nearly perfect. Ayla deserves to have you in her life forever."

"Ayla *is* in my life forever." He turned the flashlight app back on.

"I thought we needed to save the battery life," Ryann said, looking away from his dark eyes.

"I want you to see my face for this." Jackson didn't say anything else until she met his gaze. "I am Ayla's father. I am in her life."

She wanted to believe him. In this moment, he probably even meant it. But she'd had stepparents say the same thing. They'd meant it.

Until they hadn't.

"Ayla deserves two parents who can be in the same room with each other." That felt like the middle of a speech, but it was the most important part.

"I see," Jackson said. He pulled at the back of his neck with his free hand. "Did your father stop talking to you because of your mother?"

"Yes. And so did my stepfather and my stepmother and

a host of other partners that swore they were in my life forever no matter what." When she was little, she'd waited patiently for pickups and opened the mailbox for days waiting
for letters.

And each time the dream had fallen away, another little
piece of her had died.

That was not a life she wanted for Ayla.

"All right." Jackson shrugged.

"All right?" Could it be that easy? And why did her heart
feel like it was breaking from getting what she wanted, what
was best for Ayla?

He leaned his head back, inches from hers. If he turned,
his lips would rest against her head. "Do you want me to
fight this?"

"No." Two little letters. One little word. And a world of
pain. Better to wonder *what if?* than to take the risk and
find out.

"Then I won't." Jackson smiled, but there was no happiness in the gesture. "Ayla is what's most important. That will
always be the case. But if you don't trust us to be civil for
her sake no matter what, then—"

His words cut off as banging echoed in the elevator. "I
think the rescue team is here."

Flashlights peered through the top of the elevator.

"Good morning." A firefighter waved as he lowered a
rope ladder. "You guys are between levels, and the doors
are stuck. Your hospital admin swears they had this thing
inspected earlier this year. Chief doubts it."

"So do I." Jackson grabbed the end of the rope ladder and
held his hand out to Ryann. "Ladies first."

She put her hand in his, looking at the ladder. "This doesn't
seem super sturdy," she said.

"Don't worry. I got you." His words were deep, the pressure of his hand holding hers sturdy. "I got you."

The repeated words infused her with calm—Jackson had her.

CHAPTER FIVE

"I THINK AYLA'S teeth are bothering her." Jackson yawned as he drove them to the hospital. A week after the elevator incident, one the hospital CEO had apologized for profusely—before asking them to sign something releasing the hospital from damages—and Jackson's car and townhome were now fully "Ayla'd."

At least that was the term Ryann had come up with for the car seat he'd installed, the babyproofing he'd done at his condo, the bottles he'd bought and the crib in his guest room. Not that Ayla was spending much time there.

He isn't, either, Ryann thought.

She yawned. "You aren't the one she bites while feeding. Her teeth are definitely hurting her." Ryann rolled her shoulders. She needed new pillows on her bed.

Or Jackson sleeping next to me instead of in the guest bedroom.

He'd moved in. Sort of. He still spent at least one night at his condo. A way to maintain the platonic relationship she'd demanded? Ryann didn't know. And there was no way she was asking.

"Your neck still bothering you?" Jackson asked. His hand moved on the steering wheel, and for a moment she thought he might take her hand. Instead, he started tapping his thumb against the wheel.

She swallowed the pain brought on from being near him and not acting on the desires bubbling within her. It was funny—before reuniting with him she'd have sworn what they'd had was instant chemistry.

Hot. Steamy. Perfect for a vacation because then she wouldn't have to watch the fire of passion burn out. Now, though…

What if soulmates were real? The fanciful idea that her mother was always seeking. The thing that seemed too "out there" to be real. What if she was wrong? What if what she and Jackson had…

Ryann cleared her throat. If only it was as easy to clear her mind. When his hand laid on her knee, she moved her head to look at it and winced.

"So I'll take that wince as a yes." He pulled his hand back.

He'd been trying to get her attention while she was lost in fantasy thoughts about him.

Ryann placed her left hand on her shoulder and pushed two fingers into the tight ball of knots she could feel under the skin. It didn't give her much relief, but it was better than nothing.

Jackson pulled into the parking space, turned off the car and looked at her. "Put your shoulders against the back of the seat."

"Wha…?"

"Just do it," he said, gently pushing her shoulders back. "Take a deep breath."

She did as he instructed, not quite sure what he was doing as his hand rested on the top of her head. Then he gently pulled her head forward and to the left. The tight muscle burned but in such a nice way.

"Another deep breath."

This time she didn't hesitate. As she blew out, he pulled her a little further forward.

"Ooh," she moaned as the pressure released. "That feels delicious."

"It's temporary." Jackson let go. "You need an actual massage to release what I suspect are knots upon knots upon knots in your back."

Ryann laughed. "Sure. I'll just add that into my very open calendar." She leaned over and kissed his cheek, then pulled back so fast her neck let her know that even with the stretches it wasn't happy.

"I… I…" What was she supposed to say? The kiss had been unintentional. It had simply felt right, and she'd given into the impulse, something Ryann only seemed to do with him.

"Releasing muscular tension often makes you react differently." He winked, then grabbed the handle of the door and exited the car.

Grabbing her backpack, she followed him. "Is that true?" she asked. They were heading to the stairwell. The elevator where they'd been trapped had been fixed, but she wasn't ready to get back in, and so when they arrived together, she and Jackson went up the stairs.

"Yes," Jackson said as he opened the stairwell door. "Not sure why, but some people hold their emotions in tension. Releasing it brings the emotions out. I had more than one person cry on my massage table. They rarely knew why and all swore they weren't physically in pain. It was just the release."

His phone dinged, and he answered it. "Jackson." His dark eyes met hers. "She's right next to me."

Ryann could see the news in them. She picked up her speed, taking the stairs two at a time. Jackson didn't stop her, confirming her suspicions.

"Be there in ten, scrubbed in in twenty. Who's on the gas?"

She was already huffing, but Jackson was carrying on a conversation while rushing up the stairs. The man was as close to an Adonis as possible.

"Yeah, I can do it—I'm on call. Give me the details." He made a few noncommittal statements, and from the questions she heard it was clearly a crush incident.

The worst kind of accident for bones. Broken bones she could fix. Bone dust...well, that required amputation or massive reconstruction.

Jackson hung up just before they hit the sixth-floor entrance. Two more floors.

"Thirty-two-year-old female. Crushed left hand. Hang-gliding accident."

"Hang gliding?" How did you crush your hand doing that? When they'd done it in Hawaii they'd listened to a safety briefing, been warned that if they had to choose between crashing into the beach and landing in the surf they needed to crash on the beach. Though their pilots had been the ones driving the machine. A crushed leg made some sense, but a hand?

"All that really matters is that she's getting prepped now." Jackson's voice was tight, his face devoid of emotion. "We can ask after the details after surgery."

It was a surgery face. Prepping for entering the OR. Putting emotions away and focusing on what you could control—which was less than what most people thought their doctors controlled.

A cold hard truth: sometimes fate controlled things.

"Breathing is normal. She's under." Jackson rolled his shoulders behind the paper curtain separating him from the rest of the surgical staff. He used to joke that he'd become a CNA because he got to sit during surgeries.

"Scalpel." Ryann's voice was tense. He'd seen the patient's hand, knew the bone saw for amputation was already ready to go.

And he knew that Ryann wouldn't amputate unless it was absolutely necessary.

"All right," she said. "The thumb is mostly intact. Middle and distal phalanges on all four fingers crushed. The rest of the hand is also mostly intact, though I will need pins."

"Amputating the fingers?"

A sigh followed.

The question came from Dr. Ian Prots and the sigh from Ryann. It was surprising how much one could pick up from behind the curtain.

"We're not getting that bone saw out, Dr. Prots." Ryann asked for another tool, and the room took on an uneasy silence.

The bone saw was not something anyone should want to use. It was a necessary tool, but many residents were a little too eager to see it the first time. After that...well, reality set in quick.

"Ry—Dr. Oliver." Jackson looked at the monitors, then over the curtain to watch a few breaths. They were shallower than he liked.

"Yes?"

"Her breathing is shallow. Still in the normal range, but..." He had a weird feeling, an uncomfortable pull in his chest. One learned not to ignore those.

"I need at least another two hours to pin and reconstruct. Am I going to get it?"

"I don't know." There was nothing on the system that showed extreme distress. The patient was healthy. The arm was an extremity. No surgery was without risk, but this was minor compared to open-heart surgery.

"All right, we go as long as we can," Ryann said. "Jackson will tell us the moment she needs to be brought out."

He smiled behind the curtain. He wasn't surprised that she was trusting his suspicions, but it was always nice when surgeons accepted the feelings he had.

But he'd put hundreds of patients under. He had a sixth sense about these things by now. One he did not take lightly.

The God-complex stereotype was a stereotype for a reason after all.

"This is a hand surgery. I mean, come on. What is the actual problem, Jackson?" Dr. Prots proving that stereotype as a surgical resident didn't bode well for his future patients.

"I need a pin for the distal four." He heard the sound of Ryann's breathing over the hum of the surgery. It was like he was keyed into her, like they were one.

It had been that way from the beginning. A draw. A need. And he knew how stressed she was right now.

"Dr. Prots."

Jackson knew Ryann was looking at the hand, but her tone felt like it was daggers. At least it wasn't focused on him.

"If you question the CRNA or any of the team again you will exit my OR," she said. "Pin for distal five."

The sputtering was too easy to hear. "So, I'm not allowed to ask questions? This is a teaching hospital."

"It is. But I'm in private practice. Residents don't have to be in here. And ask any question you like about the surgery, about what we're doing, about why Jackson might have a bad feeling. But do so the right way." There was a clink as Ryann dropped something onto the hospital tray.

Jackson smiled behind his mask, but the feeling was short lived. "Ryann!"

The seizing started at the same time as his call.

The next few minutes were a blur as they attempted to stabilize the patient. It took less than three minutes and felt like three lifetimes.

"Two more pins, then we close," she said. "It will take me ten minutes, Jackson."

"All right." His eyes didn't leave the monitors. The patient would need additional surgeries, but that was likely even without the seizure. Some days the fates had more control of the OR than the surgeons.

Ryann slipped into the post-surgery recovery suite, her eyes meeting Jackson's in the semi-darkened room. "How is she?"

"Lauren is sleeping," he said. "She woke about an hour ago. Groggy, unsure of what happened. Not surprising. She was calling for her fiancé." Jackson watched the monitors. It was standard protocol for Anesthesiology to sit with any patient who'd seized on the table.

He'd be here anyway, but the few minutes she'd been awake had been heartbreaking.

"Is her fiancé here?" Ryann asked.

"No." Jackson didn't know the full situation, but based on Lauren's few wakening moments it sounded like what he'd experienced with Marie.

"Has anyone called him?"

"No," he said again, then sucked in a deep breath. "Her fiancé called off the wedding two weeks ago. No reason— just called it off. At least that's what I gathered. She wasn't really coherent."

"Oh." Ryann crossed her arms. "She was groggy. Maybe she'll remember why when she's fully awake. There had to be a reason."

"No, there doesn't." Jackson shook his head. This wasn't

the place to talk about Marie. But Ryann was cautious. She wanted order, and she was putting her wants aside for the benefit of their daughter.

He understood. Jackson also knew that you couldn't control much in this world. Sometimes there were no answers. Maybe the woman's fiancé had had a reason. Maybe he hadn't—either way it didn't matter; the end result was the same.

Heartbreak.

"Jackson…" Ryann said. There was a hint of pity in her eyes. That was the last thing he wanted from her, the last thing he needed.

"It's fine, Ryann. But sometimes there aren't answers," he said. "One of the nurses was able to reach her mom. She's on a plane right now. Hopefully the next time Lauren wakes, she'll be here." He looked at his watch. The anesthesia had cleared her system. The patient was stable, and he needed a walk.

"I need to see to a few things. Is there anything else, Ryann?"

He could see the questions floating in her eyes. The wonder. She knew there were things he wasn't saying, but she didn't press. "No. See you tonight?"

"Of course."

Ryann kissed Ayla's cheek as she sat her in the swing. It was her daughter's new favorite spot. Ayla would spend all day on the motorized contraption if they let her.

"I see she's in her happy space." Jackson was smiling, no hint of the unhappiness she'd witnessed in Lauren's room. And he was carrying… Ryann wasn't sure what.

"What is that?"

"Massage table." Jackson hit the side of the large contraption on his left side. "This is a mobile one I used to use for house visits."

"Do you need a place to store it?"

"No," he said. Jackson made a face at Ayla, and she giggled. "Mommy is so silly."

The conversation in the car snapped back into Ryann's memory. How could that have only been twelve hours before? It seemed like days ago.

"My shoulder is better," she said. She wanted to talk to him tonight. To find out what had happened today to drive such sadness into his eyes. And why he'd seemed so sure there was sometimes no reason for a relationship to end.

There were always reasons for things. Sometimes you just didn't want the answer. That was her mother's issue. The end of her relationships was always one hundred percent her partner's fault...at least in her version.

Jackson set the table down and walked over to her, looking at her shoulder. "Can I?"

"Sure." Her shoulder really did feel better. Her neck was still sore, but it was always sore. That was just life now.

Two fingers pressed against her shoulder, and she nearly fell into his arms as pain radiated down her back.

"That sure seems like you're fine."

"If you don't push on it, then *it is fine*," she said. Ignoring the shoulder ache or popping a few pain pills before bed would help. It wouldn't fix it, but it would help.

"Let me help you." Jackson turned and started setting up the table.

No argument came to mind to stop this. "Jackson—"

"I'm going to go to the bathroom. Get undressed, lay on the table and cover with the blanket."

"Undressed?" His hands running over her body with thin

cotton between them was going to be torture enough. But skin to skin?

Her throat burned, and her body tingled with just the memories of his touch.

"Yes. We need to get those muscles loosened, which won't happen nearly as fast with clothes on."

"Ayla—"

"Is yawning and almost down. And is also the reason that this shouldn't feel weird," he said. "She's proof that I've seen a lot more than I'll see tonight. I promised we'd keep this platonic. I meant it."

What if that isn't what I want?

"Let me take care of you," Jackson said, tapping the bed. "If you don't feel better after the massage, you can berate me all night."

"I would never."

He nodded, then disappeared down the hall to the bathroom.

Ryann stood there for a second, looked at Ayla, then at the bed. She rolled her neck, then pulled off her pants and shirt. Her bra fell to the ground, but she left her panties on. It wasn't much, but it was something.

She shimmied under the blanket and took a quick look at Ayla. She had nodded off.

"Ready?" Jackson asked.

No.

"Yes."

His steps were quiet, and when she put her head in the table's face hole she could see his bare feet. So she was getting a real massage from the only man who'd ever made her body sing.

"Take a deep breath for me."

She followed his command as he oiled his hands. The moment he laid them on her back she let out a whimper. The next hour was going to be the most blissful form of torture.

Ryann waited for him to ask if the pressure was too hard and didn't know how she was supposed to respond when he'd barely touched her. But thankfully Jackson started working on her upper trapezius.

When she let out the next moan, it was due to the tenderness of her flesh, not from desire.

"That spot is tight, honey."

Honey. He'd called her that in Hawaii, had said it was because she tasted like honey.

"All right, I need to move these knots, so take a deep breath and let me know if this pressure is too much." His elbow lay between her shoulder blades, and he pushed his elbow along the edge of blade.

It hurt, but in the best way. What an odd feeling to crave the pain knowing how much better she'd feel tomorrow.

Then when his thumb trailed the same path, the pressure was different. Lighter. Little circles tracing lines across her tight tendons. It felt delicious, and her body liked it in a much different way.

"How did you learn to do this?" she asked. She needed conversation, anything to keep her focus off the hot hunk rubbing oil down her body as much possible.

"I went to school." He pressed his elbow into her other shoulder, following the same path. "It took about nine months. I worked as a home health aide in the morning, went to night school for my RN and worked as a massage therapist on the weekends. I was willing to work Sundays, so I made bank."

She laughed but still felt her mouth fall open. "So, you took no breaks ever?"

"I was young and figured I could get all the work done early in life then so I could relax later."

"And then you became a nurse anesthesiologist. Not exactly relaxing." She sighed as his fingers worked their way down her spine. He was really good at this.

"I got into the CRNA program when my fiancée walked out on me. I had free time and needed something to focus on." He said the words automatically, like they didn't really matter. But was that because he'd pushed aside the feelings or because it no longer caused pain?

"Why did the relationship end?" And why was there a bead of happiness in her belly that he'd never wed? What kind of person was happy that the man who'd fathered their child had been dumped?

"Because she didn't want to marry me."

Jackson rolled a knot in her shoulder with his thumbs, and when it released, Ryann let out a massive moan.

"That one felt good," she said. He leaned closer, and for a moment she thought he was going to kiss her head.

But he pulled back, and she barely bit back her whimper.

"I bet it did."

She sucked in a deep breath as he gripped the blanket. "All right, time to roll over."

"Roll over?" Her eyes met his dark gaze. He was holding the blanket up—head turned away—to give her modesty.

"Yes. Come on."

She did, sliding down the table as he adjusted a pillow under her knees. He was exceptional at this—like everything else he did.

"What was the actual reason she left?" Ryann should drop it. She knew that. But she craved information about him. The good and the bad. The past and the present. She knew about his job, knew his love for Ayla, but he seemed far too good at shifting topics away from his past.

"I wasn't what she wanted." Jackson let out a sigh as his

thumb worked its magic on her back. "There is no sensational story, Ryann. A few years ago, she married a neurosurgeon, an upgrade."

"An upgrade." Ryann nearly shot off the table. "That isn't possible."

"It was years ago, honey. Water under the bridge," he said. "Take a deep breath—your neck is really tight."

She followed the directions, giving in to the care he was providing. Her body felt so much looser. The pinch of a headache that seemed her constant companion was gone.

He was taking care of her, taking care of Ayla…but who took care of him?

CHAPTER SIX

JACKSON ROLLED HIS SHOULDER, trying to push away the sleepiness and touch of sadness that had been with him since Ryann and Ayla had reentered his life. The sleepiness likely wasn't ending until Ayla was a little older.

The sadness? He worried that might be with him for the rest of his days. Ryann didn't want him—not in the way he wanted her. She thought it best for Ayla.

That was a nice sentiment, but it also meant that she thought they were temporary. A bright flame that warmed the heart but didn't ignite the soul. Meaning she didn't want to keep him, either.

He cleared his throat as he finished charting. It was fine. It was. This was nothing he hadn't dealt with before. He was Ayla's father and Ryann's friend. That was more than he'd had a month ago.

More than he ever thought he'd get.

Maybe it was selfish to want more.

"Good afternoon, Jackson," Miranda stated as she walked up with Ryann.

"Hi." Ryann waved, a hint of color in her cheeks.

"I didn't think you were working today, honey." Jackson looked at Miranda and grinned. "And I know Miranda is on the schedule...because when are you not?"

"Ha-ha." Miranda wagged a finger. "I'll have you know

that Knox and I never work overtime these days. Well, almost never."

"*Almost never* means they went from working all the eligible hours they could to only picking up one or two extra shifts a week." Jackson wagged his finger back to Miranda. "But I thought you were at the office this morning, Ryann." He'd called her honey a few seconds ago, just like he'd done last week during the massage—an hour he'd spent working out the knots of her body while fighting every feeling racing through his.

He was still waking from dreams where he'd spent the night worshipping her body after the massage. An alternate universe he'd give nearly anything to live in.

"I came in to see Lauren," Ryann said.

"I thought she was discharged." Jackson turned back to his computer. Lauren's seizure had been small, and after multiple neurological tests they'd released her with orders for physical therapy.

And Jackson had gone over the notes he'd placed in her chart with her and explained what to tell any future anesthesiologist or CRNA. Seizing on the table once didn't mean it would happen again, however she needed to be treated as a potential seizure risk from this point forward.

"Did something happen?" he asked.

The hand injury was tough. It would need months of physical therapy and at least one follow-on surgery. However, it wasn't an injury you generally worried about sending you back to the hospital after discharge.

"Only profit in the health-care system." Ryann rolled her eyes and sighed. "If I see her here, the cost to her out-of-pocket is about a hundred dollars. At the office, it's three hundred. So I agreed to meet her here. I'm going to see to a few patients and make rounds."

Her pager beeped, and she bit her lip as she read the message. "I guess word is out that I'm in the hospital."

"What is it?" Miranda looked at her own hip as the pager on it started buzzing.

"Handsaw accident," Ryann said. "We're needed in OR three. When he sliced his hand, he stumbled. So, we're tag-teaming this one." Her eyes met his, and she looked at her watch. "I'll have someone call Lauren—looks like we're going to be in surgery for hours."

"Good luck," he said. Time in the OR passed in a weird way, flying by and slowing down all at once. When your day shifted from a routine check-in to the OR with multiple surgeons, you could use all the luck possible.

"Thanks. If I can't get out by pickup time, can you grab Ayla?"

"Of course." He'd never met the babysitter, but Ryann had asked to place him on the backup list last week, something Jackson had immediately agreed to.

"You sure?" she asked.

He understood why she might ask the question. Jackson had been in Ayla's life for less than a sixth of his daughter's life. But it still stung.

He was her father—that meant everything. "I'm not on call. I won't get held up here. This is one worry you don't need to have."

"Thank you!" She waved a hand over her shoulder as she and Miranda took off running.

She didn't need to thank him. No one thanked mothers for doing what needed to be done for their children. Picking his daughter up from the babysitter, handling the evening routine was not a thank-you moment. It was a parenting moment. No matter who was doing it.

About an hour later, the final chart was clear when his

cell rang. He didn't recognize the number and nearly sent it to voicemail, but something pulled at him.

"Hello?"

"Is this Jackson? Ayla's dad?"

Jackson's face turned to the clock, seeing it was eleven thirty. No reason for a call except trouble. His stomach dropped, and years of working in trauma sent a flood of horror through his mind. "Is she all right?"

"Yes, but I have been trying to reach Ryann for an hour."

"She's in surgery. I'm the backup."

And if I'd been given your number, then I'd have answered immediately.

That was a frustration he'd keep inside and bring up to Ryann.

"We've had a power outage. We aren't legally allowed to keep the kids here once it goes past the hour mark," the babysitter explained. "Almost everyone else has been picked up."

"I'm on my way." Jackson hit a few buttons and sent an email to the floor supervisor, Kelly. He was only on for another half hour; still, he'd take a half day if they wanted him to.

Though he suspected Kelly would just tell him not to worry over the thirty minutes.

"Thank you." The woman hung up the phone without waiting for another comment, her attention clearly jumping back to one of the other kids who hadn't been picked up yet.

Ryann had three panicked messages from the sitter. Luckily Jackson had texted her a picture of him and Ayla in the swing at the park by her place. He really was the perfect father.

"That was a rough shift" Miranda said as she pulled her scrub shirt off and threw it into the laundry bin.

"And I wasn't even supposed to be here." The Lowery

Group had rearranged her schedule for the patient today. The fact that it was a local politician who'd needed the surgery was probably why they'd been so willing to shift her day to the hospital.

The hand surgery had been successful—at least as successful as possible with a reattachment. He'd have some nerve damage and his hand wouldn't work the same as before.

But the hand was a minor injury compared to what Miranda had dealt with.

"Falling forward on the saw was beyond unlucky." Miranda bit her lip. The initial call had claimed he'd dropped the saw when the hand injury had occurred, but with his injuries it had likely been intentional.

The mental health staff had been alerted, and his public relations team was already spinning the story. Which was interesting when he was in the ICU, critical, and might not make it through the night.

"Unlucky." Ryann muttered. "Mind if I shift topics?"

"Please!" Miranda threw a blue shirt over her head and pulled her dark curls into a ponytail. "The sillier the topic the better!"

"Not sure this is silly," she said, "but what can I do for Jackson as a thank-you or to make him smile because he's so helpful, you know, because of Ayla. Or…" She'd almost said because she wanted to see him smile.

Not that she didn't see him smile all the time. The man was always beaming when he looked at their daughter. But ever since she'd kissed his cheek—

Ryann shut down that line of thought. She was trying to do something nice for Jackson. He did a world of nice things for her. There was nothing more in-depth to it than that.

"Or…" Miranda raised her hands and smiled.

"I want to do something nice for him." Ryann's cheeks

were hot, and Miranda was looking at her with a knowing smile.

She looked at her watch and then pulled out her phone. "I need to check with Knox—I don't keep the schedule on this as well as he and Jackson."

Ryann had no idea what schedule she could possibly be talking about. But if it was something Jackson tracked, then it was important and she wanted to know.

When Knox answered on the other end, Miranda asked, "Is it tots night?"

Tots night? What does that mean? Ryann wondered. *Toddlers?*

"No, I'm sure that Jackson is not headed to Mulligan's tonight. But I am sure they can make them to go." Miranda made a face that Ryann couldn't decipher.

That was a bar name.

"They don't taste that good at the bar, but he loves them." Miranda winked at her as she said, "Yes, Ryann is asking."

It was weird to hear the conversation from one side. She wasn't sure what Mulligan's was or tots night, but the conversation was one Miranda was enjoying. After the day they'd had that wasn't nothing.

"Love you, too. See you soon. No, I am not bringing tots home, Knox."

"Did he want tots, too?" Ryann asked as Miranda pushed her phone into her back pocket.

"No." She grabbed her backpack, clearly ready to put this day behind them. "Jackson loves tots. We don't understand it, but we roll with it. Like Knox needing to compete at darts or lately pickleball." She rolled her eyes.

"All right, so Jackson loves them," Ryann said. "We are talking about the little potato things right?"

"Yep. The bar food." Miranda pulled notebook from her

backpack and made a quick note, ripped it out and passed it to her. "Tonight is tots night at the bar. It's five dollars for all-you-can-eat. I'm sure that you can ask the bartender for a to-go box. It might not be what they usually do, but if they give you any trouble, mention that it's for Jackson."

"Does he spend a lot of time at the bar?" Her mother's second husband had basically lived in one. But Jackson didn't seem the type.

"*A lot* is relative," Miranda said. "He and Knox used to go once or twice a week, mostly to play darts and for the tots. They each nursed a beer. When I pointed out that you can eat tots anywhere…well, I will let Jackson explain why they taste better at Mulligan's."

"I see." Ryann put the address into her phone. Grabbing some tots on the way home was now priority one.

"They're in a new season of life." Miranda opened the stairwell and waited for Ryann to head through. "Knox and I were residents together. Jackson was in his first year as an RN then, working in the ER. We were so young, and yet now, with years of experience behind us, there are days I still feel like that twenty-five-year-old resident. The more I learn, the less I know."

"A new season." Ryann liked that phrase. "It is weird. I'm a mom, and I remember thinking adults must have the answers." Not her mother, but other adults. Those were the people she'd wanted to be when she grew up.

The ones who knew what they were doing. Who had the answers. Who didn't worry because they'd figured everything out. Adults with their lives together, who knew what they were doing was right. At least she'd thought so.

"And now you realize they were all just doing their best and winging it at just about every step." Miranda laughed.

"Some kind of universal joke, right!" Yet she understood

it. Particularly with Ayla at home. She wanted so badly to do her best for her. No matter the sacrifices for herself.

Opening the door to her condo she almost wanted to call out, *Honey, I'm home.* It felt nice and weird and somewhat unfulfilling to know Jackson was here with their daughter and they were just friends.

Who was she trying to fool? She and Jackson were more than friends. Less than what her body craved.

"Hi." Jackson rounded the corner with Ayla on his hip. Their daughter was squirming, trying to get back to whatever game she'd been playing just a moment before.

"Nice to know she doesn't care that I'm home," Ryann said. She kissed her daughter's cheek, then let out a gasp as she stepped into the kitchen area. The pots were on the floor along with her wooden spoon and the chair they let Ayla sit in.

"It's one way to keep her busy while making dinner!" Jackson said, chuckling as he put her back into the chair.

Their daughter immediately grabbed the spoon and started banging on the pots.

"It does add to the number of dishes I have to clean, though. Good thing you're worth it, little miss." He booped her nose, then turned his full attention to Ryann.

"I'd ask how your day was, but I already heard from Knox." He opened his arms.

She hesitated only a minute before putting the tots and her bags on the counter and stepping into them.

Her body seemed to exhale the tension in her life as his strong arms wrapped around her. Nothing seemed like it could get to her, like when she was standing in his arms she was protected. Really protected.

Her heart yearned to lift her face. Kiss him. Lose herself in the longings only Jackson had ever brought out in her.

"I have something for you," she said. She needed to move, or she'd give in to all those urges.

"For me?"

The tone of surprise cut. He never expected anyone to treat him. That was changing. He was caring for her, and she was going to do the same for him. Friends and co-parents could do that.

Couldn't they?

"Yes, for you." She pulled away and headed for the bag. "I'm not sure they'll be any good. Bill wasn't sure, either. But hopefully…"

She handed him the to-go box. She was not sure how tater tots were going to make his day, but she was trusting Miranda and Knox.

"Are these…?" Jackson shook his head and popped one into his mouth.

"They probably need to be warmed," she said. She enjoyed tater tots occasionally. But only hot. They were not great otherwise.

"Nah, they're always a little chilly at the bar," he said. "Since food isn't really their thing."

That seemed like a reason not to get them, even for the low price of five dollars for all you could eat. "Miranda mentioned you only like them from Mulligan's."

"Yeah," he said. "Silly, I know, but they're greasy and a little cold, just like my mom used to make them. Well, *make* is relative—she'd pop them in the microwave and then set them on the counter and forget." He sighed as he chewed. "Weird how this is the thing that I miss."

Ryann understood that sentiment. Children, even those with parents who didn't care enough about them, found things they missed. It was random ice cream nights for her.

"Were there any other things she made often?" Anything else Ryann could do for him. Any insight into his past.

"Nope. Tots though…" He popped another into his mouth. "Thank you." Jackson leaned forward, like he was about to kiss her cheek, then pulled back.

How she wished he'd close the distance. She'd give in to the impulse. But the man across from her would always respect the boundaries she'd placed. As he should.

Grabbing another one, he said, "I hate that you can't share one."

For the first time she was more than a little happy that she was on the elimination diet. She was glad he enjoyed the tater tots and glad she had a reason not to share.

"Those are all yours!"

CHAPTER SEVEN

"THINK SHE NEEDS her diaper changed?" Jackson did his best to keep the smile on his face while their daughter screamed from the back seat. She'd started about ten minutes into their hour-and-a-half drive to the outlet store Ryann wanted to visit.

"She didn't when we checked ten minutes ago, or five minutes after that. So far we've stopped twice in forty minutes, and as soon as we get her out of the car seat she's fine. Maybe car sickness?" Ryann leaned over the seat and made some cooing noises to their daughter.

Ayla either didn't hear her over the screams or didn't care. With the car seat rear-facing it was difficult to know which it was. Weren't car rides supposed to calm babies?

Their daughter sounded nearly desperate, and it broke Jackson's heart.

"How about we stop off here?" he said. "There's a roadside attraction. They'll have bathrooms, and you can maybe see if she's hungry." The signs for the largest fork in Arizona and spoon museum were plastered all around the area. Jackson had never been, but desperate times…

"And if she just wants out of her car seat?" Ryann looked at him, her eyes stating that she was fairly certain that was the main issue here.

He agreed, but what other choice did they have besides letting her scream for an hour?

"If that is the case, I can drive us back to your place. She and I can hang out there, and you can enjoy a solo trip to the outlet." That way Ayla didn't lose her voice from screaming, Jackson and Ryann didn't lose their hearing, and Ryann still got to enjoy part of her day off.

Pulling into the attraction, Jackson couldn't stop the laugh. A giant four-story fork stood next to a small building with the words *Spoon Museum* written in bland script. Somehow he'd expected more.

"Oh! This is fantastic. How did I not know this was so close?" Ryann clapped and made an oohing sound that was very at odds with the sight before them.

"Why do they have a large fork and a spoon museum? Shouldn't it be the largest spoon?" Jackson turned off the car, and Ayla's screams turned to sniffles.

"Oh, it's a marketing strategy so that you say exactly that." Ryann hopped out of the car and went back to Ayla. She lifted their daughter from the seat and rubbed her nose against Ayla's, eliciting a laugh.

"So it is the car seat," Jackson said. He wasn't sure what they were going to do about that. Until she was old enough to tell them what the problem was, there was no good way to know why she was intent on only spending a few minutes in the seat.

"Looks that way." Ryann rubbed Ayla's belly as their daughter babbled. "So, plans change."

They did. Jackson was hoping to spend the day with Ryann and Ayla. Shopping wasn't his first choice of entertainment, but spending time with them was. "So, I'll run the two of us home."

His throat tightened on the word *home*. He'd meant to say *I'll run the two of us to your place.*

Ryann's condo was not home, something he shouldn't have to remind himself of. Yes, he was staying there most nights—in the guest room. But that was to help Ryann, not because it was his place.

"Today is a family day. Shopping isn't super necessary. I can order the shoes I was looking at online. I mostly wanted out of the house." Ryann pointed to the fork. "You have to take our picture!"

Family day.

His soul vibrated with the two words. The thing he'd wanted most—family.

Maybe this family didn't look like the one he'd wanted, but Knox was his brother even though they shared no DNA. Family didn't have to be some standard picture-book definition.

"Smile!" Ryann beamed as she looked into his phone, and he snapped a picture. "Ayla isn't looking. Look at Daddy."

"Da—" Ayla started.

Jackson held his breath.

"Can you say *Dada*? Dada? Dada?" Ryann looked at him. "I hope you're rolling the video."

Only the one in my mind.

He didn't want to move an inch, look away for even a second to change to video in case he missed it.

"Dada?" Ryann parroted, but Ayla just giggled.

She was babbling. A happy baby who didn't know exactly what the sounds meant...yet. It wouldn't be long before the word *Dada* turned to *Daddy*.

Time would pass so fast. She was already bigger than when he'd met her three weeks ago. Soon she'd be seven months old and, in the blink of an eye, seventeen. He didn't want to miss a minute.

He pushed the button on the phone, grabbing several pictures of the happy scene in front of him. "I've snapped several pictures. You want me to keep going?"

"Was she ever looking at you?" Ryann asked.

He wasn't sure he'd gotten one of them looking at him together, but several were perfection of mother and daughter giggling at each other.

"I don't think that ever synced, but look at this one." He pulled up his favorite. Their heads were both tilted the same way, the wind picking up their curls, smiles as wide as possible.

It should simply be titled *Happiness*.

Ryann leaned her head against his shoulder. The motion felt so right. He wanted to lean in, wrap his arms around them both. Kiss their heads and just be.

Instead, Jackson forced himself to step away. "So, are we going to try diaper changes or feeding or just walk around out here?"

"The spoon museum." Ryann pointed. "I assumed we'd do that instead. You know—family day."

"You want to go to the spoon museum? It probably isn't great," he said.

The sign needed to be repainted. The windows could use a dusting. The place had certainly seen better days.

Ryann slipped her hand into his and pulled him toward the back of the car. She opened the trunk, got out the wrap she carried Ayla in, put it on and fastened their now very happy child in.

"I'm counting on this place being a little bad," she said. "That's part of what makes it so fun. Anyone can go to a fancy museum—only a few actually stop at roadside attractions. That's what makes them so special."

She clapped her hands and kissed Ayla's cheek. "Baby's first roadside attraction." She snapped a photo with her phone.

"Wow." Jackson chuckled. "I would never have guessed you liked these."

"Love them. My mom used to stop at all of them. I saw more baby alligator farms, thimble collections and even the second-largest taxidermy collection in the US."

"Second largest?"

"Right." Ryann was practically bouncing. "I have no idea where the largest is or how you even measure that. But their sign clearly marketed them as the second largest. Mom thought it was fun. Even with everything else, I still love these. Kind of like your tater tots, but with four-story forks."

"Four-story forks." Jackson laughed. "There is a phrase I never thought I'd say."

"Then this is going to be quite the experience for you, Jackson Peters. Ready?" She slid her hand back into his.

He looked down at it. It would be so easy to pretend that they were the perfect little family today. And rather than pull away, Jackson was going to give in to it.

Just for the afternoon.

"You have to admit that was something." Ryann was swinging Jackson's hand in hers, very aware that she'd held it the entire time they'd been in the museum. She should have released it, should have put a little distance between them.

Yet Ryann felt incapable of letting him go. Today had felt different.

No. Her life had felt different from the moment the man beside her had stepped back into her life—into their daughter's life.

If she leaned over to kiss him, what would happen? Their passion had burned so bright in Hawaii. But what if the spark stayed alive? What if she could have this little family? Forever…

"*Something* feels like an apt description," Jackson said. His laugh seemed to touch the center of her body as he leaned forward.

He's going to kiss me.

Instead, he beamed at their daughter, then pulled back and released her hand. Disappointment flared and heat burned her cheeks as she fought every fiber in her body screaming for her to take it back.

He was focused on Ayla. That was what was most important.

"I mean, it isn't every day you see a spoon that was used by a president." Ryann started to laugh, trying to get back to the happiness she'd had all afternoon before covering her giggle with her hand. Ayla had fallen asleep halfway through the museum—which was the loosest description of that word as possible. Besides the gift shop, the place had three rooms, none of which was larger than her living room.

"I'm not sure we have seen a spoon used by a president," Jackson said. He opened the back door and got the buckles ready so they could transfer Ayla as quickly as possible. Hopefully she'd sleep all the way home.

"The artifacts did seem to have a bit of a dubious origin," she said. Most of the signage looked like it had been printed on regular computer paper with an ink cartridge in desperate need of a change.

"Artifacts, Ryann, honey." Jackson chuckled before sliding into the front seat and starting the car. "Those were junkstore finds put behind glass—in need of dusting—and given a new 'history.'"

He was right. That was part of the fun she always had at places like this. It was random and weird and usually someone's passion that they hoped sparked passion in others. Roadside attractions were leftovers of the days of cross-country road trips. Most were either out of business or closed.

The few that remained relied on major gimmicks. Like the largest fork next to a spoon museum. Ryann would still stop at them, though, gimmicks and all.

"The admission price was perfect!" She clicked Ayla's seat belts into place, letting out a little sigh as her daughter kept sleeping. Hopefully the car ride home would be less eventful.

For all three of them it had cost five dollars to walk around the museum for forty-five minutes. Ayla, like all children under twelve, had gotten in for free.

"Yes, they're clearly hoping you'll spend your coin in the gift shop." Jackson pulled out of the parking space as she was clicking her own seat belt closed.

"If the frame hadn't been broken, I would have bought the 'my first visit to the fork' picture frame." Ryann had one picture of herself and her mother that had survived countless moves, life on communes and couch surfing. It was of them at a building in Ohio shaped like a giant basket. Faded and the corners creased, it represented one of the few happy times in her childhood.

A time that had passed so quickly. She always knew her mother's focus would vanish the second her mother found a new partner or "path of life."

It was that happiness she was giving Ayla. Without the worry.

"So, what's for dinner?" Ryann asked. She had a few things in the fridge they could make, or Jackson had done some research on which takeout places had options for her.

"Oh." Jackson looked in the rearview mirror and cleared his throat. "I'm…um… I was going to go back to my place tonight. I haven't stopped by in a few days."

"Need to water plants?" It was a weak joke, but she didn't want him to see the pain the statement brought.

"No." Jackson looked at her briefly before turning back to the road. "I just a need a night away. A night to put myself back in the place I need to be for you."

"Oh." Ryann understood, and she appreciated his honesty. After all, it was she who had held his hand. She who had called this a family day. She who was setting the boundaries he was honoring. She who should've been happy right now.

Or at least content.

"I'll bring the tea first thing tomorrow, help with morning shift before sitter drop-offs," he said. The staccato words punctuated the quiet car.

"Sure." Ryann looked back at Ayla, then turned her attention to the road. Forty minutes in a silent car with Jackson… it was going to feel like an eternity.

"Such a good girl," Jackson cooed at Ayla as he finished up her bath. Ryann was fixing them dinner, and after today's trip it would be so easy to let himself keep pretending that they were the happy family that did day trips, came home for dinner, then went to sleep without one parent in the guest room. The whole white-picket-fence-without-the-fence idea.

It was what he wanted more than anything. But that wasn't the relationship he and Ryann had. He needed a little distance, to spend tonight in his condo. *His space*. Force his brain and heart back into check.

That was why he'd panicked when she'd asked him about dinner. He'd seen her eyes widen when he'd said he wasn't staying, watched hurt race across the dark hues of her eyes and seen her cover it so quickly, too. That wasn't fair. It was a simple question, one they'd asked nearly every day. A blasé phrase that resulted in him hurting her feelings.

Grabbing the ducky bath towel, he lifted Ayla from the bath. She laid her head on his shoulder, and his heart melted. "You had a busy day, huh, sweet girl?"

Most of that busyness was due to screaming on both sides of the trip. Her eyes had popped open just as they'd hit the highway. The screams had started moments later.

She yawned and put her thumb in her mouth as he got her ready for bed.

"Think she'll eat any of the oatmeal I made for her?"

Jackson lifted Ayla, passing her to Ryann. "No idea. She's a very sleepy girl." He used a singsong voice that he swore he'd never had before finding out he was a father. It was like the knowledge had unlocked some gene that forced silly voices. "If you nurse her, she'll probably go down, and then you can have a nice low-key night," he said.

The words should've been right, but he saw the same look of hurt pass through Ryann's eyes. The urge to pull them both into his arms, hold them until the world righted itself and they were the family he'd always dreamed of wrapped through his soul.

A host of words were trapped in his mind. But none of them were the right ones. Remaining platonic co-parents was one of the hardest things he'd ever done.

"Stay."

Had she truly whispered the word, or was his brain pushing the fantasy he was desperate to seize?

"Ryann, if you want me to feed her and get her to bed for you—"

"No." The curls bounced as she shook her head. "No."

"What do you want, Ryann?" he asked.

She bit her lip, her eyes focusing on Ayla. "I don't know. But I don't want you to go yet."

What was he supposed to say?

They stood there looking at each other, a mountain of unsaid words standing between them.

"Okay. I'll stay," he said.

Tomorrow, though, for his own sanity, he was going to spend time at his place.

CHAPTER EIGHT

"GOOD MORNING." At least Ryann's voice was bright as she welcomed her first appointment into her office, and that was what her patient needed. The rest of her…the rest of her was exhausted and torn and dealing with emotions she'd never expected—or wanted.

Today was the first time in almost two weeks that Jackson hadn't stayed at her place. She'd gotten Ayla ready without him, actions that she'd done for months alone. Ryann could do it; it was just better with him.

In fact, everything was better with Jackson Peters around. The whole condo felt less homey without him.

Her day felt off, and it wasn't yet nine.

"Morning, Doc." Her patient seemed to have no issue smiling. Or perhaps she was faking it just like Ryann.

"You're here because your fingers are hurting, Ms. Laird?" she asked. She'd read through the chart a few times, but the family doctor who'd recommended Ms. Laird see an orthopedic surgeon had put precious little in the notes.

"Peggy, please. I'm here because my niece is worried about my arthritis and hands cramping."

"Your niece, Peggy?" Now Ryann was more confused.

"Yep. The rascal is also my family doc," she said. "Super proud of her, but she's very straitlaced and a bit of a worry wart. I know why my hands hurt, and I'm all right with it."

"All right?" Ryann leaned against her desk. "Why do your fingers hurt?"

"Arthritis." She smiled and held up hands. Her knuckles were noticeably swollen but far from the worst Ryann had seen.

"Is it getting worse?" Arthritis was common. If you were lucky enough to see your seventies, the odds you'd get the diagnosis were more than seventy percent.

Peggy chuckled.

Ryann wasn't sure what was so funny, but patient reactions could swing wildly on the emotional spectrum.

Her patient smiled as she looked at her hands. "I'm seventy-two." Peggy's eyes filled with tears, but Ryann didn't think it was physical pain. "I'm painting every morning now and every night and sometimes for almost eight hours at a time."

"That amount of painting would hurt anyone's hands. I'm surprised your wrists aren't burning."

"Oh, they are." Peggy laughed again. "I made the mistake of asking my niece if the pain pill recommendation on the bottle was serious or if I could double it without issue." She pointed at Ryann. "That face. That face is the one my niece made. Guess it's a doctor face."

Ryann closed her mouth and took a deep breath, hoping that her face looked more normal now. "Have you considered painting less?"

"I've spent the last thirty years not painting, thirty years behind a desk doing a job I hated." Peggy blew out a breath.

"So you started painting again when you retired?" Ryann asked. That was actually good. Many people lost themselves in the early days of retirement. But keeping a work schedule for a hobby wasn't necessarily healthy, either.

"No." She pulled her phone and held up a picture. It was of

a young Peggy and another woman dressed in paint clothes. "This is Molly. We ran a small artist's shop in San Francisco in the nineteen eighties." Peggy looked at the image, then put it away. "Molly wanted to have a commitment ceremony and spend our lives together, but I... I didn't want to disappoint my family."

It was a tragic story. And one that was all too familiar for so many people.

"She died about a year ago." Peggy closed her eyes for just a second. "Left a note for me with her partner, a lovely woman named June. Anyway, she wrote that she hoped I got what I wanted."

And I didn't.

Ryann didn't need to hear the words to know what they were.

"I retired the next month, bought my weight in oil paints and just started. And my hands ache. There are days that my wrist burns, but my soul is at peace for the first time in my memory."

She wiped a tear away, and Ryann handed her a tissue. "I don't want surgery, and I'm only here so I keep my cool Aunt Peg cred with my niece. Which I think she knows, but..."

"Have you tried sleeping with a carpal tunnel brace?" It would keep her wrist in a neutral position, help the carpal tunnel in the wrist and maybe even alleviate some of the finger pain.

"No. Which one do you recommend?"

Ryann smiled—at least there was something she could do for Peggy to give her a little relief.

They spent the rest of the appointment going over options, all of which Peggy turned down on the side of not wasting any more time. But between the brace and anti-inflammatory meds, she was going to get at least some relief.

* * *

"All right, Ayla is down." Jackson rolled his shoulders as he stepped into the living room. He needed to use a racquetball on his sore shoulders. Unfortunately, that was at his place.

He'd make do though because Ryann wanted to watch some home-decorating show tonight. The woman loved them, even though he really thought the rooms all looked the same after it was done.

"Glad she's down because *Small Homes, Big Future* is starting," Ryann said. "Not that we couldn't stream it later, but somehow live it feels different."

"Sure." He didn't care what they watched. He was just looking forward to the evening. Jackson slid onto the couch beside her, wincing as his shoulders complained at their first position.

"You okay?" Ryann's curls shifted as she stared at him.

Her dark gaze called to him, and his soul ached for him to reach over and run a hand along her cheek, then ask to kiss her.

Instead, he smiled and carefully shook his head, making sure not to aggravate the muscles any further.

"I'm fine. What kind of name is *Small Homes, Big Future*?" he asked. He'd spent two nights at his place and probably should've gone back tonight. But he didn't want to.

He wanted to be here, having a random night with her.

"They all have names like that." Ryann threw him a look as the program started. Then she hit Pause.

"Thought you wanted to watch this live? It's better that way, remember." Jackson shifted, and his neck and shoulders reminded him that he'd chosen poorly.

"It's only a little delay—we can skip the first couple of commercials," she said. "Don't change the subject. Your neck is sore."

"Happens. I sit still in weird positions during long sur-geries. You get lower back pain, and I get neck pain. Which you also get." He winked. This wasn't a big deal. Just a fac-tor in his life.

"Move up." Ryann moved before he could process more than her soft scent wrapping through him. She slid behind him, wrapping her legs around his waist as she pushed on the base of his neck.

"Oh." Her fingers found the exact right pressure point.

"I might not have massage background, but I know where each muscle connects to the bones."

"A built-in bonus." Jackson sighed as her thumb followed the trapezius muscle pushing hard enough to hit the smaller muscles under it.

"All right, I can do this while we watch the show." She reached around him.

Her hands brushing his shoulder lit up his skin. He hadn't reacted to a woman like this since high school.

He'd felt this way every second with her in Hawaii, like he'd never be able to get enough of Ryann. He'd chalked it up as vacation fun, but what if it wasn't? What if they could be so much more?

Not that that mattered, since it wasn't what she wanted.

"What color of gray will they paint the bedroom?" Jack-son chuckled as the camera panned the currently dark red bedroom, trying to focus on anything other than the woman wrapped around him rubbing his shoulders and neck.

"They have other colors!" Ryann's hand hit his chest, rest-ing on it for a moment before she pulled it back and started rubbing his shoulder again. "And you have to admit that red is horrid." Her soft words were breathed against his ear.

"No one can argue that," Jackson said. He preferred brightly colored rooms. Probably because he'd never been allowed to paint any room a color of his choice until he'd become an adult.

He was decent at interior decorating...provided you were going for something with personality. His kitchen was a nice shade of light green. His bedroom was a dark blue—for the relaxation and to keep as much light out as possible when he worked nights. His bathroom was pink with flamingos because it made him smile every morning,

And the extra room that was now Ayla's was light yellow with clouds on the wall. The light yellow had been there before. The white clouds were wall clings he'd found the day after discovering he had a daughter.

Not that Ayla had ever slept there. One day he hoped she'd like it. But if she wanted a different color, he'd do it immediately.

And thinking about interior decorating was doing nothing to stop his growing desire for the mother of his child as she ran her hands over his sore muscles.

"I bet they paint it any other color than gray." Ryann pointed to the screen, then pushed her elbow into his shoulder.

"Oh." That felt like heaven. Torture, but heaven.

"The homeowners don't look like they want gray." She kept rotating her elbow, thankfully unaware of the turmoil cascading through him.

"Fine. If it is gray, what do I win?" he asked. Focus on a bet. That would be something to draw his attention—maybe.

Ryann looked around the living room, then made a face. "Umm, there isn't a lot here to bet. Oh...how about a question. You win you get to ask me any question and I have to answer. And if you lose, you have to answer mine."

His stomach flipped, and he thought of just playing it off, then shrugged. How bad could one question be? And he was going to win.

Because they were painting this house gray. Now he had thirty minutes to come up with the perfect question while she loosened the muscles in his shoulder. Not a bad way to spend a night.

"I told you!" Ryann squealed as they picked out the purple paint that the designer was begging the couple to consider as just an accent wall. "Sorry—that was way too close to your ear."

It was, and he didn't care. "Not a problem. Why have these two agreed to be on a show with designers they had no intention of listening to?"

"Money, ratings, as a dare," she said. "Who knows, but it did make for a far more interesting show. Most importantly..." Her lips were right his ear. "I was right—they're not gray-loving people."

She was. And he was a man of his word. "So, what is your question?" They'd gotten closer over the last few weeks—so much, but there was still a wall between them. A distance they seemed to be trying to keep in order to maintain the balance they had.

She leaned her head on his shoulder and took a deep breath. "What would you do if I kissed you?" Ryann's cheeks darkened, but she didn't look away.

That wasn't a question he'd been expecting. She shifted, the soft scent of her soap hitting his nose as he tried to see if any of the synapses in his brain would fire.

"Ryann..." He wanted to kiss her. Wanted so badly to hold her, to see if the magic they'd had in Hawaii, the magic that had created Ayla, was still there.

It was. He was nearly certain of it. But he didn't want one night, didn't want to release the pressure because for him, it would still be there tomorrow.

"If you kiss me," he said, "I would kiss you back and then

push you away. I don't want a night, Ryann. I want you. I want to give this a real go. I know you don't…"

"What if I did?"

Ryann's fingers twitched. From rubbing his shoulders, or because she wanted to do something else with her hands?

"What if…" Ryann paused. The quiet seconds stretching on forever between them. "What if I did want to see what happens with us? But you can't leave Ayla if we—"

He put his finger over her lips. "Ayla is my daughter. I will be in her life for the rest of my life. I swear it."

Then her lips were on his. The universe sang as she slid into his lap. His arms wrapped around her waist, anchoring her to him.

This was heaven, pure and simple. "Ryann…"

"I love when you say my name between kisses." She trailed her lips down his throat as he lifted the shirt over her head.

Her tan skin was perfection, but he saw her hesitate.

"Ryann…" Jackson put his hands on her hips. If she'd changed her mind, they'd stop.

"My body is different," she said. She grabbed his hand, tracing it along one of the dark stretch marks on her belly. "Pregnancy and…umm."

"You're the most beautiful woman in the world." He traced his hands along the dark stretch marks. They'd probably lighten with time. But even if they didn't, they did nothing but add to her beauty.

"My breasts aren't sensitive like they were." Ryann bit her lips. "From feeding…"

"Then I get to rediscover what turns you on." That was a chore he was very much looking forward to completing.

"Jackson…" Ryann's mouth captured his. "You're so perfect."

No one was perfect. And he knew that he was devastatingly far from it. After all, if he'd been perfect his life would look so much different. People would have stayed.

Her fingers traced his chest before she lifted his shirt off. "If I remember correctly…" Her lips skimmed the hollow between his neck and shoulder, her tongue flicking just the right place.

She moved her hips, rubbing against his already painfully hard erection. "You are very hard."

He was. His body wanted nothing more than to rip the tiny white shorts from her body, slide into her and feel her crest into oblivion. But Jackson wasn't rushing a single moment of this.

"I haven't been with you in almost two years, sweetheart." He wrapped his hands through her hair, pulling her mouth to hers.

"I haven't been with anyone since you." She purred, "I feel like I might burst with need."

Burst with need.

There were no sexier words.

"I haven't been with anyone, either." Despite Knox's attempts to set him up with someone, no one had compared to the woman in his arms now.

Her tongue met his, and she wrapped her legs around his waist. When Jackson moved his hands to her bra strap, she grabbed his hand.

"I leak." She bit her lip, color that he knew had nothing to do with passion erupting across her features.

"Do you want to keep your bra on?" he asked. This evening was about pleasure. For both of them. He wanted Ryann to enjoy every minute.

"Yes."

"All right." He grinned and moved his hands to her shorts,

the elastic band allowing him easy access to her bottom. "You are so gorgeous," he said.

Ryann let out a giggle before kissing him again. "I certainly feel that way with you."

"Good." He gripped her hips, sliding her off him and onto the couch. Jackson needed to taste her. He pulled the shorts off, and then the plain white panties dropped to the floor.

Lifting her legs, he ran his finger across her folds, enjoying the flickers of desire running through her dark gaze.

She lifted her hips, moaning as his thumb found her clit. "Jackson…"

His manhood screamed as she called out his name. Dipping his head, he ran his tongue along her folds before suckling her. Ryann bucked against him, panting out his name.

"I need you, Jackson!" She sat up, grabbing for his pants, unbuttoning them and releasing his manhood.

He was so close to losing himself just from her touch.

"Jackson…" She pulled him close, then paused. "I don't have condoms."

He took a deep breath. He hadn't carried a spare condom in his wallet in years. "Then tonight is just about you."

He bent his head again, capturing her mouth. He wanted her, but waiting wouldn't kill him.

"Jackson." His name echoed in the room as she came again. Then she sat up, kissing him the whole time.

"It's about you, too." Her mouth trailed down his neck, down his chest, his stomach. She pulled his jeans and boxers off in one touch.

Then her mouth was on him. "Ryann…" Jackson took a deep breath as she ran her fingers over his shaft, moving with her mouth in a way that was as close to divine as possible.

"Sweetheart." He gripped the couch as his orgasm overtook him.

CHAPTER NINE

JACKSON ROLLED OVER, his hand reaching for Ryann, only to find an empty pillow. He blinked, then stretched. His back and neck were sore, but it was like the feeling the day after a good deep-tissue massage. Ryann certainly knew what she was doing with her fingers…and her mouth.

They'd spent the night pleasuring each other. It had been a lovely experience. One he planned to repeat, once he had condoms. Now, though, he needed to find Ryann.

If Ayla had gotten up last night, he'd not heard her. Pulling on his boxers, he went in search of Ryann and Ayla. The baby's nursery was empty and so was the living room. They were probably just running an errand.

Jackson went back to the bedroom to look at his phone. No message. All right, look in the kitchen.

No message there, either. His skin prickled as his brain reminded him of all the times he'd woken up alone. Not alone in his place, where it was expected, but alone at a foster home or on the few occasions when his mother had had custody.

It had never been a good sign. He'd had two families who'd taken their biological kids out to breakfast without telling him. When his case worker had showed up, he'd been told to pack his bags.

The case worker had been sweet each time, but the message had been clear: *you're not enough—get your stuff.* It was weird how he hadn't considered that for years and now it was all his brain could remember.

His chest tightened. He was an adult, forty years old with a doctorate in nursing. This was a morning errand. Nothing more. Breathe.

Breathe!

The front door opened. "Jackson?"

Oxygen filled his lungs as Ryann rounded the corner with Ayla in her car seat in one hand and a bag of groceries in the other. "I thought you might still be asleep. Knox said you like to sleep in."

"Knox?" He wiped his face, trying to clear the cobwebs of panic from his brain.

"Yeah. Are you okay?"

"Fine." Jackson took a deep breath. Damn, he hadn't had a panic attack in years. And he wasn't having one now—not when everything was going so well.

"Not sure I believe that," Ryann said. "But yes, I texted Knox this morning to find out your favorite doughnut."

"Doughnut?" He'd never been a huge breakfast person. He usually grabbed coffee, or tea now, and a granola bar. Mostly because he usually slept until it was time to leave for work.

Or he had before Ryann had walked back into his life with a cute bundle of joy on her hip.

"Yep. I didn't just want to buy contraception." Ryann laughed and raised both her brows in a funny motion. "I'm turning forty this year. I have a six-month-old, and there is almost no one there, but somehow walking in to grab only condoms made me feel like someone was looking over my shoulder the whole time."

"Like your mother was watching?" Jackson lifted Ayla from her car seat, kissing her cheek. He'd never had a parent who cared about what he did, but he'd heard friends at school joke about it.

Or complain.

Never realizing how lucky they'd been to have parents who worried, who were frustrated when they made bad choice, who wanted the absolute best for them. It was a gift you only really understood when you were outside looking in.

"No. My mother would never judge contraception," Ryann said as she chuckled. She pulled a chocolate cake doughnut from the container, then lifted a pastry that was marked as dairy and wheat free. "Figured you wouldn't eat it if I didn't have a treat, too."

He might not have. So far, he'd stuck to her diet exclusively, except for the tots she'd brought home. Ayla was doing so much better, too. So now it was time to start adding back in a food a week to see if they could identify the item, or items, that upset her.

"So your mother wouldn't have judged you for buying contraception?" Jackson was always fascinated by parental reactions.

"My mother gave me the talk, as it was, at twelve," Ryann said. She bit into her pastry and gave a sigh. "Not sure this is that good or if I'm just missing doughnuts!"

Twelve wasn't that young, and it was good for parents to have an open communication line. But there was something about the phrasing that made him shudder.

Ayla giggled and reached for the pastry in Ryann's hand.

"No, sweet girl, you're not big enough for this, and it might hurt your belly." She tapped their daughter's nose. "My mother would say it was no big deal and give her a little piece, damn the consequences." Ryann shuddered. "At twelve, she gave me six boxes of condoms."

"Six!" Jackson shook his head. "Did she not realize they expire?"

"Oh, she knew. But Mom is a free spirit," she said. "At

least that's what she calls herself. I call her wildly irresponsible. The woman let me do whatever I wanted."

"I guess you plan to be super strict with Ayla?" Jackson asked. He wasn't opposed to rules. Boundaries were helpful, but you could overcompensate, too.

"Not super strict. But I do want to know what she is doing. And protect her."

Protect her.

"Your mom didn't protect you?" He'd seen some of the worst the world had to offer—both in foster care and in medical work. Jackson would do everything possible to keep their daughter safe.

But experiences were important, too. And hurt happened. No life was lived without it. Ensuring his daughter always had a safe place to land was his priority.

"My mom wanted to be my friend. And she wanted to laugh and do whatever she wanted. And she rarely wanted to pay bills or keep house or pay attention to schoolwork."

"And yet you're a surgeon. An orthopedic surgeon," he said. That was impressive as hell.

"Yep. I succeeded, but I struggled. And I never felt safe," she said. "Ayla will never feel that way. She is never going to be hurt."

That wasn't possible. Ryann had to know that. But pressing the point now wouldn't do any good. Instead, he held out his hand to her, pulling her close. His little family. "Thank you for the doughnut."

"It's almost the best way to start the day." She winked at him, then playfully covered Ayla's ears. "Tomorrow we'll do the best way."

His body heated as her lips brushed his.

"You look happy." Miranda closed her locker door and leaned against the locker bank. "In fact, you're glowing."

"Don't say that." Ryann tossed a surgical cap at her. "The last time someone said I was glowing I got an eight-pound baby girl."

"Oh!" Miranda shook her head and made a waving sound with her hands toward Ryann. "I release any of that energy. I release any of that energy." She shrugged as Ryann raised a brow. "My sister swears by energies. No idea, but no wishing babies around here."

"So there won't be a little Miranda or Knox dressed as a surgeon on Halloween in a few years?"

"Nope. And Knox would shudder as hard as me. Jackson is the one that always wanted a family, and now he has one."

He does.

"I wanted a family, too." The words felt funny as she let them out. But it was true. When she was alone and wondering where her mother was, she'd dreamed of having her own family, one that loved her.

In the brief times she'd gotten that dream, she'd clung to it tightly hoping this time it would last forever. Except it never did.

"Well, Knox and I are family. Us and Icy—my cat, who kind of likes Knox. He would argue that she puts up with him. I would say that Icy putting up with you is her liking you."

"Drama-queen cat?"

"Yes." Miranda's vigorous nods were silly.

The light moment was one Ryann hadn't shared with another woman in so long.

"But I can never tell Icy that." Miranda giggled. "Do you have any pets?"

"No." She'd had a lizard once. Sort of. She'd begged for a turtle. Ryann wasn't sure why now. The whims of a child.

Her mother had said maybe, then she'd come home with

a bug-catching kit. Not exactly the same. Or even in the same ballpark.

"Maybe one day. But right now, a six-month-old is plenty of excitement."

"Ryann?" Jackson's voice on the other side of the locker room door nearly made her jump. She and Miranda instinctively looked at their pagers as they both raced to the door.

"What?"

"Mr. Nigili's having the surgery." He was beaming so bright.

"Jackson, I thought something was terribly wrong," Ryann said. "We both did!"

His smile made her desire to lightly push him disappear. This was good news.

"Not sure I'd say *terribly*, but you should know better, Jackson." Miranda pulled her left arm in front of her, stretching it, then doing the other. "Time to start rounds!"

"Ryann, this is good news."

"It is like you're reading my mind." She winked. She was a little stunned. The man had seemed more determined to avoid surgery than just about any patient she'd ever seen.

"Sometimes the unexpected is good news." Jackson put an arm around her shoulder and squeezed tightly before releasing her.

"Sometimes," she said. Unfortunately, it was often an emergency or tragedy. If one were to rate the likelihood that an excited call in the hospital was good news versus bad the metrics would look tragic.

Looking at her phone, she frowned. "Wait, I don't have a message from the office. Is he not on my schedule?"

"He will be. As soon as the scheduler gets it on there." Jackson put his hands in front of him and mimicked taking a deep breath. "Think positive thoughts."

"Why do you know before his surgeon?" That didn't make sense, even if she was only focusing on positive things.

"Because he had questions about the anesthesia. The office called me and patched him through. I answered everything. He thanked me and told me to make sure it goes exactly like I told him."

"And you told him you would?" Ryann was stunned. Doctors rarely spoke in absolutes. Routine procedures became emergencies. Things that looked unsurvivable sometimes beat the odds. You could never count the fates out.

"I told him I would do my best." Jackson bopped her nose. "That's all I can do. Ryann—"

"Right. Of course that's what you did. You're perfect." She blew out a breath. Jackson was so close to it.

"No, not perfect," he said. "But I do a pretty good job. After we were done, the scheduler picked him back up. I suspect you will see him on your books shortly."

"Thanks." Ryann hit his hip with hers. "And you are pretty perfect." She liked telling him that. No one had. She knew that.

Rationally she knew no one met the actual definition of the word *perfection*, but Jackson was pretty damn close.

He gave a her a playful salute. "Happy to be of service." Jackson looked at his watch, then said, "Time to prep a little one for tonsil removal."

Jackson headed down the hallway. Watching him walk away was not difficult. His backside was delicious.

Still, her belly twisted. What if he walked away...

It was an intrusive thought. A small one. Easy enough to ignore. Mostly. Clearing her throat, she moved her fingers, doing anything to change her brain's patterns and trick it into focusing on something else.

"Dr. Oliver." Dr. Jenks raised his hand as he started toward her. "I just got paged. They need two orthos in the ER. Now."

"I didn't get paged." She looked down. She was on call here today.

"Nope." Dr. Jenks motioned for her to follow him as he started for the stairwell. "They tried reaching Lewis Anderson first—he's hospital staff. However, he's somewhere else, so you're with me."

"Any idea what we're walking into?" she asked.

"The ER didn't specify, just called it an emergency. Always a good sign." The words were dripping with a sarcasm she understood. The ER was the most overworked place in the hospital. When they said it was an emergency, they had a whole different meaning of that word.

"Dr. Jenks, Dr. Oliver. Here." Mandy Plar, an ER resident, flagged them down. "I have a little boy, age three, in bed six with a broken left tibia. Was playing with his brother and fell off the porch. Can you follow me into the consult room?"

"All right." Dr. Jenks looked at Ryann, and she just shrugged as they followed Mandy. That sounded like a terrible day for the little boy and his family, but broken bones were not uncommon in children. "Is the break that bad?"

A fall from the porch could break a leg, but it often didn't need more than a plaster cast.

"I don't know what I'm looking at, but I'm pretty sure it isn't cancer. Which is why I called the bone guys…and gals." Mandy pulled the X-ray up on a tablet, then pushed it to the consult room's big screen.

Technology!

Ryann blinked as she stared at the image. "How old did you say the patient is?"

"Elijah is three—just had a birthday. Despite the pain,

he'll tell you he had balloons at his party." Mandy smiled. "Kids are fun."

"CPT is rare. Extremely rare. And it almost always presents before three." Dr. Jenks ran his finger over the bow in the leg. "I've never seen this."

"Me either."

"Great—something you know but haven't seen." Mandy clapped. "Now clue in the ER doc?"

"It's congenital pseudarthrosis of the tibia, or CPT." Ryann pointed to the bow in the tibia. "It's a rare presentation, and it means Elijah will need multiple surgeries to lengthen his leg."

"Or amputation." Dr. Jenks shook his head. "Only three."

"Amputation is typically reserved for failed reconstructions." Ryann wanted to shake Dr. Jenks. Amputations happened. They were things that orthopedic surgeons were trained to perform early on. They were also the last resort. They hadn't even met Elijah or his parents.

"Amputations happen with this diagnosis," Dr. Jenks said. "Not unrarely, either."

Unrarely isn't a word.

That wasn't a line that needed to be stated so Ryann kept it to herself.

Dr. Jenks wasn't wrong. However, the parents had come in today thinking their little boy was going to get a cast and were probably wondering how they were going to keep a toddler calm and off the foot for six weeks or so. Now they were finding out their life was changing.

There were worse diagnoses to receive, but that didn't change the fact that this was a difficult day,

The fact that the first fracture hadn't occurred until he was closer to three might mean his bone would heal easier. It could also mean that this first break would be so bad grafting the bone back would be difficult. It was far too early to tell.

"Right now, the important thing is to let them know what we see. Because this treatment isn't happening in the ER." Ryann looked at Mandy. "You need to refer them to an ortho. Splint the broken bone. There's nothing else that can be done today."

"Come with me to talk to the parents?" Mandy asked, looking at the X-ray.

"You don't need both of us." Dr. Jenks lifted a hand and headed off.

He was right. This wasn't an emergency consult, but Mandy was young and this was a condition she might never see again. Even as an orthopedic surgeon, this was likely the only time Ryann would see it.

If the boy came to the Lowery Group, one of the surgeons specializing in legs would be recommended. This wasn't a condition Ryann was ever likely to treat, but she could answer some questions now. And assure the parents that while this was a tricky diagnosis their son was going to live a close to normal life.

It might not be overly comforting today, but she'd do her best.

"So, what food are we thinking of introducing first?" Jackson laughed as Ayla reached for his spoon. The cereal they'd given her over the last week was working well. It was rice-based instead of grain, but she was tolerating it.

"Maybe bananas? Or sweet potatoes?" Those were safe foods because Ryann had eaten them and Ayla hadn't had a reaction.

He bopped Ayla's nose, then turned to Ryann. She was looking at her phone, focusing on it intently. "Ryann?"

"Did you know that an allergy to bananas can mean you're allergic to latex?"

"No." He'd spent time in many specialties but never dealt with allergists. It was an important, vital area of medicine but held little attraction for him.

"Did you have a patient with a latex allergy today that was discovered through bananas?" he asked. He really wasn't sure where the train of thought was coming from, but some days were hard at the hospital.

And it didn't take a tragedy for the day to be heavy.

"No. I saw CPT today—a first." Ryann bit her lip as she looked up at him.

"CPT? Honey?" Jackson was certain she didn't mean chest physiotherapy, which helped cystic fibrosis patients break up the excess mucus in their lungs. What one specialty meant with acronyms did not always transfer.

"Congenital pseudarthrosis of the tibia." She moved her fingers like he'd seen her do several times—twitching the first few fingers, then pulling at them. He wasn't even sure she was aware of the motion.

"All right. I have doctorate, but that is not a diagnosis I know. Rare?"

"Very. I'll probably never see it again in my life," Ryann said. "The little boy broke his leg jumping off a deck. And it probably won't heal. Not without pins and grafts, and he's in for multiple surgeries until he stops growing just to keep his left leg close to the same length as his right."

"Did the parents miss any signs?" he asked. It sounded like a rough diagnosis, but he wasn't sure what it had to do with bananas and latex.

"No, there were no signs. Nothing they could have done. They did exactly what they should have done—brought him to the ER with a broken leg." Ryann put her hands on her hips and blew out a breath. "Sorry. This doesn't have a point. I just… I don't know. You asked about food and said bananas, and my brain just leapt." She tapped the side of her head and rolled her eyes. "Nothing like thoughts running wild, right?"

Maybe that was all it was, but maybe not. "Nothing wrong with a wild thought every once in a while."

Ryann rubbed her arms. "But…"

"But maybe its anxiety." It was a common enough condition, and Ryann saw things the general public didn't every day.

"It isn't."

The certainty in her voice surprised him.

"It isn't a problem if you have anxiety. Lots of people do." Jackson stepped a little closer. "In fact, more than sixty percent of people report—"

"I know the stats, Jackson. You don't have to play nurse with me." Ryann reached for Ayla. "It was a rough day, that's all."

She kissed his cheek. "Now, how about we get this one down and we spend a fun night watching the home and garden channel? I've got a few episodes of *Tiny Home, Big Dreams* saved. I know how much you enjoy it."

"I enjoy spending time with you." Jackson kissed her cheek.

It was only when the show ended that he realized they'd never gotten back to the conversation about which food to start Ayla on.

CHAPTER TEN

RYANN RAN HER hand along Jackson's solid thigh. He let out a soft sigh in his sleep. She couldn't take her eyes from the stunning man. In the light of the early morning, everything seemed relaxed and easy.

The worry that was her constant companion hovered in the very back of the mind as she traced patterns on his dark skin. She wasn't necessarily trying to wake the hot man in her bed, though as his manhood sprang to attention her mind turned to all the delicious ways her body sang when he touched her.

"Jackson Peters." She whispered his name, loving the sound of his name on her tongue. He was such a beautiful man.

"Good morning," he said. His eyes weren't open, and his tone still held all the vestiges of sleep.

"Morning." She dropped a kiss onto his nose. "Did I wake you?" Ryann gripped his manhood, stroking the hard skin. "I didn't mean to."

"I think you got exactly what you want." Jackson grinned as he shifted to his side. His fingers found her folds and stroked her, each pass mimicking the motion she made on him.

When his thumb found her most sensitive spot, she couldn't control the gasp. "I want you." She shuddered as he matched every rhythm on her body.

"Mmm-hmm." Jackson nuzzled against her shoulder, molding his lips to the spot by her throat that sent tingles from the tip of her head to the bottom of her feet. "I want to savor you."

She pushed on his shoulder, rolling him to his back. "We have a six-month-old who is sleeping but might wake any moment," she said. "Savoring is something we get to do in a few years."

A few years...

The phrase was out and she held her breath, but Jackson didn't seem bothered by it. They hadn't talked long-term plans. They were in each other's lives for forever because of Ayla. But this...just like in Hawaii...they'd slipped into it.

Because it felt so natural.

"Ryann..." Jackson ran a hand along the outside of her breast.

She whimpered as his spellbinding touch held her in rapture.

Grabbing a condom, she slid it down his length, then she slipped down his erection, slowly taking him deep within.

His large hands wrapped around her waist, guiding her but not forcing her motions. Jackson looked at her like she was the definition of beauty, his eyes holding hers as she took him.

Ryann let out a breath when they were fully joined. She hadn't misspoken—Ayla could wake any moment. But right now, in this moment, she agreed with Jackson.

Savor...

Her body molded to his. She was a siren, a goddess, a mythical female united in harmony with him.

Jackson's thumb found her clitoris again. He filled her, and she arched, enjoying every bead of pleasure.

"Ryann." His voice was gruff.

He was on the edge of orgasm; she was on the edge, too, but now she wanted this to last forever.

Their daughter had other plans.

Her screech echoed just as Ryann tipped over pleasure's edge. Jackson came seconds later.

"Guess you were right," he said. His lips brushed hers as she slid from him. "You think it's five years or ten before we can safely savor?" Jackson chuckled as he rolled over and waited for her to clean up before following.

Five or ten years.

Tears coated her eyes. Could this be her life…forever?

She wanted to hope so.

Please.

Ryann looked at the jars of baby food Jackson had pulled out last night. Pureed bananas, sweet potatoes, peas and carrots were all in tiny jars with cute cartoon baby faces. Ayla was able to swallow the rice cereal they'd had her on for a few weeks, so this was the next step. Today was a big deal, but not as big a deal as Ryann's brain was screeching.

"Are we trying something for breakfast?" Jackson walked in with Ayla on his hip.

She was wearing a little yellow dress with flowers, and he'd put a headband in her curly hair. She was happy and content, and the image of her in Jackson's arms was a memory Ryann wanted to hold on to for forever.

"I thought maybe." The jars were right there. It was pureed food, and Ayla would have to try something new eventually. Today was as good a day as any. And if there was any reaction, she and Jackson would watch her. Not like her own mom had.

But what if Ayla's tongue itched? That was the feeling

Ryann got with peaches. The allergy made her itch, and if she ate them in high enough doses, she got hives.

It wasn't life-threatening, only uncomfortable. But her mother had told her it was in her head, that the itchy feeling was in her brain—when she'd listened to Ryann at all. Often, she'd waved away the concern.

"Ryann, why is this making you anxious?" Jackson asked.

"She can't tell us if something is wrong," Ryann whispered.

The odds of any of these fruits causing a reaction was slim. But rare outcomes happened. Look at Elijah—his parents had thought he'd broken a bone, only to find out he had a chronic illness that would impact the rest of his life.

"Yes, she can." Jackson's hand rubbed Ryann's lower back, reminding her that she wasn't alone in this.

"Not with words. Not with statements that let us know when she's uncomfortable. Look at the diet I've been on. Her stomach must have ached when I breastfed her with dairy in my system. It must have." And she'd been too tired to catch it until the diaper rash and screams had become unmistakable.

If she'd noticed sooner, her daughter wouldn't have been in such pain.

"Ryann—"

"My tongue itches if I eat peaches." She needed him to understand that this wasn't just an anxiety reaction. She knew what she was talking about, knew the uncomfortable feeling it left her with, even if it didn't send her into an anaphylaxis reaction.

"Oh." Jackson kissed the top of her head. "Well, peach allergies aren't uncommon in those with Mediterranean heritage. Do you know if your mother or father had an allergy?"

Ryann couldn't contain the sad laugh. "Jackson, my mom

never discussed anything that might be helpful or that didn't have to do with her. She still doesn't. She told me until I was eleven that that peach allergy was all in my head."

"In your head." Jackson lifted up Ayla, made a funny face for her, then walked her over to her swing.

After strapping her in and getting the swing going, he moved back to Ryann and pulled her close. "I know she can't say *Mommy, my tongue is itchy*, but there are other ways that she'll let us know."

"Like pushing away a spoon or spitting it out," she said. "Babies do that for things they love when they're testing boundaries. It isn't that simple." There were a million ways for parents to miss things, even when they looked and monitored all the time.

"Yes, and those boundaries are important whether they are because she doesn't like the food, because she isn't hungry, because she is hungry but doesn't want that right now, or because her tongue itches," he said. "We should try the same food with her eight times—that's what the parenting books recommend. That way if it is a new texture or something she might change her mind. But we don't like every food, and neither will she."

"You read a parenting book?" Ryann pursed her lips as her eyes coated with tears for the second time today. This man really got to her. In all the right ways.

"No." Jackson winked. "So far I've read *four* parenting books—well, read two the traditional way and listened to two with audiobook credits."

"Perfection, thy name is Jackson." She'd been with Ayla since the first twist in her belly. The first breath. First diapers, baths, breastfeeding. And yet she wasn't nearly as confident as the man standing beside her.

"Not perfect," he said, the tone shifting, but the darkening of his cheeks was unmistakable.

He liked being called perfect, and for her, he'd certainly been.

"So…" Jackson gestured to the jars. "What's the first pick?"

Ryann looked at them, then over at her daughter. "What if we let Ayla pick? All of these are good starts, so we can make a game of it."

"That's a perfect plan."

The pea puree hit Jackson square in the eye, and if his glasses hadn't protected him Ayla would have scored a direct hit to his eyeball.

"I did tell you not to try the peas again. I know the baby book suggests introducing the food to them several times, but she hates peas."

Ryann didn't even attempt to cover the grin on her face as she poured their tea into travel mugs. She'd been sprayed with peas last night and swore it was still in her hair after her shower. It hadn't been—Jackson had made sure of that for her before going to bed.

"Ah. Ah." Ayla pointed to the cupboard where the banana puree she adored was hidden out of sight. The kid liked carrots, would tolerate the sweet potatoes, but the peas…those were simply weapons in her tiny fingers.

Ryann wandered to the cabinet and pulled out the carrots. "I know that at six and half months she can't technically be a tiny dictator."

"Oh, I think she certainly can. She just isn't trying to be." Jackson took the washcloth and the carrots from Ryann, opening the can as soon as his glasses were clear—again.

He started feeding Ayla as Ryann whispered the day's plan to herself.

"The surgery is going to go fine. Tell Mama that she's going to do great." Jackson spooned the carrots slipping down Ayla's chin back into her mouth.

"I know it will be fine."

He wasn't sure she heard her heavy sigh at the end of her sentence. "It's standard."

"I know," she said.

"The patient is healthy." Jackson could list a million reasons why Mr. Nigili's hand surgery would turn out fine. Unfortunately, there were a dozen reasons it might not.

A dozen reasons compared to a million didn't sound like much—unless you were the patient or the one holding the scalpel.

"I know." Ryann looked at her watch and tapped her foot. They weren't due at the hospital for another hour. And he was technically due first, as he needed to get the sedation prep done.

But she was already antsy.

"It's standard. Minor in the grand scheme of things, but he's terrified." Ryann pulled her curly hair out of the ponytail and then put it back up again. "I mean, he's heard *standard* before."

His wife's surgery had been back surgery. Even routine back surgery was not routine. The same argument they'd made that day in her office to Mr. Nigili hung in the back of Jackson's throat. It hadn't done any good that day, and he doubted it would help here.

"Sometimes I just wish life had a fast-forward button." Ryann playfully picked up the TV remote and pointed it at herself. "Nope. Fast-forward doesn't work on me." Her dark gaze found his. "Want me to try it on you?"

"Don't you dare." Jackson tossed the rag with peas at her, deliberately aiming a foot in front of her feet so it didn't cause any actual damage. "I'm having too much fun in my life. I already missed months—I'm not rushing anything else."

Last night when she'd joked that it would be years before they could trust their intimate times wouldn't be interrupted by a baby's cry had been the third happiest of his life.

Third only to meeting Ryann and then meeting Ayla. Two things that could never be topped.

"Yes, yes, Mr. Perfect wants to live every moment," she said. She grabbed the rag and kissed his cheek on the way to drop it in the sink.

"Not perfect." Jackson grinned at Ayla, enjoying Ryann's favorite description of him a little too much. It wasn't true, and that was something people always seemed to realize about him at some point.

And then they disappeared from his life.

Jackson blinked, forcing the uncomfortable thoughts away. They were both just antsy today. Or maybe Ryann's antsy was rubbing off on him.

"Spall!" The sound his daughter made was the only warning he got before she grabbed the spoon and threw it over the high chair onto the floor.

"I guess breakfast is over, then." Jackson kissed her head, reached for the spoon and handed it back so she could throw it a few more times.

Ryann picked it up on the fourth throw. "Time to go," she said. She bent down and kissed the top of Ayla's head while passing him the wet rag.

"Making me the bad guy that has to clean her up?" he said. How a tiny human could manage to fight off a wet rag so well while strapped to a chair was an answer only the heavens could give.

"I'm the bad guy putting away the spoon. We each play

our roles." Ryann's smile showed that she knew which was the better role…and this morning she'd taken it.

The music floated through the surgical suite as a nurse pressed a cloth to Ryann's forehead. The sweat on her brow was from the surgical lights, nothing more, because this was going routinely.

"I'm going to close." Ryann looked to Jackson and saw him nod as his gaze stayed focused on the patient.

Everything about this had been textbook. There were two surgical residents who'd asked to watch from the gallery, and what they'd seen today was how surgery was supposed to go.

"Closed," Ryann said as she passed the tool to the nurse at her side and stepped back from Mr. Nigili. She'd be able to give his daughter the good news, and when he woke his family would be at his side.

"All right, let's get him to recovery." Jackson's deep voice echoed in the room, and she looked over her shoulder.

The man was hot in anything. But the blue surgical scrubs that looked drab on everybody else made him mouthwatering. Because he was in his element here.

In the surgical suite he was confident, in total control, and it was intoxicating.

She wasted no time giving Mr. Nigili's family the update and letting them know that a nurse would be out to take them to his recovery room shortly.

Today was exactly the kind of day a surgeon wanted.

"Ryann!" The call came from behind her.

Knox was running. Never a good sign.

"ER page—all hands on deck."

Damn. When was she going to remember that the good times always were warning signs of the bad to come?

Knox pushed open the ER doors, and the sound of chaos

echoed through the halls. To the uneducated eye, the ER always looked a little chaotic, but it was a well-oiled machine that functioned in that kind of chaos.

This kind. The all hands on deck, the waiting for multiple traumas. Trauma situations like this were what television show thrived on and what every doctor feared.

"Crane collapsed downtown. Four inbound with internal injuries. Two head traumas, one amputation and others to be determined!"

The head nurse's call echoed in the hallway as Miranda ran up next to them, followed by Dr. O'Sullivan and Dr. Jenks.

"Are they all coming here? What about County Hospital?" Knox crossed his arms, them uncrossed them. The wait was the worst. Knowing each moment counted in trauma but unable to start supporting the patients until they arrived and were assessed.

"Every hospital in the city with a trauma bay will be full. And it still might not be enough. It is going to be a long, hard day." Dr. O'Sullivan let out a sigh as the first siren sounded in the distance. "All the elective surgeries are canceled, and I've got every available suite readying to put patients under."

"The crane hit a building, going through a boardroom before crashing to the crowded street. Many were hit while videotaping and the debris field." One of the nurses called as she started passing out details for the cases they knew were headed to Hope.

Dr. O'Sullivan looked at his watch. "The first priorities are the internal injuries. I'll take the first one, Knox number two, then Miranda, then Stephen. Amputations go to Ryann and then Dr. Jenks. After that, we each handle whatever triage sends us next."

The siren sounded in the parking lot. "All right, people. Here we go."

CHAPTER ELEVEN

EXHAUSTING WAS NOT a descriptor for today. *Exhausting* didn't even come close to the feeling deep in Jackson's bones as he stared at what was hopefully the screens of his last patient.

"Everything all right over there?" Ryann's voice was strained. She'd done six surgeries in the last twelve hours. This one was minor—reattachment of ligaments torn when a woman had pushed her daughter out of the way of the crane.

The woman was a hero. The video of the incident had already gone viral—at least according to the nurse, who'd heard it from one of the techs, who'd heard it from someone in triage, who'd heard it from a patient. Or that was the trajectory of the rumor.

"She's fine," Jackson said. She'd waited longer than any of the other patients, which meant she'd been in pain for longer than any of them but also meant that she'd been stable enough to wait.

"The tendon was already inflamed. Her shoulder must have hurt for months." The nurse's mused thoughts were probably designed more to keep her focused following the long day than to produce actual conversation.

"We're almost done, Renee." Ryann asked for a scalpel and then let out an expletive.

"She's still out," Jackson said. He wasn't sure what Ryann

was seeing, but his monitors were all showing the patient was stable, which was most important.

"The ulnar nerve is entrapped."

"At her shoulder?" Renee sounded shocked.

"It's less common than wrist or elbow entrapment, but it still happens," Ryann said. "But it means this went from a short tendon repair...to an entrapment repair. How did I miss this on the X-ray?"

"It's been a long day." Jackson could tell from her tone that she was mad at herself. Ryann's perfectionist streak ran deep.

"It's standard," she muttered.

It was. Sort of. If it had been an X-ray of the wrist or elbow it would have been spotted immediately. Still, Ryann felt she should have seen it. But then so should've the ER doctor. She wasn't solely at fault here.

"She'll be okay." Jackson kept his voice level. He was a colleague in this situation, not her...his mind blanked on terms.

They'd never actually discussed what they were. He was practically living at her condo. They were sleeping together, and not just in the intimate way but falling asleep in each other's arms. They were raising their daughter.

Boyfriend...partner...baby daddy? Certainly not that last one. It was technically true, but he wasn't a fan of the term.

"The compression is significant. I'll have to clear a larger area." Ryann sighed. "She must have used all the force she could to push her daughter out of the way."

Nerve compression caused weakness, tingling and eventually muscular wasting.

"That's what moms do." The nurse's voice was bright, and he heard the awkwardness that followed when Ryann didn't say anything.

He was glad the nurse seemed to have had that kind of

mom. When she was an adult, Jackson hoped Ayla would have the exact same reaction.

Growing up without such a figure hurt. Children knew when their mom didn't want them or was exasperated by them. Everything reinforced the societal expectations that moms protected their children.

And neither of their mothers had done that. In fact, those women had pretty much taken society's expectations and stuffed them.

"She should feel better once she heals." Ryann cleared her throat. "I need my forehead wiped, please."

She was tired. If today had gone the way they'd expected, they'd have been back at the condo, eating dinner, getting Ayla ready for her nighttime routine. The babysitter had been alerted to the emergency, though it was apparently all over the news. Ayla would be with her until they were cleared to leave.

"Why didn't I catch this?" Ryann's words were barely audible over the pop music they'd piped into the surgical suit. Every song was above eighty beats per minute, a weird trick to force the brain to stay active.

"Are you close to closing?" He rolled his shoulders. They both needed some sleepy-time tea and decompression.

"Is there a problem?" she asked.

Not with the patient.

"No, she's handling anesthesia well." It was Ryann who Jackson was worried about. She blamed herself for things others let slide away.

"All right, I've got about twenty minutes left."

Then they were finishing up the paperwork and going home. They'd both earned the rest, and he was going to spend the evening reminding Ryann that she didn't need to never make mistakes to be the best version of herself.

* * *

Jackson flipped on the news and looked at the damage the crane had done in downtown Phoenix. The tallest crane in Arizona…at least until yesterday afternoon. It was a miracle only one person had lost their life, though dozens of lives had changed forever.

The anchor's solemn tone shifted, and he offered a smile. "There are many harrowing videos from the tragedy. However, one video is giving people a sense of awe and showing the world a mother's love."

Jackson reached for the remote; Ryann didn't need to see this.

"No, wait. That's Priscilla." She grabbed the remote before he could. Slowing the screen down to half speed.

"Remember when we had to watch the television in real time?" Jackson leaned toward Ayla. "Once upon a time, you had to watch a show when it was on, and if you missed something…oh, well."

Ryann gave him a look, but she didn't say anything. "Look. Right there." She pointed to the grimace Priscilla made before she pushed her daughter.

A few milliseconds later the shrapnel hit Priscilla and then screen of the camera.

"That video already has over six million views." The anchor's voice started then stopped as Ryann ran the video back.

"The pain in her shoulder was there before."

"Just like you said it would be." Jackson reached for Ayla as she made a face that was nothing more than a warning sign. They had about three minutes to get her fed before she decided to try to bring the walls of the house down with her cries.

He walked into the kitchen and grabbed the bananas. "If

you think about it, she's lucky the crane went down in a weird way."

"How?" The horrified look on Ryann's face made it clear what she thought of his statement.

"It's clear she was in pain before the incident, and that pain was picked up by the ER."

"Who misdiagnosed a tendon tear." Ryann crossed her arms. "Then I looked and didn't…"

"Let me finish before you castigate yourself for something that is not your fault." Jackson took a deep breath. That was not what he'd meant to say. "I just mean, let me explain."

Ryann rolled her hand toward him, fire blazing in her eyes.

"She was in pain for a while, maybe years. The crane crash means that her injury gets fixed, and it's likely the crane company, or rather their insurance, will have to pay for it. Those are bright points."

"A crane collapsed!" Ryann looked at the television, then back at him. "The thing fell on twenty people, and it hit five in the boardroom, the shrapnel struck an additional six and then there was the four car accidents caused from rubbernecking."

"I know." Jackson held up the spoon with banana puree enjoying Ayla's smile. This tragedy hadn't touched her but others would. It was unfortunate but no life was lived without pain and loss. "I'm just looking for the silver lining."

"Silver linings are a myth." Ryann sucked in a deep breath, then turned on her heel. "I'm taking a shower."

He stared after her for a second, then looked at Ayla. "Any ideas?"

Ayla made a few gibberish noises.

"Sounds reasonable." Jackson tapped her nose, keeping the smile he didn't really feel on his face for her.

* * *

The sun was streaming through the window when Ryann rolled over. Her hand hit Jackson's empty pillow, and she immediately sat up. She'd told him she hadn't wanted to talk about what had upset her yesterday morning.

He'd agreed. Half-heartedly.

She could tell he'd wanted to argue, wanted to have out whatever issue had been standing between them. But the issue wasn't his fault. Nothing about what he'd done or said was wrong.

Hell, the man was perfection. She almost wished he'd forced the argument. Then she might feel better about over-reacting to his statement about silver linings.

Don't get upset; look for the silver lining.

Her mother's voice echoed in her head as Ryann slid out of bed. She needed to find Jackson, apologize for getting upset and then for spending the day quiet and upset.

"Morning." Jackson handed her a cup of tea as soon as she stepped into the kitchen. Ayla was asleep in her swing.

"She got up about two hours ago," he said. "Wanted a bottle and then went back down."

Jackson smiled at their daughter, answering the unasked question before Ryann's brain had even formed it.

Sometimes it was tough to live up to the flawlessness that was the man in front of her. "Aren't you mad at me?"

She'd spent yesterday brooding and rethinking and just sad. No, mad. She'd been mad at herself, mad at the world and mad at...

"Do you want me to be mad?" Jackson leaned against the counter.

"Maybe." That wasn't rational. "No. Of course I don't." She blew a curl away from her eye. "It's just... Don't you have anything in your past that you just can't stand now? A phrase, a food?"

"I try to keep the past in its place." Jackson shrugged.

Maybe he had put everything from his past in a nice box marked Do Not Open, but she wasn't able to.

"I… I…hate silver linings." She was tapping her fingers against the tea mug. "Not the actual things but the words. I hate that phrase." Ryann shook as she drew in a breath. "There's nothing positive about suffering, about resiliency."

She set the mug of tea down, worried that she might drop it or spill it as her hands shook. "*Resiliency* is a fancy term for surviving. What other choice do you have?"

"Ryann—"

"No. No. I don't want you to *Ryann* me in that sweet voice that tells me everything is going to be fine. I messed up. I didn't see it on the X-ray. I messed up. And…"

"And it happens. The patient, Priscilla, is fine. Better than fine. She is going to make a full recovery and have little to no pain moving forward." Jackson said. "Yes, you should have seen it. So should the ER doctor. So should her primary care physician."

"Her primary care physician wasn't there." Being pedantic wasn't a great look. But her argumentative side didn't seem to want to shut the hell up.

How many times had she just let words like this roll over her?

Have you considered that your upbringing prepared you for the hectic life a surgeon leads?

Maybe everything happens for a reason and it made you the person you were supposed to be.

Ever thought that maybe the universe chose you for that life because you could handle it?

All platitudes to make others feel better. If it was a grand plan or something that made her stronger, then it was okay that she'd had a rough childhood. It was okay that people had missed the signs, let her fall through the cracks.

That made them feel better, not her.

"I looked at her records after surgery while you were finishing up your paperwork," Jackson said. "She's complained to her primary care physician about the weakness and tingling for almost two years. He told her to lose weight."

Now Ryann really was seeing red. Women's complaints were often overlooked. Add in someone who society labeled *fat* and you got a recipe for pushing aside any issues.

As much as she hated the term *silver lining*, this one actually did have one. For Priscilla.

"You looked at her records for me, didn't you?" Of course he would pick up on her beating herself up in the operating room. The man seemed to miss nothing.

"I looked at her records as her anesthesiologist," Jackson said. "We missed the nerve compression—I wanted to make sure there wasn't anything else."

He doesn't miss anything.

"This isn't your fault, Ryann. And she's fine."

"I know." That was the thing. She knew Priscilla was fine. She knew there was nothing she could have done once she'd gotten her open. But her brain kept playing things back, asking what-ifs that had no answers.

It kept looking for a sign she'd missed. Except in this case, it knew exactly what the sign was. The X-ray and what she'd missed in it. So it had a latch. Something to cling to.

"I know she's fine," Ryann said. "And I even know that given the day, there's nothing I could have done differently. I was looking for obstructions and broken bones on that X-ray, not nerve compression. She was the last patient on a day when triage saw the worst. I know all of that."

"But your brain won't shut off."

"Spoken like someone who can shut theirs off." Ryann shook her head. "I'm sorry. I don't know why I'm hyper-focusing on this."

"Maybe because it's the easy case to hyper-focus on, the one that turned out all right." He tilted his head.

Had he ever considered going into one of the therapy career fields? Ryann wondered. He'd be an excellent therapist.

And he was right. The night's other cases had not been nearly as straightforward. The change in those patient's lives less rosy.

She'd saved one hand from amputation...for now. But the odds were not in the gentleman's favor. And she'd had to amputate a teenager's foot. Priscilla's shoulder had been the easiest, the one where the oversight had mattered least.

"You should be a therapist, Mr. Perfect." Ryann took a deep breath, mentally releasing the anxious thoughts. Or trying to.

Jackson chuckled. "I never felt called to the mental health field. I love nursing, love learning. Most of it is listening."

"You're an excellent listener."

"Well, when no one listens to you growing up, you either listen to everyone or no one." Jackson grabbed the cup of tea she'd sat down and put it back into her hands.

"Jackson," she said, laying her hand over his. "I'm sorry no one listened to you."

"I turned out fine." He winked.

"Jackson..." It felt like he was close to giving her more information, to opening himself up to her. Outside of knowing that no one had responded well to his outreach on the DNA-matching sites, she knew next to nothing about his past. It was like he'd erected a solid wall around that part of his life.

All of it locked away, never to be visited or discussed. But that didn't mean it didn't impact him.

"So do you think we should take Ayla to the balloon festival tomorrow?" he asked. "I know she's too little to get the full experience, but they are brightly colored."

"You don't have to change the subject." Ryann squeezed his hand.

"I'm not." He kissed her cheek. "There's nothing to discuss."

"I think there is," Ryann said, seeing his jaw twitch. It was the first time she'd seen him frustrated with her. And it was tiny, barely even noticeable.

"There isn't." He let out a heavy sigh. "I was foster-care kid. My parents abandoned me. My fiancée left me for reasons only she fully knows. I love my job, my daughter and…"

And me?

She saw words dance through his eyes, but he didn't say anything else.

"And?" Ryann shouldn't push, but she wanted to. She loved him. Maybe she had from the moment he'd sat on the plane next to her. Everything with Jackson came so easily.

Scarily easily. Like it was fate. Her mother would love that analogy.

"My life in general. It's pretty close to perfection." Jackson set his teacup down and pulled her close. "So, Ryann…"

Her heartbeat accelerated. He was going to say he loved her, going to kiss her. Maybe hearing those words, knowing someone like Jackson loved her would drive out the voices that never seemed to quite let her think she was enough.

"Do you think Ayla would like the balloon festival? Or should we find something inside so the heat doesn't get to her?"

"Oh…" Ryann blinked. Of course that was where this conversation was going.

Ayla let out a cry, and Jackson kissed Ryann's head, then went to get their daughter.

"Mommy is trying to figure out what we're going to do on our day off tomorrow." Then he looked at his phone. "Oh… um… Knox needs me."

"Is he okay?" Ryann took Ayla, hating that she was a little happy that he needed to leave. That would give her some time to compose herself, to get the feelings, the urge to tell him she loved him fully under control.

"I think so. He's being secretive, which probably means he's planned something for Miranda. The man's favorite hobby is spoiling the woman he loves."

"Sounds nice." Ryann nuzzled her head into Ayla's curls. "Let's get you changed, sweetie."

CHAPTER TWELVE

JACKSON DRUMMED HIS fingers on the steering wheel as he drove up to Knox and Miranda's condo. He'd nearly told Ryann that he loved her this morning. He'd wanted to tell her. His entire soul ached with the desire.

But the woman was a flight risk. She hadn't even wanted to date him. She'd given into that urge, but would she worry about his love ending?

Her mother's relationships all seemed to evaporate after she and her partners pledged their undying love.

Jackson would love Ryann for the rest of his days. There wasn't a single doubt in his body. But Ryann's body was riddled with worry. He wouldn't add this to it. The second she told him she loved him he'd make sure she understood the depth of his own devotion.

But until then, he'd keep the feelings—and the worry—to himself.

Pulling up to the condo, Jackson couldn't stop his mouth from falling open. Outside, there were at least three dozen balloons and boxes upon boxes stacked. What had Knox gotten himself into?

He parked on the street, got out and wasn't surprised to see Knox look over a box as he heard the car door slam.

"What is going on?"

"That is a good question." Miranda sighed as she moved a box to the side. "Knox?"

"I won a bar in an online auction. Or rather, I won the bar's contents."

"That clears up nothing." Jackson looked at the boxes.

"I thought I was bidding on a vintage Maitland-Smith dartboard. I mean, that is what I was bidding on. Who clears out a bar for two grand?"

"Two grand?" Miranda's leaned against the box in front of her. "You spent two thousand dollars on a dartboard? Knox! You can get a super nice board—one that doesn't have holes in it—for less than a hundred."

"I know, but I mean, come on, sweetheart. A Maitland-Smith."

Jackson crossed his arms and didn't manage to catch the laugh in the back of his throat. "I don't think that means anything to anyone but you, man."

"It should." Knox looked to Miranda, who just shook her head.

She threw up her hands before walking over and kissing his cheek. "I love you. I'm going on my spa day as planned," she said. "Any chance you and Jackson can get this gone before I'm back? And not in the house," she added. "Other than the very impressive Maitland-Smith dartboard."

"She's perfect." Knox said. He waved as he watched Miranda walk to the car.

When she was gone, Knox looked at Jackson. "What exactly am I supposed to do with this?"

"Bit off more than you could chew, huh?" Jackson laughed. "Your love of darts finally got you."

"Think Ryann needs barstools? You can probably get the cigarette smell out of them."

"You heard yourself, right? The thing I want to ask the

woman I love—honey, want some old barstools? Knox thinks they won't always smell of smoke." Jackson laughed. "I'm sure our baby would enjoy pulling them over."

He could see Ryann's exasperated face. Hell, it would look almost identical to Miranda's.

"Love." Knox leaned against a box. "You love her."

"Yes," he said. Knox was the one person in the world who understood the childhood he'd had. Sort of. They'd become brothers as teens. Inseparable. The rock each had needed.

But even Knox didn't know everything. No one but Jackson needed those memories.

"And she loves you?" Knox raised his brows, enjoying this too much.

"Don't know." Jackson opened a box and made a face at him. "This is trash."

"Probably. I think they legit packed everything but the booze and just shipped it." He pointed to a pile by the side of the house. "If nothing is salvageable, it goes in that pile. But don't change the subject. You're too good at that."

"Ryann agrees on that," he said. But it wasn't true. Not really. Or maybe it was, but he'd had to get good at shifting topics. It was survival skill in care—and life.

"So you love her but don't know if she loves you?" Knox opened the box in front of him, made a face and closed it back up.

"Woulda been cheaper to just toss this rather than ship it."

"I paid for shipping. That was one thousand of it."

"And that didn't raise your brow? Really, Knox." Jackson opened another box—this one had glasses in it. He didn't need them and they weren't Ryann's style, but someone would use them. "Where is the donation pile?"

His and Knox's first place had been stocked with odds and ends picked up for free on the side of the road or dirt cheap at garage sales. They knew every place that took donations to help out those needing to start fresh…or just start period.

"Over there," Knox said. "Stop changing the subject."

"No, I don't know if she loves me. And I don't want to tell her that I love her because then she might run. She thinks love doesn't last." Jackson pulled at the back of his neck. "And the worst part is I can't even take that worry away from her. I mean, who do I know that has stayed together more than a few years?" he said.

"My parents rotated through partners, most of the foster homes I was in weren't exactly loving relationships and Marie left with little warning, never telling me exactly what I'd done wrong." She'd wanted him to talk more, to open up to her. When he had, when he'd told her his whole story, she'd looked at him like he was broken. Like she hated that she had the burden of knowledge. Two weeks later she'd told him she didn't think they were a good fit.

When he'd asked why, Marie had just said the words again. Not a good fit. Then she'd left.

"Maybe you didn't do anything wrong. Maybe it was just Marie." The words were quiet, and he was glad Knox's head was buried in a box.

Jackson's stomach was at his feet and tears threatened. It was comforting to think he hadn't done anything wrong. Comforting, but wrong. Everyone left him eventually. So that meant it had to be him.

"And Miranda and I are still in love." Knox held up a hand. "Before you say, *Oh, but it's only been six months*. So? The woman had thirty-two boxes of trash, sixteen barstools and one very nice vintage dartboard delivered to her condo this morning, and she still loves me."

"No small miracle there," Jackson said. He opened a box containing nothing but old rags. Seriously, who packed this?

"Yeah, she really is the best."

"You make good points," he conceded, mostly to end the conversation.

"I know." His brother's smile was bright and happy. "So you are going to tell her that you love her?"

Jackson shrugged. "Sure."

"I don't believe you." Knox sighed. "All right. Let's open each of these, see if there is anything salvageable."

Ryann waved at Jackson as he wandered down the hallway, unable to stop the worry pressing at the back of her mind. He'd been different for a week…since getting an emergency call to help Knox with one of the most off-the-wall scenarios she'd ever heard of.

"Why the long face? Do you also have a 'vintage' dartboard hanging in your living room?"

"Miranda." Ryann bit her lip to keep the laughter in her chest from slipping out. "You are the last person I would have expected to see use air quotes."

"It is fitting." She pulled her phone from her scrub pocket. "Look at this."

The screen showed a picture of a dartboard—an ugly one, though were any dartboards cute? Aesthetics were in the eye of the beholder.

"It's something." Ryann bit her lip, unsure of what else she was meant to say.

"It's ugly as hell," Miranda said as she slid her phone back into her pocket.

"Then why is it in the living room?"

"Because that's the only place in the condo big enough for the man I love to stand regulation distance to throw the darts."

"I see." She didn't.

"He loves darts. And I love him." Miranda chuckled. "Good thing he never misses."

"Never?"

"No, he hustled in bars growing up." She paused. "He and Jackson had a rough upbringing. But you know that."

Ryann knew some of it but really nothing more than the basics she'd learned the day he'd met Ayla. And the fact that he'd had a fiancée who'd "upgraded," as though that was even possible. The man was a pro at shifting the topic.

"Jackson doesn't talk about it." Ryann whispered the words—somehow that felt like a secret, though it wasn't. Not really.

Miranda reached out, rubbing Ryann's shoulder as she said, "Jackson protects people."

"Yes, but I'm not people, I'm…" Ryann lost the words. What was she? The mother of his child. The woman he woke up next to every morning.

The woman who loved him. That was terrifying. Love was an emotion without control. You couldn't stop it, couldn't hold it. There was no way to manage it, only the effects of its loss.

Her mother had managed by falling for another person fast, dancing between loves. Ryann had never felt this way, so certain that Jackson was hers and terrified that one day he might not be. It was as if her body was simultaneously thrilled and terrified.

"You are—" Whatever Miranda might have said was interrupted by both their pagers. "Damn."

They took off toward the ORs. Whatever today might have been was morphing fast into something much worse.

Ryann pulled the surgical cap off her head and leaned against the locker banks.

"I hate days like today." Miranda threw her surgical cap to the ground and wiped a tear off her cheek.

"Me, too," she said. Ryann's patient had a traumatic brain injury. She'd repaired the damage to the leg, putting it in traction, while the neurosurgeon had done everything they could. To say it had been touch-and-go was an understatement.

And even if he survived, his life was going to look different.

One patient was gone, the other fighting for their life.

"I want to go home, hug my cat, eat a pint of ice cream and scream into the shower." Miranda slammed her locker closed. "I don't know what's worse—the days where the trauma feels routine… I mean, hell, this was a car accident. They happen every hour."

"Or days like today?" Ryann wrapped her arms around herself. "When it feels personal."

It was always personal, but to survive in this field you had to be able to put it away. At least somewhat. Or it would drive you from the profession.

"Ice cream. Cat. Hugs from Knox."

"Sounds like a good plan." Ryann grabbed her keys. Jackson wasn't off for another few hours, but she was going to get Ayla. And then lose herself in design shows.

She waved to Miranda as she headed to the stairwell.

"Oh!" Ryann grabbed the door before it could hit the young woman sitting in the stairwell. "Are you okay?"

The answer was no. The tear streaks on her cheeks, the runny nose and the red eyes should have clued in Ryann's brain. But it was a phrase you uttered automatically when you nearly hit someone with door.

"My boyfriend died." The woman choked back a sob. "Boyfriend. We lived together for six years. He asked me to marry him half a dozen times, but I don't—didn't—believe in marriage." She leaned her head against her knees. "But he did. And I…" She lost herself in sobs.

Ryann pulled her phone from her back pocket. She sent a quick text to the head nurse, requesting the assistance of a counselor or chaplain. Then she sat on the step beside the woman.

"He wanted it, and I just... I just never did. I think he thought I'd come around." She hiccupped. "And I would have, too. I would have. I almost said yes last time. He never pushed. Not Kellen. He just said *you let me know when*."

Ryann made some noncommittal noises. There wasn't much to say. There was little she could do to provide comfort right now. The woman was in shock, and Ryann was a stranger, a person she'd never remember—or if she did, her brain probably wouldn't be able to place her.

"I should have said yes. Why didn't I say yes? Life is so short, and I just..."

The stairwell door opened, and the chaplain slipped in. The older white woman motioned to the step where Ryann was sitting. She got up, changing seats with the chaplain without the sobbing woman noticing.

The chaplain squeezed Ryann's hand before she put her hand on the crying woman's shoulder. "I am so sorry for your loss."

Ryann started down the stairs; she made it a flight before her own tears started. Life wasn't fair. She'd known that since she'd been a child.

Today, though, today was a reminder that it was short. Miranda wanted her cat, a pint of ice cream and Knox. Ryann needed Ayla, a pint of ice cream—which she couldn't have—and Jackson.

CHAPTER THIRTEEN

"WHY DO YOU have a dozen balloons?" Ryann backed out of the doorway as Jackson pulled the balloons through the door.

"It was a rough day. I thought you might like them." Jackson's laugh was full, but there was a look in his eye that sent a bead of worry across her skin, like he was assessing something.

Was this the day he said she was too much?

Ryann, come on! she told herself.

Everything was fine. Mostly. Yes, over the last few days she'd caught him watching her, a pensive look in his eyes, like he was waiting for something.

And her brain was intent on filling the questions it developed with the worst-case scenarios, despite there being no evidence that would make anyone else worry.

"I love balloons," Ryann said as she smiled at the pink, purple, blue and black balloons in the bunch.

"I remember." Jackson grinned.

His smile lit a flame in her soul. Today had been rough as he'd said, but there was good in just about every twenty-four hours.

And balloons from the man she loved would always count as good.

She pushed one, unable to contain the laughter as it moved. "This is so silly." She pushed it again. How many times had she asked her mom for a balloon after her first stepfather had left, just because it was something happy he'd brought? Probably hundreds.

And no balloons had ever appeared.

But Jackson remembered a throwaway comment from before they'd ever gotten back together. Something he'd had no reason to lock away in his memory. He'd remembered, for her.

"Of course. You were so jealous of the get-well balloon. Who gets jealous of a get-well balloon?" His strong arms wrapped around her. His head rested on her shoulder, and she leaned into him. "Your text said you were craving ice cream and can't have it for Ayla. I walked through the frozen section. I didn't find anything that would work, then I thought—balloons!"

This was peace. This was perfection.

"I love you, Ryann," he said. "You don't have to say anything. I just need you to know I love you."

Such simple words. Words people had told each other in some form from the beginning of time. Words they believed in the moment.

Her mother had said them to countless partners—repeated them, then screamed them, then cried over them, then moved on from them. Ryann wondered if she'd ever had the deep peace of them.

And if she did, does that mean the words are still cursed?

"I love you, too," she said. Turning in his arms, she wrapped her hands around him, holding him.

It was such a small moment. Yet part of her expected the heavens to start singing, for the world to hold its rotation for a second. A recognition of this important step.

But maybe this was what love really was. The peace of knowing you were with the person you were meant to be with.

"Where's Ayla?" Jackson's hand slid down her stomach. Even through the cotton of her shirt her skin flamed.

"Sleeping. Not sure how long she'll stay down." Ryann captured his lips. She relished the way their bodies fitted, the need to be with him, to push away the day's unhappiness with him.

His arms shifted, and the next thing she knew she was cradled in his arms. His tongue traced her lips as he carried her back to their bedroom.

Their.

"Ryann…"

Her name on his lips sent her body into pleasure. He laid her on their bed, stripping her clothes from her piece by piece. When she reached for his shirt, he grabbed her fingers, kissing the tips of each one.

"I plan on enjoying every single second with you, honey, and I can't do that if you touch me. Because…" He leaned his head into hers, swirling his tongue on the sensitive spot where her neck met her shoulder. "…I'm already on a knife's edge just from your words."

"Jackson…"

"I do love when pleasure makes you slur my name." His fingers danced across her breasts, teasing one nipple and then the other before tracing the curvature. The touch was not enough and too much all at once.

"Ayla?" As much as she loved the idea of spending the evening being worshipped by the man she loved, they might have all night or just a few minutes.

"Will wake when she wakes. If tonight is about your pleasure only, that's fine with me." His fingers skimmed her inner thigh, stroking ever closer to her core. "Let me pleasure you, honey."

Then he dipped his head to her mound, and Ryann lost the ability to track anything but the cascading waves of pleasure falling over her.

* * *

The morning sun was basking Jackson in all his glory as she lay on her side looking at him. Ayla had cooperated last night. And she'd only been up once all night. She'd likely make her presence known in a few minutes, but for now, this precious time was Ryann and Jackson's.

She let her fingers trail along his stomach. Not enough to wake him. Not enough to drive pleasure through him. But enough to remind her that he was here. In her bed. A man she loved, who loved her.

The twinge of uncertainty pressed at her core, but with the sun dancing on his features it was easy to ignore.

Just because her mother had terrible luck with men didn't mean Ryann had, too. She bit her lip as the memories of her mother, tears spilling down her cheeks, screaming at a partner, filled her mind. Her mother's life.

And mine.

But not in the same way. It wasn't the same. Jackson wasn't the same.

"If you bite your lip any harder, you're going to taste blood." Jackson ran his hand down her back. A morning ritual between comfortable lovers, not a passionate touch. It was weird to like this one as much as the other.

"I wasn't," she said.

His finger reached up, pulling her bottom lip from between her teeth.

"I… I wasn't even aware."

"I believe that." Jackson sat up, grabbed his glasses from the bedside table, then pulled her into his arms. "So, what were you not-thinking about?"

"My mother's failed relationships." Ryann let out a sigh, curling into him. "I know I'm not her and you aren't any of my stepparents, but I only ever saw one kind of relationship growing up."

"The kind that ended." Jackson kissed her forehead. "Yeah, me, too."

"Your mother got through a lot of relationships?" Ryann wrapped her arms around his waist, leaning her head against his shoulder. She felt the deep pull of his breath, heard the start of his statement and then a pause.

"Not sure."

The words were crisp. But there was a hint on the end of them. Like it wasn't the truth. Or at least not the whole truth.

Her tongue felt dry. "Jackson?"

"I'm here for you and Ayla. Forever." Jackson kissed her head.

Forever.

That sounded nice. It was exactly what she should want to hear. Her soul craved the idea, but her brain seemed determined to think the word had meant very little in the past.

Not with Jackson.

"I can see the wheels spinning," Jackson said. He tapped the side of her head, then kissed the same spot. "It's okay."

"Right." Of course it was. She was letting a past that wasn't even technically hers cloud today's pleasures.

"If you didn't see your mom's relationships—"

Before she could finish the question, Ayla whimpered over the baby monitor. Jackson was out of bed in a flash.

"Give her a second." Ryann ached for him to come back. The noise wasn't a cry. It might be one in a few minutes, but often Ayla let out a few soft noises and then drifted back to sleep for a few minutes.

"I love getting her in the morning," Jackson said. "And if you go in, she'll want to eat immediately. This way I can get her changed and ready while you either relax or get ready for the day."

He grinned as he strutted through the door. The look of an incredibly proud father.

It was everything she should want, everything people craved in a partner. Yet part of her couldn't help but question if he'd used it as an excuse to avoid answering her questions.

"Patty, where exactly am I supposed to put all this?" Jackson held up his hands as the woman who'd raised a community pulled a sixth box from the ancient van that he was certain ran more on fear that Patty would scream at it than actual ability.

"Ever think of getting a new ride?" He asked this every time he saw her. And so, he mouthed along her response with her.

"This one works fine. I get along." She held up a finger, wagging the now crooked digit at him. "Don't sass me. I can still send you to the corner, young man."

"Uh-huh." The corner. He remembered the first time Patty had threatened him with that at the community center that everyone lovingly called Patty's Place, even though the meetings had outgrown her home where she'd started her work years before she'd taken in Knox and Jackson.

When he'd gone to "the corner" in the community center, it had been filled with books, coloring pads, knitting supplies—things to occupy an overstimulated mind without feeling like punishment.

She handed him the box and went back to the trunk.

"If you pull out another one without letting me help…" he warned.

She had unloaded the boxes onto his condo driveway before he'd arrived and sworn there was only one left…three boxes ago. The woman took care of everyone but still did things her own way. Eighty or not, she didn't stand for help when she didn't want it.

"This is the last one." She winked as she rounded the corner of the van with what was the supposed last box.

"Heard that four boxes ago now." He took it from her, setting it with the others, happy when she didn't rush back to the van.

Tapping her forearms, Patty gave him a grin, "If you don't use these they wither, and I got too much left to do." Her smile broadened, then fell a little as she pushed on her dentures. "Damn things are loose again."

"The story of your life." He gave her a hug. "Tell the community I appreciate the donation, and I'm sure Knox and Miranda will, too, but I think we're good on the supply closet for a while."

The supply closet, Miranda had asked for more space for. Because the little one-cabinet closet Knox and Miranda had set up when she'd first gotten to Hope to give their patients something to do besides watch television was an ever-growing thing. It had a little of everything now.

And following this donation—a lot of everything.

Ryann pulled into the drive, and he saw the look of confusion pass her eyes as she stared at the boxes. He'd mentioned that he'd be over after meeting Patty, that there wasn't a need for her to stop by. Honestly, he hadn't wanted Patty and Ryann to meet.

These parts of his world were separate, a divider that he rarely crossed. Yes, he still volunteered with Patty's Place. Yes, he and Knox both helped the community to navigate the medical world and sat with someone at Hope when they had no one else. But they were pillars of the community to the people there.

To Patty, they would always be the scrawny, hungry boys

who'd been chased out of every coffee shop for trying to study without purchasing more than one drink. The library had been a haven, as long as the ancient Mr. Ilona hadn't been there. The man had been convinced every student—particularly every student of color—was a delinquent.

Never mind that they had just wanted to study.

Patty had taken them in. She'd seen and tended to the bruises, physical and mental, that life in state care brought. She'd given them the upstairs room and told everyone to leave them be so they could study. She'd seen them both at their absolute worst and had shepherded them to their best. She knew the trauma—and the things he kept hidden from everyone else.

"This the girlfriend you're hiding."

"I'm not hiding her."

Patty gave him a look that said *You keep telling yourself that*.

"I'm not."

"I didn't say anything." Patty winked. "But your past is your past. It isn't my place to share." She laid a hand on his arm; her skin was so much thinner than he'd remembered. She was old, elderly. All the spirit in the world wouldn't stop Father Time. "But you've got nothing to be ashamed of."

"I thought you might like some help with the boxes and then you could just ride over to the condo with me." Ryann shook her head. "But, umm, there's more here than I thought there would be."

Patty held out her hand. "I'm Patty. Don't suppose you've heard much about me."

Ryann looked at Jackson and then shook her head before taking Patty's hand. "No. Sorry. I'm Ryann. Have you heard much about me?"

"Nope." Patty hit Jackson's thigh. "He's a good one,

though." She waved, then started back toward the van. "Give me a holler when you need more stuff. We got it coming out of the woodwork."

"That was a lie," Jackson whispered. "She holds drives for it."

"And the people were very generous," Ryann said. She privately felt the hospital should fund the supply closet, but given that the it did nothing to up profit, she doubted that would ever happen.

"Yes. Still willing to help me sort it?" Jackson asked. He grabbed the first box and started toward Ryann's car. They had the next two days off and no need for his car, so riding over with her would be nice. Some quiet time before the nighttime routine with Ayla started.

"Of course." She grabbed a box, and they loaded them in silence.

"You okay?" Jackson asked as she slid into the driver's seat. Ryann wasn't the overly chatty type, but her silence as they'd loaded the boxes sent off warning signals.

She looked at him, then started the car and backed out of the driveway.

No immediate answer. Warning signal number two. And not a subtle one!

"Ryann?"

"It's like you have two lives." Her fingers tightened on the steering wheel, her eyes never leaving the road.

"No. I have a past—one that isn't very pleasant. And my present." Jackson touched her knee, grateful that she didn't pull away. "Which I love very much."

"And never the two shall meet, right?" Ryann drummed her thumb on the steering wheel. She rolled her head from side to side, like she was stretching out her neck.

"Do you need another massage?"

"No," she said. "Or yes, but that's not what we're discussing."

"It could be, though. That's far more fun to talk about." Jackson didn't want to talk about the past. His present was lovely—the only thing his past had ever caused was loss. "So, massage tonight?" he asked.

"Jackson."

"Let it go, Ryann." He heard his tone and wanted to slap himself. "I love you, and I want to focus on the present. On us."

"All right." She offered him a smile, but it didn't quite reach her eyes.

"Did you pack Ayla's extra clothes?" Ryann looked through the diaper bag for the fifth time.

"The clothes are in the bottom, just like—"

She laid her hands on the clothes, touching them, reminding herself they were there. "Just like the other times." Biting her lip, she ran her hands over the clothes one more time and tried to calm her heart. This was silly.

It was just an intrusive thought. A focus that they'd get out on the hike and her daughter would need clean clothes and they wouldn't have them and then.

She stroked the clothes one more time hoping this time it would imprint on her brain that they had extra clothes available and the anxiety bubble would finally pop.

"We can skip hiking." Jackson ran his hand on her shoulder.

"No." Ryann would push through this bout of anxiety. It was only because it was their first outing. "I'm fine."

"It's okay if you're not," Jackson said, then kissed her temple.

The scent of his shampoo wrapped through her, and she tried to focus on that.

"Any idea why the extra clothes bother you so much?" Jackson turned to the fridge, pulling out the water bottles he'd filled last night. They were frozen but would melt along the hike today, giving them cold water all day.

She looked at the clothes, fingering them. "My mom was… is…forgetful. On more than one occasion when we took spontaneous road trips, she'd forget extra clothes." Ryann remembered having to wear the same clothes for almost a week one time. Her mother "washing" them in rest stop sinks and then having to put on damp clothes.

"You are not forgetful," Jackson said. He tapped his head. "You store everything up here." He went over to Ayla's swing and picked her up. "We're going to have a blast today. Aren't we, sweetie?"

Ayla cooed at Jackson, her little hand wrapping around his nose.

Jackson made a honking noise. He'd done it a few nights ago, and Ayla had laughed for almost a minute. Now he did it whenever she touched his nose.

This was perfection. There was no reason to look for worries. Ryann had everything under control.

"Right." She clapped her hands. "We're ready for a fun day. Hiking, here we come."

"Ayla giving you a headache yet?" Ryann laughed as her daughter continued to drum on Jackson's head. This was her first time in the backpack carrier that Jackson had bought. She was strapped in tight, enjoying the sights and the easy access to her daddy's head.

"Nope. And even if she was, I don't think I'd mind."

That wasn't a lie. Jackson probably wouldn't even tell anyone that he was bothered. He'd just let it go—never tell anyone and keep it to himself.

And if he was upset with Ryann, would he ever tell her? Probably not.

"Why don't we stop at the rest point? She's having a blast, but I think a diaper change might be in order." Jackson pointed to the exit then playfully held his nose.

"We can eat lunch, too." Ryann's needed substance and the heaviness in her chest indicated that Ayla needed to breast-feed too. The trail they were on was a short one, designed for families—and luckily within twenty minutes' drive, the exact time before Ayla's lungs opened on car rides, ending anyone's enjoyment.

"Sound good to you, missy?" Jackson tilted his head.

Ayla wasted no time. She grabbed his prescription sun-glasses and threw them.

"Not a bad arm," he said. Jackson patted her, then looked in Ryann's direction. "Any chance you saw were those landed? I'm afraid the ground looks like one big blur to me."

Ryann grabbed them, dusting them off before gently put-ting them back on his face. Pressing her lips against his, she laughed as Ayla's hands wrapped through her hair. "She's enjoying herself."

"The feeling is very mutual." Jackson kissed her forehead. "But I think the diaper change may have become more im-mediate."

The smell wafted her way, and she backed up. "Let's get moving."

Ryann pulled the sweaty shirt off Ayla and grinned as she pulled out one of the extra outfits. "See, there was a reason I was so focused on these today." Subconsciously her brain must have been tracking the heat. It was a fine day, but ba-bies' bodies didn't control their temperature as well as adults. She stripped the diaper, cleaned Ayla, then reached for the diaper cream.

She reached around the bag, keeping one hand on Ayla on the changing table.

"Give me one moment, sweet girl." Her wiggles were much more vigorous than the newborn stage. And now that Ayla could sit up on her own, lying on her back had lost all its appeal.

Ryann rummaged around the side pouch where she always kept the cream. Nothing. Then her mind flashed with the memory. The cream was on the kitchen counter. Ayla had spilled water and rice cereal all over herself last night. Jackson had stripped her, and Ryann had grabbed the diaper bag supplies because they'd been closest.

She'd repacked new clothes and left the cream. She quickly finished dressing Ayla and went to find Jackson.

"We need to leave."

"Is she sick?" Jackson's eyes went to their daughter, the back of his hand to her forehead.

"She's fine. But I forgot the diaper cream." Ryann couldn't believe it. How could she have not remembered that? She'd looked in this bag more times that she wanted to count this morning. She'd counted the clothes six times. Six times. And never looked for the cream.

"Her rash is back?" Jackson tilted his head, but this time he was focused on Ryann.

Heat crested in her cheeks, but she wasn't sure why. "No." Why wasn't he more concerned? Because this wasn't a big deal. Except with the heat and the lunch, Ayla's rash could come back any time. And it had before. At the height of her allergies, one rash would clear only for another to start without warning. And each one was uncomfortable.

"Then why don't we eat?" he said. "She needs to eat, and you must be uncomfortable."

He said the words as her breasts' ache punched through

her foggy mind. She was very full, and Ayla did need to breastfeed.

"Then we hike back down. We'll change her diaper before we leave."

Ryann lifted her shirt, letting Ayla latch. "I can't believe I forgot it."

"It happens, Ryann." Jackson pulled out the sandwich he'd made. It was technically a lettuce wrap with meat and a vegan cheese that Ayla tolerated well. But he always called it a sandwich. He pulled his out and bit into it before taking a swig of water. "It's a small mistake."

"It's my mistake. But Ayla is the one that suffers the consequence. She had no say in it, but that won't matter if she gets a rash." Ryann had paid for all her mother's mistakes, borne the brunt of decisions she'd had no control over.

"Ryann, you cannot protect her from everything."

"Yes, I can." Ryann smiled at him, tears coating her eyes. "No one protected us, but I can and *will* protect her."

"Life won't let that happen," he said. "And if you try, you'll suffocate her." Jackson reached his hand across the table, but she pulled it back. "There has to be a balance, honey." He looked at his hand, sitting on the picnic bench.

Was he hoping she'd reach for it? Should she?

"This is anxiety."

"It's not," Ryann said, shaking her head. "Or if it is, does it matter? If it helps keep Ayla safe."

This time when he reached for her hand, she let him take it. "Anxiety hurting you doesn't help Ayla. We can talk about this," he said.

"Why? You going to tell me about your past? Are we going to talk about that?" She was upset with herself and lashing out. That wasn't fair. "Sorry. Let's just eat and get going. I'm fine. Really."

"Again, it's okay that you're not." Jackson squeezed her hand.

"I know it *would* be okay if I wasn't, but I *am*. I'll just make sure the diaper bag has two tubes of diaper cream. Problem solved."

Jackson opened his mouth, but he closed it without saying anything. Finally, he said, "All right."

CHAPTER FOURTEEN

JACKSON WENT OVER his plans again. He'd rehearsed this evening's plan a hundred times. Ryann was only seeing patients at the office. Her schedule was light, and there were no upsetting cases. Miranda and Knox were watching Ayla. They'd stopped by to pick up her things a few minutes ago.

He had reservations at a vegan restaurant that specialized in food allergies. He'd already cleared the elimination-diet issues with the manager. They'd confirmed that Ryann would have multiple options.

They were going out on a date. As a couple. A real couple.

He enjoyed their nights in. Loved them. But he wanted a night for just them.

A night to recapture—

No, he was not going to think that. They weren't recapturing anything. They were fine.

He wanted to believe that, wanted to pretend there hadn't been a disconnect between them lately. Since the hike.

Except that wasn't true. It had started after she'd met Patty.

Ryann wasn't asking after his past. In fact, other than the comment on the hike, she'd intentionally dropped the topic since he'd asked her to let it go. It was what he wanted, what he needed, but part of him hated it, too.

She was already so worried about Ayla, worried that she

might not have the perfect life Ryann wanted for her. But no life was perfect.

Perfect.

The word only Ryann had ever associated with him. A descriptor she hadn't used since Patty had dropped off supplies.

A descriptor he missed.

"I'm home."

Ryann's call sent flutters through his belly. This was a good idea. But the idea of springing it on her suddenly made him feel like it was a misstep.

"Wow." Ryann's smile was brilliant as she took in his suit and the flowers in his hands. "This is a surprise."

"Glad you like it," Jackson said. He walked over, pulled her into his arms and dipped her back into a kiss.

"It's nice." She pushed a curl behind her head as he straightened. "Kisses and flowers—a nice surprise."

"It's not only kisses and flowers." He took a deep breath, then said, "I have dinner reservations at Ines."

"Ines?" Ryann crossed her arms. "The upscale vegan restaurant that Nicola and the other nurses were talking about last week?"

Her posture made his tongue thick. She was already on the defensive. Why? "Yes," he said. "Though I didn't know the nurses were discussing it. I could have asked them instead of doing research on my ancient laptop."

"You need a new laptop, but we aren't shifting the topic now."

He tilted his head, but before he could work out that statement, Ryann continued. "Not exactly the kind of place to bring a baby."

"Oh. Well, that's part two of the surprise. Knox and Miranda are watching Ayla."

"What!"

Okay, that was way more of a reaction than expected. "Honey, it's just for a few hours. She's at the babysitter's for way longer than that sometimes."

"That's the babysitter, not a strange—"

"Miranda and Knox are not strangers," he said.

"They are to Ayla! They aren't to us, but they are to her. What if she doesn't think we're coming back?" Ryann uncrossed her arms and then crossed them again. "What if she eats something that upsets her? What if—"

"Take a deep breath," he said. This night had morphed and they probably wouldn't get to dinner, but she needed to breathe, acknowledge the anxiety and find a therapist.

"Don't tell me to take a deep breath." The words were rushed, like she wasn't getting enough air. Panic attacks were frightening, and she was on the verge of one, if not in a full spiral.

"Ryann, take the breath with me." He overexaggerated his breath, then started again.

The color was draining from her face.

"This is a panic attack," he said. "I've had them. You are safe. You are fine."

"But is Ayla?"

Jackson pulled out his cell and called Miranda.

"Hey, did Ryann like the surprise?" Miranda's cheery voice was at odds with the situation here. But that wasn't the point now.

"She's panicking because Ayla is there. Is she okay?" Jackson's words were firm; he did not drop eye contact with Ryann.

"Um…"

"Not the time for 'um,' Miranda." God, if something had happened…

"She's fine."

"But!" Ryann's voice echoed in the room.

"She has a small bump on her head," she said. "Icy went past while we were sitting on the floor. Ayla reached for her tail and lost her balance. She cried for a second, then laughed. *Bump* is even too big of a word. It's a little red mark. She and Knox are currently dancing in the kitchen. She's fine."

"I'm on the way." Ryann grabbed her purse and was already moving toward the door.

"She really is fine, Jackson."

He felt the same sense of disappointment that he could hear in his friend's voice. "I know. Thanks, Miranda."

Jackson jogged to catch up Ryann. "I should drive—you're close to hyperventilating."

"I'm going on my own," Ryann said, pushing a tear from her cheek. "I know you meant this as a surprise, but Jackson, she is our daughter. She is hurt."

"She has a small bump from reaching for a cat's tail," he said. "She is a child. This will happen. We can't protect her from everything."

Jackson had seen some of the worst cases in foster care— at one point he'd even been a worst case.

"Ayla is loved and cared for, Ryann, but you can't smother her," he tried again.

"I'm not smothering her. I'm protecting her. We didn't get that. Not everyone can just move past their past trauma and let it mean nothing, let it roll away and be unbothered."

He wasn't unbothered. Was that what she thought? Jackson was trying to protect her! Protect Ayla.

Not burden them with memories they couldn't unlearn.

"I am her mother, I will always protect her,". Ryann said. "If you don't want that, then don't be here when I get back."

And with that she got into the car.

Jackson stood on the driveway long after her gray car had

faded away. He looked at his car, then shook his head. He wasn't leaving.

Tonight was a shift, not the one he'd expected but the one he needed. He was right—Ryann needed to find a way to deal with her anxiety. Therapy, medications, a combination of both. He would support her through it.

But she wasn't the only one who needed to stop overprotecting. He'd been so worried that she'd find fault in him, see his past as an anchor, because mentally that was how he still saw it.

His anchor. His burden.

If he and Ryann were to be partners—and he wanted that more than anything—then he needed to share, too.

Jackson walked to the door. He needed to cancel their reservations, make some dinner and put on a pot of tea. Tonight was going to be long.

Ryann swiped at the tears running down her face. Not that it mattered. Her eyes refused to stop doing anything but leak.

The idea had been sweet. A date night out. A surprise. But it was too soon. They needed to do more planning, make sure their daughter was safe.

Yes, she went to the sitter's house, but Ryann had investigated every available option in the city. And the house kept nanny cams going all day while the kids were there. Anytime she wanted, she could use her code to log in and check on Ayla.

There were no nanny cams at Knox and Miranda's. She couldn't just check in on Ayla.

Ayla was so little, and she didn't know Knox and Miranda. When she'd tipped over, had she been scared? Probably. And Ryann hadn't been there to comfort her.

Ryann pulled up to Miranda and Knox's place. She sat in

the car for a minute. She didn't want Ayla to see her crying, though she doubted she'd be able to hide it for long.

Icy was sitting in the front window. The white cat twitched her tail as she looked out. The feline judgment sent an uncomfortable laugh through Ryann.

Her cell rang, and she tried not to flinch when Miranda's name popped up. She answered, and the video started. Ayla was in the kitchen, on Knox's hip.

"Any idea why she keeps hitting his nose?" Miranda didn't comment on Ryann's tears, but she offered a comforting smile.

"Jackson makes a honking noise every time she presses it." Her daughter's father, the man she loved. She'd told him to leave, given him an out. So many people had walked out on her, but this was the first time she'd told someone they had her permission to do so.

"She really is okay." Ryann laughed as Ayla hit Knox's nose, then squealed when he made the most obnoxious honking noise.

"She's fine," Miranda said. "Though we don't have to live with that honking, warn Jackson that she might expect more of a production when his brother is done here. Knox is nothing if not competitive."

"Over nose honks?" Ryann couldn't imagine that, but she'd never had a sibling.

"Over anything!" Knox called, then made another honking noise. "Yep. Uncle Knox is your favorite, right? I'm your favorite."

The image was lovely but tinged with sadness. She looked at her daughter, happy and fine. She was going to get bruises and scrapes as she started to explore the world. Physical scars and some mental. That was life.

Ayla would never fear that she'd be left. Never fear an

eviction notice that meant living in the car for a while. Never worry that the stepparent her mother swore was her soulmate was a little too quick to touch her.

But Ryann couldn't protect her from the world. She shouldn't.

Tonight should have been perfect. Yes, until tonight, Ayla hadn't done more than meet Knox and Miranda. But Jackson and Ryann knew them. Hell, Jackson and Knox were basically brothers.

Knox had started referring to himself as her uncle immediately, and Miranda had taken on the role of aunt. She'd even playfully teased Ryann that she fully planned to embrace the fun-aunt mode and to be prepared for her to side with Ayla on everything when she was older.

Controlling everything—or attempting to control everything—was breaking her. Had broken her. She needed help.

For Ayla.

And for me.

"Can you watch her for a little longer?" Ryann needed to see Jackson, needed to put things right tonight.

"For as long as you need. Jackson sent a literal house full of stuff for this playdate with Uncle Knox. I swear we have enough stuff for a week, but come before then." Miranda winked, then showed Ryann Ayla and Knox dancing one more time.

"Thank you."

"Jackson! Jackson!" Her voice felt hoarse as she screamed his name as soon as she'd opened the door to the condo. She'd gone to his place first—no Jackson. His car was here.

"Hi, honey." He'd taken off his suit. Now he wore loose sweatpants, a white T-shirt and no shoes. And it was just as sexy as the suit. "Where's Ayla?"

Ryann wrapped her arms around herself. She wasn't sure the script she was supposed to follow. "I…umm, I got to Knox and Miranda's place, video chatted, and she is fine. Knox learned about the nose boops. His noise is very over the top."

"Of course it is."

"I went to your condo, and you weren't there." Such an obvious statement. He wasn't there because he was here. And if her nose wasn't mistaking, he'd made dinner.

"Why would I leave?" Jackson held out his arms.

She didn't hesitate. She fell into him. She let out all the tears. Years of tears. The first person she'd given permission to leave had refused. The man would always be here. For her and Ayla.

The realization healed a piece of her tattered childhood heart. The scar was still there, would always be, but it didn't feel as close to the surface.

"I'm never leaving, Ryann. Not you or Ayla." He stroked her back.

"You're right," she said. "I am trying too hard to protect her. I want the world to be easy for her. To be fair. To be perfect. And I can't grant any of those wants."

"You can't." Jackson kissed her head. "But it's sweet that you want to try."

"I think I should talk to a doctor. Maybe it's postpartum anxiety or maybe it's childhood trauma triggered by having my own kid, but help might be good." Saying the words was a little scary but also freeing.

"I will help you find one, if you want help," he said.

"Thank you. Sorry I overreacted tonight. I love you." She kissed his cheek.

"I love you, too." His arms tightened around her. "But I have been holding back a part of myself. Protecting you from my past. I didn't want it… I didn't want you to see me differently when you hear."

Her hands went to his face, resting on his cheeks. "You don't have to protect me from your past," she said. "I love you. All of you. And I want to be part of your life, know the stories you want to tell. Though I do want to know Patty. That woman seems fun."

"Very."

She dropped a light kiss onto his lips. "I know others have judged your past—that says more about them than it does about you. You are amazing. You have accomplished so much, but more importantly you are an empathetic and caring human to everyone you meet. You're extraordinary."

"*Extraordinary*. I think I like that descriptor."

She chuckled. "Good. Because it fits you."

"Want some dinner?"

"Yes, I'm famished. I can't believe you cooked all this after our fight," she said. "Actually, that isn't true. I completely believe it."

Ryann fixed their plates while Jackson got the drinks.

They sat at the table. Jackson picked up his water glass, took a deep breath and looked at her. "I was five the first time my mom abandoned me…"

EPILOGUE

"You're a beautiful bride." Miranda reached up and adjusted the flower in Ryann's hair.

She looked at the mirror over her shoulder and couldn't believe she was seeing herself standing in white. "I never planned to be here," she said.

"Life certainly looks different when you love someone, doesn't it?" Miranda reached for the small bouquet.

"It does." Ryann took the bouquet, and her eyes filled with tears. "No—my makeup." This was not a fancy wedding. In fact, it had exactly ten invited guests, and they were heading to a local restaurant as soon as she and Jackson had said their vows.

"You need to make a run for it?" Miranda asked. She winked as she pulled the veil over Ryann's face. "I can get a getaway car here in seconds."

The jest made her laugh. "Happy tears are such a curse when you don't invest in waterproof mascara."

"Momma!" Ayla waddled in, her curls already escaping the bows Ryann had placed this morning. She was holding the basket that would hold flowers in just a few minutes upside down.

"Maybe we should have waited for her to turn four before doing this." Ryann leaned down and tapped her daughter's nose. She instantly made a honking noise.

Ayla looked at the veil, then held up the basket. "Flowers."

"Yep. We're putting the flowers in there. Just like you and Daddy practiced." She reached for her daughter's hand. "Daddy has the flowers. Let's go see him."

"There's my girls."

Dashing didn't begin to cover the description of her soon-to-be husband in his dark gray suit and the pink tie that Ayla had insisted on to match her sash.

They'd decided to walk down the aisle together—the family they were highlighted—rather than alone.

"Ready?" Ryann slid her hand into the crook of Jackson's arm as Miranda put a handful of rose petals into Ayla's basket, then headed down the aisle to take her place as maid of honor with Knox.

The music began, and Ayla started down the aisle. She dropped a few rose petals, then a few more.

"See, just like we practiced." Jackson kissed the top of Ryann's head.

"Don't mess up my veil," she playfully chided. "And she isn't even halfway down yet."

As if on cue, Ayla looked at the basket, then at them. She dumped the remainder of the petals into the aisle, then raced to Miranda's open arms.

"Still perfect." Jackson beamed as they started down the aisle.

"Yes," Ryann said. "It absolutely is."

* * * * *

MILLS & BOON MODERN IS
HAVING A MAKEOVER!

The same great stories you love,
a stylish new look!

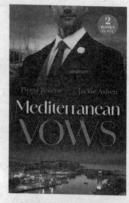

Look out for our brand new look
COMING JUNE 2024

MILLS & BOON

COMING SOON!

We really hope you enjoyed reading this book.
If you're looking for more romance
be sure to head to the shops when
new books are available on

Thursday 23rd May

To see which titles are coming soon, please visit

millsandboon.co.uk/nextmonth

MILLS & BOON®

Coming next month

UNBUTTONING THE BACHELOR DOC
Deanna Anders

'Dance with me,' Sky said, her blue eyes dancing with a fevered excitement that flowed over onto him.

He knew he shouldn't. This wasn't a date. They were there purely as professional colleagues. Nothing more.

But as her arms wrapped around his neck, his own arms found their way around her waist, pulling her closer. And when she laid her head against him, he let himself relax against her. What could it hurt to share one dance?

It only took a minute for his body to answer that question. It was as if a fire had been lit inside him as his body reacted to the feel of Sky against him. His muscles tightened and he went stone hard. He tried to keep his breathing as even as possible as they swayed to the music, her body rubbing against him with each movement. He glanced down and their eyes met. As she drew in a breath that appeared as labored as his, his eyes went to her lips, the same lips that had teased him for months. For a moment he considered tasting them. Would they be soft and supple? Or would they be firm and needy? He had just started to lean down when the couple next to them bumped into him, breaking whatever spell he'd been under.

What could one dance hurt? It could destroy his whole reputation if he let himself lose control on the dance floor.

He pulled himself back from the brink of doing something that would scandalize the whole room with a willpower he hadn't known he possessed. But when the song ended and she stepped away from him, his arms felt empty. It had only been one dance. The fact that her body had molded so perfectly to his didn't mean a thing. But he'd danced with many women before Sky and he'd never felt anything like this before.

'We should go,' he said, though his traitorous feet refused to take a step away from her.

'Why? Do we have plans?' she asked, her voice soft and breathy. His body responded as once more she stepped toward him.

He wanted to pull her back into his arms, to kiss that mouth that had teased him for the last six months. Only he couldn't kiss her now any more than he could have kissed her all those other times. He had to step away from her now just like he'd done over and over when she had tempted him. He needed to put things back to the way they'd been before that dance. Before he'd felt how right her body felt against his.

It should be simple. One step. Just take one step and walk away. But this was Sky. Nothing about the woman was simple.

Continue reading
UNBUTTONING THE BACHELOR DOC
Deanne Anders

Available next month
millsandboon.co.uk

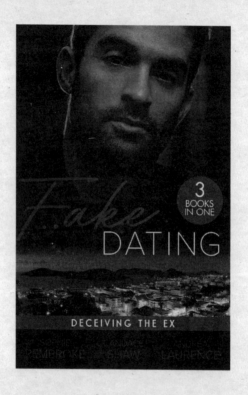

OUT NOW!

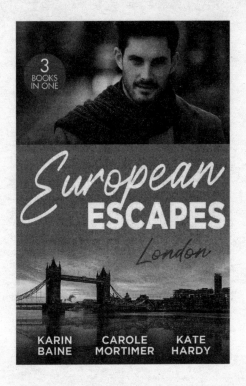

Available at
millsandboon.co.uk

MILLS & BOON

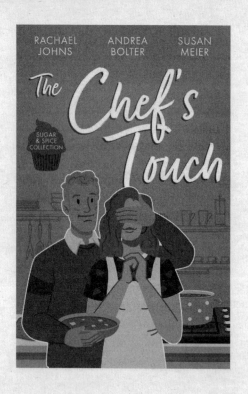

LET'S TALK
Romance

For exclusive extracts, competitions
and special offers, find us online:

f MillsandBoon

X @MillsandBoon

◎ @MillsandBoonUK

♪ @MillsandBoonUK

Get in touch on 01413 063 232

MILLS & BOON

THE HEART OF ROMANCE

A ROMANCE FOR EVERY READER

MODERN

Prepare to be swept off your feet by sophisticated, sexy and seductive heroes, in some of the world's most glamourous and romantic locations, where power and passion collide.

HISTORICAL

Escape with historical heroes from time gone by. Whether your passion is for wicked Regency Rakes, muscled Vikings or rugged Highlanders, awaken the romance of the past.

MEDICAL

Set your pulse racing with dedicated, delectable doctors in the high-pressure world of medicine, where emotions run high and passion, comfort and love are the best medicine.

True Love

Celebrate true love with tender stories of heartfelt romance, from the rush of falling in love to the joy a new baby can bring, and a focus on the emotional heart of a relationship.

HEROES

The excitement of a gripping thriller, with intense romance at its heart. Resourceful, true-to-life women and strong, fearless men face danger and desire - a killer combination!

From showing up to glowing up, these characters are on the path to leading their best lives and finding romance along the way – with plenty of sizzling spice!

To see which titles are coming soon, please visit

millsandboon.co.uk/nextmonth